Plumber's Gap

THE LOST GOLD SHIPMENT OF 1882

EDITED ADDITION

Parts 1, 2, 3, and 4
The Whole Story

MARION DEES

Copyright © 2024 Marion Dees.

All rights reserved. No part of this book may be reproduced, stored, or transmitted by any means—whether auditory, graphic, mechanical, or electronic—without written permission of both publisher and author, except in the case of brief excerpts used in critical articles and reviews. Unauthorized reproduction of any part of this work is illegal and is punishable by law.

ISBN: 979-8-89419-274-1 (sc)
ISBN: 979-8-89419-275-8 (hc)
ISBN: 979-8-89419-276-5 (e)

Because of the dynamic nature of the Internet, any web addresses or links contained in this book may have changed since publication and may no longer be valid. The views expressed in this work are solely those of the author and do not necessarily reflect the views of the publisher, and the publisher hereby disclaims any responsibility for them.

One Galleria Blvd., Suite 1900, Metairie, LA 70001
(504) 702-6708

Acknowledgments

I want to thank my wife of thirty-five years for her continued support in this project. I also want to thank my granddaughter Makayla, who is a big part of this book, for she was the inspiration for the character Mary Plumber.

Introduction

This book is based on fictional events.

Parts 1, 2, 3, and 4

In 1875, gold was discovered in French Creek, near what is now known as Custer, South Dakota. But larger amounts of gold were found in the Deadwood and Whitewood Creeks the same year. Although the Black Hills and the land around it all belonged to the Sioux Indians and the Lakota tribes, white men poured into the area, staking claims on bits and pieces of land. Most came to the Deadwood Gulch area; this illegal settlement was known as Deadwood, the most dangerous settlement in the United States at the time.

By the year 1905, most of the smaller gold mines had played out or had been sold to the larger outfits. Also, by now, most of the land granted to settlers by the government's Homestead Act had already been claimed by farmers and/or ranchers and ex-miners. However, some of the homesteads had been reverted to the government because of the death of the homesteader, and some just gave up and left their homestead. The land around Deadwood and Lead was rough land for farming, too rocky and hilly for most farmers. This land was now for sale at $1.25 per acre from the federal government. The railroad had moved in and was also selling land along their right of way for cheap, helping towns spring up all along the railroad tracks.

Mary ran over to where the gravel had been spread, bent down, and picked up a gold coin. "This, Mama, this is what I was talking about. They were everywhere, hundreds of them."

"Oh my god," said Kathy as she picked one up. "This is unreal." She picked up another one and another.

Kattie and Troy came running over.

"Holy mother of Jesus," said Troy.

Kattie had frozen. "Wait, stop! Where are we going to put them in? Hold up." Kattie was in panic mode. "Okay, I need to go call Sara. Yawl go to the barn and get some buckets, bags, or something."

Mary Plumber found out she had a half sister and who her father was. She had proven that her ability to work with and understand horses was more than normal. She tested her theory of team riding out on barrel racing, and in the process, Mary also learned that her love for helping others wasn't always in her best interest. But through all her efforts, Mary had created a name for herself and had set her sights on the future.

Kattie learned that unspoken words could change one's life. Rose became a vet like Kattie. Troy and Kathy had a little girl, and they named her Tommie.

Mary and Billie had already set up the arena for barrel racing. Jim brought Billie's horse to Plumber's Gap. They had been running every afternoon with Kathy coaching them. Rose liked to watch the girls but was not interested in participating at all. Jim spent time at the arena watching the girls also; he was amazed at how good Mary was at handling the horses.

Part 1

Chapter 1

The Gold Rush

In 1875, gold was discovered in French Creek, near what is now known as Custer, South Dakota. But larger amounts of gold were found in the Deadwood and Whitewood Creeks the same year. Although the Black Hills and the land around it all belonged to the Sioux Indians and the Lakota tribes, white men poured into the area, staking claims on bits and pieces of land. Most came to the Deadwood Gulch area; this illegal settlement was known as Deadwood, the most dangerous settlement in the United States at the time.

So begins the story of the lost shipment of gold coins belonging to one James Leighton Gilmore. Gilmore came to the Deadwood Gulch in 1876 and took over one of the existing mining camps, the Cleveland, by forcing the owner into signing over his claim or be shot. The owner chose to do as he was told but was then shot in the back of the head by one of Gilmore's men. His body was never found. A story was widely told that the Cleveland was sold to Gilmore by the owner, who left and went back home to the east.

Gilmore was a mean, loud-talking man who would curse a lot. He would cheat, lie, steal, or kill to get what he wanted. He built a makeshift gambling hall and a boarding house on his stolen claim. He bought most of the gold found by the miners in return for credit notes or gold coins. Currently, there were no established banks in the Deadwood area. The nearest bank was in Hill City, over forty miles away to the south of the gulch.

The township of Hill City was established in 1874 by George Armstrong Custer and his men, the only township in the area at this time. So some of the other claim owners would sell their gold to Gilmore to keep from making the dangerous trip down to Hill City. Gilmore's gold handlers always seemed to spill a little gold on the floor while weighing it up, but dealing with Gilmore was safer than making the trip.

By the year 1882, Gilmore had obtained a great amount of gold from the miners in the settlement of Deadwood. The settlement had started to form a township of sorts, along with a local law enforcement paid for by the mine owners. In late September, Gilmore decided it was time to cash in a large amount of his raw gold. Coins were easier to store in his safes, and he needed more gold coins to buy more gold dust and nuggets. Gilmore's men—Jake, Pete, and Carl—loaded down the bottom of a freight wagon with bags of gold, then built a wooden subfloor above it, hiding the gold. On top of the subfloor, they placed dry goods and hay. The three men then set out for the Hill City bank to cash in the Gilmore gold.

With two men on the wagon and one man on horseback, they left the next morning headed south. The ramrod of the outfit, Carl, was on horseback. He was a rugged man. Carl was tall and amazingly fast with a gun. He was devoted to Gilmore, and they were like brothers. Then there was Jake, strong and also fast with a gun, but he was best known for handling horses and mule teams. He was driving the wagon. Pete was Pete, a short barrel-shaped man willing to do anything for money to buy more liquor. He was a heavy drinker, but not on this trip.

Gilmore wanted no drinking whatsoever on this ride; he wanted the men to be alert and ready for trouble.

They followed the established wagon road through the hills and valleys leading out of what would become the city of Deadwood. The men would have to camp at least two nights on the trail before they got to the bank in Hill City. Their orders were to head straight back to Deadwood as soon as they reloaded the wagon with the coins. They were to hide them under the subfloor of the wagon. There were 5,400 $20.00 gold pieces loaded onto the wagon—over $100,000.00, a small fortune—along with more supplies on top of the subfloor to be sold to the miners.

They headed back with their minds at ease, knowing that even if they were stopped by bandits, they would never find the gold coins. Before they reached the foothills, it was getting dark again, so they stopped to camp for the night, hoping to get an early start the next morning. Just as they got their fire going, another wagon pulled up to their camp. Carl and Jake pulled their guns.

"Hello, boys," called out an old man with dust-covered clothes. "What's for supper?" He laughed as he climbed off his wagon. The old man's name was Dodger. People called him that because he was the best around at dodging the local Indians. Dodger had been hauling freight for over six years all by himself, from north to south and east to west, and had never lost a load. He knew these boys were from Deadwood; he also knew they worked for Gilmore. "What you boys doing? Hiding bodies?" he asked with a laugh.

Carl laughed back. "No, we had to go get some dry goods and supplies for the boarding house in Deadwood. You know, Mr. Gilmore will not buy from the general store there. He says those people are cheats." He laughed out loud. "You know, he thinks he is the only one who should make a profit in Deadwood."

"Yup," said Dodger. "Well, boys, y'all better be in a hurry come morning. There's a big snowstorm coming. Oh, by the way, you know, there is a shorter way back to Deadwood. It might save you half a day or so."

"No, we didn't know that. We've always just taken the main trail."

"No, there is another shorter trail northeast of here. It cuts straight through Lead Valley. Not many people use it, but I do. Less likely to see other folks, if you know what I mean."

"That's great," said Carl. "We will have to think about that."

The next morning when they woke, old Dodger had headed out.

Carl said, "Well, what do yawl think about that shortcut Dodger was telling us about?"

"Okay with me," said Jake.

"Pete, what do you think?"

"I am not sure. What if we have trouble along the way and nobody knows which way we went?"

"Oh, hell, the only trouble we are going to have will be if we get caught by that snowstorm."

"You're right," said Pete. "Let's go. I am ready to get back home."

The boys headed west like old Dodger said, then turned northeast onto a dim wagon trail through the valley headed to Lead, South Dakota, then on to Deadwood.

"Looks like we were lucky running into old Dodger like that. This is some nice-looking country," said Jake.

"Yep, sure is," said Carl. "Real nice."

About midway of the valley, they could see the dark clouds building to the southwest behind them.

"Okay, boys, we got to move," said Jake. "Get up, mules."

They drove on. As the sun had started to fade behind the clouds, the storm was getting closer.

Carl said, "We better keep going as long as we can. The weather is looking rough."

Just as they stopped near a small creek to camp, light snow had started to fall.

Pete said, "I sure wish we had stayed on the main trail. We could have kept going with a torch to light the way."

"Oh, stop complaining," said Jake, "and help me unhook these mules from this wagon."

Carl said, "I will get the tent out. We better get a fire going soon." Carl yelled at Pete, "Come help me unfold this tent! The snow is getting bigger."

"I'm coming."

"I'll get some firewood," said Jake, "and get us a fire going. It's getting colder fast."

The men ate and then crawled into their tent and fell off to sleep.

The next morning, everything was covered with snow. Luckily, the snow was not that deep. The wagon would not have any problem traveling through it, but there was no trail. It was gone; the snow had covered all traces.

"Well, which way do we go now?" asked Pete.

"Northeast," said Carl. "We just follow the valley."

"Okay," said Jake, "but which way is northeast?"

"It's that way." Carl pointed to the north.

"Okay, let's get everything loaded," said Pete, "so we can get moving."

They rode off headed north, not knowing the trail went northeast for ten more miles, then turned due north to Lead-Deadwood, only about twenty-five miles from where they camped last night. Not knowing for sure where they were or where they were going, they rode on through the snow. As they rode up over a ridge, they could see something up ahead.

"What in the world is that?" asked Pete.

"Kinda spooky-looking," said Jake.

"That's how the Indians bury their dead," said Carl.

"Do we go around these things?" asked Jake.

"No, I'm ready to get back."

7

"Yeah, me too," said Jake. "I heard bad spirits live around graveyards."

"Me too," said Pete.

"If we don't get this gold back to Gilmore today, he is going to make spirits out of us. Just follow me," said Carl. "Be quiet and go slow."

As the men made their way through the Indian graveyard, the snow began to fall again, this time harder and bigger flakes, covering the tree limbs.

As the men rode out of the graveyard, the land turned flat and open; they could hardly see in front of them through the snow. As they kept going north, they were unknowingly getting farther and farther away from Deadwood instead of closer. The land seemed endless, just open plains, no hill, no valleys, just flat. As they rode on, the snow stopped, and the sky cleared, but everything was covered with a white blanket of snow. It was getting harder for the mules to pull the wagon through the deep snow; they had to stop from time to time to beat the ice off the wagon's wheels.

To the south, the men could see small hills and trees.

"Let's go that way," said Jake. "There are trees. Maybe we can build a fire. I am freezing."

"Okay," said Carl, "let's go look."

They made their way to the wooded area; they could hear water running nearby.

"Hey, look," said Carl, "there is a creek and a waterfall over there."

The sun had already set, and it was getting darker fast.

Carl said, "Let's go to the falls and make camp. We are not going to make it back today."

"Gilmore is going to be so mad," said Jake.

"Well, maybe he will send someone out looking for us in the morning," said Pete.

"He will send somebody all right," said Carl, "to find his gold."

"It is not our fault it snowed," said Pete.

They backed the wagon up close to the edge of the creek before they unhooked it from the mules. They moved all the dry goods to the front of the wagon so they could lay in the back of the wagon, off the snow-covered ground. Then they pulled the tent canvas over themselves. As the snow began to fall again, they went off to sleep.

The next morning, they woke up and started digging their way out from under the snow-covered canvas. Pete went to get the mules as Jake and Carl rolled up the tent canvas. Pete came back with the mules. "Hey, Carl," he said, "I think we got company."

Carl turned and looked on the ridge across the creek. "Jake, up there!" Carl shouted as he pointed to the ridge.

"It's Sioux Indians," said Jake.

"What do we do?" asked Pete.

"Nothing," said Carl. "Just be still. Maybe they are just passing through."

"Yeah, and maybe they are mad because we went through their graveyard," said Jake.

About that time, an arrow flew by Pete and hit Jake in the neck. Blood began to run down as he gasped for air and then fell.

"Oh god," said Pete as an arrow hit him in the back, then another and another. Pete fell.

Carl pulled his gun and ran for the horse as the Indians came down the hill and across the creek. Carl untied the horse and climbed on its back with no saddle. He fired at the Indians as he took off on the horse, but the Sioux braves were catching up fast. He fired again. Carl screamed as an arrow hit his back, then one of the braves rode up beside him and hit him in the head with a tomahawk. The Indian took the reins of the horse just as Carl fell to the ground. The Indians took all the dry goods from the wagon, the mules and the horse, and the men's guns. They picked up the tongue of the wagon and pushed it into a deep hole at the bottom of the waterfall. The wagon slowly sank to the bottom of the hole with all the gold coins still in it.

After a week and no sign of the three men Gilmore sent to cash in his gold, he sent three more men out to find them. The men rode the main trail to the bank in Hill City, where they learned that the gold had been traded for gold coins like Gilmore had requested. But there was no sign of Carl and his crew anywhere along the way or in Hill City, and no one had seen them since they left the bank. The search party returned to Deadwood and reported to Gilmore that the three men and his gold coins were nowhere to be found. Gilmore went into a rage and said he would kill Carl's crew if he ever found them. He assumed that the two men, Jake and Pete, must have gotten the drop on and killed Carl and had headed south to Mexico with his money.

Gilmore decided after losing the gold coins that he needed another gold mine to make up for his losses. He offered to buy out the Deadwood Mining Company's mines, not knowing that the mines had been mined out and truly little gold was left. He made an offer to the owners of the Deadwood Mining Co., and they accepted. Papers were drawn, and the deal was made.

Gilmore spent most of the gold he had left in his safe to buy the claims. Gilmore thought he was back on his way to being on top again. After one month of mining, Gilmore realized that the Deadwood mines were worthless; he was getting more gold out of the Cleveland, his smaller mine, than he was the Deadwood mine. He was devastated. He went looking for the men who sold him the mines but found out that all but one of them had left the area to parts unknown.

Mr. Lewiston was still around and living in Deadwood and now building *the Bank of Deadwood*, the first bank to be built there, which would also compete with Gilmore's gold-buying operations.

Gilmore rode up to the building site. Lewiston walked out. Gilmore said, "You sold me an empty hole!" Then he shot Lewiston in the chest, then walked up to him and shot him in the head.

All the men working on the building were watching. It did not take long for the new town marshal to show up at Gilmore's gambling hall to arrest him. A gunfight broke out, and Gilmore was shot in the leg. They took him to jail and locked him up.

Two days later, they had his trial, and he was found guilty of murder and sentenced to death by hanging. It took two more days to build the gallows, and he was hanged on December 15, 1882, just five days after he shot Lewiston. Gilmore was laid to rest in Mount Moriah Cemetery and became the first man to be buried there.

The next spring, after all the snow was gone, two miners working the creek found what was left of three bodies near a waterfall. After the bodies were found, a story spread far and wide about the large shipment of gold coins taken by Indians.

Chapter 2

The Plumbers

By the year 1905, most of the smaller gold mines had played out or had been sold to the larger outfits. Also, by now, most of the land granted to settlers by the government's Homestead Act had already been claimed by farmers and/or ranchers and ex-miners. However, some of the homesteads had been reverted to the government because of the death of the homesteader, and some just gave up and left their homestead. The land around Deadwood and Lead was rough land for farming, too rocky and hilly for most farmers. This land was now for sale at $1.25 per acre from the federal government. The railroad had moved in and was also selling land along their right of way for cheap, helping towns spring up all along the railroad tracks.

Two such 460-acre plots that were once homesteaded for a while became available just west of John Plumber's mining claim. Across the wagon trail, going from Lead, South Dakota, to Deadwood, South Dakota, the Plumbers bought the 920 acres of land for $1,150.00 from the federal government with options to buy more later. The land lay in a small creek valley, between government-owned national forest land on each side. These two plots were part of more than 5,000 acres of connected land available for sale.

There were the beginnings of two cabins, one on each plot, which was great for the Plumbers. John and his two sons, Eric and Paul, had been living in tents at the mining claim for more than twelve years, through rain and snow. John's wife, Mary, had died eight years earlier from fever. She was a small woman, but tough as nails. John and his two boys had nowhere else to go and little money when John's wife and the boys' mother died. All they had was the claim, a hole in the ground, and whatever nature would provide for them.

After years of working the mine and barely getting enough gold to buy coffee, flour, meal, and salt monthly, in 1906, they found a large vein of quartz gold, about forty-five feet down from the entrance of their mine. They knew that they had to keep quiet about their find; they only sold small amounts of gold at a time so no one would notice. They kept mining, and over the next two years, the Plumbers saved over $3,000.00 in gold coins, which was a lot of money back then. They also had quite a bit of mined gold hidden away for safekeeping.

The two boys, Eric and Paul, were grown by now. Eric was nineteen and Paul seventeen, but men. All they knew was mining, hard work, hunting, and trapping, but that was all they needed. Their mother had taught them to read, write, and add before she died. Their father had taught them how to work, how to handle a gun, and how to survive. The two brothers had taught each other how to fight, and they did a lot of that when they were younger. Now they had a land of their own and a roof over their heads.

"I wish Mama could see us now," said Paul.

"She can. She is watching us right now," said John as he hugged his youngest son.

The cabins were small and not complete. Eric took one, and Paul took the other to work on. John, however, would not leave the claim no matter how hard the boy tried. John just stayed in his tent. He said, "I bought them plots for you two boys. Anyway, somebody's got to watch the mine. We do not want no trespassers coming around here."

The boys each got their cabins weathertight knowing that winter was coming soon. They got together and came up with a plan to build their father a cabin on the claim.

John said, "I don't need no dang cabin. I am fine." But the boys would not have it; they were not going to sleep under a warm roof while their father slept in a cold tent all winter. John said, "Yawl do what you want to." As he climbed down into the mine shaft, they could hear him grumbling on his way down. "Damn kids won't let me alone."

The two boys got started cutting and notching trees. Eric came up with the idea to build the cabin over the entrance to the mine.

"That is a great idea," said Paul. "Dad will love that. He can go in and out without even leaving the cabin."

"Yeah," said Eric.

"We can build a trapdoor in the floor. No one will ever know," said Paul.

When John came out of the mine that afternoon, the boys had two rows of logs stacked around the mine's opening.

"What the hell," said John.

The boys laughed, then told him of their plans. John was so impressed with their ideas that he decided to stop working the mine and help his sons until the cabin was finished.

Once a month, John and one of his boys would go into town to sell some gold and get supplies, while the other son stayed and watched the mine. In the spring of 1909, the Plumbers bought two more plots of land connected to what they already had. Eric and Paul both cleared a spot on their land for vegetable gardens. Then Paul bought a milk cow and some chickens and built a small barn to keep them in.

Both boys still worked the mine with their father most of the day and then worked their land in the afternoons. They now owned 1,840 acres of land, with a plan to buy more by winter and get more cows. Things were going great for the Plumbers until fall and John got sick.

John told the boys, "It is this dang cabin. I've been sleeping in a tent for twelve years, and I haven't been sick, not one day."

Paul said, "Aw, Pop, you are getting older. You cannot keep pushing yourself as hard as you do."

"I will pop you in a minute. Here, pour some more coffee and then get out of my hair."

Paul and Eric worked the mine without their father for a week. That was all the time John would stay away. He was some better but still had a hard time breathing.

Eric asked, "Hey, old man, what are you trying to do? Get us all sick?"

John was only forty-six years old, but the last fourteen years had been hard on him. Living outside and working long days had taken their toll on him; he looked more like sixty.

Winter came and went. John got over being sick, and the boys were in hog heaven. Eric had bought some pigs, and Paul had bought five cows. They did not get to buy more land last fall like they wanted. With John being sick, they put it off until spring, but John and Eric were going into town today to the land office to buy more. They bought two more plots, another 920 acres, which made 2,760 acres they owned now, but this time, the land was $1.50 an acre, $1,380.00. John was happy. He had set the boys up for their future, and the boys were happy too. Life was good, and all their hard work was paying off.

For the next four years, things went good for the Plumbers. They were still getting good gold from the mine, just not as much of it. Eric was twenty-five years old now, tall and strong, a good-looking young man, clean-shaven. Eric had started talking to a young lady at the general store when he and his father would go into town for supplies. The young lady was the daughter of the store owner and had long brown hair, blue eyes, and a sweet smile. She had been off to college and had just come back home. She and Eric were about the same age.

Eric did not know much about how to act around her or how to read the signs she was throwing his way, but Marsha Leann Tindall knew exactly what she was doing and how to do it. She was sweet with Eric, and she wanted him to know it. Without a word, she could make him blush. Eric would leave the store red-faced every time. The more he saw her, the more he thought about her, and the more he thought about her, the more he would find a reason to go to town.

Paul was content to stay at home and work the mine and work his land. Paul was twenty-three now, also tall and strong. But Paul looked more like a miner with long hair, beard, and mustache, like his father. Deadwood was still a tough town currently. Saloons, gambling halls, and prostitution were prevalent there. Paul would not go to town unless he just had to. Last summer, a man picked a fight with him in the street, and Paul beat him half to death before John could pull him off. Although it was not his fault, Paul was reaching for his knife when his father pulled him and would have killed the man if his father hadn't stopped him.

Mr. Tindall did not like Eric, not because he had ever done anything but because of his daughter. Eric was a miner's son and a miner himself. He felt his daughter was too good for him. But not Marsha Leann. To her, he was just what she wanted—tall, strong, good-looking, and hardworking. What else could a woman need? The trap had already been set, and Marsha was just waiting for Eric to step in. On June 15, 1912, Marsha Leann Tindall married Eric Lamar Plumber in the Methodist Church in Deadwood, South Dakota, at 3:00 p.m.

Eric took his new bride to his cabin in Lead, South Dakota, only about fifteen miles away. Eric's father and brother were proud of him. Paul mostly hoped she would start doing the cooking. That had always been his job, and he would be more than glad to give it up. However, Marsha was a town girl, and not only that, but her family always had a cook and a housekeeper. The young couple got along fine for a while. Eric and Paul added a room to Eric's cabin for a bedroom. Everything was new and exciting for Marsha, and she absolutely loved Eric.

Winter came, and Marsha was still having fun playing house, but when all the trails were covered with snow and most traveling had stopped, things began to change. Eric would spend his days working the mine with his father and brother, while Marsha stayed at home and cried all day because she could not see her father and mother. Homesick and alone in a small cabin covered in snow was not what she had planned for herself.

John had always shared the gold they found with his sons. He kept half, and the other half was split between Eric and Paul, which was fair because John paid for all the supplies and the land out of his share. Nevertheless, Eric and Paul were wealthy by now, though no one knew it but them. The mine was starting to play out, they felt, by the amount of gold they were getting out of the quartz now. But John was determined to buy the rest of the homestead land before someone else did. He wanted to leave his sons something he never had—land and money. As soon as the snow melted and the trail cleared, Marsha had Eric take her to her folks in Deadwood.

Eric bought some supplies in town while Marsha visited with her mother and dad. Marsha was so glad to see them; she never got homesick like this while she was at school, but she had so many other girls around her there. Spending the winter with only seeing and talking to three men was more than she could take. When Eric came back to get her, she would not go.

"I am sorry," she said. "I just cannot do it. I thought I could, but I cannot. Please understand, I love you, Eric, but I cannot... I just cannot."

Eric rode off alone, heartbroken and confused. "What did I do wrong? She knew I was a miner and that I lived in a cabin in the middle of nowhere. What did I do?"

When Eric showed back up without Marsha, no one said a word. John knew she was unhappy and was not surprised. He was hurt for his son and knew his son was hurting too. The next day, as they worked the mine, Eric was just going through the motions, not there; his mind was back in Deadwood, remembering what was said and trying to understand why the love of his life would not come home with him.

John watched for a while, then pulled Eric to the side. John said to Eric, "Son, you don't need this mine. You have more money than most, but you do need that woman! You do what you got to do, son. This was mine and your mother's dream. You go find your own."

They hugged each other. Eric walked over and hugged Paul. As tears rolled down all three men's cheeks, Eric climbed out of the mine for the last time. Eric packed a bag, got on his horse, and headed straight to Deadwood.

Eric and Marsha bought a house in the town of Deadwood. Eric started working in the store with Marsha and her father; her father liked him now. Marsha was expecting a baby in December, and Eric was becoming quite the businessman.

Paul and his father, John, bought the last of the homestead land connecting to theirs, and now what little gold they found, they split fifty-fifty. Paul bought twenty-five more head of cattle to put on the place.

On the morning of March 5, 1915, Paul climbed into the mine and found his father, John, curled up in the bottom, dead. Paul put his father's body on his shoulder and carried him out of the mine; he laid his body on his bed in the cabin. He took all the gold and coins that belonged to his father and placed them down in the mine. He climbed out of the mine, then took a hammer and some nails and nailed the trapdoor shut and placed a rug over it and then the table. He went to his cabin, got on his horse, and headed to Deadwood to tell his brother, Eric.

Paul rode up to the general store, got off his horse, and went inside. Eric and Marsha were behind the counter. Eric looked up at Paul, and a big tear formed in his eye.

Marsha looked at Eric. "What's wrong, honey?"

"Daddy is dead," said Eric.

"How do you know?" asked Marsha.

Eric pointed at Paul standing in the doorway.

"Come on, buy your brother a drink," Paul said as he walked out and headed to the saloon.

Eric met Paul in the saloon, and they ordered drinks.

"How did it happen?" asked Eric in a low voice.

Paul took a sip of his drink. "When I climbed in the mine this morning, he was lying there."

"Well, he died doing what he loved," said Eric.

"Yep," said Paul as he took another sip.

"Daddy's gold?"

"I put it back in the mine and nailed the door shut," said Paul as he took another sip.

Eric started to ask, "Do you think—"

"Nope," said Paul before Eric could finish. "That man worked half his life for that gold. Don't seem right to just take it."

"Okay," said Eric. "What about the land?"

"What about it?" asked Paul.

"Well, I would like to keep the two plots Dad gave me and the cabin. Who knows, my kids might want it someday. You can have the rest and the mine claim," said Eric.

"That's fine," said Paul, "but I will not ever enter that mine again." Paul finished his drink, got up, and walked out. He climbed on his horse and headed out of town.

The next day, Paul and Eric dug a grave on the mine site, wrapped their father's body in canvas, and placed him into the ground. They covered him up and placed a big rock for a headstone. Paul took some white paint and wrote, "John Plumber."

The two brothers never saw each other alive again. Eric kept buying up businesses in Deadwood; his riches were growing as fast as the town. Paul took an Indian woman from the reservation and had two kids with her, a boy and a girl. Eric and Marsha had two sons. Paul died in the spring of 1925 at the age of thirty-four years old. No one ever knew why. Eric said Paul mourned himself to death over their father's death.

Eric dug a hole by their father's grave and placed his brother's body in the ground, as Paul's woman and two kids watched.

The woman told Eric, "We go home now." She and her two kids went back to the reservation.

Eric had a gravestone made that said,

Father and Son

John Plumber
Father

Paul Plumber
Son

Eric did not know what else to say; he felt like he had abandoned his brother and father. After all the years they were together, it was hard to know they were both gone now. It was like he was the only one who had escaped the mine and made a better life, and he did. Eric made a promise in the memory of his father and brother to make sure that someone in their family would build the ranch that he, his father, and his brother had always dreamed of when they bought the land years ago—a cattle ranch, a 5,000-acre cattle ranch, with a large ranch house big enough for the whole family. He knew he would not be able to do it alone and prayed for him and Marsha to have a couple of sons to help him later.

Chapter 3

Eric Plumber

By the end of 1925, Deadwood was a real town, only around three thousand people though. Eric Plumber had several successful businesses in town and was one of its most respected residents. Marsha Plumber, Eric's wife, was still running the general store and had added a dress shop. They now had two sons: Timothy (Tim), who was twelve years old, and his younger brother, Theodore (Tom), who was ten years old. Tim helped his mother around the store, and Tom aggravated Tim as much as he could.

Most signs of the old mining town were gone, and the mud streets were gone. The new streets were cobblestone and/or brick on the main streets. Horses and wagons had given way to cars, trucks, and motorbikes. It was a whole new world. Well, not really. There were still gambling halls, saloons, and some prostitution houses behind every closed door, even though they were all illegal now. Other than random fistfights, things were quiet. Guns were no longer aloud in town, except for law officers and bank guards.

Eric would go out and visit the old mine claim and his cabin sometimes on the weekends. He even took his sons a time or two and told them about how he, his father, and his brother used to live there. John's old cabin was falling in and was not safe to go in. Eric's cabin surprisingly was in good shape. Paul's cabin was still standing, but not much better than John's. As Eric was looking around the old places, he happened to think about Paul's kids, the boy and the girl. They would be about the same age as Tim and Tom, his two boys. He went to take a closer look at Paul's cabin and pushed the door open. Inside was a rotten floor, some old clothes, an old bed, and a lot of dust.

"Not much to see here."

Eric made his way out to Paul's old barn. The roof looked okay; the loft was still up. He made his way inside—an rotted old saddle, some leather straps, old buckets, and spiderwebs. As Eric was walking back out, he saw something in the front corner. *What is that?* he thought. As he moved closer, he could tell it was some old wooden box with rotted burlap sacks over it. He walked over to it and started pulling the old sacks off. They were coming apart as he pulled at them.

Under the sacks was a wooden box. It had an old padlock on it, and the box had rope handles on each side. Eric tried to pick up the box with the handles, but the rope handle on the side broke. It was like the box was stuck to the ground. Eric looked around trying to find something to hit the lock with. He walked through the barn kicking the ground, trying to find something under dirt and hay. Finally, he hit something with the toe of his boots. He picked it up. It was part of a hoof nipper. "All right," he said. He walked back over to the box, took the nipper, and hit at the lock repeatedly until the lock popped open. He slowly raised the lid on the box, more burlap. "Oh my god," he said, "how has no one found this in all these years?"

He started trying to gently remove small bags from the box. He had not opened one bag. He did not have to; he knew exactly what was in those bags. He helped fill them up years ago with his brother—six five-pound bags of gold, a fortune. It was Paul's stash. There was no sign of Paul's gold coins. Paul, when he died, must have hidden them somewhere else. *Oh my god,* Eric thought, *why did Paul not tell his woman or his kids about the gold?* He could not believe his eyes. Eric started carrying the bags of gold to his truck, still not knowing what he would do with it. He could not just leave it there after finding it. Besides, there were Paul's son and daughter. Surely, they could use the gold.

Eric drove back to town, trying to decide what he should do with the gold. The next day after the bank opened, Eric put a bag of the gold in a leather bag, then carried it into the bank, rented a safe deposit box, and placed the gold inside. "One down," he said to himself. The next day, he took two more bags to the bank and placed them into the safe deposit box. It was full, no more room. *What now?* he thought. Then he decided, *The kids.*

The next Saturday, Eric put the last three bags of gold in the leather bag, placed it in his truck, and headed to the Indian reservation, not knowing what he might find. He stopped at the Indian affairs office just inside the reservation. Eric went inside and asked the lady behind the counter if she had ever heard of Paul Plumber from Lead, South Dakota.

"No, I do not think so, but ask the chief."

Eric expected a small dark man with a headdress, but a tall well-dressed man with short hair walked into the lobby.

"Can I help you, sir?" asked the man.

"I hope so," said Eric. "I am looking for my brother's family. Paul Plumber, he passed away seven years ago. He had an Indian woman wife and two kids, a boy and a girl."

The old man smiled. He looked at Eric and asked, "What took you so long?"

Eric looked down at his own feet, then looked up at the man and, with a red face, said, "No excuse, but I am here now."

The man walked up to Eric and reached out his hand. "My name is Black Cloud, but my friends call me Chuck."

"My name is Eric, Eric Plumber."

"Nice to meet you, Eric."

"You too, Chuck."

Chuck said, "Come to my office. Let's talk."

Eric told Chuck how he had buried his brother for his wife and kids and asked them to stay on Paul's land, but all the woman would say was, "Home, we go home now." And they turned and walked away.

"What do you want with them now?" asked Chuck.

"Well, it turns out my brother had some money put back, and I thought it should go to them."

The man smiled. "You think the Sioux people live like they do because they have no money and cannot afford to live like the white man in big houses with stone streets?"

"I mean no disrespect, sir," said Eric.

"I know you do not," said Chuck. "I can tell that you are a good man trying to do a good thing. But there is no need. The Sioux and the Lakota have been here a long time. The white man thinks he has found all the gold. We have more gold than there are stars in the sky.

Silver, cooper, and turquoise too. We do not sell to the white men in buckets and bags. Our people make jewelry to sell. We live like this because we want to, not because we must. It's our way."

"Well, can I see them?" asked Eric.

"Why?" asked Chuck. "It won't help them. They will never live like the white man. Just know my daughter and my grandchildren are fine." He smiled.

Eric got up, shook Chuck's hand, and walked out of his office.

Eric left the reservation and headed straight to the old mine claim. He got out with the three bags of gold. He went to the headstone at his father and brother's graves, dug a deep hole under the headstone with a shovel, placed the three bags into the hole, and covered it up. "Here, Dad, you and Paul look after this for me." Then he drove home.

The Prohibition Act was repealed in 1933, and gambling once again flourished in Deadwood. Then in 1934, the Federal Gold Reserve Act was passed, setting the price of gold at $35.00 per ounce. While the rest of the country was in a severe depression, the Lead-Deadwood area was prospering greatly. Eric and Marsha Plumber were prospering with the area. Their sons Tim, now twenty-one years old, was at college studying law and Tom, now nineteen years old, was running the store with his mom. Tom was not sure yet what his plans were, but it was not more school, he said. He never did like school much away.

Tom was more like his uncle Paul, whom he never knew, than Eric, his father. Tom loved the outdoors, hunting, fishing, hiking, and skiing. He was good at building things; he said one day he would build his own house. No matter how much money Eric and Marsha had, Eric always made the boys work to earn their spending money, except for what their mother would slip them from time to time. Tim planned to come back to Deadwood after graduation and start a law firm; his father and he had already made plans to build a building on the main street. Eric owned several lots in town. Tim had hopes of later going into politics, maybe a state senator or something like that. Marsha wanted a grandchild, but that was not happening soon claimed the boys.

In the year 1938, Tim graduated from college and came home to a proud mother and father. But to everyone's surprise, he was not alone; he brought a wife he met and married back east. She was from the city, wearing a beautiful dress, shawl, gloves, and hat; she looked like she had just walked right out of a magazine. Tim was smiling from ear to ear as he introduced her to his family.

"Mom, Dad, Tom, this is Abby, my wife."

Tom was not impressed; she was too preppy for his taste. But Marsha was in awe and so excited; she could not wait to steal her away from

Tim and talk about all the new dress styles and all that was happening in the east. Abby (Abagail) and Marsha hit it off from the start; they talked for hours while Tim and his father looked over building plans.

That same year, a group of motorcycle enthusiasts held a rally in the nearby town of Sturgis, South Dakota. Around nine bikers came to participate in the event, with over fifty spectators. It was a great boost to Sturgis's economy, and plans were made to repeat the rally the following year. Also, that winter, a group of ski enthusiasts organized the Bold Mountain Ski Club and installed a rope to help climb the slope.

A lot of good things were happening in the area, but not for Tom. At twenty-three years old, Tom was no longer content to just being a store clerk. He began to spend a lot of time in the gambling halls, gambling and drinking. His father, Eric, who did not approve of his son's activities, was concerned, along with Tom's mother, Marsha. Two years later, Abby and Tim announced that they were expecting Eric and Marsha's first grandchild. Eric was proud, and Marsha was ecstatic. She had hoped and prayed for so long. Tom shook his brother's hand and congratulated him, then announced that he also had some news.

"I have signed up with the Army. I leave at the end of the month."

Dead silence filled the room. A tear rolled down Marsha's face.

Tim said, "But why?"

Eric walked over and hugged his son. "I know why. I'm proud of you, son."

Tom looked at his brother Tim and said, "I'm not like you, brother. I've got to leave this town, or I'll die. War is coming. I'm going to go fight so that you won't have to. If I'm going to die, I want it to be for a good reason."

At the end of the month, Tom got on the train. All the Plumbers were there to see him off. Just like before, history repeated itself. Tim and Tom never saw each other again. Two years later, Tom was killed in the war. Tom's body never made it home, just a small box of his belongings. Tim buried the box by his grandfather's grave and put up another headstone at the mine that said,

> Three Generations of Plumbers
> John, Paul, Tom
> Rest in Peace

Tim and Abby's baby girl, Sara Ann, was one year old now. She was such a sweet child, and she looked just like Marsha did when she was a baby, with brown hair and blue eyes. By now, all the gold mines were shut down; nothing seemed the same for the man who spent twelve years in a tent and crawled around in a dark hole. Tim's law practice was growing, and Abby was expecting again. This time, they hoped for a boy. Eric went to the old mine claim mostly every day now; he just sat there by the graves. The land across the now blacktop road sat empty, no sign of the cabins or the barn that were once there. They were all rotted away, just tall grass with trees along the bottom of the ridge. Eric wished he had helped Tom build a house there and gotten him out of Deadwood.

Abby and Tim had their second child, another little girl; this one looked just like Abby, with blond hair and bluish-green eyes. They named her Leann Elizabeth, after Tim's mother, Marsha Leann Plumber. Sara Ann, now two years old, was so excited to have a little sister to play with. She ran to her every time she made a sound. She loved her baby sister and was even learning to change her diapers. Abby was not quite ready to turn that responsibility over to Sara yet.

After the war ended and the men came home, there were more people than there were jobs in America. Women had to work in the factories during the war to keep the economy going. Now men wanted those job back, but the women were not just going to give up and move out of the way for the men. Some had lost husbands, fathers, and brothers in the war and needed the income to support their families now. The government made plans to create more jobs for men and women to ease the tension created by the war. This would cost money, and the war had already cost a lot. The government's gold reserves had financed the war and would now be needed to finance more jobs.

The government needed more gold knowing that there were people still holding on to gold that they needed. They raised the price of gold to over $100.00 per ounce, which made their reserves worth more and gave incentives to the gold holders to sell their stash. It worked; old miners were lined up at the banks, along with businessmen who had invested in raw gold. Eric Plumber fell in line with everybody else and sold the three bags of gold he had in the safe deposit box. The only problem was that the cost of everything else—food, gas electricity, cars, and homes—also went up during the next two years. The cost of living just kept growing, and the value of the dollar went down.

Chapter 4

Kattie Plumber

In 1953, Eric turned sixty-four years old. He loved spending time with Sara and Leann, but Tim and Abby had their third child five years ago, another little girl. Abby said, "That is it, no more kids." But Tim was not giving up yet on a son. The girls—Sara Ann, ten years old; Leann Elizabeth, eight; and Kattie Lynn, five—were the light of Eric and Marsha's life. Kattie had long red hair and green eyes. Eric loved all his granddaughters, but that little Kattie Lynn stole his heart. From the time she could walk and talk, Eric knew she was different than the other two girls. She loved her pops and followed him everywhere; she would go to his office with him and color and play while he worked. Sara and Leann did not like to get dirty and stayed inside most of the time. But not Kattie Ann. Give her a spoon to play with, and she would dig a hole to China. She stayed outside always. Her sisters said she was dropped on her head when she was a baby, and that was why she was so crazy, but she wasn't! She was just wild and free, no cares. The only thing she cared about was what time Pops was coming home or where

Pops was or what Pops was doing. Nothing else mattered to her. She was Pops' girl, and everybody knew it.

It was time for Kattie to start school like her sisters. The first thing she wanted to know was, "Is Pops going?"

"No," said Abby.

"Then I ain't neither," Kattie said.

"Yes, you are, young lady," said Abby. "You go to school and become smart and make your pops proud."

"My pops is already proud of me," said Kattie.

Abby looked at Tim and said, "Call your father!"

Eric came right over. "What is it?" he asked.

"Your girl," said Abby. "You take her to school." And she walked out with Sara and Leann.

"Come on, baby girl."

"But, Pops, I don't need no school. I'm already smart."

"Yes, you are," said Eric, "but there's things Pops can't teach you. I never went to school. There was no school here when I was your age. My mother had to teach me to read, write, and add, but I'm still not that good at reading and writing. I'll tell you what. I'll make you a deal. I'll come get you and take you to school every morning and pick you up in the afternoon for the first week. If you don't like it, we will get somebody to teach you at home." Kattie spat in her hand and reached out to her pops. Eric spat in his hand, and they shook hands.

Eric and Kattie walked to school. He took her to her classroom. Inside, there were about ten other kids her age, boys and girls, laughing and playing. There was a teacher at the chalkboard writing her name. Eric walked up to the teacher with Kattie.

"Excuse me, ma'am. This is my granddaughter Kattie. She is a little reluctant about school."

The teacher looked at Kattie and said, "Hi, my name is Ms. Andrews. You and I are going to be great friends." Kattie smiled. The teacher said, "Here, you sit right in front of my desk."

Eric took the teacher's hand and said, "Thank you." As he walked out, a tear formed in his eyes.

That afternoon when the bell rang, Eric had been there for thirty minutes. When Kattie walked out, the first thing she saw was Eric smiling at her.

"Hey, Pops," said Kattie, "let's get ice cream."

"Okay, baby girl."

The next morning, Eric was at Tim's house to walk Kattie to school. She ran out and took his hand. They headed down the sidewalk to school. That afternoon, Eric was right back at the school, waiting for the bell. Kattie came running out. She took Eric's hand and said, "Come on, Pops." They walked down the sidewalk heading home. Kattie was just jabbering about her teacher and this boy and that girl.

Eric did the same every day for the rest of the week. As Eric walked Kattie up to her door on Friday afternoon, Kattie stopped, looked up at Eric, and said, "Bend down, Pops." He did, and she gave him a kiss on the cheek and said, "I got this now. I'll go with Mama and my sisters next week." Again, as he walked away, a tear formed in his eye.

Kattie never complained about going to school anymore. They just never knew what she would be wearing to school. In the fall, she would wear a dress, but come cold weather, she would show up in overalls and a ball cap. Her third-grade teacher once told her that all little girls had to wear a dress to school. The next day, she did over her overalls. When Tim and Abby told Eric about it, he just smiled. "Kattie is not like the other girls. She never will be," said Eric. Kattie's two sisters, Sara and Leann, made Kattie walk about a block behind them on the way home from school in the afternoons. They were ashamed of her in her overalls and cowboy boots. Besides, Kattie was only in the fourth grade, and they were both in junior high, seventh and eighth grade. Kattie did not care. She would rather not be seen with them either; they were too prissy.

One afternoon while walking home, Kattie had fallen behind. A boy jumped out at Sara and Leann from the bushes. Kattie heard them scream. The boy was in Leann's class and a known bully. Kattie started walking faster. He was poking at Leann with a stick. Sara was trying to make him stop. Leann had started to cry; Sara was screaming at the boy to stop. Kattie kicked off her cowboy boots and broke into a run straight for the boy. She leaped and hit him in the chest at a dead run, knocking him to the ground. When they stopped rolling, Kattie was on top and punching him in the nose repeatedly. Sara ran up and grabbed Kattie's arms.

"Stop! You're going to hurt him," said Sara.

"I sure am," said Kattie as she got a hand free and hit him again. Kattie stood up, put a foot on his chest, and said, "If you ever touch one of my sisters again, I'll kill you!" The boy got up and ran off. Kattie turned and walked back to get her boots.

Leann ran after her, hugged her, and said, still crying, "I love you, Kattie."

Sara hugged Kattie too. "Where did you learn to do that?" they asked Kattie.

"Learn what? I was born this way," said Kattie.

The three girls held hands as they walked home. Kattie never had to walk behind her sisters again.

Chapter 5

The Will

At the age of sixty-seven years old in 1956, Eric went to his son's office.

"Hey, Dad, what are you doing?"

"I just came by to talk about some legal stuff."

"Okay, Dad, what do you need?"

"I think it's time to make a will."

"Okay, we can do that, but I'm not sure I understand why. I mean, your assets will go to me, and when I die, they will go to the girls."

"Yep, let's talk about that," said Eric.

"Okay," said Tim.

"I want you to write up papers that make sure Kattie gets the mine claim."

"Dad, wait a minute, Kattie is only nine years old."

"I know how old she is, son. I want you to write up papers that say when she turns twenty-one, she gets the mine and the 5,000 acres across the road."

"Well, what about the other girls?"

"I'm sure you will take care of them when the time comes. Look, we own half this town," said Eric. "We have more money than we could ever spend. Just write up the papers so I can sign them. Kattie gets all the Lead property. You get everything in Deadwood and whatever money is left."

"Okay. What about the gold in the mine and the gold under the headstone?" asked Tim.

"Kattie's, it's all Kattie's. I'll write her a letter and tell her about the gold and where it is. You give the letter to her when its time," said Eric.

"Okay, Dad, I'll write it up, and you can sign it, but you will be here for a long time yet."

"I plan to be, but write up the papers anyway!" Eric didn't tell Tim about his promise to his father and brother.

Kattie was always into something. She loved animals; she would bring home stray dogs and cats, fatten them up, then give them away. At least that was the plan. Some stayed a long time. Her grandfather, Eric, had gotten Kattie a horse when she was about eight years old. She named him Dawg. Dawg was a pinto, a paint horse with long black mane and tail. An Indian horse, said Kattie. Now thirteen, Kattie lived on that horse; they went everywhere. Eric and Tim were always getting calls from other business owners about Kattie and that horse walking down the sidewalks. Kattie would say, "Yawl get them cars off the street, and I'll ride there." Kattie and one of the bar owners in town, Bob Clark, were good friends. He kept bottles of soda pop in his cooler just for Kattie. Sometimes she would ride up to the bar, tie Dawg to a parking meter out front, then go inside and belly up to the bar. Bob would hand her a bottle of pop and smile as he watched her drink it down, then she would walk out and climb on Dawg and ride away, hollowing "Yeehaw" as she rode off down the street. On Saturday afternoons, when the bar was full of customers, Bob would have both doors open, the front and back. Kattie would ride Dawg in the front door, Bob would pitch her a pop, and she would ride out the back of the bar. The customers loved it.

Sara, Kattie's oldest sister—Kattie called her Ms. Priss—had gone off to college but came home for two weeks every year to help in the store during the Sturgis Bike Week. Over five thousand bikers came through Deadwood during that week. Some would stay in Deadwood or close by or in nearby towns. Kattie loved bike week. She'd say, "You can see some crazy stuff on bike week." She said, "It's like watching a bunch of crazy Indians on firewater round here." Kattie would pull her bar ride every afternoon during bike week, dressed up like Calamity Jane.

Kattie and Eric were still as thick as thieves as she started her first year in high school. She was still wearing overalls and a ball cap. Nobody even thought anything about it now. They just accepted her and how she was. Kattie's other sister, Leann, helped Abby run the store and dress shop now. She would graduate in two years. Leann was seventeen now and had a boyfriend, Bobby Joe Thornton; his father sold cars. Kattie said that they were the stupidest people she had ever seen. Bobby Joe hung out around the store, sometimes making googly eyes at Leann. Kattie would say, "Somebody shoot this boy and put him out his misery, please!"

Marsha had turned the store and the dress shop over to Abby about six years ago. Eric and Marsha had spent the last few years traveling the country and just being together. They were seventy-six years old now. Eric was having some health problems, so he and Marsha stayed close to home now. Tim was now forty-nine years old. Not only did he have his law firm but he also had control of Eric's business dealings. He had to hire more help in the office and hoped Sara would follow him and go to law school so he could one day turn the firm over to her. Leann had no college plans and hoped to take over the store and dress shop from her mom after high school. Eric had told Tim to try and sell off some of the other businesses to lighten the load. But this year, in

1961, the town of Deadwood was declared a national monument. The stipulations of this made selling of property harder and more costly.

Eric took Kattie out to the mine claim. They sat there by the graves. Eric told Kattie the story of his father and brother. Eric looked at Kattie and said, "You see that field across the road there?"

"Yeah, Pops."

"There's over five thousand acres there."

"Really?" said Kattie.

"Yep, it's yours, baby girl."

"Mine? What do you mean, Pops?"

"I'm giving it to you."

"But, Pops—"

"But nothing. It's yours, along with this old gold mine claim."

"How?" asked Kattie."

"Your dad knows."

"Is there any gold left?" asked Kattie.

Eric laughed. "You will have to find out." Eric said, "Let's just keep this between your dad and us for now, okay?"

"Okay, Pops."

On the way home, all Kattie could talk about were all the horses and cows she was going to have on the land. Eric smiled; he knew she was the one to take over the family land. He knew she would bring it back to what it was supposed to be from the start.

In 1962, at the age of seventy-seven, Eric Lamar Plumber was laid to rest in the Mount Moriah Cemetery. Over three hundred people came out to tell him goodbye. Kattie Plumber was the only one of the family members who did not cry at the funeral. She stayed at Eric's grave all night. Tim stayed with her. He picked her up off the ground and carried her home the next morning at daylight. They both cried all the way home.

Two years later, Kattie graduated from high school and had plans to go off to veterinarian school the next fall. Before she left for college, she went to Eric's grave. She sat there and talked about her plans after school. After a while, she got up, leaned over, kissed his headstone, and said, "It's okay, Pops. I got this now!"

Kattie started college in the fall of 1967. She attended the University of Wyoming in Cheyenne, Wyoming. She was going to be a horse doctor, she would always say when she was young. She still came home every weekend. She and Dawg still ride through the bar at times, but not as much.

"You're getting too old for such foolishness," said Abby, her mom.

Marsha, her grandmother, was still living. She still tried to spoil Kattie like Eric did. She once told Kattie, "I don't know who your pops loved more, you or me."

Kattie would hug her and say, "It was you, Grandmaw. It was you."

In Kattie's second year of college, she found a place to board her horse Dawg near the university. She didn't come home as much after that; she would compete in the school rodeos on weekends. Abby told Marsha, "I think the only reason Kattie came home before was to see that dang horse." Marsha would just smile. Kattie became quite good at the rodeo thing, winning buckles and ribbons for barrel racing, pole bending, and breakaway roping. Marsha and Abby would sometimes go watch her at some of the bigger events.

Kattie came home to her sister Leann's wedding. "The dumbest thing I ever heard of," said Kattie. "Mama, are you going to let her marry that stupid boy?"

"Yes, I am, honey. And when you find someone, I'm going to let you marry him."

"Well, that's not happening."

"Do not hold your breath for that one! Just be happy for your sister."

Kattie said, "Okay, I'll try, but I'm not promising nothing."

Sara came home also for the wedding. Tim walked Leann down the aisle to give her away to Bobby Joe. "More like throwing her away," said Kattie to Marsha. Marsha just smiled. When the preacher asked

Leann if she took Bobby Joe to be her husband, Kattie said under her breath, "Run, Leann, run."

Marsha started to softly giggle. "Hush, child," said Marsha.

Abby and Sara cried as the preacher said, "Now you can kiss the bride."

After the services, at the reception, Kattie walked up to Bobby Joe as he stood by Leann. She reached out to shake his hand. She took his hand, swung his arm around behind his back, and said, "If you hurt my sister, you're dead." Then she smiled and walked away.

Bobby Joe shook his arm and looked at Leann. She kissed him on the cheek and said, "She's not joking." Leann walked off with a big smile, thinking, *Oh, Kattie, how I love you.*

Within three months, Leann and Bobby Joe were expecting their first child. Abby and Tim were excited; as were Sara and Kattie. Kattie told Marsha, her grandmother, that she hoped the baby didn't take after his father. Marsha laughed. Kattie was genuinely happy for them, but she loved to give Bobby Joe a hard time; it was so easy. Kattie was there when Leann gave birth to her first son.

"Such a sweet baby boy," said Kattie.

"Don't you want one?" asked Marsha with a smile.

"No, thank you. I'll just spoil this one, then give him back," said Kattie. "I am not putting up with no stupid man just so I can have a baby."

Chapter 6

The Letter

In 1973, Kattie graduated from the University of Wyoming with a veterinarian degree. She and Dawg moved back home to Deadwood. Sara Ann had finished college in 1968 and was now a female lawyer working for Tim at his law firm. Leann and Bobby Joe had two little boys now.

Kattie was glad to be home but was ready to get her life started, so she went down to her father's office. "Hi, Dad," she said.

"Hi, sweetie," he replied. "You glad to be home?" Tim asked.

"Yes, sir, I am," replied Kattie. "I wanted to talk to you about some things."

"Okay, shoot," said Tim.

"Well, I want to start my own veterinarian office and hospital here in Deadwood. I was hoping you would help," said Kattie.

"Okay," said Tim, "what were you thinking?"

"Well, that empty lot at the edge of town would be a good spot, I think," said Kattie.

"Okay," said Tim, "I'll have to check and see who it belongs to."

"Dad, you know who it belongs to."

Tim laughed. "I'm sure we can work out something, but first, I've got something to give you."

"What?" asked Kattie.

Tim went to his file cabinet, unlocked a drawer, and pulled out a file. He sat back down at the desk. "Your pops said to give you this when you turned twenty-one, but you were in school, so I held on to it."

"Is it the mine?" asked Kattie.

"Yes," said Tim.

"Pops told me he was giving it to me before he died," said Kattie? "But he told me not to say anything to anyone but you."

"Well, it's yours now." Tim pulled out a letter from the file; it said "For Kattie" on the front and was stamped Confidential below her name. Tim slid it across the deck to Kattie. He said, "Take this, go out to the mining claim, and read it. When you come back, we will talk about your hospital."

Kattie took the letter and walked out of Tim's office. *What could this be?* thought Kattie. She got in her car and drove out to the old claim. She got out of the car with the letter, walked to the grave site, sat down on an old bench, and opened the letter.

Dear Kattie,

If you are reading this, I've gone, and you are now grown, a young woman. You know you always had a special place in my heart. I wanted you to have this place, the place where it all started, where my brother Paul and I made plans to build a beautiful ranch with cows and horses. Things did not work out for us, but I felt like if anyone could make that dream come true, it's you. With your love for animals and the outdoors, I felt you would like this place. There is a lot of good grass across the road for grazing, good water supplies—the creek runs all year. Everything you need to get started is here at this old mine. Behind the first headstone, right in the center, about two feet down, is a small wooden box with three bags of gold. There is enough there to get you a good start. Your dad will help you sell the gold. After that is gone, under my dad's old cabin, there is a door built in the floor. My brother Paul nailed it shut after Dad died. Under that is the entrance to the old gold mine. Paul put Dad's share of gold and his gold coin in the bottom of the mine. It's yours. Use the money from the gold mine to make my brother's and my dream of a ranch come true. I love you, Kattie. You're still my little girl. God bless you!

Love, Pops

Kattie looked around until she saw an old shovel leaning on a tree; she took the shovel and started digging. Just as Pops said, about two feet down, she hit something. She got on her knees and started removing the dirt with her hands. She cleared the dirt away and pulled up the box. She carried it to her car and placed it in the trunk. She went back to the graves, filled in the hole, took some leaves, and covered the fresh dirt, then placed the shovel back where it was. As she drove back to Deadwood, she thought of how she and Pops had been so close. She made an oath to build his dream; she would call it Plumber's Gap.

Kattie pulled back up to Tim's office and went in. Tim smiled at Kattie. "Well?" he asked.

"I need to sell some gold." She smiled from ear to ear.

"I thought you might," said Tim.

The next day, Tim sold the three bags of gold for $185,937.50, about six times more than what it was worth when it was mined. Kattie now had the money she needed to build her hospital and start the ranch. The building went up fast, then the stalls and pens were built for the animals. She put new equipment inside, and before winter, she was now open for business. Marsha came to the grand opening and was so proud of Kattie. Marsha passed away that next spring, leaving a son, three grandchildren and two great-grandchildren. They placed her beside Eric.

Kattie Plumber's Veterinary Service was a success, although most of her time was spent at the clinic, she had hired some men to build fences on the 5,000 acres, with catch pens and corrals, getting ready to put some cows on it.

Then came Jim Hatcher, a Montana cowboy with a cow pony that was sick. Kattie checked out the horse. "What have you been feeding him?" she asked.

"Just hay and all-grain."

"You better check that hay," said Kattie. "It might be moldy. This horse has a tummy ache." Kattie gave the horse a couple of shots and told Jim that he would be fine in a day or two.

While Kattie was checking out the horse, the cowboy was checking out Kattie, and one of her assistants noticed. After Jim left, she told Kattie about how he was checking her out.

"Well," said Kattie, "he can just look somewhere else. I don't need anything else to have to take care of. Most men are useless anyway, especially cowboys."

Carol, the assistant, said, "Hmm, I like cowboys."

"Not me," said Kattie. "I had one once. I was not impressed." They both laughed as Kattie was helping a dog have puppies.

The very next week, the old truck and horse trailer with Montana plates pulled back up at the clinic.

"Oh, Kattie, your cowboy is back."

"What?" asked Kattie. She looked, and sure enough, Jim was unloading his horse. Kattie walked outside. "What's wrong now?"

"Well, Doc, he's still not acting right."

Kattie took the lead rope and led the horse inside. "Okay, pretty boy, let's check you out," said Kattie.

"You think I'm pretty?" asked Jim.

"No, the horse," said Kattie.

"Well, what's wrong with me?" asked Jim, smiling.

Kattie said as she felt the horse's joints, "Your head's too big, your butt's too small, and you smell like a cow."

Jim busted out laughing. "Well, Doc, at least you're looking."

Kattie gave the horse a vitamin shot, then turned to Carol and said, "Charge him $50.00 for the shot plus the examination." Jim just smiled.

After Jim left, Carol asked Kattie, "Hmm, $50.00 for a vitamin shot?"

"Well, he will either give up or run out of money," said Kattie. "There was not a thing wrong with that horse, and he knew it. I don't have time for games. If he wants to play, I'll play, but it will cost him."

Kattie went out to the ranch after work one afternoon to see how the fences and pens were coming along. She hauled Dawg out with her. She unloaded the horse and climbed on his back. "Let's check this place out," said Kattie. They headed off through the tall grass to the creek, then followed the creek bank deeper into the valley. Along the creek bank, she saw a lot of deer, elk, wolf, and bear tracks in the soft sand. The water was about one and a half feet deep with a gentle, steady flow. As she rounded a bend in the creek, she could not believe her eyes. "Oh my god," she said as she got closer, "a waterfall." It was the most beautiful thing she had ever seen.

She thought, *I must be about five miles in by now.* The sun was starting to set. She could not believe it. *I have my own waterfall,* she thought. "Okay, Dawg, let's go. We do not want to be here when it gets dark." She and Dawg galloped back the way they came. When they got back to the truck, it was almost too dark to see. Kattie climbed down. "Load up, Dawg," she said. She latched the door, started the truck, and headed out back to Deadwood. She could not stop thinking about those falls. *What else could be back there?* she thought.

"Oh, Kattie, he's back. This time no trailer. He got out of the truck with a blue heeler puppy, a cow dog puppy. Oh, how sweet," said Carol as Jim walked in with the puppy. "What can I do to help you?" asked Carol.

"This little baby needs her shots."

"Okay, just have a seat. Kattie will be out soon."

Jim sat down with his puppy and waited and waited. Finally, Kattie came out from the back. "What, no horse?" asked Kattie.

"No, he's fine, but this puppy needs her shots."

"Okay, come on back."

Jim was watching Kattie walk all the way back to the examining room.

"Okay, let's check her out," said Kattie. "A pretty baby? Yes, you are." She eased the thermometer up the puppy's behind. "Good girl, you're a good girl." And she kissed the puppy's nose. "By the way, do you know any ranches in Montana that are looking to sell their herd of cows?" asked Kattie.

"No, but I can do some checking around. Why?" asked Jim.

"Well, I have inherited some land, and I want to put a herd of cows on it."

"Well, I'll make you a deal. If you let me buy you dinner tonight, I'll find you some cows."

Kattie's mind said no, but her mouth said, "Okay. What about your puppy? What will you do with her?"

"That's not my puppy. It's yours."

"What?"

"Yeah, I got five more just like her at home."

Again, her mind said no, but her heart said yes. She placed the puppy in one of the kennels and said, "I'll meet you here at seven."

"Okay," said Jim, "I'll be here."

About six o'clock, Carol said, "Come on, girl, you've got to go home and clean up and change for your date."

"It's not a date," said Kattie, "just dinner."

"Oh, really?" said Carol.

"Yep, I'll take my lab coat off, but I'm going in my scrubs, and they ain't coming off!" said Kattie.

Carol laughed. "You're so crazy. Why do you hate men?"

"I don't hate them. I just don't trust them. They always have an ulterior motive for everything they say or do."

"Give the boy a chance. He might fool you," said Carol.

"I doubt it," said Kattie.

At 6:45 p.m., Jim was waiting outside of the clinic for Kattie.

"Oh, Kattie, he's here," said Carol.

Kattie removed her lab coat, fluffed her hair, and walk out. Jim jumped out of his truck, ran over, and opened the passenger door for her. Jim had on dress slacks, a starched shirt, a bowler tie, and no hat. He had his black hair cut short, a clean-shaven face, and a small mustache. He closed her door, then ran around to the other side and got in. "Where are we going?" asked Jim.

"Go straight for three blocks, then turn left."

They pulled up at a local steak house. They went inside and got a table. Along the way, all the men spoke to Kattie by name and all the women hugged her.

As they sat down, Jim said, "Wow, you are a very well-known young lady."

Kattie said, "Well, I don't know about being a lady, but yes, I've lived here my whole life."

"Well, what's good here?" asked Jim.

"Everything," said Kattie.

"Hi, Kattie," said the waitress. "How are you today?"

"I'm fine," Kattie replied, knowing the waitress was wondering about the man with her. Kattie ordered a beer and a steak.

Jim said, "That sounds good to me."

As they waited for their steak and beer, Jim asked, "Well, how many cows are you looking for?"

"Oh, about 250 head to start with," said Kattie.

"Wow, you're jumping in headfirst, aren't you?"

"Yup."

The waitress came back with the beers. "Anything else right now?" she asked.

"No, just our steaks," said Kattie with a smile. "So what do you do in Montana?" asked Kattie.

"Well, my family has a small cow operation there."

"Oh, really?" said Kattie.

"Yep, we have feedlots. We buy yearlings, feed them out, and sell them, about 2,500 head at a time."

"Wow," said Kattie.

"Well, I'm just working there with my father and brothers until I can afford to start my own place. I'm the youngest of six boys. I want to raise cattle and create my own bloodline, but my brothers don't."

"Oh, that's interesting," said Kattie.

They finished their meal and then got up to leave. Jim paid the check and left a tip. They walked to Jim's truck. Jim opened her door and then closed it. Jim went around to his side and got in. Jim drove her back to the clinic where her car was at, got out, and opened her door. Kattie tensed up, thinking Jim would try to kiss her, but he closed the door of his truck and then said, "Well, Doc, that was fun." He walked around to the driver's side, and he opened the door to get in. "A deal, a deal, I'll let you know about those cows." He got in and drove off.

Kattie stood there relieved he didn't try to kiss her but wondered why not. She got in her car and drove home. *The last thing I need is a man,* she thought but could not stop smiling.

The next day at work, Carol said, "Tell me everything. How did it go?"

"How did what go?" asked Kattie.

"You know," said Carol, "the date."

"It was not a date."

"Okay, the dinner. How did the dinner go?"

"It was okay. He was nice, opened my doors, pulled out my chair. We ate and talked. He drove back to the car and left."

"Left? Left?" said Carol. "He didn't try to kiss you or nothing?"

"Nope," said Kattie.

"Oh my god, I cannot believe that," said Carol, "after all the trouble he went through."

Kattie laughed. "Well, at least I got a puppy." She pulled her out of the kennel. "What are we going to name you, little girl? I know what we will call you. Pepper. You look like someone sprinkled pepper all over you."

Two weeks went by, and no word from the cowboy. Kattie assumed he had changed his mind and moved on. Then she heard coming from the front, "Oh, Kattie, he's here."

She stopped what she was doing and ran to a mirror, fluffing her hair. Then she thought, *What am I doing?* She walked out front, and there he was walking in the door.

"Hey, Doc," he said.

"What, no sick animal?" asked Kattie.

"No." Jim smiled. "I got some news for you about some cows."

"Oh, great," said Kattie. "Come in my office, and we'll talk."

"Okay, lead the way," said Jim. Carol was smiling from ear to ear.

Kattie said, "Okay, what you got?"

"Well, I found a man who has a herd of about 180 head of Angus cows for sale. Ages range up to six or seven years old. About sixty head are yearlings. He is getting about sixty calves each spring. You could do more if you would split the herd and get another bull."

"When can we go look at them?" asked Kattie.

"How about now?" asked Jim.

"Let me check," said Kattie. She went out front to talk to Carol. "He has found me some cows to buy. What have we got this afternoon? I need to go see them."

"Go," said Carol. "We got this."

"That's my line," said Kattie.

Jim and Kattie drove across the state line into the edge of Montana. They turned down an old gravel road.

"Where are you taking me?" asked Kattie.

Jim just smiled.

As they drove on for about ten more miles, Kattie was getting concerned, then she could see a small ranch house up ahead. *How quaint,* she thought. They pulled up to the barn by the house. Jim got out.

"Mr. Smith, Mr. Smith, are you here?"

An old man walked out of the barn. "That was fast," said the old man.

"Well, you know how women are when they think they want something," said Jim.

"Man, do I," said the old man.

Kattie got out of the truck.

"Mr. Smith, this is my friend Kattie," said Jim.

"Are you a nurse?" asked the old man. "My wife was a nurse."

"No, sir. I am a vet."

"Well, how about that?" said the old man. "I guess you want to see some cows?"

"Yes, sir, if you do not mind."

"Come on, yawl, follow me. I'll open the gates. Yawl close them."

"Yes, sir," said Jim.

They went through one gate into a small lot to another gate and, through it, into a larger lot to another gate into an open field. As they drove down an old trail, soon they started seeing the cows.

They made a big circle around the field, then the old man led them back through all the gates.

The old man got out of his truck and said, "Yawl come sit on the porch with me." Kattie and Jim followed behind him. The old man said, "Look, I started this herd twenty years ago, with forty cows and one bull. Over the years, I sold off yearlings, mostly steers. When the mama cows stop producing, I sold them or put them in the freezer. This was a good life. I made a good living here. The doctor says I got about six months before I join my Martha. That boy there said if I sold you my cows that you would take care of them. Is that true?"

"Yes, sir, I will."

"That boy also said he would buy my place here. I got two girls, one in Colorado and one in Wyoming. They have their own family now. Don't see them much. They never did like this place anyway. So I'm going to put the money in the bank for them to fight over. So here's what I want for my cows." He wrote on a piece of paper with hands shaking, then slid it to Kattie.

She picked up the paper and looked at it. "No, sir, that's not enough."

"Look, girly, I know what I want. Do you want them or not?"

"Yes, sir, I do," said Kattie.

"Well, write me a check. That boy and I already made our deal. Make that check out to me, but give it to that boy. He is going to put it in the bank for me."

Kattie made out the check and handed it to Jim. Jim had the old man sign it, then he put it in a yellow envelope. He pulled out a bill of sale and handed it to Kattie. It had already been made out with her name and the amount on it.

The old man said, "Girl, you can get your cows anytime. I am not going nowhere yet. Make that boy help you!" The old man looked at Jim and said, "Now go get that money in the bank and fill them papers that lawyer man wrote."

"Yes, sir," said Jim. Jim got up and said, "Come on, Doc."

Kattie could not believe what just happened. She followed Jim to the truck. He had her door open for her.

As they drove back down that gravel road, Kattie asked, "What just happened?"

Jim said, "You got a herd of cows, and I got my ranch."

"Oh my god," Kattie said.

They headed to the bank in Cheyenne, Wyoming. Jim said, "I got to do this before I take you back to Deadwood." They drove to the bank. Jim went inside, and when he came out, he said, "One more stop." He went to the courthouse, went in for a while, then came out. "Well, it's a done deal," said Jim. "Let's get you home."

Kattie said, "You know, I went to college here."

"Really?" said Jim.

"Yup. It's my turn to buy you dinner."

"Okay," said Jim.

They drove to a place Kattie knew, and they had dinner, but Jim would not let her pay. As they drove back to Deadwood, Kattie asked Jim, "Why didn't you just buy the cows for yourself?"

"I couldn't afford them and the ranch too," said Jim.

"You could have gotten a loan," said Kattie.

"I could have," said Jim, "but I want to build my own herd of crossbreed cows."

As they pulled up at the clinic, it was after 10:00 p.m. Jim got out, came around, and opened Kattie's door. "Well, I've got to get home. I've got cows to pen in the morning."

Kattie raised up on her tiptoes and gave Jim a kiss. She looked in his eyes and said, "Thank you!"

Jim said, "You're welcome, Doc." As he walked around his truck, he added, "Let me know when you're ready to move those cows."

Kattie stood there as Jim drove off, wondering what this cowboy really wanted.

Chapter 7

Plumber's Gap

"A little higher on the right," said Kattie as the men raised up the sign in place that she had made for the ranch. The sign was placed above the road leading into the 5,000 acres. The sign said Plumber's Gap. *Plumber's Gap Ranch will be the ranch my great-grandfather always wanted,* thought Kattie. *I've got to make a call to that man about some cows,* thought Kattie as she drove off.

She went to the clinic. Kattie asked Carol to pull Jim's file and get his home phone number. Carol brought the number to Kattie's office.

"What are you doing?" asked Carol in an inquisitive voice.

"I've got to get my cows brought to the ranch," said Kattie. She dialed the number.

"This is Jim. Leave a message," she heard on the other end.

"Hi, this is Kattie Plumber. Call me at the clinic, please."

The next morning, Jim called, "Hey, Doc."

"Hi," said Kattie. "I am ready to come get my cows and move them. You told me to let you know."

"Sure," said Jim. "How can I help?"

"Well, I might need some help rounding them up."

"That's no problem," said Jim. "Give me until Monday, then send the trucks. I'll have them ready."

"Can I come help?" asked Kattie."

"Sure. You need a horse?" asked Jim.

"I've got one, but he's never been around cows, and he is getting old."

"No problem. I've got one you can ride. We start at daylight."

"Thanks," said Kattie. "See you in the morning."

The next morning, Kattie pulled up to Jim's ranch just before daylight. There were six pickups with horse trailers already there. The men were saddling their horses and getting ready to go.

Jim called out, "Kattie, over here!"

She looked and saw Jim at his truck. She walked over.

"Hey, Doc," said Jim.

"Morning," said Kattie.

He was saddling a beautiful buckskin horse. Jim said, "Kattie, this is Ginger. Ginger, this is Kattie."

"Hi, sweetheart," said Kattie as she rubbed the horse's nose. "You are a pretty girl."

Jim said, "Let's mount up." Kattie climbed up on Ginger. Jim adjusted her stirrups, then got on his horse. "Let's go," said Jim.

They rode through the three gates into the open field. The sun was just coming up over the trees. Kattie rode close to Jim as they started to round up the herd. Kattie had no idea what she was doing, but Jim did. Kattie watched as Jim and the other men and four dogs worked the cows, pushing them into a tight group. It was like magic—no one talking, everyone just doing what was needed. There were cows mooing, dogs barking, horses neighing, and men whistling and pointing. Kattie watched in awe. Once the cows were bunched up, they started driving them into the big lot. One rider closed the gate as the last cow ran in. One man was filling up the water troughs. Two more were throwing hay out. The other two had gone back looking for strays.

By now, it was around 2:00 p.m. Jim rode up to Kattie and said, "Let's find a shade." They rode through the small lot and out to a group of large trees. Kattie was sweating; as was Jim. "Here, Doc." He handed her a canteen of water.

"Oh god, thank you," said Kattie.

Jim reached back into his saddlebags and pulled out a paper sack and handed it to Kattie.

"What is this?"

"Lunch," said Jim.

Kattie looked back to the lots. The men all sat on the top rail eating something.

"Eat," said Jim. "We are not through yet." He took a bite off his sandwich.

Kattie opened the sack and took out a ham-and-cheese sandwich. She started eating it. No dressing, just ham, cheese, and bread; it was the best sandwich she had ever tasted.

"Let's go," said Jim as he eased out from under the trees. The other two men had just come back with three cows with calves and put them in the lot. One man was at the gate of the small lot, two more eased into the big lot on their horses, Jim and Kattie got on the outside of the lot, and two more men got on the other side.

"What are we doing?" asked Kattie.

"We have got to keep the herd off the fences while they separate the mama cow and calves. We do not want the babies stepped on by the other cows."

Kattie thought, *Man, there is a lot I do not know about cows yet.*

The two men in the lot cut out one cow and one calf at a time, then pushed them into the smaller lot. When they were done, there were thirty-three pairs of cows and calves in the smaller lot. It was now 6:00 p.m.

"What now?" asked Kattie.

"Now rest and eat."

"Oh, thank you, Lord," said Kattie. Jim laughed.

All the men tied their horses to their trailer, pulled off the saddles, and brushed their horse down. They then gave them grain and hay to eat. Kattie brushed down Ginger and talked to her while she did, then fed her. Some of the men had already built a big fire with a grate over it; others had brought out their ice chest of cold beer. Kattie had a new understanding of the way cowboys took care of their horses before their selves. Today had been a learning experience she would never forget. One of the men was throwing thick slabs of beef steaks on the hot grate; she could hear the sizzle of the meat. Another was prepping baked potatoes, and one was stirring a big pot of beans. It all smelled so great.

"Here, Doc," said one of the men as he tossed her an ice-cold beer.

She was amazed at how everyone worked together. Each took a task, and each performed it, just like when they were working the cows. The ice-cold beer was so good. Before she knew it, Kattie was on her third one.

"Ladies first," said one of the cowboys as he handed her a plate. "Come on, we are all waiting for you."

She filled her plate and started looking around for somewhere to sit. Jim walked over by her and said, "Watch. Like this." He crossed his feet, then slowly sat down on the ground.

"Oh," said Kattie as she did the same. Kattie ate all she could. It was so good; the meat just melted in her mouth.

After Jim was finished eating, he let out a shrill whistle. One of the four dogs that were helping came running over. "Kattie, this is Cowley. Cowley, this is Kattie. That's Pepper's mom," said Jim.

"Oh, well, glad to meet you, Cowley."

Jim placed the two plates in front of Cowley and said, "Eat." She lapped all the leftovers up, then lay down beside Jim.

All the men ate, then cleaned up the area and fed the other dogs the scraps. They started loading up their horses and dogs, all but Jim.

One of the men handed Kattie another beer before he picked up his ice chest and loaded it. One of the other men said, "Good night. See you in a couple of days, Doc." They all got in their trucks and headed out.

"Are we leaving?" asked Kattie.

"No, we got to look after them cows until the trucks get here Monday morning."

"Oh," said Kattie.

"Just rest," said Jim.

She set down the half bottle of beer she had in her hand. She lay back on the ground and looked up at the stars and passed out.

"Kattie, Kattie, wake up," said Jim. "It's time to go to work."

"Okay, I'll be there in minute," she said as she rolled over. Then she opened her eyes. "Oh, where am I?"

"Mr. Smith let you use one of his daughters' rooms. Come on, get up."

Kattie started to slide out from under the covers and realized all she had on was her bra and panties. "What…where…who took off my clothes?"

"I don't know," said Jim. "Come on, get a shower and get dressed. We got work to do." Jim walked out of the room with a big smile. "Coffee's on the stove," said Jim on his way out.

Kattie took a shower, then put her clothes back on and headed out of the room. "Jim. Mr. Smith." Nobody replied. She went into the kitchen, poured a cup of coffee, and walked outside.

"Still glad you got those cows?" asked Mr. Smith with a smile.

Kattie stretched her arms above her head and said, "I'm not sure." The old man laughed. "Where's Jim?" asked Kattie.

"He's out there tending your cows," said the old man.

"Oh," said Kattie as she set down her coffee cup and headed out to find him. Jim was filling up the water troughs. Kattie walked up. "Sorry, I'm late."

"It's okay. Not much of a drinker, are you?"

"No, I'm not," said, Kattie. "By the way, how did I get in that bed last night?"

"I picked you up and toted you in the house and laid you on it."

"So you didn't take off my clothes?"

"No, ma'am," said Jim with a smile.

"You liar," said Kattie.

Once they got all the cows watered and fed, Jim said, "Okay, come on, Doc, let's go inside."

Jim and Kattie went inside the kitchen. Jim poured them both a glass of iced tea, then sat down at the table. Mr. Smith came out wearing a suit and tie; he handed Kattie a small dress.

"Found this in my girls' closet. Try it on. Go get ready, boy," said Mr. Smith.

"Where are we going?" asked Kattie.

"Well, I don't know about you people in Deadwood, but round here, we all go to church on Sundays. Hurry up now," said Mr. Smith.

Kattie got up and went to the room she slept in last night. She changed into the dress. *Perfect fit,* she thought. She brushed her hair and put back on her boots while Jim changed into dress pants and dress shirt. They met back in the kitchen. "That sure is a pretty dress," said Jim.

"Okay, let's go," said Kattie as she rolled her eyes.

They drove out to the highway, then drove down the road a way to a little white church. After church, they drove into town to get something to eat.

That afternoon, Jim and Kattie refilled the water troughs and threw out more hay. Then they sat on the porch and drank iced tea and talked for a while.

Jim asked, "What time will the trucks be here in the morning?"

"Around 8:00 a.m.," said Kattie.

"You got your med crew lined up?" asked Jim.

"Yes, I even got another vet coming to help too," said Kattie.

"Okay, let's do a walk around before dark," said Jim, "to make sure the cows are all right." "Okay," said Kattie.

Kattie was kicking the ground as they walked around the lots. She said, "You know, I really appreciate everything you have done to help me."

"You do?" asked Jim.

"Yes, I never knew there was so much work involved in moving cows."

Jim stopped and turned around. He took Kattie's hands into his and pulled her up close, leaned down, and kissed her lips. He then kissed the tip of her nose, then her forehead, then back to her lips. Kattie just melted in his arms. She could not move; she had no control of her body. Jim picked her up and carried her into the barn. They fell into the hay, still clinging to each other.

The next morning, Kattie woke to the smell of bacon and coffee in the house. She got up and got dressed. Pulling the last boot on, she stumbled out of the room. In the kitchen, Mr. Smith was sitting at the table drinking coffee and Jim was taking up scrambled eggs.

"Something smells good in here," said Kattie.

"It's me," said Mr. Smith. "I took a bath last night." Then he chuckled.

"What can I do to help?" asked Kattie.

"Nothing," said Jim. "Just have a seat."

Kattie could not look Jim in the eyes but could not take her eyes off him.

Just as they were finishing breakfast, the cowboys started showing back up. As they walked out onto the porch, one of the men said, "Morning, Doc."

"Good morning," said Kattie.

Jim had already saddled up his and Kattie's horse. Jim walked over to the older man in the group; his name was Bill. Jim said, "When the first two trucks get here, let's load the calves on one and the mama cows on the other one and send them first."

"Okay," said Bill.

As the last cowboy got saddled up, they could hear the first cattle truck coming. As the first truck came, they flagged him over to the smaller lot. As they opened the truck and let down the ramp, Bill rode up and said, "Just the babies on this one." The crew started pushing the babies out of the lot and onto the truck. After it was loaded, the second truck was there. "Okay, move that truck. Let's get the other one in here." They dropped the ramp on the second truck and loaded the mamas. "Okay now let us get those yearlings in this pen. Just hold the truck," said Bill. After about thirty head were in the lot, they started. "Let them load up with the mamas. Okay, ship them out."

Jim told Kattie, "You need to follow these two trucks to Plumber's Gap and get your crew started. We will bring the rest. Just let the mamas and yearlings out first into the lot, then as you run the calves through, they can find their mamas."

"Okay," said Kattie. Another truck came in as Kattie and the other two trucks left.

When they got to Plumber's Gap, Carol and the clinic crew were there, along with the other vet. They brought the trucks in and started unloading the yearlings and the mama cows in the lot. They sent that truck back for another load, then started unloading the calves. They had to run them through the chute to vaccinate and deworm them. Jim showed up with the third truck and the horses; he unloaded the horses. Jim backed the third truck up to a larger catch pen and unloaded the cows into it. When the fourth truck got there, they were through with the calves. Two of the other cowboys showed up with that truck. Jim asked them to put the yearlings in the catch pen with the chute. Jim unloaded the fourth truck, then sent those two trucks back. When the fifth truck got there, Kattie and her crew were almost through with the yearlings. Those two men went down and relieved Jim and unloaded the fifth truck.

Jim came back up and told Kattie he needed her help. She got on Ginger and followed Jim. They went to the cow and calf pen. Jim said, "We need to turn them loose so we'll have more room." Jim opened the gate and went in. He said as they came out, "Just push them slowly deeper into the field."

Kattie was thinking, *What? Me?* Ginger fell in behind the first group of mamas and babies and eased along behind them. Kattie did not know what to do, but Ginger did. The other mamas and babies followed along, and Jim filled in behind them. They worked their way back until they couldn't see the lots anymore.

Jim rode up to Kattie and said, "That's good, Doc. Just let them go." The mamas and babies stopped and started eating the tall grass. "Good job," said Jim as they rode back to the lots.

The sixth load was there, and all the other cowboys came with it. Jim told Bill, "Cut them steers out of the yearlings, then let the heifers out. Just push them down to the mama cow. I'll cut out the bull and put him in a pen by himself for a while."

"Okay," said Bill.

The last truck left. The vet crew had been gone for a while. It was midafternoon.

Jim said, "Here, Doc." He handed her a brown sack. She did not have to ask; she knew what was in it. The rest of the men rode back up to the pens and pulled out their brown sacks.

"It was a good day," said Jim.

"Yup," said Bill, "smooth."

Kattie asked Bill, "What do I owe you and your crew?"

"Well, what are you going to do with those twenty yearling steers?" asked Bill.

"I don't know," said Kattie, looking at Jim.

"They should do it," said Bill.

"Okay," said Kattie and shook Bill's hand.

"Nice working with you, Doc," said Bill.

"It was my pleasure," said Kattie.

Bill told his crew, "Load up them steers, boys. Let's go home."

Each one came by and shook Kattie's hand. She told them all her thanks. They loaded up and headed out, honking their horns as they drove off.

"Well, what about you, cowboy?" asked Kattie.

Jim smiled and said, "Let's put these horses in this empty lot, brush them down, and give them some food and water." Jim pulled the saddle off his horse and started brushing him down. Kattie did the same with Ginger. They put out food and water for the horses, then put out some food and water for Cowley. Jim locked up his truck but left the trailer open for Cowley. Jim said, "Okay, Doc, let's get a room and a bath." They got into Kattie's car.

"Can we please go by my house so I can get some clean clothes?"

"Sure," said Jim, "but I don't think you're going to need them."

Chapter 8

The Surprise

Kattie was making plans for a house at Plumber's Gap. She had an architect working on the house plans. She wanted to build her house on the ridge of the valley in sight of the waterfall she found back in the spring. She was having a road built back to the site and reworking the fencing. Kattie had taken her father, Tim, out to see the cows and showed them the spot where she wanted to build. Tim told her that he was enormously proud of her and that her pops would be too. Kattie said, "Well, Dad, I need some help getting the gold out of the old mine shaft."

"Oh, okay, I'm not sure what that's going to take," said Tim. "I'm sure the old ladders have rotted. We will have to get the old cabin debris off the floor. We left it there to hide the entrant."

"I know," said Kattie. "It's going to be hard, but Leann and Bobby Joe have the old Tindal house, and Sara will want yours and Mom's house, so I need my own house. I need the money to pay for my house and finish building the ranch."

"Give me a couple of days. I'll come up with something," said Tim.

The next week, Tim called Kattie and told her that he had had the debris removed from the old floor so they could open the old hatch.

"Great," said Kattie. "What are we waiting for? Let's go get it."

"Not so fast," said Tim. "It might be dangerous. We need to plan this out. I don't think I'm able to go down in the mine. I am getting too old for climbing in holes."

"I'm not," said Kattie.

"No, but if there is trouble, who is going to help you get out?" asked Tim.

"I know someone I think I can trust," said Kattie. "I'll call him."

"Are you sure you can trust him?" asked Tim.

"Yes!" Kattie dialed Jim's number.

"This is Jim. Leave a message," she heard.

"This is Kattie. Give me a call, please." She hasn't heard from him in over three weeks.

Late that afternoon, Jim called. "Hey, Doc," he said, "what's up?"

"Well, I need some help," said Kattie.

"Okay, I'm on my way."

"Wait," said Kattie. "Just you, no horses."

"Okay. Where at?" asked Jim.

"Plumber's Gap," said Kattie. Kattie called Tim. "I've got help coming."

"When?" asked Tim.

"Now," said Kattie. "He'll be here in a couple of hours."

"Okay, what do you need?" asked Tim.

"Lights, ropes, ladders, hammers, and crowbars," said Kattie.

"Okay," said Tim, "I'll meet you out there."

Kattie drove out to the ranch and parked in the driveway. Tim showed up later with the supplies. They sat and talked for a while; they waited for Jim.

"So who is this guy?" asked Tim.

"Just a friend, Dad. He helped me find my cows and get them moved," said Kattie.

About that time, Jim pulled up. Kattie and Tim got out and walked to his truck. As Jim got out, Kattie walked up and kissed him.

"Hey, Doc," said Jim.

"Oh, Dad, this is Jim," she said, blushing. "Jim, this is my dad, Tim."

Jim reached out and shook Tim's hand. "So, Doc, what you got this time?"

"You didn't tell him?" asked Tim.

"No, not yet," said Kattie.

"Well, let's move this stuff across the road," said Tim.

They all got in Tim's truck and drove across the road and up to the mine.

"Okay, Doc, what's up?" asked Jim.

"Okay, well, you see, there's this old gold mine here, and I need to get some gold out of it."

"Do what?" asked Jim. "You don't just get gold out of a mine. There is a little more to it than that. Mr. Plumber, sir, will you tell her."

Tim laughed. "Okay, look, Kattie inherited this claim. First of all—" said Tim.

"That's good," said Jim, "at least we are not stealing the gold."

"No, no," said Kattie, laughing. "Okay, my grandfather's brother put his father's gold back in the mine and seal it up when his father died. That's their graves right over there," said Kattie, shining a light. "And now it belongs to me."

"How much gold are we talking about?" asked Jim.

"No one knows for sure," said Tim.

"Okay, what do we do?" asked Jim.

They walked over to the old door in the cabin floor.

"We need to get that open," said Tim as he pointed at the floor.

"Okay, here goes," said Jim. He took a hammer and a bar and started working on the door.

Tim walked over by Kattie and said, "Just a friend, huh?" Kattie blushed as her dad got a hammer to help. They got the nails out and started prying the door open. It finally gave way and opened. "Be careful," said Tim. "That hole is deep."

They all shone their lights down in the hole. All they could see was a landing about twenty feet down and lots of spiderwebs. The old wooden ladder was still up.

"Well, who's going down the old routine ladder into the creepy hole?" asked Jim. Neither Kattie nor Tim said a word. "Oh, okay, I see," said Jim. Jim took one of the ropes and tied it around a big tree, then dropped it down into the hole.

Kattie said, "Okay, I just needed yawl here in case I need help getting out and pulling up the gold. I'll go down. God, I hate spiders."

"Nope," said Jim, "there ain't no way you are going down in that hole. I've got to have that gold to finish what I started."

Tim said, "No, he is right, Kattie. It's not worth it. It's too dangerous, baby."

"Okay, look, let me get my truck. It has a winch on it. We can pull it up here and use the winch," said Jim. "But I'm going down in the hole."

"Good idea," said Tim.

Kattie said, "But—"

"But nothing," said Jim, pitching his truck keys to Kattie. "Go get my truck, Doc."

Jim tied a piece of rope around his waist, then hooked the winch line to the rope. Jim showed Tim how to work the winch line, then started down, while Kattie shone a light down the hole.

"The ladder is not going to hold," said Jim. "Tell your dad to stop."

"Stop, Dad," said Kattie.

Tim walked over to the hole. "What is wrong?" he asked.

"The ladder," said Jim, "it won't hold."

"Hold on," said Tim. He went to his truck and came back with an aluminum extension ladder and started it down in the hole.

Jim asked, "Why are we just now doing this?" He got over on the new ladder and said, "Okay, let's go."

Tim was letting out on the winch cable while Kattie was shining the light. Jim made it to the landing. He shone his light down the tunnel leading off from the entrance hole.

"Okay, I'm down," he said.

"Stop, Dad," said Kattie. "What do you see?" asked Kattie.

"Just rocks, dirt, and spitters. Lots of spitters. You want one?" asked Jim, laughing.

"Do you want out?" asked Kattie, not laughing.

"Okay, what am I looking for?"

"Bags of gold," said Kattie.

"I know that. Get your dad."

Tim came over to the hole. "Yeah?"

"Where do you think the gold would be?" asked Jim.

Tim said, "The story was that my uncle put the gold back in the bottom of the mine. I assume that means the lowest point."

"Okay," said Jim. He headed deeper in the hole at the very end of the tunnel; he could see something. There were three wooden boxes. "I think I found it," said Jim.

"What?" asked Kattie.

Then Jim's light went out. "Oh, shit," said Jim. "Kattie!" Jim called.

Kattie could not hear what Jim was saying. Tim said, "There is something wrong."

Jim called out, "Kattie!" They could hear him but could not understand what he was saying.

"We've got to do something," said Kattie. She climbed into the hole and started down the ladder.

Tim said, "Wait, let me tie a rope on you."

"No time, Dad," said Kattie. She made it to the bottom of the hole, and she shone her light down the tunnel. She saw Jim on his hands and knees crawling her way. "Jim!" she called out. "Are you okay?" she asked as she ran to him.

"Yes," said Jim, "my light went out. It was dark." They both busted out laughing with tears in their eyes.

"Oh my god," said Kattie, "I thought you were hurt."

"Nope, just scared the shit out of me."

Kattie went back to the hole. "We are okay, Dad," said Kattie. "Drop us another light."

"Okay," said Tim.

Kattie went back to Jim.

"I think I found it," said Jim.

"Really?" said Kattie, all excited.

He led her to the end of the tunnel. There, they saw three boxes. "There," he said.

Kattie slowly opened one of the boxes. "Holy cow," said Kattie.

"What?" asked Jim.

Kattie moved over. Jim could see gold coins, hundreds of them. They each grabbed one side of the box and headed out to the landing, then went back to get the others. Once they had all three boxes at the landing, Jim sent Kattie up to her dad.

Tim hugged her. "Are you okay?"

"Yes, Daddy, I'm great."

"Did you find it?"

"Yes, Daddy, you're not going to believe."

Jim got a rope, saddled under the first box and told Tim to winch it up. As the box got to the top, they grabbed it. Jim put a rope on the second box while the cable was coming back down, then did the same on the third. By the time they got all three boxes up out of the hole, it was getting daylight. They loaded the boxes in Tim's truck first. They pulled up and untied all the ropes, rolled them up, and put them and the ladder in Tim's truck. They closed the hatch door and nailed it back shut.

Tim said, "Yawl follow me to my house. I will get Abby to cook us some breakfast."

Tim pulled into his carport and closed and locked the door. Kattie and Jim went inside the house.

"Mom," said Kattie.

"In the kitchen," said Abby.

They walked in the kitchen holding hands. "Mom, this is Jim. Jim, this is my mom, Abby."

"Nice to meet you, Ms. Plumber," said Jim.

Tim came in and poured three cups of coffee and set them on the table. They sat down.

"Abby, did you meet Jim, Kattie's friend?" Kattie blushed.

"Yes, I did," said Abby. "So how did you meet each other?"

"Well, ma'am, there was this horse, then there was this puppy, then there were some cows." Kattie busted out laughing.

Sara walked in. "What's all the laughing about?" she asked.

Tim said, "Jim, this is my oldest daughter, Sara, Kattie's sister. Sara, this is Jim." Jim stood up and pulled out a chair for Sara. Tim said, "Sara is a lawyer."

He took a sip of his coffee. "I might need one if I keep hanging out with you two," Jim said, talking about Tim and Kattie. Tim choked on his coffee and laughed.

Sara got up and helped her mom put everything on the table. As they started eating, Sara asked, "So what have you been doing all night?" Nobody said a word. "Mom?" said Sara.

"I do not know, dear. All I know is, your dad stayed out all night with Kattie and her friend," said Abby.

"That sounds interesting," said Sara.

"It was," said Tim. They all laughed.

Kattie asked Jim, "So how is your ranch coming?"

"Okay," said Jim. "Mr. Smith, still hanging on, got me a few cows for breeding, all from different bloodline."

"That's good," said Kattie. "Do you have a bull yet?"

"No, not yet. I found one in Nebraska," said Jim, "at the Three Bar Ranch. Right bloodline, but the wrong price."

"How much?" asked Kattie.

"Oh, just $20,000.00," said Jim.

"For a bull?" asked Tim. They all started laughing again.

"Yep, that's what they said. It will take a while to come up with that."

"What breed of the bull is that?" asked Kattie.

"A Braunvieh," said Jim.

"Oh," said Kattie, "a German cow."

"How do you know? Oh, right, vet." Kattie just smiled.

After breakfast, Kattie and Jim said their goodbyes. Kattie did not want him to go, but he had things to do. He promised he would come back soon. Tim shook Jim's hands and told him if he ever needed anything to just call; he gave him a business card. Kattie walked him to his truck, holding his hand. He had to pull his hand away.

The next day, Kattie called the rancher in Nebraska and made a deal to buy the Braunvieh bull Jim was wanting and had him shipped it to Jim's ranch in Montana with a note that simply said, "Surprise! Thank You! Love, Kattie."

Chapter 9

The House

"Kattie, line 2," said Carol.

"Hello, this is Kattie."

"Hey, Doc, it's Jim. How are you?"

"I'm good," said Kattie. "And you?"

"Well, I'm standing here looking at a beautiful bull somebody sent me."

"Oh, really?"

"Yep, thought you might want to come see him."

"I do. I think a weekend trip would do me good."

"Well, come on, we'll be here."

Friday afternoon, Kattie packed a small overnight bag and headed across the Montana line. Kattie got there right at dark. Jim and Mr. Smith were sitting by a fire in the firepit, drinking beer. Jim got up and got her a chair, then handed her a beer.

"You know, the last time you drank beer, you lost your pants," said Jim.

"Yep, looks like I'd know better, but I don't," said Kattie.

"Well, boy, you ready to burn them steaks?" asked Mr. Smith.

"Yep, bring them on."

Kattie said, "I'll get them." She got and went to the kitchen and got the steaks off the counter, then took them to Jim. She turned and headed back to the house.

"Where are you going?" asked Jim.

"To fix the potatoes and get some plates."

Jim looked at Mr. Smith and smiled. "She's learning, boy," said Mr. Smith.

They ate, then sat and watched the fire for a while. Mr. Smith said, "Well, I'm going in."

"Good night," said Kattie.

"Good night," he replied.

After a while, Kattie said, "Well, I think I'll go in too." She picked up the plates, gave the leftovers to Cowley, and headed inside.

Jim just kept sitting at the fire. Kattie could tell he was in deep thought about something. She washed up the plates and started to go back outside but stopped in the doorway. She turned and went to the bedroom; she took off all her clothes and crawled under the covers. She thought to herself, *He knows where I'm at if he wants me.*

She woke up the next morning to the smell of breakfast cooking and coffee. She got up, went to the bathroom, then got dressed. As she walked into the kitchen, Jim and Mr. Smith were filling their plates.

"Morning, Doc," said Jim.

"Good morning," she said back.

"You better hurry up," said Mr. Smith. "Last person gets the least."

Kattie laughed as she poured herself some coffee and sat down. "So tell me about this bull you got," said Kattie.

"Nice bull," said Mr. Smith as he sipped his coffee.

Jim said, "We will go out and see him after breakfast."

They finished eating. Jim got up, and Kattie followed. She followed Jim out to the barn.

"Oh, how beautiful," said Kattie. It was a large brown-colored bull with short, stubby horns. Jim just stood there. "What's wrong?" she asked. "I know something is bothering you." Jim kicked the dirt floor. "Did I do something wrong?" asked Kattie.

"No, Doc." In a soft voice, Jim said, "It's just I don't know how to feel about you buying me this bull."

"Feel happy," said Kattie. "That's nothing compared to what you've done for me. You saved me more than that on my herd."

"I know," said Jim. "Don't get me wrong, I love the bull."

Kattie walked over and kissed him. She looked into his eyes and said, "Thank you for everything! Besides, I'm rich now thanks to you." She smiled as she walked back to the house.

Jim saddled up his horse and Ginger, then led them up to the house. Kattie was on the porch with Mr. Smith. "Come on, Doc, let's go check things out."

Kattie jumped up and climbed on Ginger. They turned around and headed to the main pasture. "What are we doing?" asked Kattie.

"Just looking to see what we can find."

They rode along and told each other about their own plans. Kattie talked about her house, and Jim talked about the herd he was going to build. After an hour or so, they headed back. Jim told Kattie that he was sorry about the way he acted earlier and thanked her for the bull.

They made it back to the house, unsaddled the horses, brushed them down, and put them up. Jim said, "Let's go to town and get us a burger or something."

"Okay," said Kattie.

They got in Jim's truck and drove off down the gravel road. They got their food and sat there in the truck and ate with the radio on. Once they finished, Jim cranked up, and they took off, heading back. Jim turned off the radio and said, "Looks like we are both going to be busy for a while."

"Yup, but it will be worth it in the long run," Kattie said, not seeing what he was trying to say. When they got back to the house, Mr. Smith had gone inside, probably for a nap, said Jim.

Jim and Kattie sat in the porch swing side by side as a cool breeze was blowing across the porch. Kattie took Jim's hand and placed it on her leg between her knee and thigh as they sat and talked. Jim just kept talking and made no effort to move his hand. Kattie had unbuttoned her top shirt button and was lying back against Jim's chest, trying to give him a view. She then took his hand and pulled it up to her thigh, still no attempt to move his hand. Kattie sat up, then stood up.

Jim asked, "What are you doing?"

"I'm going home," said Kattie.

"Home? But why?" asked Jim.

"Because I got things to do. I got contractors coming Monday. I got… I got…bye, I got to go." Kattie went inside, got her bag, and stomped out to her car. She cranked it up and drove off. Tears filled her eyes. As she headed down the gravel road, she hit the blacktop squealing tires and headed to Deadwood.

Kattie stayed in bed all day the next day. Come Monday morning, she was up and ready to go. The contractors were moving in today to start building her house; she could hardly wait. She didn't know what was wrong with Jim, but she did not care. She had things to do. The last thing she needed was a man to get in her way. Kattie spent her days at the clinic and the afternoons at the ranch. The house was coming along great; they should have it done by winter. That was the plan anyway. It had been four weeks since her trip to Montana. She still didn't understand what had happened but tried not to think about it.

Kattie's dad came to the clinic to see Kattie. "So how are things going?" asked Tim.

"Good," said Kattie. "The house is coming along."

"What about your fall roundup?"

"Yep, I got Bill and his crew lined up," said Kattie.

"What about Jim?" asked Tim. No reply! "Well, if I can do anything to help, let me know," said Tim as he kissed her cheek.

*****

"Kattie, are you all right?"

"Yes, I'm fine," said Kattie as she came out of the bathroom.

Carol said, "You need to go see your doctor. Something's wrong. You have been sick every morning for two weeks now."

"I am a doctor," said Kattie.

"Not a very good one if you won't take care of himself," said Carol.

"Okay," said Kattie, "call and get me an appointment. I'll go." Kattie went out to the ranch. The men were putting in the windows and doors.

The next day, Kattie went to the doctor's office to get something for her upset stomach. "I'm sure it's just a bug of some kind," said Kattie.

"Well, it was a big one," said the doctor. "You're pregnant."

"No," said Kattie, "I can't be."

"But you are, about six weeks," said the doctor.

"Oh no," said Kattie.

When she got back to the clinic, Carol asked, "Well, what did the doctor say?"

"Nothing, just a bug," said Kattie. Kattie told no one; she tried not to even think about it. She was mad at herself. *How could I let this happen?* she thought.

In the spring of 1978, Kattie finished building her house. Now six months pregnant at the age of thirty years old, she was now having a hard time hiding her baby bump from everyone. Tim and Abby were now eighty-four years old. Kattie prayed they would live to see her baby. Her sister Sara and her assistant Carol were the only ones she had talked to about the baby. Kattie decided to have an open house at Plumber's Gap and announce that she was expecting. It had been over five months since seeing Jim. She had been so busy that she had not thought much about him. After Kattie announced the open house, Tim took it upon himself to invite Jim. Jim tried to refuse, but Tim would not take no for an answer. After all, he did help him and Kattie get the gold, and he hoped maybe them seeing each other might get them back together. Tim had no idea what happened with them. Kattie would not talk about it at all.

On the day of the open house, all of Kattie's family was there, as well as the staff at the clinic and the law office. She also had a lot of her friends and customers show up. Everyone toured the house and was awed over it and the size—six bedrooms, five baths, a den, a living area, and a study, with a large kitchen and a porch that wrapped all the way around the house. Once everyone had gathered in the living and den area, one big open room, Kattie announced that she had news for everyone. The end door opened, and in walked Jim, but Kattie didn't see him.

Kattie said, "I know you all think I'm just getting fat, but the truth is, I'm six months pregnant." You could hear a pin drop, but the thing they heard was the side door close as Jim went out. After a few seconds, everyone went to her to congratulate her.

Tim, her father, had seen Jim come in and went out looking for him, but he was gone. Kattie never knew Jim was there. Tim went to her and hugged her; he would not let go. He just kept saying, "My sweet, sweet baby girl."

After everyone else left, Carol and the clinic staff stayed and helped Kattie clean up. Now that it was out, Kattie felt a weight had been lifted off her shoulders and was now looking forward to having her child.

The next week, Jim showed up at the clinic. He walked straight back and found Kattie. "We need to talk, Doc," said Jim in a stern voice.

"No, we don't!" said Kattie. "Get out of my clinic now!"

Jim dropped his head. "Just talk to me, Kattie, please."

"Go to my office," said Kattie. "I'll be there in a minute."

Kattie walked into the office and sat behind her desk. "What do you want?"

Jim said, "I know you know."

"What?" asked Kattie.

"I know about the baby," said Jim.

"How do you know?" asked Kattie.

"I was there at the open house."

"Why…how?"

"Tim invited me, more like forced me to come or else."

"I didn't see you there," said Kattie.

"I left. I didn't think it was a good time. I didn't know what to say. All those people were there," said Jim.

"Well, what do you want to say?"

"What do you want me to do? I mean, what can I do? Do you want me to ask you to marry me, or what?"

"No!"

"I want you to want to marry me."

"Do you?" asked Kattie.

Jim dropped his head.

"Well, it's a simple question, Jim. Forget all that cowboy horror bull crap," said Kattie.

"Well," Jim started to say, "I got plans."

Kattie stopped him. "I've got plans too, and it looks like you're not going to be in them. So get this straight. This is my baby, not yours. I don't want or need your help. My father and my sister are both lawyers. They will make sure you have no responsibility at all. Go back to your breeding ranch. Your job is done here!"

Jim got up, head down, and walked out. Kattie walked out behind him, not realizing that she was screaming at Jim and that everyone in the place had heard what she said. As Jim walked out the front door, everyone stood up and clapped as Kattie walked in the room.

Chapter 10

The Baby

"The Lord gives, and then he takes away." Kattie had her baby, a little reddish-blond-haired, green-eyed girl, just like her mom. Tim and Abby were so happy to have their third grandchild. Abby would sit all day and just hold her if they would let her. Kattie named the baby Marsa Marie Plumber. They called her Mary, after Tim's grandmother, but Abby just kept calling her my little Kattie. Two months after the baby was born, Tim passed away at home; he just went to sleep one night and didn't wake up. "Such a sweet man," said Abby. "He was such a sweet man." In the spring of 1979, Abby passed away at the age of eighty-five years old, holding her little Mary—Marsa Marie Plumber.

Kattie had to put Dawg out to pasture that spring. He was now twenty-five years old. He just walked around grazing with the mama cows and their babies. Pepper was over a year old now, just right for Mary to play with. Sara was still single and had the law firm. Leann and Bobby Joe's two sons were teenagers and now driving; Leann still had the stores. Kattie had hired two more vets and spent most of her time with baby Mary and at the ranch. She had just hired an older Mexican American couple to help her around the ranch. They were raising a granddaughter who was fourteen.

She moved in a small house trailer by the barn and corrals for them to live in. Kattie couldn't pronounce their names, so she called the man Pete and the woman Alice. "That's close enough," she said. The little girl's name was Rose, with paper sack-colored skin, long black hair, and brown eyes. Rose loved following Kattie around the ranch. She never stopped asking questions, but her favorite thing to do was play with Pepper. The man helped take care of the horses in the barn and kept up the yard around the house; the woman kept the house and cooked for everyone. Rose helped her grandfather and grandmother and watched after Mary. Mary was three years old now and loved the horses and the dog. Pep, she said.

Kattie had met a woman who owned a small place just out of Spearfish, South Dakota. She boarded and trained horses for a living. The woman would buy young horses, work with them for a year or so, then sell them to the local ranches for stock horses. Kattie bought four horses from the woman this spring. Her favorite was Dusty, a yellow gilding. She asked the woman if she knew of anyone she could hire to work with her horses part-time.

"My daughter," said the woman, "she's a schoolteacher but was raised helping me with horses. She's very good."

"Great," said Kattie. "When can I meet her?"

"I'll send her over to see you this afternoon after school. Her name is Kathy."

That afternoon, Kathy showed up at the ranch. She got out of her car in a dress and high heel. Kattie thought this wouldn't work. Kathy walked around to the back of her car, opened the trunk, and pulled out a pair of jeans. She slid into the jeans under her dress, then pulled the dress off over her head. She pulled out a zip-up shirt, then sat on the bumper and pulled on a pair of an old cowboy boots. She then tossed the dress and heels in the back seat of the car and shut the trunk. "Hi, I'm Kathy," she said as she walked toward Kattie.

Wow, Kattie thought. She was already impressed with this girl. "Hi, Kathy. My name is Kattie. This is Rose, and the little one is Mary. Oh, and that's Pepper." The dog smelled Kathy's boots.

"So Mom says you need someone to work your horses part-time."

"Yes," said Kattie.

"Okay, let's look at these horses."

They walked into the barn. They walked to the first stall where Dusty was kept.

"Hey, sweetie," said Kathy as she opened the stall. "I remember you." She reached out and rubbed his nose. She walked by and looked at the other horses. She spoke to each one, rubbing their noses. "I'll be here Monday afternoon at 4:00 p.m. to get started." She stuck out her hand to Kattie. She and Kattie shook hands.

"Sounds good," said Kattie. "See you then." Kattie said to Rose, "Now I just need a foreman to take care of the cows."

They headed back to the house. "Alice should have dinner ready," said Kattie.

They all sat at the table and ate—Kattie, Mary, Rose, Pete, and Alice—just like a big family. Alice cooked twice a day, breakfast at 6:30 a.m. and dinner at 5:00 p.m. If one ate in between, then they were on their own. Of course, Alice spoiled Mary and would cook her whatever she wanted whenever.

Kattie put up signs at the clinic and an ad in the local paper for a foreman, but not many responded. Most men just didn't care about working for a woman back then. Kattie called Bill, who had been doing her roundups since she first started the ranch. She asked if he knew anyone he would recommend.

"No, I can't think of anyone," said Bill. "Wait, there is one guy who has been helping me when I needed extra help. A good cowboy, a little older than most, but so am I." Bill laughed. "His name is Troy Petit. I'll give him a call and see if he is interested."

"Okay, thanks," said Kattie.

Two days later, Rose and Mary were watching Kathy work the horses in the corral when they saw an old raggedy pickup truck and horse trailer coming down the road.

"Wonder who that is," said Rose. He pulled up to the front of the barn in his old truck; he got out as they all stared at him. "Can we help you?" asked Rose.

"Yep, I'm looking for a Ms. Plumber."

Rose said, "I'll go get her." She picked up Mary and headed toward the house. Rose yelled "Kattie!" as she entered the house.

"What?" asked Kattie.

"There is an old man up at the barn looking for you."

"Oh, okay."

"He's in an old truck with a trailer."

Then Kattie remembered her talk with Bill. Kattie and the two girls walked back out to the barn. "Can I help you, sir?" asked Kattie.

"Hi, my name is Troy, ma'am. Bill told me you might be needing a ranch hand."

"Well, he's right. Bill said that you are a good cowboy."

"Well, ma'am, I do my best."

"How old are you, sir, if you don't mind me asking?"

"Well, not as old as I look, ma'am. I'm forty-three years old. I know look older. You see, I've been hit in the face a few times by bulls and other cowboys. I'm an old rodeo hand."

"Well, that's fine. I want to hire you, not marry you," said Kattie. "Come on down to the house and let's talk about this job."

"Yes, ma'am," said Troy.

Kathy told Rose, "Oh my god, he is gorgeous. So weathered and tall, um, um, um."

"You're crazy," said Rose. "He looks like he is a hundred years old."

"I don't care. I like older men."

"Well, he is that," said Rose. "Well, I'm going take Mary back down to the house. Come on, Mary."

"Come on, Pep," said Mary.

Kattie told Troy, "Look, I started with about one hundred and sixty head. I got one hundred calves last spring. Around forty were males. We cut and sold them. We put the heifers back in the herd this spring. I've got about fifty calves on the ground already this year, so by next spring, I'll have over three hundred head. I need someone to manage the roundups and work the cows, along with making sure the fences stay up. Oh yeah, and cutting and putting up the hay, plus everything else that goes with it. And we need a bunkhouse built. Do you think you could handle all that?"

"Yes, ma'am," said Troy. "What about hands?" he asked.

"You hire them when you need them and fire them when you don't. Build the bunkhouse back down the road about halfway over by the creek. I don't want to hear them at night, and I don't want them in my yard. I got kids here."

"Yes, ma'am," said Troy. "If it is okay with you, I'll go back and pick a spot for the bunkhouse, and I'll camp there until it's built."

"Sound good," said Kattie. "Welcome aboard, Troy. Good luck."

Troy headed back out to his truck. Kathy was there waiting. "Hi, my name is Kathy."

"Nice to meet you, ma'am. My name is Troy."

"I tend the horses here," said Kathy.

"Well, looks like I am gonna be tending the cows now," said Troy.

"Good," said Kathy. "Maybe we will see each other."

"Spec so," said Troy. Troy got in his truck and drove back down the road. Kathy twisted her behind back to the barn.

The next morning, Kattie went down to see the spot Troy had picked out for the bunkhouse. "That's good," said Kattie, "away from the road and out of sight. Get me a list of materials, and I'll get them coming. Make sure you build a kitchen in it. When you hire a crew, make sure one of them can cook. I'll buy your groceries, but I ain't cooking them."

The next week, Troy hired a couple of men, and they started building the bunkhouse.

Kathy wanted to help Troy, but Kattie told her to keep away from there, that she didn't need her distracting the men while they were trying to work. "I guess I'll go ride a horse then," she said, sticking her tongue out at Kattie.

The bunkhouse was finished well before time for the winter roundup. Troy spent his days riding the fences; sometimes he would be gone for two days or more days. He said there were a lot of fences around 5,000 acres.

Kathy was a plain-looking girl; she was twenty-three years old, twenty years younger than Troy. But she didn't care. She did everything but ask him to sleep with her. When he was there alone, Kathy would cook for him, clean the bunkhouse, and they would sit by the fire and talk. She loved hearing about his old rodeo days.

Winter was getting close; it was almost time to round up the cows and bring them to a pasture close to the house and barn. Troy brought in some hands. It was the first time that Kattie didn't have to help. After the roundup, Troy kept two hands to help through the winter. One of them was named Douglas; he was nineteen years old. Rose, now fourteen, was in love.

"He's too old for you," said Kathy.

"Shut up. No, he's not."

"That's what you always tell me."

"Yeah, but Troy is a hundred years old."

"What in the world is going on here?" asked Kattie.

"All the girls on this ranch have gone crazy. Not me," said Mary, who was now four. You want me to have Pep bite 'em?"

"No, baby, it wouldn't help."

"I will," said Mary.

"There's only one cure for this, and that's just to let it happen. They will have to learn the hard way. Except for you, Ms. Rose. You're too young," said Kattie.

The next day, Kathy asked Kattie, "What can I do? I've tried everything. He just will not pay me any attention."

"I know how that feels," said Kattie. "Look, talk to him. Just tell him how you feel. Don't try to trick him into something. Just be honest."

The next day, Kathy rode one of the horses back down to the bunkhouse. Troy's crew were out mending fences, and he was alone. Kathy got off the horse and tied him.

"What are you doing?" asked Troy.

"I wanted to talk to you."

"Okay, what's on your mind?"

"You," said Kathy. "Before you say anything, let me finish."

"Okay," said Troy.

"Look," said Kathy, "I know you're a lot older than me, and I know you have probably been with girls a lot prettier than me, but I love you, Troy! I truly do. I don't care how old you are or what you've done before. I just want to be yours and you mine." Tears were pouring down her face.

Troy walked over, put his hands on her face, wiped the tears with his thumbs, leaned down, and kissed her. He picked her up and carried her inside the bunkhouse and locked the door.

The next afternoon, Troy was at the barn when Kathy got there. Kathy was blushing as she looked at Troy.

"I want to tell you something," said Troy. A big lump rose up in Kathy's throat. Kathy just nodded; she couldn't talk. "I know I'm not much to look at," said Troy, "but I'm a hard worker, and I'll always be good to you if you want me."

Kathy ran over and hugged and kissed Troy. "Yes, yes, yes," said Kathy.

"Well, okay, I got to go back to work now," said Troy as he walked off. Kathy smiled and cried at the same time.

A year later, Kathy asked Troy to marry her, and he said yes! They had a small wedding in June. Kattie put them in a trailer house on the old mine claim across the road from the ranch.

Chapter 11

The Lost Gold Coins

In 1986, Mary was now eight years old and Rose was now eighteen and enrolled in college next fall. Kattie was sending her to veterinary school in Wyoming. Alice was so excited that her granddaughter was going to college; she said it was more than she could have ever hoped for. Rose grew up to be a very beautiful young lady, responsible, and strong-minded. Rose said she didn't know where that came from, but she did. Kattie raised Rose like her own daughter. Kathy and Troy were still living across the road from the ranch, tending horses and cows, and Kathy was still teaching. Dawg died last summer; they buried him up on a hill overlooking the valley so he could still watch over the baby calves. He was thirty-three years old, unheard of for a horse. Kattie had a tombstone made that said, "Dawg, the best horse ever."

Mary had her own horse now, and like her mother was when she was that age, she lived on that horse's back. Kattie always had to send out a search party for Mary's clothes and boots. She dressed her up in little cowgirl outfits every morning, but by lunchtime, when she came back to the house, she was only wearing her panties. Kattie asked her, "Where are your clothes?"

She pointed out. "That way."

Pepper was nine years old now. He never left Mary's side. They rode together, slept together, and would eat together, but Alice wouldn't have it. They even took baths together. Kattie said, "You both smell like that horse. Go take a bath."

Kattie had been appointed to the local Cattle Men Association. She only accepted because most of the members were her customers at the clinic, plus it was a status thing for the ranch.

In the summer of 1987, it rained for weeks on end. All the local creeks, rivers, and lakes were overflowing. The bunkhouse was flooded, large trees fell, and the main road going to Deadwood washed out. The force of the water was so strong that it washed rocks and grovel out of the creek bed up into the pastures. It took weeks for the water to reseed. Once it had, Troy and his crew got started removing the big rocks from the pastures. When they started working downstream from the waterfall, there were parts and pieces of an old wagon—old, waterlogged wagon wheel, old board, and metal straps.

Troy sent one of the men to get Kattie. When Kattie got there and saw the old wagon wheels, she said, "I wonder where that came from." They could tell by how wide the wheel was that it must have been an old freight wagon built for heavy loads. They knew it was old; they didn't know how old. Kattie said, "Save what you can of it and take it to the barn. I'll do some research on old wagons."

"Okay," said Troy.

The next morning, Troy decided it was going to take too long to scoop up all that gravel and threw it back into the creek. So he decided to just put a drag behind the tractor and drag the piles of gravel out flat where grass could grow through it and just leave it there to help with erosion. As Troy was dragging the gravel out flat, the other two men were putting hay up in the barn.

Kattie, Mary, and Kathy rode down to the falls on horseback to see how it was coming. As they rode up, Troy stopped the tractor. "What do you think?" he asked.

"Looks like it's working," said Kattie.

"What's that over there?" asked Mary as she slid down off her horse.

"What?" her mother asked.

About that time, Kathy saw it too. "What is that?" she asked.

Mary ran over to where the gravel had been spread, bent down, and picked up a gold coin. "This, Mama, this is what I was talking about. They were everywhere, hundreds of them."

"Oh my god," said Kathy as she picked one up. "This is unreal." She picked up another one and another.

Kattie and Troy came running over. "Holy mother of Jesus," said Troy.

Kattie had frozen. "Wait, stop! What are we going to put them in? Hold up." Kattie was in panic mode. "Okay, I need to go call Sara. Yawl go to the barn and get some buckets, bags, or something." Troy told the hands to go on to the bunkhouse, that they were through for today. "The fewer people that know, the better," said Kattie.

Kattie and Mary rode back to the house. Kattie called her sister Sara, the lawyer.

"This is Sara," she heard.

"Sara, this is Kattie. Come quick."

"Where?" asked Sara. "What wrong?"

"Nothing, but I need you to come to Plumber's Gap. Hurry."

Sara thought, *She is as crazy as she ever was.*

Kattie waited at the house until Sara came.

Troy and Kathy were gathering up containers of all kinds. "Where did it come from?" asked Kathy.

"I don't know," said Troy. "It has been in the creek." Troy and Kathy headed on back to the falls.

When Sara got there, Kattie, Mary, and Sara got in the truck and drove down to the falls. Sara asked the whole way, "What is it?"

"You've got to see this for yourself," said Kattie.

When they got out and walked down to Troy and Kathy, Sara saw what they were picking up. She almost fainted. "Oh my," said Sara, "how many are there?"

"I don't know," said Kattie as she pointed down the creek bank.

"They're everywhere," said Sara. "Who else knows?" asked Sara.

"Just us four and you now."

"Okay," said Sara, "let's get them picked up and put in something, and I'll be thinking about the legal side of things."

"You have got to buy a safe," said Troy as they picked up coin after coin as fast as they could.

After four hours of picking up coins, they stopped. They loaded what they had in the back of the truck.

"That's most of it," said Troy. "We've had to dig in the gravel to find any more." They took what they had to the house and put the containers in Kattie's closet.

Sara said, "Everybody, stay calm, and I'll start looking into this tomorrow."

Mary said, "I don't know what the big deal is. It is just a bunch of yellow quarters." As she went to watch TV, they all laughed.

Troy said, "I'll go back in the morning and drag some more and see if any more turn up. I'll have my crew go back to stacking hay in the barn."

"Okay," said Kattie. "Kathy, I need you to help me count tomorrow."

"Okay, no problem."

The next day, Kattie, Mary, and Kathy locked themselves in the bedroom. Mary watched TV, while Kattie and Kathy counted out the coins. They counted 2,643 $20.00 gold pieces, $52,860.00 in face value, but these were hundred-year-old coins dating from 1870 to 1876.

The hundred-year anniversary coin, centennial, was priceless! Kattie, Mary, and Kathy went to check on Troy when they finished counting.

Troy was still dragging the gravel; he had picked up about half a bucket full there at the falls. Troy said, "I think we need to go over this good, put up some marker, and then move on downstream and do the same. The gravel stops at the turn about five hundred yards downstream."

"Okay," said Kattie.

They spread out and started working their way across what Troy had spread; they put up a marker. They loaded what they had, then took it to the house to count, while Troy spread the next spot. Kattie and Kathy counted it out—806 more $20.00 gold pieces, $16,120.00 in face value. The girls loaded up and went back to Troy and started picking up coins in that area he was working on. They all stopped at dinnertime, loaded up, and went to the house. Kathy and Troy ate dinner with Kattie, Mary, Alice, and Pete.

"What are you doing down by the falls?" asked Pete.

Troy said, "Well, the creek folded and washed gravel out into the field. I'm spreading it out were the grass can grow through it."

Kattie looked at Mary and put her finger over her lips and made a key-turning signal.

"Oh," said Pete, "the boys about got all that hay stacked."

"Good," said Troy.

"So what are you bringing up here in those buckets?" asked Alice. "You better not be making a big mess in that room."

"No, we are getting the pretty round rocks and washing them off in Kattie's tub, then taking them out to dry," said Kathy.

"I'm going to put them in my flower bed just as long as I don't have to clean it up," said Alice. Alice cleaned off the table, and she and Pete left.

Mary said, "I ain't never heard so much storytelling in all my life. I'm going to watch TV." They busted out laughing.

Kattie, Kathy, and Troy counted the rest of the coins—1,486 more $20.00 gold pieces, $29,720.00 in face value, a total of 4,935 coins with a face value of $98,700.00.

Kattie called Sara, "So what did you find out?"

"Well, you can't go sell them. We must find out somehow where they came from."

"Why?" asked Kattie. "We found them on my land. They're mine."

"Not so fast, little sister. We must prove that they did not belong to a bank, some bank robbers' loot, or in any way belong to the government when it was put there. If they did, all you will get is a finder's fee."

"Well, that's not fair," said Kattie.

"It's not about fair. It's about the law," said Sara. "Anyway, how many coins did you find?"

"There are 4,935," said Kattie. She could hear Sara's phone hit the floor. "Sara, you okay?"

Sara finally came back on the phone. "Okay, you've got to hide them, and don't tell anyone until I can do some investigating. I may need to hire some help on this one," said Sara.

"Okay, just let me know what you find out."

*****

"Where are we going to hide all those coins?" asked Troy.

"At your house," said Kattie.

"What?" said Kathy.

"Troy, do you remember the old mine I told you about when we put the trailer in there?"

"Yes, ma'am."

"Well, that's where we are going to hide them."

"When?" asked Troy.

"Now," said Kattie.

Kattie told Mary that she would stay with Alice and Pete tonight, that she was going out with Troy and Kathy. But she couldn't tell them anything about all the yellow quarters they had found. She said, "Promise me."

"I promise. Can Pep go?"

"Yes, baby, Pep can go too. I'll be right back," said Kattie. "And we will load up the coins."

"Okay," said Troy.

Kattie took Mary to Alice, then went back to the house. They loaded the container of coins in the back of the truck. Troy said he had a ladder and lights. They drove across the road and backed up to the old shaft. Troy got the ladder and lights. They started pulling the nails out of the door, then pried it open.

"What's the plan?" asked Troy.

"We will put the ladder in. I'll climb down. You and Kathy lower the containers in. I'll untie them."

"Okay," said Troy. "Here is the ladder." Troy got a rope.

Kattie started down the ladder. "Well, I see the spiders are still here. Yuck."

Troy and Kathy let down the first container, then another and another until they had all of them in the mine.

"Okay," said Kattie, "I'm coming up." Kattie got out. They pulled the ladder out, shut the door, and nailed it back. By now, it was after midnight. They put everything up, and Kattie headed home.

The next morning, Troy went to the barn and got ten bales of hay, took it back across the road, and stacked it over the door on the wooden floor. Then he put plastic over it and tied it down.

Chapter 12

The Lost Gold Shipment Found

More than three months after Kattie put the gold coins down into the mine, her sister Sara called. "Well, we have our proof, baby sister. We now know where the coins came from and who they belonged to," said Sara.

"That's great," said Kattie.

"Come to my office, and I'll tell you the story."

"On my way," said Kattie.

Mary was in school, so leaving the house was not a problem. She drove into Deadwood to the law firm office.

"Hi, Kattie," said Sara. "I want you to meet Dave. He has been helping me with this. Let's go into the conference room. We have everything laid out in there. It took some digging, but we finally found the proof. The gold coins belonged to a man named James Leighton Gilmore. Mr. Gilmore was a gold miner and gold buyer in Deadwood Gulch back in 1876. He had bought up so much gold for a cheap price that he had run out of money and all he had was gold. With no bank in Deadwood at this time, he had to send gold to Hill City for more gold coins. The preferred currency was a $20.00 gold piece. The silver dollars were too heavy, and twenty silver dollars would weigh a man down. So Mr. Gilmore had his most trusted man load down an old freight wagon with bags of raw gold and sent him and two more men to Hill City to cash it in for gold coins. The men made it to the bank. We have a copy of the bank's copy of the receipt that the men were given, the amount of raw gold's weight and the value at the time of the exchange, and for the 5,400 $20.00 gold pieces the bank paid. Now the shipment was lost."

"How?" asked Kattie.

"An old freight hauler they called Dodger told the local law in Deadwood, which was investigating it as a robbery, that he saw the boys the day they left Hill City at the foothills and camped with them and that he told them about a shorter route back to Deadwood. We also have a copy of his statement."

Sara continued, "Now nobody hears of or sees these three men again until 1883, when miners found three bodies, skeletons, by a small waterfall west of Deadwood close to Lead. They also found arrows. Now here is the tricky part. It was assumed that the Indians killed the men and took everything, including the wagon, but according to historical data, there was over two feet of snow on the ground at that time. So the Indians most likely just took what they could carry and the horse and mules. According to the miners who found the skeletons, there were no guns, wagons, or animals, just the skeletons. So the only thing we can assume is, the Indians pushed the wagon into the falls. Either way, we have proof that there was a shipment of gold coin that left Hill City. The men took a shortcut, and the rainstorm washed up over 4,935 gold coins from somewhere along your creek. If this is correct, there are still 465 coins out there somewhere."

"So what now?" asked Kattie.

"We petition the state of South Dakota for ownership of the gold coins found. We will send all our proof with the request. The only thing is to protect you. Personally, we need to form a corporation for ownership and distribution of the coins," said Sara.

"Okay," said Kattie. "I want Troy and Kathy to have shares in the corporation."

"How much?" asked Sara.

"Fifteen percent each," said Kattie.

"Okay," said Sara. "I'll take 10 percent for legal fees. That will leave you 60 percent. Where are the coins now?" asked Sara.

"They're around somewhere," said Kattie.

In 1988, the state of South Dakota declared ownership of the James Gilmore lost gold shipment to P&P Gold Recovery Inc. and their shareholders. Of course, the state required the corporation to pay taxes on the coins as they were sold.

Part 2

Chapter 1

The Rodeo

Kattie Plumber and the P&P Gold Recovery Inc. had sold most of the lost coins recovered on Kattie's property. She saved back some of the more valuable ones for Mary to have when she was grown. The proceeds were divided between the shareholders. Some of the older coins were sold individually and brought large amounts of money for each coin, but most were sold in lots of ten, which sold for ten to twenty times their face value, making Sara and Kattie Plumber even wealthier. Troy and Kathy both got a share, which, combined, made them wealthy as well. Troy and Kathy bought an 80-acre spread about five miles from Plumber's Gap. They were now building a new house on their land. They now had a beautiful little two-year-old girl whom they named Tommie Ann Petit. They both still worked for Kattie. Kathy was still teaching in school and worked the horses in the afternoon. Rose had come back from college and was now a veterinarian. She was living in the house with Kattie and Mary. She now worked for Kattie as an intern vet at the animal hospital in Deadwood. Her grandmother and grandpa were still there at the ranch working for Kattie also.

Mary, now thirteen years old, was an avid horsewoman. She helped Kathy work with the horses. She had also started running the barrels, and with Kathy's help, she was training her own horse. She was getting pretty good. She and Kathy made trips to Cody and Cheyenne, Wyoming, just to get the horse used to the crowds and the other horses. Kattie would sometimes go with them when she had time. The name of Mary's horse was Quick Gold Cash, but she called him Bob! Bob was a beautiful palomino paint with a long white mane and tail. Mary kept him groomed and braided his mane. Bob was just five years old, but Mary and Kathy had been working with him since he was born. At five years old, Bob knew what he was doing but was learning how to do it with Mary on his back. Mary was also learning how to move on Bob as he ran to help him make the turns. Running the barrels was not just riding a horse; it was a team sport, horse and rider working together. That was the hardest part to do well, and you must be connected to your horse and your horse to you to be any good at it.

At an event in Cheyenne, Mary and Bob took third place. "We're getting better, Bob," said Mary.

The next week, they were set to run in Cody. She and Bob were waiting in the back. A horse trainer came up to Mary and said, "I've been watching you. You're pretty good, but you just need a better horse, one that's been trained for running the barrels."

Mary smiled and said, "I think I'm the one that needs more training."

The man said, "I've got a good horse for sale that I trained. I'd love to sell him to you."

Mary rose up, swung out of her saddle, and stepped down on the ground. She took and tied a knot in her reins and put them behind the saddle horn. They called her name. She told Bob, "Show him boy," as she popped him on the rump. Bob took off like a bullet, with Mary still standing there. He ran the course without a bobble. As he got shut down at the end of the alley, Mary climbed back on Bob.

The announcer said, "Whoa, folks, a 14.62 run. Too bad it doesn't count. The riders must be on the horse."

Mary looked at the man and said, "I think he'll be all right." And she rode to her trailer.

Kathy came running to the back to see if Mary was all right. "What happened?"

"Oh, that jerk over there tried to sell me a horse. He said Bob wasn't good enough, so we showed him."

"You're a crazy little shit, Mary," said Kathy. "Well, Bob, you won," said Kathy as she laughed. They loaded up their gear and headed home. "I'm sure Troy is ready for Mama to get home."

Leann's two boys were in high school now; they came out on the weekends sometimes to ride horses while their mother visited with Aunt Kattie and Rose.

"So how is Bobby Joe?" asked Kattie.

"He's okay. Still working for his dad selling cars." Leann laughed. "You know, he still remembers what you told him at our reception."

"I still mean it," said Kattie.

The next day, Mary was working with Bob in the arena. She had long reddish-blond hair just like her mom, and when she and Bob ran around the arena, it looked like yellow and orange flames shooting out of the back of her head. Kattie was watching her, wishing Mary could have had a pops growing up like she did. Growing up, just like her mom, she didn't have much use for boys. Kattie worried about her though. Pepper was getting older and didn't do much playing anymore. Mary liked spending time with Kathy and Troy, but once they got their house built, they probably would not be around as much. Rose was the perfect big sister, and she rode with Mary a lot when she was off on the weekends. She took Mary to town for clothes shopping and to movies and such. Kattie sometimes felt she made a mistake keeping Mary from her father, but then she thought, *Well, he never bothered to try.*

Mary and Kathy heard about a big rodeo coming up in Billings, Montana. That was a lot closer than Cody, Wyoming, so they started making plans to go. Bob and Mary ran barrels every day for a week. "We're ready," said Mary. This was a three-day event—Thursday, Friday, and Saturday—with the top five riders competing Saturday night. Troy, Kathy, and Tommie, the baby, would pull the horse trailer with Kattie, Mary, and Rose following. They had rooms reserved, and everybody was so excited just to get away for a few days. This was Mary's first big event, and she would be fourteen in three days, the last day of the event. She and Bob were ready.

Kathy and Mary got Bob ready to be loaded. They left out early Thursday morning. Mary wanted Bob to have time to rest from the trip before the event started. Kattie told Mary, "Try to get some sleep. It's going to be a long day." Mary lay back and closed her eyes, thinking about all the things she and Bob had been working on.

"Wake up, Mary. We're here," said Rose.

Mary rose up and looked out the window. Troy was backing the trailer up under the shade of a big oak tree. "How's that?" asked Troy.

"Great," said Kattie. "A little far from the arena, but Bob will like it."

They unloaded Bob and tied him to the trailer. Mary started brushing him down, then gave him some oats. She hugged his neck and said, "This is going to be a good weekend, buddy."

They sat out lawn chairs under the tree. Kattie said, "Okay, it's two more hours until this thing starts. Rose and I will go to town and get the rooms and unload the luggage. Mary, have you got your entry fees?"

"Yes, ma'am."

"Okay, we will be back."

Troy crawled in his truck seat, rolled down the windows, and said, "I'm going to get a nap."

Little Tommie was on the ground playing in the dirt. Kathy and Mary were just sitting and watching the other cowboys and cowgirls show up. Before long, Mary and Kathy would have to go to the draw. The girls ran based on their standing in the circuit, but if they had no standing, their names would go in a hat to be drawn.

Kattie and Rose had just come back. It was time to go register and get their draw.

Mary told Kathy, "I hope I'm not last."

There were fifteen entries in the barrel racing event. Seven of the girls were ranked, so the others had to draw. Mary got tenth; she was smiling from ear to ear. She went back to the trailer to get Bob ready for the grand entrée. The girl who drew eleven was a little blond-haired girl about Mary's size. Mary could tell that she was nervous. The girl was walking along with Mary headed to the back. Mary stopped and said, "Hi, my name is Mary. What's yours?"

"Billie," said the little girl. "Guess my dad wanted a boy." They both laughed.

"Have you run the barrels much?" asked Mary.

"Just at home. This is my first competition."

"Well, don't worry. You will be all right. It doesn't matter how good you do your first time. Just stay on your horse."

"Thank you," said Billie as she hugged Mary.

"If you need help or to talk, just let me know. I'm right over there," Mary said, pointing at her trailer. The girl turned and walked off. Mary got to the trailer and started saddling up Bob. She checked his feet and his shoes, making sure none were loose.

Mary lined up for the grand entrée. Kattie, Kathy, Troy, Rose, and Tommie all went to the stands. They started the grained entrée. The crowd sang the national anthem, then prayed, and the riders headed out of the arena. Mary saw Billie up ahead of her. The other horses were crowding her horse. Her horse was not used to this, and he started crow hopping. Mary rode up beside her, took her reins and synced them up around her saddle horn, pulling the horse's head against Mary's leg. "I got you," said Mary. They broke the pattern and headed out of the arena. Mary let go of the reins and handed them back to Billie. "Just walk him around for a while," said Mary. "Let him calm down. He'll be all right." Mary went back to the trailer to wait for the event to start.

After a little while, she saw Billie and some man walking up to her trailer.

"Hi, young lady, my name is Jim," said the man as he stuck out his hand.

Mary took his hand and said, "My name is Mary."

The man said, "I saw what you did for Billie, my daughter. Thank you very much!"

"You're welcome. I've been there myself. The ground's no place to be during the grand entrée," said Mary.

"You're right about that. I just wanted to shake your hand and say thank you!" Billie and her dad walked out of sight.

It was time. The eighth entrée had just run a 14.40, the best so far. Mary and Bob had their work cut out for them. The ninth runner ran a 14.52 but had a barrel down. Mary got ready at the end of the alley. Billie said, "Good luck, Mary." Mary pulled her hat down tight.

The announcer said, "All right, everybody, here comes Ms. Mary Plumber from South Dakota."

Mary Plumber? thought Jim. *It can't be.* He counted the years.

Mary said, "Okay, Bob, let's go."

Bob left out throwing dirt behind him. When they reached the timing light, Bob was stretched out. He hit to turn on the first barrel. Mary leaned like they had practiced. Bob shot out the outside of the turn, then hit the turn on the second barrel, never even touching the first two barrels. He stretched out for the third barrel. He nailed it, then opened up and headed back to the alley. When Mary got Bob shut down at the end of the alley, all she could hear was the crowd cheering.

"A 14.10," said the announcer. "That's your new leader, folks." They all kept cheering.

Mary took Bob back to the trailer, pulled his saddle off, and tied him. She grabbed his neck and started crying. "Oh, thank you, Bob!"

"Mary Plumber, sixty-five pounds, soaking wet, just made an incredible run," said the announcer. "Man, what a ride."

Billie made her run and clocked a 15.19, a good run for her first time. Mary brushed down Bob and gave him some oats and fresh water. She then headed off to the stands to watch the last two runners. She saw Kattie and the rest in the stands; she walked over to them. Kattie, Kathy, and Rose all hugged her. Troy shook her hand and said, "Great job, baby girl, great job."

The last two riders made their runs. One had a 14.98, and the other had a 15.31, making Mary the leader for the night. She would get to run first tomorrow night.

Billie saw Mary and came over to her. "You were great, Mary," told Billie.

"You did good for your first big event. Billie, this is my mom Kattie, my aunt Kathy, my uncle Troy, my niece Tommie, and my big sister Rose. Yawl, this is Billie, my new best friend."

"I'm your best friend?" asked Billie.

"Yep," said Mary.

Billie had a tear in her eye. "I've never been a best friend before."

"Well, you are now," said Mary as she took Billie's hand.

After the rodeo was over, they all went back to the trailer to check on Bob. Kathy walked up to Bob and said, "You're such a good boy." Kathy asked Rose if she would take Tommie to the room with her.

"Sure," said Rose.

"Troy and I will stay tonight and sleep in the truck if somebody will come relieve us in the morning."

"Okay," said Kattie.

Kathy leaned over to Troy with a smile and said, "I might have to get you to help me do something in that horse trailer."

The next morning, Kattie and Mary were there early to relieve Troy and Kathy. "Yawl head to the motel to get some more sleep and see Tommie. We got this." Kattie had stopped on the way and got Mary something for breakfast. Mary sat in a chair by Bob and shared it with him. He loved the hash browns. Mary got up and started rubbing Bob's legs. Then she walked him around the lot on his lead rope. She brought him back to the trailer, took off his lead rope, and turned him loose. Bob walked around, then found a spot and lay down and rolled. He got up and shook his whole body, making the dust fall off. Then he walked back to Mary. She clipped the lead rope back on him and tied him to the trailer. She got his brush and started brushing him down, talking to him the whole time about tonight. When she finished, she gave him oats, hay, and water.

Troy, Kathy, Rose, and Tommie came back around noon with BBQ. They all ate, and Kattie and Mary went back to the room so Mary could rest. When they left, Tommie was sitting on the ground under Bob, playing in the dirt. Bob never moved.

That afternoon about five, Kattie and Mary made it back to the arena. Mary started getting Bob ready for the event. It was a little hotter today than yesterday and not much of a breeze blowing. Mary was all excited. She got to be the first one to run tonight. Billie came by on her horse. "So what are you running tonight?" asked Mary.

"Ninth," said Billie.

"That's not too bad," said Mary.

"You got any pointers for your best friend?" asked Billie.

"Yes, let your horse run the barrels. You just hang on," said Mary.

It was time to line up. Everybody else had gone to the stands. Mary and Bob were in the alley when they called her name. Bob took off, slinging dirt again. He hit the turn for the first barrel and slid a little—the dirt was not packed. He adjusted and hit the turn for the second barrel.

"Perfect," said Kathy to Kattie as they watched.

He turned the third barrel and headed home, slinging dirt.

"Wow, folks," said the announcer, "a 14.30, another great run." The crowd cheered. "This Mary is not riding a little lamb, folks. She's got her a horse. There's the number to beat, girls. Let's see what you got."

Mary hung around the back, waiting for Billie to come up with her horse.

"Hey, Mary," said Billie as she rode up, "great run."

"Thanks," said Mary. "I wanted to talk to you."

"Okay," said Billie.

"Last night, when I ran tenth, the holes around the barrels were packed tight. You can hit them hard, and they will stand up. So when you go into the first barrel, go at a full run, and when your horse leans to the right to make the turn on the backside of the barrel, you lean left to help him pull out of it. On the second barrel, do the same, except lean to the right. On the third barrel, just stay in the middle of the horse."

"Okay," said Billie, "I will."

"Good luck," said Mary. Mary tied Bob up and went up into the stands to watch Billie's run. Billie did just what Mary had told her to do.

"A clean run, 14.51," said the announcer. "Okay, folks, we got us a race going on." When the event was over, the announcer said, "Let's name the top five who will run tomorrow night. No. 1, with a combined score of 28.41, Mary; no. 2, 28.70, Jill; no. 3, 28.92, Paula; no. 4, 29.50, Cases; and no. 5, 29.63, Billie."

"Oh no," said Billie to her dad, "I'm in… I'm in! I can't believe it. I'm in."

"Well, that's great," said Jim. "Now let's go get some rest."

"Wait, I've got to find Mary. She told me what to do, and it worked."

"That Plumber girl?" asked Jim.

"Yes," said Billie.

"I'm not sure it's a good idea for you to be hanging out around her."

"Dad, I have to. I'm her best friend. I've never been a best friend."

"What about me?" asked Jim.

"Dad!"

"Okay, meet me at the truck."

"Okay," said Billie as she disappeared. Billie rode her horse to Mary's trailer.

"Hey, Billie," said Mary.

"Oh, Mary, thank you. Can you believe I made it?"

"Yeah, I believe it. I had no doubt you could."

"My dad said we must go home and get some rest."

"What's your daddy's name, honey?" asked Kattie.

"Jim, Jim Hatcher," said Billie.

Kattie almost passed out. "And how old are you, sweetie?"

"I'm fourteen. I'll be fifteen in two months. Well, I better go. Thanks, Mary," said Billie. Billie took off on her horse. "See you tomorrow," said Billie as she rode away.

That no good SOB had a little girl while he was sleeping with me?

Oh, I'm going to kill him, thought Kattie.

Mary and Kattie stayed with Bob that night. Troy, Kathy, Rose, and Tommie went to the motel. Mary unsaddled Bob, brushed him down, and gave him some oats, hay, and water. Then she turned him loose and let him graze around the area. He rolled a couple of times and grazed some more while Kattie and Mary sat and talked.

"I'm so proud of you," said Kattie. "I saw how you've been helping those other girls too. So have you met Billie's daddy?"

"Yes."

"What's he like?"

"Oh, his okay," said Mary.

"What about Billie?"

"Oh, she's great. Did you know this is her first big competition too? That's why I'm helping her. It's just her and her dad. She has no mother, like us, but opposite."

"Oh," said Kattie, "do you know what happened to her mom?"

"Not really. Billie said she just up and left them there by themselves about twelve years ago." Mary yelled, "Bob!" Bob came walking over to her. She clipped the lead rope on him. "I'm ready to get some sleep," said Mary. She crawled into the back seat of the truck. In ten minutes, Mary was sound asleep.

Kattie couldn't sleep. *I've got to know what happened. Why didn't he tell me? Was he married?* Thoughts kept running through her head all night.

The next morning, everybody showed back up. Kattie asked Mary, "Do you want to go to the room and get some more sleep?"

"No," said Mary, "I slept good last night listening to horses' nicker and with the smell of horses everywhere."

"Okay, well, Kathy and I have got to go into town. We will be back around noon."

Mary fed Bob and gave him some fresh water, then they all just sat around and talked. Tommie was swinging on Bob's tail. "Stop," said Rose.

"Do you want to ride Bob?" asked Mary.

"Yes," said Tommie.

"Okay, come on." Mary picked up Tommie and put her on Bob's back, then led him around, letting him stop and get a mouthful of grass. After about thirty minutes of that, Tommie was ready for a nap.

Rose said to Mary, "You know, those other girls are going to be coming after you tonight."

"Yeah, I know. I don't care."

"What, don't you want to win?" asked Rose.

"Sure, I want to win. And if I do, that's great. If I don't, that's fine too. I'm not going to be all sad over it. It's a sport. There's a winner and loser. I wish we all could win."

"You're crazy," said Rose.

"Yep, I know that too."

Kathy and Kattie pulled back up. "Hi, Mama," said Tommie.

"Did you miss me, baby?"

They took a foldout table from the back of the truck and set it up under the tree. They unloaded birthday cake plates and silverware. They had a big ice chest full of drinks, even some special ones for Troy. Then they unloaded fried chicken, a bucketful of it, and all the sides.

Tommie said, "Oh, goody, my favorite chicken and cake."

Kathy said, "And ice cream."

They all stuffed their faces, except Mary. She didn't want to overdo it. She just ate one piece of chicken, a roll, and a small piece of cake and ice cream. Tommie had chicken grease, cake, and ice cream from head to toe. Troy said, "We are going to have to find a water hose to wash you off, girl."

It was almost time for tonight's events to start. Billie came riding up to Mary's trailer. "Hi, Mary. Happy birthday," said Billie.

"Hi, Billie," said Mary. "Come get some birthday cake. We had some ice cream, but now it's more like milkshake." Mary laughed.

"So how was your birthday?" asked Billie.

"It was good," said Mary. "Mom said I would get my present before tonight's events started."

"Oh, hi, Billie," said Kattie. "I didn't see you come up. Did you get some cake?"

"No, ma'am."

"Well, come here. I'll cut you a piece. We have plenty."

"Okay," said Billie.

"We are going to give Mary her birthday gift now."

"Great," said Mary.

Kathy brought out this fancy-looking box and set it on the table. "Okay, everybody, come over here."

Tommie asked, "What is it, Mama? A dress?"

"No," said Kathy. "You don't worry about it, miss. It's Mary's."

Mary opened the box and folded back the fancy paper. "Oh, Mama," said Mary, "it's beautiful." She picked it up out of the box and held it up for everyone to see. It was a bright-red vest with Mary on the front lapel. On the back across the top, in bright silver letters, it said Mary Plumber, and at the bottom, it said Plumber's Gap. Mary tried it on. It fit perfectly. She gave her mom a big hug and a kiss.

"That's like the pro's wear," said Billie.

"Okay, girls, yawl better get ready."

Mary saddled up Bob, checked his shoes, and climbed on him. Mary and Billie rode to the alley. The other three girls were already there.

"Okay, folks, let's get a look at tonight's barrel racers," said the announcer. "Girls, please come into the arena." The five girls rode in the arena and turned to the grandstand. "Okay," said the announcer, "here is how this is going to work. The leaders get to pick where in the lineup they run, and the others pick from the spots left. Mary, since you're in the lead, you get to pick first."

"I want to run last," said Mary.

"Fifth. Okay, Mary is fifth."

"Okay. Jill?"

"I'll run fourth."

"Okay. Paula?"

"First."

"Okay. Cases, your turn."

"Third."

"Okay. Billie, you're second. Now go get ready. Folks, we are ready for the final run of the barrel racing. We are giving a gold buckle and a check to the event winner. Second and third place get a check also.

Okay, folks, are yawl ready for some barrel racing?" The crowd cheered. "Okay, here we go," said the announcer.

The announcer started. "Here comes Paula. Yawl help cheer her on." Paula rounded the first barrel, then went for the second. As she rounded it, her horse bumped the barrel. As she headed for the third barrel, the second barrel fell over. She ran back through the timing light. "A 14.80, folks, but with a downed barrel. We must add five seconds, making her time 19.80. Yawl give her a hand. Get ready. Here comes Billie." Billie hit the first turn. She did just as Mary had coached her. She hit the second turn, and as she headed to the third, the crowd was already on their feet, cheering. She hit the third and headed home. "A 14.35," said the announcer. "Great run, Billie. Okay, folks, here come Cases. By the way, folks, Cases got second in this event last year." Cases ran her pattern clean, but she slid a little on the third barrel. "A 14.72," said the announcer. "Okay, now comes Jill. Folks, Jill had the fastest total time last year, winning the event." Jill came out hard; she made a clean run. "A 15.13, great job," said the announcer. "Okay, folks, this next little girl turned thirteen years old today. Give her a hand. She is the leader of the first two events. Now let's see if she can take it home. M-a-r-y P-l-u-m-b-e-r!"

As Mary came out of the alley with that bright-red vest and her bright-reddish-blond hair, like she was on fire, the crowd was standing and cheering her on. Mary and Bob hit the first turn. As they came out of the whole, she said, "Perfect, Bob. Now do it again." They hit the second turn and headed for the third barrel. As they rounded the third barrel, Mary said, "We got them, boy. We got 'em." Mary and Bob cleared the timing light.

"A 13.80, folks! Can you believe it? It was a 13.80 perfect run."

Kathy, Rose, and Kattie were all crying. "Oh my god," said Kattie, "did you see my baby?" She put her hands together and looked up and said, "Thank you, Lord." The three women sat back down and hugged one another and just cried and cried.

The award ceremony wasn't until the end of the night. Mary was in the back taking care of Bob, her partner. She couldn't stop hugging him. Kathy came to the back to help her. "Oh my god, girl, that was great." As she started filling up Bob's water trough, Kathy asked, "Why did you pick fifth to run?"

"Because last night, when I ran first, Bob slid a little going around the barrels. The dirt was too soft."

"Smart girl," said Kathy.

Kathy and Mary went to the stands to watch the rest of the rodeo and to see her mom. Kattie saw her coming and ran to her, picking her up and carrying her to their sets. They all hugged Mary and congratulated her.

"What a birthday," said Rose.

Mary said, "Now that's over, I am starving."

"What do you want?" asked Troy.

"Everything," said Mary, "a hamburger, a hot dog, popcorn, cotton candy, and two drinks."

"Okay," said Troy, "I'll be right back."

Kattie hugged her again and said, "I'm so proud and happy for you, baby. You did so good."

Troy came back with Mary's food. Mary said, "Tommie, come here."

"What?" asked Tommie.

"I might need some help." Tommie crawled down and went to Mary. "Here," said Mary, "you help me eat this stuff." She handed her the cotton candy. Tommie's eyes lit up as she started pulling the cotton candy off and eating it. Mary took two big bites of the hot dog, then handed the rest to Tommie. Tommie handed the cotton candy to Kathy, her mom.

"Don't eat that!" Kathy tore off a piece and stuck it in her mouth.

Tommie said "Mary" and pointed at Kathy.

Mary said, "It's okay, baby." Tommie started eating the hot dog as Mary was eating the hamburger. Mary was letting Tommie drink out of her straw. Tommie finished the hot dog, and Mary handed her the popcorn.

"Man, you got a lot of stuff." Tommie ate popcorn until Mary finished the hamburger, then they both ate popcorn and cotton candy. "Looks like some of this cotton candy is missing," said Tommie, looking at her mom. "All gone," said Tommie as Mary sipped the last of the second drink down. They all laughed.

About midway of the calf roping, Mary noticed Billie and her dad sitting down below them about six rolls. They were sitting with an older couple. Billie's dad looked a lot like the older man, just younger. *That must be Billie's grandmother and grandfather.*

Kattie asked "Mary, have you talked to Billie since her run?"

"No," said Mary, "but she was right down there." She pointed at her.

"Oh," said Kattie, "wonder who those people are."

"I don't know," said Mary. "Must be her grandma and grandpa."

"I can't believe she didn't come talk to you, sweetie."

"Aw, she's busy," said Mary, "and so am I." She gave Tommie a big hug.

Kattie found her purse and dug out a notepad and pen. She took the pad and wrote,

Jim,

I'm not looking forward to talking to you, but we have a situation we can't control. Billie and Mary have bonded, even though they don't know why. I'll tell you from experience that there is no bond stronger than the bond of sisters. We need to talk in private. I'm free next week if you can find the time.

Kattie

Kattie folded the note up, then gave it to Rose. She told her, "Take it to that man by Billie. Just act like yawl are old friends and reach out to shake his hand. When he does, leave the note in his hand. His name is Jim. Just act normal."

"This ain't normal for me," said Rose.

"Just do it, please."

Rose walked down the aisle to the row Jim was on with the note in the palm of her hand. She said, "Hi, Jim, how are you?" She stuck out her hand. Jim took her hand, and she passed the note and then said, "Good to see you." Then she walked away.

Billie looked at her father and said, "I didn't know you knew Rose. That's Mary's sister. She's a vet."

"Yes, I took a horse to them once," said Jim. He opened the note and read it. A great big lump formed in his throat, and sweat started running across his forehead. He folded the note and stuck it in his pocket.

The last bull was in the chute. It was almost time for the award ceremony. After the last bull rider was thrown off, the announcer said, "Okay, folks, while the judges finish adding up the scores for the bull riding event, let's go ahead and announce the other winners, starting with the barrel racing event." Everybody cheered. "We all know what the winner's name is. But I have a little back story about her. Mary Plumber is thirteen years old today. She decided two years ago that she was going to run barrels on a horse that she raised and trained. As some of you may know, she was a regular at Cody and Cheyenne, she said, training herself to run barrels. Her horse's name is Bob. Not only did she compete in this event but she also coached the other girls who were competing. Your 1990 winner of the Billings Montana Rodeo Barrel Racing Competition is Ms. Mary Plumber."

Mary headed down to the arena, climbed over the fence rails, and walked to the announcer.

"Ladies and gentlemen, Ms. Mary Plumber gets this beautiful silver buckle and a check for $3,000.00. Give her a hand, folks." Mary stood over to one side out of the way. "Okay, for second place, Ms. Jill

Ward, folks. Come on, Jill, come get your check." Jill came down to the announcer and shook his hand. "Folks, Jill gets this giant check for $2,000.00. Give her a hand, folks." Jill went and stood by Mary. Mary gave her a hug. "Now for third place, this little girl came from behind and, with some help, grabbed third place, Ms. Billie Hatcher. Billie gets a giant check for $1,500.00. Yawl give all three of our winners a big hand." Mary hugged Billie and then hugged Jill again. They all held up their checks while pictures were taken.

Mary climbed back up and over the rails. Billie was behind her as she walked by the row where Billie's dad was sitting. Jim stood up to shake Mary's hand. "Great job, young lady, great job." Then he did the same to Billie.

Mary then walked up to her mom. Kattie could see the tears in Jim's eyes. Kattie grabbed Mary and hugged and kissed her. "Okay, we can go now," said Kattie.

"No," said Mary, "I can't go."

"Why not, baby?" asked Kattie.

"Seems disrespectful to leave before the others get their prizes."

"You're right, baby. You're absolutely right." Kattie told Kathy, "Yawl go ahead and go to the motel. Mary and I will bring Bob later."

"Why?" asked Kathy.

"Because my daughter just told me it would be disrespectful for her to leave before the other winners were announced. We will see yawl in a little while," said Kattie with tears in her eyes. As they sat there, Kattie kept looking at Mary, wondering, *When did my little girl grow up? Where was I? How did I miss it? She's all grown up now. I'm not ready for this.*

They sat and clapped as each winner got their buckles and checks. Most of the fans were gone. All the other barrel racers and their families were gone. The calf ropers and bulldoggers were gone. There were only four other people on their side of the arena. When they announced the winners of the bull riding, the last event, Mary stood up. She looked around the arena, then said, "See you next year." They headed to the back to get Bob. When they got out back, the lot was mostly empty. They walked to the trailer holding hands. When they got there, Mary wrapped her arms around Bob's neck. Then she unclipped his lead rope. "Go roll, boy," she said. It was now midnight. Kattie and Mary got everything ready to travel, then Mary said, "Load up, boy." Bob walked to the back of the trailer and stepped in. Mary closed and latched the door.

Chapter 2

Sisters

Sunday morning, after breakfast, the Plumber's Gap crew headed back home to South Dakota. It had been a great weekend, but everybody was ready to get back home. Mary and Billie had exchanged phone numbers and had made plans to talk at night sometimes. As they got close to the driveway at Plumber's Gap, Mary could see something hanging from their sign. Seemed Aunt Sara had had a banner made and put up there that said, "Welcome home, Mary!"

"Aw," said Mary, "how sweet." As they pulled up to the house, Troy pulled up to the barn. Mary went up and unloaded Bob and put him in his stall.

Troy and Kathy gave Mary a hug. Tommie was passed out on Kathy's shoulder. "See you tomorrow," said Troy.

"Okay, bye," said Mary. "Thank you." She walked back to the house.

Kattie and Rose was unloading the last of their stuff. "Hey, Mary," said Rose, "what do you want to do with this big check?"

"I'll put it in my room," said Mary.

"Okay, I'll hang on to this old buckle for you."

"No," said Mary, "I'll take that too!"

Kattie said, "Okay, girls, I'm going to my room. Yawl can come drag my wrinkled body out of the tub in the morning."

The next week, the *Billings Newspaper* had a front-page article about the rodeo. The winner of the Bull Riding Competition was a local cowboy named Tony Allen, one of the top-ranked bull riders on the circuit. Normally, the article each year was about the rodeo's attendance and a list of all the winners. This year, they had included an interview with the bull rider Tony Allen, in which all he could talk about was the thirteen-year-old little girl who won the Barrel Racing Competition. He said, "This little girl has more class and more heart than anyone I've ever seen. After the first night of competition, Mary was coaching the other girls on how to get better times. She also stayed after the rodeo until all the awards were given out, cheering for each one. As a bull rider, we have always had a comradery among us, along with the bronc riders. We all try to help each other if we can. But barrel racing has always been a very competitive sport. That's why Mary Plumber is such a breath of fresh air. Mary Plumber, you are no. 1 in my book. God bless you!"

Sara brought Kattie a copy of the newspaper. She said, "You need to read this."

Kattie read it, then hugged Sara. "I'll put this on her bed," said Kattie.

Jim called the animal hospital and left Kattie a massage. Kattie checked her massages and heard him say, "This is Jim. Just tell me when." Kattie dialed his number.

"Hello," she heard a little girl say.

"Hi, is this Billie?" asked Kattie.

"Yes, ma'am, this is Billie."

"This is Mary's mom, Kattie."

"Oh, hi, Ms. Plumber."

"Is your father home?"

"Yes, he is in the barn doing something."

"Okay," said Kattie. "I just wanted to call and invite you and your dad to come to our house Saturday afternoon."

"Oh yes," said Billie. "Well, I mean, I'll have to ask my dad."

"Okay, well, you ask your dad."

"Yes, ma'am, I'll go ask him. Hang on." In a few minutes, she came back. "Yes, yes, yes, he said yes."

"Okay, settle down. I'll see yawl Saturday. You bring your swimsuit. We have a pool."

"Yes, ma'am. But where? How do we get there?"

"Your father knows the way."

"Okay, bye," said Billie, and Kattie hung up.

Kattie didn't tell Mary that Billie was coming. She told Troy and Kathy that she wanted to have a cookout Saturday afternoon and needed them to help and for Troy to grill steaks.

"Sure," said Troy. "How many?"

"About ten," said Kattie.

"Okay, twelve then," said Troy.

"I'll get all the sides ready," said Kathy.

Saturday morning, Mary was up and out doing her normal chores around the barn. She got Bob out and put him in a side lot to eat grass. Then she got out a new horse she and Kathy just started to train. She put him in the round pen and started to work him.

Rose came out. "How does he look?" asked Rose.

"His okay, not too spooky, just young."

"Did you know we were having a cookout tonight?"

"No," said Mary. "What are we having?"

"Mine and your favorite steak," said Rose.

"Great," said Mary. "Who is coming?"

"I'm not sure. Mom and Kathy said ten or twelve people. So what are you going to do with your prize money?" asked Rose.

"I don't know," said Mary. "I thought about a new saddle, but I like mine. We don't need any more horses, says Mom. I don't know."

"What about one of those four-wheelers?" asked Rose.

"Mom would die," said Mary."

"No, she wants. I've already told her I was getting one next week. I told her you needed one too. She just said, 'I ain't buying one.' They're not but $3,800.00," said Rose. "I've got my own money, and you have your money. We can ride together every weekend."

"Can you haul hay on it?"

"Sure. And feed," said Rose. "They're great for farms and ranches."

"Okay, I'll buy one," said Mary.

"Great," said Rose. As she took off back to the house, Mary kept on working with the horse.

Kattie waked up to the barn. Mary was lying on the new horse's back, rubbing him all over, while she made him keep walking in a circle. "How's he doing?" asked Kattie.

"He is coming along," said Mary.

"I think so," said Kattie, "seeing how two days ago you couldn't even touch him."

"He will be okay, just needs some time." Mary eased off his back and led him over to her mom. She tied him up, then reached for the brush and started slowly running the brush across his skin, talking to him the whole time in a soft, low tone.

Kattie watched as Mary worked with the horse; she was amazed at how every move she made was direct and had a purpose. Never fast, just slow and steady. Kattie asked, "Mary, did Kathy teach you that?"

"What?" asked Mary.

"How to be like that with a horse."

"She showed me some things, but Bob taught me how to feel or sense what they felt." Mary unsnapped the lead rope from the halter, then walked to the middle of the round pen with her back to the horse. She stood there, no movement. Slowly the young horse started walking up behind Mary. Kattie was nervous but stayed quiet as the horse put his head over Mary's shoulder, then laid it against her face. Mary rubbed the horse's nose, then turned her head and kissed the horse on the side of his face. Mary slowly walked out from under the horse and to the gate, moving slow. The horse followed her until she opened the gate and stepped out.

"Wow," said Kattie, "I've got to spend more time at this barn. I guess you heard we were having a cookout tonight?"

"Yes, Rose told me. She wants me to buy a four-wheel."

"It's your money. You decide," said Kattie. "Okay, well, get through out here and come clean up before people start getting here."

"Who's coming?" asked Mary.

"Just our group and a surprise guest."

"Mom, you know I don't like surprises."

"You will like this one," said Kattie as she walked off. Mary finished up what she was doing, then put the horse back into a stall and gave him oats.

Mary went back to the house to take a bath and change clothes. As she walked inside the door, Tommie ran up to her and grabbed her hand. "What are you doing?" asked Tommie.

"I'm going to take a bath and change clothes."

"Why?" asked Tommie.

"Because I'm dirty."

"But Mama said we were going swimming. Are you going to swim?"

"Sure," said Mary,

"Then why do you need a bath?"

"I just do," said Mary.

Mary went to her room to take a bath. When she came out, everybody was out back. She went outside with them. Troy had the grill going, and Kathy had the table set. Rose was with Tommie in the pool. Rose's mom, Alice, was helping Kathy.

Tommie yelled, "Mama!"

"Yes?" said Kathy.
"Can I take off my floaty?"
"No," said Kathy.
"But I can swim," said Tommie.
"Like a rock," said Kathy.
"No!"
Mary asked Kattie, "Who else is coming again?"
"You'll see."

Then they saw a truck coming up the road. The truck pulled up to the house. The passenger door swung open, and out jumped Billie. "Mary," she yelled, "I'm here!"

Mary ran to her, and they hugged. "Come on," said Mary, "everybody is here." They turned and held hands as they walked onto the patio.

Kattie just stood there waiting as Jim slowly got out of the truck. He walked up to Kattie. She stuck out her hand. "Hello, Mr. Hatcher, let me introduce you to everyone." She turned and said, "Everybody, the is Jim Hatcher, Billie's dad."

Everybody started introducing themselves. Troy handed Jim a cold beer. Jim stood by the grill with Troy and Pete, Rose's granddad. Troy started putting on the steaks to cook. Mary and Billie had already gotten in the pool with Rose and Tommie. Kattie didn't push it; she didn't want Jim to feel cornered. *Just old friends with daughters that are best friends.*

Troy yelled at the girls, "Yawl come eat."

They all went inside the house and put on shorts and T-shirts over their swimsuits. Troy said the grace, and they all started filling their plates. Little Tommie was waiting for her mom to cut her food up. "Hurry, Mom. I'm hungry." Mary and Billie got their plates and sat side by side at the table, laughing and giggling the whole time. Kattie tried not to look Jim in the eyes, but she could see he was watching the two girls as he and Troy talked about cows. Mary and Billie were having such a good time just being together. When the kids finished eating, including Rose, they all got back into the pool. Troy and Jim kept talking about cows, while Kathy, Kattie, and Alice cleaned up. The ladies came and sat at the other end of the table and talked.

About 10:00 p.m., Kathy said, "Tommie, time for you to get out."

"Oh, Mom."

"Now, Tommie."

Rose got Tommie out and dried her off, then brushed her hair and put her on some dry clothes.

Troy stood and shook Jim's hand and said, "Nice to meet you."

"You too," said Jim.

Pete and Alice left and went to their trailer. Mary and Billie got out of the pool, wrapped towels around themselves, then they walked over to Jim and Kattie.

"Mr. Hatcher," said Mary, "can Billie please spend the night? You can come back and get her tomorrow, or we can bring her home."

Jim dropped his head. "I think that's a good idea," said Kattie. "School will be starting back in a couple of weeks."

Jim raised his head. "Okay, I'll come back around 2:00 p.m. Be ready." Billie ran over and hugged her dad and kissed his cheek. Mary hugged him and kissed his cheek too. Jim turned red. The two girls took off running and jumped back into the pool.

Kattie looked Jim in the eyes for the first time and said, "That's why we need to talk."

Jim nodded. "Tomorrow then," Jim said as he got up to leave.

Kattie and Rose sat and watched the girls play until about 10:45 p.m., then made them get out. They disappeared into Mary's room.

Kattie told Rose, "Get us a beer. I need to tell you a story." Rose did, then she sat back down by Kattie. "About fifteen years ago, Billie's daddy, Jim, and I dated."

"What?" asked Rose.

"Yes, and I turned up pregnant, and thirteen years and two weeks ago, I had Mary."

"Oh my god," said Rose, "you're kidding me."

"When I told Jim I was pregnant, he was floored. He asked if I wanted him to marry me. I said I wanted him to want to marry me. He didn't reply, not fast enough anyway. So I said a lot of hurtful things to him. I told him that this would be my child and that I didn't need him, that my lawyer family would make sure he had no responsibility for this child. We never talked again until tonight. At the rodeo, I figured out who Billie's daddy was. He never told me he had a child. So I had you give him that note telling him that we had to talk about these girls."

"So Mary and Billie are sisters?" asked Rose.

"Yes, half sisters and now best friends," said Kattie. "I had him bring Billie so she and Mary could spend some more time together. We must decide if and how to tell them."

"You've got to tell them," said Rose. "It's plain to see that they love each other. I thought to myself while we were in the pool that those girls favored and they could pass as sisters. I never thought it was true."

"I noticed it the first time I saw Mary and Billie side by side," said Kattie. "I need you to keep this to yourself until we decide what to do."

"I promise," said Rose, "no one will ever hear it from me!"

They both went inside. Kattie opened Mary's door. The two girls were curled up together in Mary's bed, sound asleep. A big tear filled Kattie eyes. She and Rose went to bed too.

The next morning, they all got up and ate breakfast. After breakfast, the girls Mary and Billie took off for the barn. Mary showed Billie all the horses. Mary took out Bob and tied him, then she took out Molly and said, "Here, Billie, you can ride her. She's nice. She is the horse I always rode before Bob." Mary got Billie a saddle. They saddled up and climbed on the horses. "We must stop by the house and tell Mom where we are going."

"Okay," said Billie.

Kattie saw them coming down the hill. She walked outside. "Where you headed?"

"Just down to the falls and along the creek," said Mary.

"Okay," said Kattie, "be safe."

"We will!" they yelled as they rode off.

"Wow," said Billie, "you have a nice place."

"Thanks," said Mary. They rode down to the falls.

"Oh, how beautiful," said Billie.

"Yeah, this is my favorite place," said Mary. "Mom and I come here for picnics sometimes. We just lie around and listen to the sound of the falls." Mary turned and headed up the creek. Billie followed. Once they got away from the falls, it got quiet. Mary said, "Back in the 1800s, there was an old trail through here that went to Hill City."

"Where's Hill City?" asked Billie.

"It's a long way on the other side of the Black Hills. Come on, let's head back," said Mary.

The girls eased back to the barn; their little ride had taken about two hours. They tied the horses, then unsaddled them. They each brushed down their horses, then put them back in their stalls, with a little bit of oats. Pepper came walking up to see what was going on.

"Hi, Pep," said Mary.

"We used to have a dog just like that when I was little, but she died," said Billie.

"Yeah, Pep is older than me," said Mary.

"That's old for a dog."

The girls went back down to the house. It was now 11:00 a.m., only three hours until Billie had to go home. They both tried not to think about it. They put their swimsuits back on and headed for the pool.

Jim decided to come a little early so he and Kattie could talk. Jim had his whole story worked out in his mind. He knew she was going to be tough on him, but he was ready. The girls were still in the pool when Jim got there about 1:00 p.m. Pepper went to barking.

Kattie looked out. It was Jim. Kattie went to the door. When she opened it, Jim was kneeling down, rubbing on and talking to Pepper. Kattie stood there and watched for a minute. "She has been a good dog," said Kattie.

"Yup," said Jim. "Her mama was too."

"Come on in. The girls are in the pool."

Jim walked in and sat down at the bar. He laid his hat on the counter. Kattie sat on the other side across from him.

"You're early," said Kattie.

"Yeah," said Jim, "I wanted us to have time to talk."

"Okay, good," said Kattie. "Let's talk."

"I know there are a lot of things you want to know," said Jim. "Just let me tell my story, then I'll answer any questions you have."

"Okay," said Kattie, "sounds good."

"Before I meet you," said Jim, "I got my high school sweetheart pregnant. She had finished college and came back home. We went right back to dating again. She told me that she was pregnant, and I loved her, so we got married. After Billie was born, she left me and took Billie. I was devastated, hurt, and confused. Everything I did was for them. My parents wanted me to file for a divorce and sue her for full custody of Billie, so I did, and I lost. I got visitation every two weeks. It was more of a fight between grandparents, her family and mine. I had wanted to just give it time, hoping she would come back, but the divorce fight ended that hope, I thought. My parents blamed me for not fighting hard enough to get Billie, but I had no grounds. Billie's mama was not a bad person. So I tried to move on.

"After a few months, I meet you at the clinic. I knew right away I liked you but was unsure if I could trust anyone again. I finally decided to give myself a chance to be happy. Then just after I helped you and your dad get that gold out of the old mine, my ex-wife came back to the ranch with Billie. They stayed for a couple of days. Yes, we did sleep together. She called every other day after that, then you bought me a $20,000.00 bull. I was confused again. I had you come out that weekend so I could tell you that my ex-wife and I thought we were going to try it again. I thought that was what she wanted.

That's why I wouldn't sleep with you that weekend. Then you left before I got up the nerve to tell you what was going on.

"My ex came back the next week, she and Billie. Her parents were dictating and controlling hers and Billie's life. She told me she had a job offer in New York and that she had to get away from her mom. I begged her to stay with me. She just said that we would talk tomorrow. The next morning, when I woke up, Billie was in the bed with me, but her mom was not. I called out her name, then got up and went into the kitchen. There on the table"—tears started to fill Jim's eyes—"were papers giving me full custody of Billie, signed by a judge and notarized, with a note that said, 'I love you both, but I can't stay.'" Jim broke down, tears streaming down his face. Kattie got up and got some tissues. She poured her and Jim a cup of coffee. Jim said "Thank you" as she set the cup in front of him. As he started sipping the coffee, he said, "Two days before that is when I came to the clinic to talk to you about you...about you being pregnant."

Tears filled Kattie eyes. "And I ran you off," said Kattie. They both just sat there sipping coffee; not a word was said for ten minutes. "What about the girls?" asked Kattie.

"I don't know," said Jim. "I just don't know." Jim looked up at Kattie. "You decide. I'll agree to whatever you say."

"Well," said Kattie, "we are not going be able to keep them apart."

"And I don't want to," said Jim.

About that time, the girls burst into the room coming from the pool.

"Oh, hi, Dad," said Billie.

"You girls get some dry clothes on, and quit dripping on my floor," said Kattie. She got up and poured her and Jim some more coffee, then fixed the girls glasses of soda.

The girls came back into the room. They came to the bar. Mary stood by her mom, and Billie stood by her dad. Kattie said, "You know, you girls could pass for sisters."

"We are sisters," said Mary, "just like me and Rose."

Jim looked at Kattie with a question in his eyes and said, "Rose?"

Kattie said, "Yes, Rose is Pete's and Alice's granddaughter, but Mary and I claimed her, and she has always been Mary's big sister."

"Now she is a vet, just like Mom," said Mary.

"Okay, girls," said Kattie, "there is only two weeks until school starts."

"We know," said the girls at the same time in a depressed voice.

"Look, here's what we are going to do. I'll bring Mary to your house next Saturday," said Kattie. The girls' eyes lit up. "Billie, you and your dad can bring her back home Sunday." "Yeah," said the girls.

Jim got up, put his hat on, looked at Kattie, and said, "Thank you!"

The next Saturday morning, Kattie drove Mary into Montana to Jim's ranch. Billie came running out to greet them. Mary grabbed her little overnight bag and gave her mom a big hug. Kattie said, "You call me if you need anything. I'm only two hours away."

"Okay, Mom," said Mary.

Jim was standing in the doorway of the barn. Kattie raised her hand, and he did the same as Kattie drive off. On the way home, Kattie was still trying to figure out how all this would play out. Seemed the man she had hated for so long was the only person who did nothing wrong. It's funny how unspoken words can change so many lives. If Jim had just been given a chance to explain back then, things might have been a lot different for all of them. Kattie decided that she was going to keep an open mind and, from now on, leave no words unspoken between her and Jim. She had no expectations; they were just single parents trying to look out for their kids.

The next afternoon, Jim and Billie brought Mary home. Mary got out. Kattie walked up to Billie's window. She reached in and gave her a hug. "Come back to see me now," said Kattie.

"Okay," said Billie. They then drove off.

"So how did it go? Did you have fun?" asked Kattie.

"Yes, we rode horses, then we cooked out over an open fire. This morning, we had a big breakfast. Billie's dad is a good cook."

"Is he now?" said Kattie.

"Then we sat around being lazy, as Jim called it. He asked about you and the ranch."

"Did he?" asked Kattie.

"Yeah, just normal stuff, but it was fun. Billie's going to use her money to buy a new dog like Pepper, a cow dog, so she can call it her own."

CHAPTER 3

The Roundup

Summer was gone! It was September in South Dakota, not real cold yet but it was coming. Troy and Kathy had their new house built and had moved in their house and off the ranch. Troy was working on fences and catch pens on the weekends. Kathy wanted to build a barn and arena next spring, but for now, they were just glad to be in their house. Tommie loved it; she had more room to run and play, and she had her own room, which she would be glad to show them if they stopped by. Mary and Kathy were still working the horses. The new horse they'd been working with was fully broke and ready to ride.

Troy and his hands would be rounding up cows soon to bring up to the winter pastures. Kattie would sell off most of the steers to keep from feeding them all winter. Then the slow times would start. Not a lot happened around Plumber's Gap during the winter. The roads got bad, and traveling was slow at best. However, Rose and Mary got their new four-wheelers and were excited for the snow to come. Mary got her four-wheeler decked out with front and back racks and a winch; Rose just got the back rack on hers. Billie came last weekend to get in on the final swim of the year. The water was still fine, but the air was cool. They had to stay in the water to keep warm, but they had fun. The girls still didn't know that they were sisters yet. Kattie and Jim agreed that they needed to know, but they just didn't know how to tell them. Kattie and Rose had been working a lot of long hours at the vet clinic and were looking forward to things slowing down some this winter.

Kathy's mom, the lady Kattie bought her first string of horses from, had gotten too old to work horses and had sold everything she had, including tacks and saddles. Kattie bought some of it for Mary. Kathy bought some too. Now Kathy's mom was just going to try and tame little Tommie while Kathy and Troy were at work. They were hoping she would move in with them; they had a room added to their house just for her, but she was not ready to leave her home yet.

The roundup used to take only a day or two; now it took about a week. The herd had gotten so big and spread out over the 5,000 acres, plus the national forest lands Plumber's Gap used during the summer months. This land must be cleared of all livestock before October each year before hunting seasons started. So Troy and his crew would do that first, then move back to the ranch. Once it started, they would be gone until all the cows were back home in the winter pastures. They would camp on the trail and stay with the cows until they had them all together, then start driving them back home. Last year, they lost two young cows to grizzlies and a steer to coyotes on the way home.

Well, Troy had set the day to start the roundup. The first cold snip was coming in two weeks, and he wanted to be done by then, so they would head out Monday of next week. Troy had Pete already staging rolls of hay in the winter pastures and putting extra rolls close by. Kattie always looked forward to this time of year. She used to go on the roundups when she first started the ranch. Now she just let Troy and the men take care of it. She always took two or three steers that she had handpicked to the meat-packers and would have them process the meat, then donate it to the orphanage of South Dakota. Kattie was once asked, "Why do you give cows to the orphans?" Kattie said, "If I raised corn, I would give them corn, but I raise cattle. We should all give something."

Monday came, and the crew left to go after the cows. Troy led the way like always; he knew it better than anyone else. He had made this trip many times. Down by the falls then up the old trail to the first gate, all the men and horses went through the gate and then closed it behind them. They were not going to worry about any cow right now; they needed to make it to the back end of the ranch. There was a gate going off Plumber's Ranch onto the national forest land. It would take them all day to get there, and once there, they would set up camp. They had a couple of catch pens and an old line cabin there Troy built years back. Not much but it was dry. There was a corral for the horses. The men would set up their tents and fold out the cook wagon, a kitchen on wheels. Tomorrow morning, they would cross over onto the national forest and find those cows. They only ran about one hundred head on the forest; it shouldn't take long. The older cows started heading back to the meadow nearby when cool air came. They would know it was about time to go home. The next morning, they all saddled up and got ready to head out.

"Okay, guys, lesson. We are going on to government land. If you find a cow being eaten or attacked by a wild animal, you can't shoot it. You can shoot to scare it off, but you can't kill it. Understood? Most of you know where the meadow is. We want to get the cows there in a bunch, then we will push the back here."

Troy headed into the meadow. When he got there, most of the cows were there waiting for him. "Good girls," said Troy. He started easing through them, counting. "Eighty-six head," said Troy. "We just have fourteen more to find." One of the men came back with five, another with four, and the last men brought back the other five. "Good deal," said Troy. "Let's take them home."

They eased the cows through the trees to the gate at Plumber's Gap. They opened the gate and let them in the catch pens. It was now 3:00 p.m. "Well, that went good," said Troy. "Let's get a fire going."

The next morning, they ate and packed up. Everybody got saddled up and ready. Troy said, "We will look for strays along the way. Just push this group down the middle of the valley. Hopefully, the other cows will hear them and come to them." They turned the cow out and started pushing through the meadow. Cow after cow came out of the trees and joined the herd. Two riders, one on each side, worked their way up through the tree, pushing out any cow they find.

Everything was going smooth just like Troy planned, then Troy heard a "Yup, yup, yup!" as one of his men came running out of the trees. It was Jeff. His horse crossed the creek and headed into the valley. A big grizzly was hot on his tail. Troy grabbed his rifle and shot, then Ben shot, then Troy shot again. The bear folded up and slid to a stop. Ben, Troy's right-hand man, made sure the bear was dead with a shot to the head. He rode back to where Troy was at. "That was close," said Ben.

"Yeah, too close," said Troy. "Take one man and gut the bear, then put him on the wagon. I will keep the cows moving."

"Okay," said Ben, "will do."

Troy and the others kept moving, even Jeff the cowboy, who was being chased by the bear. About an hour before dark, Troy stopped and told the men to set up camp. Ben and the wagon had just caught up with the herd. Ben and Troy dragged the bear off the wagon. They started skinning him out. They cut enough meat off the bear for supper. Then they cut up the rest and put the meat in cloth bags. "Let's put the meat in the creek until morning to stay cool," said Troy.

"Okay," said Ben.

Troy rolled the bear hide up and tied it with a piece of rope, then put it on the wagon. *There's me rug for my new house,* thought Troy.

They cooked up the bear meat with beans and sat around the fire and ate. One of the cowboys told Troy, "I thought you said not to kill the bears."

"That was on government land and if they were after a cow, not a man."

One of other ones said, "You should have just let that old bear eat Jeff." They laughed.

Troy was chewing his meat and then said, "I would have, but I didn't want to lose a good horse." Laughter filled the camp.

Ben said, "I think it was my shot that killed that bear."

"Well," said Troy, "he was still running pretty fast when I shot the last time." They all laughed again.

The next morning, they ate. Ben got the bear meat and loaded it on the wagon. They got packed up. "Saddle up, boys" said Troy. The herd size had grown and grown along the way, over four hundred head now. They started easing along again through the valley alongside the creek. Jeff wouldn't go back across the creek into the tree; he stayed in the wide open. Ben had to take his place in the trees. Troy planed his next stop to be about half a day from the winter pastures. He wanted to make it back by noon the last day with plenty of time to separate the herd. They made it to their last overnight stop just before dark. They set up camp.

"Guess what's for supper," said Ben.

"Bear," said one of the hands.

"Yep." They got a fire going and set up their tents.

"We'll be home tomorrow," said Troy.

"Good," said Jeff.

Ben said, "I think we need to send Jeff back in the trees to find us another bear. I like this bear meat."

"No," said Jeff.

Ben said, "Well, I don't know what you're so worried about. You are about the best I've ever seen at running from a bear."

"How many others have you seen?" asked Troy.

"Well, none," said Ben. "Just old Jeff there." Laughter filled the camp again.

The next morning, they ate, packed up, saddled up, and headed home. The cows were clam and ready to go. They pushed them slow and steady the rest of the way home.

Midday, Kattie heard the cow bawling over the hill. She fixed Troy a big glass of tea and a jug for refills. She got in her truck and drove to the corrals to meet them. Troy came riding up. Kattie gave him his tea. "Oh, thank you, Lord," said Troy.

"Any problems?" asked Kattie.

"Not really, other than a grizzly bear tried to eat old Jeff there, but we didn't want the bear to get sick, so we shot him."

"Very funny," said Jeff. "I almost died, and yawl make jokes."

"I see… I see how you are." Troy looked at Kattie with a serious look. "It was close, bad close. We almost lost him and his horse."

"I'm glad everybody is okay," said Kattie. "Let me know when you get the steers separated, and I'll make my picks for the orphanage."

"Okay," said Troy. "Hey, you want some bear meat?" asked Troy.

"I don't eat bear meat," said Kattie.

"You have before. You just didn't know it," said Troy, smiling.

"Well, I don't want to know it next time either," Kattie said as she walked to her truck.

The next morning, Troy went to the house and told Kattie that they had the steers separated. "Okay, I'll be there in a minute," said Kattie.

"Those are some nice-looking steers," said Kattie. "What's the count?"

"Ninety-eight," said Troy.

Kattie picked out three steers. Troy wrote down their tag numbers. "Send those to the meat-packers. Make sure they know they are for the orphanage."

"I will," said Troy.

"How is the herd count?"

"All here but one, number 107, but we got two late calves with no tags," said Troy.

"Tag 107? That's the old bull that came with the herd," said Kattie.

"Yep," said Troy. "If his not back in a couple of days, we'll go looking. If he is still alive, he should come home to the cows. It's probably what that bear had in the tree, and Jeff got too close to his kill."

"Okay, cut out another steer for the bunkhouse. I don't need one this year, and you have bear meat," she said with a laugh. "Send the rest to Kansas and sell them. We will need the money. It looks like we might need to buy a new bull come spring."

"Okay," said Troy. Troy told Ben, "Here, cut out these three steers, plus two more. Take them to the meat-packing plant. Tell them to send these three to the orphanage and that the other two are for the ranch. Take the hams and shoulders off that bear. Tell them to grind it up for hamburger."

"That will make some good chili and stew meat for winter," said Ben.

"I'll go call for the trucks," said Troy, "so we can get them other steers gone."

Three days and no sign of the bull. Troy told Ben, "Take one of the boys and find that bull. He is probably back where we killed the bear, somewhere up in the trees."

"Okay," said Ben.

Ben and Clark, one of the hands, rode back up the valley. With no cows to slow them down, they made it to where the bear was killed before dark. They stopped and built a fire. Ben told Clark, "We will start looking first thing in the morning. I'm not going up into those trees this late in the afternoon."

The next morning, they got packed back up and headed into the trees. As they were riding along the ridge through the tree, Clark yelled, "Over here!"

Ben went to Clark. "Yep, that's him, or what's left of him." Ben got off his horse, walked over, and cut the ear tag off the bull and stuck it in his pocket. "Okay, let's go home," said Ben. The men took off back down the valley.

*****

Mary got a bright idea for a winter project. Last spring, Kattie picked out a bull calf to keep and raise for breeding. Mary named him Randolph. She decided to move him into the barn where she could work with him this winter. She wanted to train him to be ridden like a horse and maybe even do tricks. She had seen one in Cheyenne last year, but he was a Brahman, not an Angus.

Kathy told her she was crazy. "I'm not helping you with that bull."

"Oh, but it will be fun."

"Yeah, it's always fun until somebody gets a broken bone."

Mary just laughed. Mary got Kathy to take her to town to get a cow halter.

"You need a nose ring," said Kathy.

"No, that would hurt him." She picked out a nice show halter and bought it. "This will work. I'll have him be gentle as a lamb in no time," said Mary.

"You better not be putting my baby on that little lamb."

It took about a week of working with Randolph before Mary could lead him around the arena. He was just a baby, about nine months old, too small to ride now. But Mary wanted him to be gentle before he was very big. At this stage, he still pulled away sometimes, but he was doing so much better.

The first snow came, and Rose and Mary were having a ball on their four-wheelers in the snow. They went all over the ranch on those things, sliding and jumping small hills.

"Looks like winter is here," said Kattie. "I hope we're ready." She and Kathy watched the girls ride.

Billie called Mary that night. "Did you get snow?" asked Billie.

"Yes," said Mary. "Me and Rose played in it all day on our four-wheelers. It was great. What about you?" asked Mary.

"I played in it some, then Dad dragged me around on a sled behind the horse."

"Oh," said Mary, "I'm training a bull calf."

"A what?" asked Billie. "Training it to do what?"

"To ride," said Mary.

"Why?" asked Billie.

"I just thought it would be fun to have a bull to ride." Mary laughed out loud.

"You're crazy, Mary Plumber," said Billie.

"I know," said Mary.

Chapter 4

Spring 1991

Most of the snow was gone! Calves were starting to drop. The grass was peeking out from under the snow patches. This was a busy time for Kattie and Rose—helping cow birth, vaccinating, and tagging calves for ranchers and farmers. Troy and Kattie had started looking for another bull to replace 107 before the cows were turned out into the summer pastures.

Tommie would be four years old soon and thought she needed her own horse to ride. Mary told her, "I have a bull you can ride."

"No," said Kathy, "you better not, Mary Plumber."

"But, Mama—"

"No," said Kathy. "No!"

Mary told Tommie, "I was eight before I got my first horse. You need to grow some more. We will get you one when you're ready, I promise. You've got old Molly to ride now," said Mary. "What else do you want for your birthday?"

"A four-wheeler," said Tommie. Mary and Kathy both busted out laughing.

"Girl, you keep dreaming," said Kathy.

"I'll let yawl fight this out. I'm going to fight with a bull calf for a while."

Ben and his crew were in the big lot separating the mama cows that had already dropped calves and putting them in a smaller lot. Troy came up and told Ben, "When yawl get those mamas out, go back and get the heavy cows and put them in that other small lot so we can watch them."

"Okay," said Ben.

The weather was getting warmer. No snow left. Kattie decided it was time for a cookout this weekend. She had Mary call Billie and invite her and her dad to come. Kattie called Sara and Leann, her sisters, and invited them and theirs. She had Kathy invite her mom and had Troy invite the ranch hands. Troy said, "It's a good thing I didn't listen to you, and I went ahead and had that steer butchered for the house."

"I knew you would," said Kattie, laughing.

Kattie and Jim had been talking some over the phone. Jim had asked Kattie to go out with him several times, but Kattie would just say, "Not until we figure out what to do about the girls." Jim had apologized for not telling her about his wife while they were dating. Kattie had told Jim that she was sorry for keeping him from Mary, his daughter. She had also told him that she had not been with any other man or dated anyone since him. Kattie told him that she never trusted men before she met him, and now she didn't know if she ever could again. Jim said that he would do whatever it took to work things out; he wanted her and both his daughter.

Well, Saturday arrived. Jim and Billie came early so Jim could help Troy and Pete get things ready for the cookout. Billie went straight to the barn to see the bull Mary was training. "Hey, Mary," said Billie. They went to each other and hugged.

Jim started helping Troy get the grill set up. Rose and Kathy were in town getting drinks iced down and picking up some last-minute items. Kattie came out of the house. She and Jim just looked at each other and smiled. Kattie said all the grilling forks and utensils were in the kitchen sink. Jim said, "I'll go get them." He followed Kattie back in the house. She walked over to the sink to show him, and as she turned around, Jim pressed her against the countertop. They kissed and held on to each other for a few minutes, neither one wanting to let go. When they did pull away, Jim was smiling. Kattie just tried to act like nothing had happen and handed Jim the utensils. Jim went back outside. The kiss reminded Kattie of so many things, good and bad.

Mary and Billie came to the house. "Where are yawl headed?" asked Kattie.

"Swimming," said Billie.

"It's too cold to swim," said Kattie. "You're going to freeze."

They laughed and ran to Mary's room. Kattie tried to think of what it would be like with both girls living there. Would knowing that they were sisters break up their friendship?

Kathy and Rose got back and, of course, Tommie. "Where are those girls?" asked Tommie. She stomped off heading to Mary's room.

"You just leave them girls alone," said Kathy. "Go aggravate your daddy outside." Tommie turned and headed outside to her dad. After everything was unloaded and put away, Kathy went out back to check on the men.

Rose asked Kattie, "What are you doing?"

"What do you mean?"

"Billie and Jim, everybody together," said Rose.

"I just thought it was time to have a cookout."

"No," said Rose, "that's not it. You've been talking to him, haven't you?"

"Well, we've talked some on the phone, just about the girls though."

"You're lying, Kattie Plumber, and you're not even good at it."

Kattie said, "Okay, he wants to work things out. I don't know what to do."

"Oh my god, you still love him after all these years, don't you?" said Rose.

"I don't know. Maybe," said Kattie.

"Are you going to tell the girls tonight?" asked Rose.

Kattie said, "Nothing."

"Look, they are going to figure it out," said Rose.

"How?" asked Kattie.

"Well, Billie knows you've been calling her dad and that her dad has been calling you. She has told Mary, and Mary has told me. They think it's sweet, but they don't understand. Also, the girls have spent enough time together to realize that they look alike and have the exact same birthmark in the exact same place on their butts."

"What?" said Kattie. "How? Oh my god…"

"Yes, Mary told me," said Rose. "They know, Kattie. They just don't know the details."

"I've got to tell Jim," said Kattie as she headed out back.

Kattie went outside. She stopped and talked to Kathy for a minute. When Jim looked her way, she pointed inside the house. She then went back inside. In a few minutes, Jim came in. She grabbed his arm and took him into her bedroom.

"What?" asked Jim.

"The girls know," said Kattie.

"Know what?" asked Jim.

"Well, they don't know, but they know something."

"Slow down," said Jim. "What do they know?"

"They know that we have been talking on the phone to each other."

"Okay," said Jim. "So?"

"They also know that they look a lot alike and…they have the same birthmark on their butts."

"Oh," said Jim, "I didn't know that. Well, let's tell them before they figure out everything, because if they do and we haven't told them, they are going to be even more hurt."

"When do we tell them?" asked Kattie.

"Right now," said Jim. "Let's get them in here with us and just lock the door."

"Okay," said Kattie, "I'll go get them." When Kattie opened her bedroom door, the girls were standing right outside.

"Why are you and Billie's dad in your bedroom?" asked Mary.

"I thought you were swimming," said Kattie, trying to act normal."

"The water is too cold," said Mary.

"Well, we're waiting," said Billie.

"You girls come into my room. Jim and I need to tell you both something."

The girls followed Kattie into the room. Kattie closed and locked the door. Jim was sitting in a chair beside the bed. Kattie went over and stood by Jim.

"What was yawl doing?" asked Billie.

"You girls just sit on the bed, and we will tell you," said Jim.

"We know that you girls think the world of each other," said Kattie.

"That's because we are sisters," said Mary. "We know that much already."

"Yes, Mary," said Kattie, "you are half sisters. Jim is yours and Billie's father." A tear ran down Kattie's face. "It's all my fault. I'm so sorry we didn't tell you. But there are things that I didn't know about Jim until now."

Billie said, "So you and my dad made Mary?"

"Yes, sweetie," said Kattie. "But I didn't know about you and your mother. Look, your dad and I dated years ago after your mother took you and left your father. He didn't think she was ever coming back to him. About the same time as when you and your mother came back, I found out I was pregnant with Mary. When your father found out I was pregnant with Mary, he thought that your mother had come back to work things out so yawl could be a family. Although, I didn't know why at the time your father didn't want to marry me. So I got mad and told him that I didn't need him and that Mary was mine alone, not his." Tears were now running from Jim's and Kattie's eyes. "I loved him so much," said Kattie. "I was hurt that he didn't want me and my baby. I didn't know he had you, Billie. I didn't know."

Now Billie was crying big tears too. Kattie was sobbing out loud. Jim looked at Mary and said, "Mary, I want you to know I'm sorry I didn't fight for you like I should have. I'm sorry you had to go through life without a father. I thought of you every day even though I didn't know you."

A single tear rolled down Mary's face. "So you are my real father?" asked Mary.

"Yes, sweetie, I'm your dad," said Jim.

"Can I hug you?" asked Mary.

"Yes, baby, I wish you would," said Jim. Mary walked over to Jim and climbed on his lap and curled up with her arms around his neck.

Billie crawled down from the bed and got on the floor by Kattie. "Are you going to be my mama now?" asked Billie.

Kattie grabbed her and hugged her and kissed her face. "Yes, I'm your mama now, baby."

Jim got up with Mary still clinging to him and got on the floor with Kattie and Billie. He wiped the tears from Kattie's eyes. "Let's make it official then, Kattie. Will you marry me? Let's try to make up for what these girls have missed!"

"Yes," said Kattie, "yes, yes, yes!"

They all got up and went outside, Billie holding Kattie's hand and Mary holding Jim's hand. Jim said, "Hey, folks, we have an announcement to make." Everybody turned. "I've asked Kattie to marry me, and with the help of our daughters, she has said yes!" Everybody cheered. Rose and Kathy ran over and hugged Kattie. Sara and Leann were there and hugged their sister too. All the men shook Jim's hand, then everybody hugged Mary and Billie.

Then Troy yelled, "Let's cook some steaks and celebrate, everybody!" They all cheered again. Jim grabbed Kattie, and they kissed over and over.

Later, Kattie told Kathy and Rose, "Well, girls, looks like we have a wedding to plan."

"It's going to be grand," said Kathy.

Kattie walked over to Mary and Billie and hugged them both at the same time. For the first time in years, she felt complete and happy, truly happy!

That night, after everyone left, Rose went to her room and Mary and Billie went to Mary's room. Kattie went to check on the girls. She knocked and then opened the door. The girls were lying on the bed talking. "What are yawl doing now?" asked Kattie.

"Well," said Mary, "I think we are going to take this big bed out of this room and get two regular beds to go in here."

Kattie said, "Billie, you know, you can have your own room down the hall."

"Me and Mary want to room together for now," said Billie.

"Okay, whatever yawl want," said Kattie. She walked over and kissed them both and said, "Good night. Love you both."

"We love you," said the girls in unison.

Kattie closed the door and went back outside with Jim. "Well, too late to back out now," said Kattie. "The girls are already making plans for their room. No backing out now."

"So when do you want to get married?" asked Jim.

"I told Kathy, Rose, Sara, and Leann as soon as possible," said Kattie. "We don't want to give you time to change your mind." Jim laughed. "What about your ranch?" asked Kattie.

"I don't know. We will worry about that later. For now, I'll just go there every day and work it, then come back here at night."

Kattie leaned over and gave him a kiss. "Take me to bed," said Kattie. Jim picked her up and toted her inside her bedroom.

The next morning, Kattie woke up to the smell of coffee and bacon. She got up and went into the kitchen. Rose, Mary, and Billie were all sitting at the bar eating breakfast—pancakes, sausage, bacon, and scrambled eggs. Jim was fixing Kattie and himself fried eggs and toast. Kattie sat down by Billie. Jim brought her plate and set it in front of her, leaned over, and gave her a kiss.

"I like this," said Kattie.

"Well, ma'am, I'm just the weekend cook," said Jim. "Rose told me her grandma cooks during the week."

"We might have to fire her," said Rose. "She can't make pancakes like these. Yum, these are so good."

"They are so good," said Mary.

"Well, I guess after breakfast, we need to go to Montana and get Billie's and Jim's clothes and whatever else they need from their house."

"Okay," said Billie and Mary.

"What do you think, Jim?" asked Kattie.

"Whatever you say," said Jim with a smile.

"Okay, girls, eat up," said Kattie.

Well, the date was set. On May 15, 1991, Kattie and Jim would be wed. Sara would rent the venue and would furnish the decorations and flowers. Leann would pick out and furnish the dresses of the bridesmaids, which included herself, Sara, Kathy, Rose, Billie, and Mary, and the maid of honor, Carol. Also, the dress of the ring bearer, which would be little Tommie. Leann's two sons would be the ushers, and Troy would give Kattie away. Jim hadn't named his best man yet, but Kattie would furnish her own wedding dress, Jim's suit, and the best man's suit. Jim's family had met Kattie and Mary now, and his mother and father were happy to have another granddaughter, Mary. Jim's brothers and their families had all agreed to take care of the reception. A lot to do in three weeks, but Kattie had a lot of help from friends and family.

Mary and Billie had already set up the arena for barrel racing. Jim brought Billie's horse to Plumber's Gap. They had been running every afternoon with Kathy coaching them. Rose liked to watch the girls but was not interested in participating at all. Jim spent time at the arena watching the girls also. He was amazed at how good Mary was at handling the horses. It was like she could read their mind.

One afternoon, Billie's horse was acting up and was hard to control. Rose checked him out. "I don't know what wrong with him," said Rose. "Everything checks out. He seems to be fine, but something's wrong."

Mary got off Bob and tied him. She walked over to Billie's horse. She rubbed his nose and asked the horse, "What's wrong with you, buddy?" The horse nickered and shook his head. "Okay, okay," said Mary. She took his reins off his head and the bits out of his mouth. Mary told Kathy, "Get me a hackamore." And then she asked Rose, "Do you have a light and a small pick?"

"Yes," said Rose. She went for her bag.

Kathy came into the arena with the hackamore bridle. Mary handed Kathy Billie's bridle. "What's wrong with it?" asked Kathy?

"Look at the bit," said Mary.

Kathy looked at the bit. "Yup, that will do it."

"Do what?" asked Billie.

"See here where the chrome has gone off the metal bit?" said Kathy.

"Yes," said Billie.

"Feel how rough that is. You feel that?"

"Yes," said Billie.

"So does your horse."

Rose came back with her bag. Mary opened the horse's mouth and shone the light inside. "See that?" Mary asked Rose.

"Yes, I see it." Rose took the pick and plucked a piece of chrome flake from between two of the horse's teeth.

Mary put the hackamore on the horse and told Billie, "Use these today. We will get you some new bits." Billie got on her horse Toby and made another run.

"Perfect," said Kathy. "Good run, Billie."

Rose asked Mary, "How did you know?"

"When I asked him what was wrong," said Mary, "he opened and twisted his mouth like he had something stuck in his teeth. Then he was gumming his bits and shaking his head, which told me something was wrong with his bits."

"They don't teach that in vet school," said Rose.

That night in bed, Jim told Kattie about Mary's ability to understand horses and what was bothering them even when a vet couldn't. Kattie smiled. "I know she has always had that knack. Nobody understands it, but it's real. She took a wild horse that no one could touch, and in two days, she was lying on its back while she made it walk around the round pen. She told me that Bob taught her how to understand the horse and what they are feeling. As a veterinarian, it's not possible, but as her mother, I've seen it over and over. She has a gift."

"That's for sure," said Jim. "I wouldn't have believed it if I hadn't seen it. She asked the horse what was wrong, and then she knew what to do. Amazing."

Mary altered an old saddle to fit her bull and made a bridle to fit him. She was now riding him around in a round pen, teaching him to turn and back up. The bull had really grown since she started working with him; he probably weighed around eight hundred pounds now. "Just a big kid," said Mary. Kathy still didn't like him; she was afraid Mary was going to get hurt. Troy thought it was funny that Mary wanted to train a bull to ride. "If anybody can do it, I think she can."

Billie was happy about having Kattie as her mom now. She spent a lot of time with Mary still, but she also liked hanging out with Kattie. She asked Kattie if she could go to work with her sometime at the animal hospital. "Sure," said Kattie, "anytime you're not in school." But now it was all about getting the wedding over and getting ready for rodeo season. Mary wanted to compete the Cheyenne Frontier Days Rodeo this year and run with the best of the best in the barrel racing.

Kattie was already thinking about a big new horse trailer with living quarters and a new truck to pull it.

Well, the day was here. Total chaos in the Plumber household as they all tried to get ready for the wedding. Jim and his family all met at Sara's house to get ready so Kattie and the girls—Rose, Mary, and Billie—could get ready at home. Kattie was going to put her dress on at the church. She was trying to help the girls with their hair and makeup. Pete and Alice had already left with Kattie's wedding dress and were taking it ahead to the church. Everyone that was in the wedding were to be there an hour before the service. The decorations were already done at the church. Jim's brothers and their wives had everything set up at the reception hall.

"Come on, girls, we've got to go," said Kattie.

"We're coming."

Kattie had on a jogging suit. The girls were so beautiful in their dresses it made Kattie want to cry. All four got loaded in the truck and headed out to the church. Once at the church, Kattie got out and ran in the side door to the prep room. Sara, Leann, and Alice were waiting there for her. They sat her down and started doing her hair and makeup. The dress was hanging there; it was white with white lace, pearl buttons, and a ten-foot train. The veil would run halfway down her back to cover her hair, with a lip up in front. The bridesmaids' dresses were also beautiful, all peach-colored with white lace. Kattie hadn't seen the decoration in the church yet; she had been told how beautiful it was.

"Who has the rings?" asked Kattie.

"We have them tied to the pillow and ready for Tommie."

"All four?" asked Kattie.

"Yes, all four," said Leann. "Just calm down, sweetie."

"Oh my god, I'm sweating like a horse." They all laughed. "I can't believe I'm getting married and to a younger man at that. I'm forty-three, and he is only thirty-eight. What am I doing?"

"It's just nerves. You're doing the right thing. Calm down."

Kattie didn't want a ring with a big diamond stone; she said it would get in her way working with the animals. So she and Jim both just got gold bands for each other and two small gold bands for the girls, Billie and Mary. It was going to be a special service for the girls also. Mary, Kathy, Tommie, Rose, and Billie were all in the hallway waiting for Kattie. Jim got his oldest brother, Scott, to be his best man. They were in the sanctuary, ready to go. Most of the guests were already there, along with Jim's family and the preacher.

"It's time," said Sara. "Get your dress on. Hurry up."

Kattie was thinking, *Run, Kattie, run.* But then she thought of those two beautiful little girls. "Okay, I'm ready," said Kattie. "Yawl get my train."

"We got it. You just go to the hall."

Troy was waiting at the front door of the church. They all came out the side door with Kattie. They lined up outside—Little Tommie in the front, then Mary and Billie, then Troy and Kattie, then Leann and Sara holding the train, then Rose and Kathy behind them. Two of Jim's nephews opened the double doors to the church. The organ started playing the march. Tommie started in the door as they rehearsed, with the pillow. Mary and Billie followed, dropping rose petals, then Kattie and Troy with the four bridesmaids behind. Kattie saw Jim and his brother standing there as they all made their way down the aisle. Tommie handed the ring pillow to Scott, Kattie stopped, and Troy put her hand in Jim's. Kathy moved up behind Kattie, and Troy took Tommie and sat down. Billie stood beside her father, Jim, and Mary stood beside her mother, Kattie.

The preacher started the service. They both said yes, and he pronounced them husband and wife. Then the preacher said, "Jim, you can kiss your bride." Jim raised the veil and kissed Kattie. The two girls had tears in their eyes, as well as Kattie and all the maids.

Jim said, "Hold up. There is something else Kattie and I want to say to the girls." Scott pulled the pillow from behind him. Jim took one of the rings and said, "Mary, I promise to love and honor you just as your mom. I will try to be a good dad, and I will always be here for you as long as I live, so help me, God." He put the ring on Mary's finger and gave her a kiss.

Then Kattie took the other ring and said, "Billie, I promise to love and honor you just as your dad. I will try to be a good mom and will always be here for as long as I live, so help me, God." She put the ring on Billie's finger and gave her a kiss.

There was not a dry eye in the church. All four hugged and headed out of the church. The bridesmaids threw bird seed in the air as they came out. Kattie, Jim, Billie, and Mary all got in Kattie's truck and headed to the reception hall. It was a beautiful wedding and a beautiful day for them all.

At the reception, Jim and Kattie danced, then Jim danced with Mary and then Billie. Rose was sitting at one of the tables with Pete and Alice. Jim walked over and reached out for Rose's hand. She took his hand. "Can I have this dance?" asked Jim. She smiled and stood up. He walked her to the dance floor, and they started dancing. When the dance was over, he walked her to where Kattie was waiting.

"Everyone," said Kattie, "I have an announcement to make." Everybody got quiet. "Most of you know Rose, my other daughter. For those who don't, Rose is Pete's and Alice's granddaughter, but I have loved her and thought of her as my daughter since she was fourteen. She has always been Mary's big sister and now Billie's. She is now a veterinarian and a very good one. She works for me at the veterinarian clinic. But not anymore…" Rose looked up at Kattie. "Now she is my partner. I'm giving her part ownership of the business. Sara has the paper ready, and we will sign next week."

Rose hugged Kattie and said, "Thank you so much. I love you, Mom."

Chapter 5

Rodeo Season 1991

Mary and Billie got Kattie to buy them a new horse trailer with a living space built in. Kattie also got Jim a new truck big enough to pull the new trailer. The four were planning to go to Cody, Wyoming, next weekend so Billie and Mary could run three nights to get ready for the Cheyenne Frontier Days Rodeo coming up next month. Jim and Kattie got Billie a blue vest like Mary's red one made with Billie Hatcher on the front and Hatcher Cattle Co. on the back. Kattie had reserved two rooms in Cody, one for her and Jim and one for the girls. She said the bunks in the trailer's living space would be fine for resting and napping but that she wanted something bigger to sleep on.

Thursday morning, Billie and Mary loaded up their horses in the new trailer. Jim had hay and oats on top, and Kattie had stocked the cabinets and fridge inside the living space. They headed out with Jim driving, Kattie in the front with him, and the girls in the back seat. It was 342 miles from Deadwood to Cody, Wyoming, about six hours. They should have time to make a couple of practice runs before time for the rodeo once they got there.

They finally made it to Cody. Jim parked the trailer, and Billie and Mary unloaded their horses. Jim leveled up the trailer and started up the generator. Mary started saddling Bob, and Billie started saddling her horse, Toby. They rode to the arena and rode around, warming up their horses. Then they set up the barrels. There was no time clock set up yet. They both made two runs before the crew started dragging the arena.

They rode back to the trailer, unsaddled their horses, and brushed them down. Jim and Kattie were in the trailer with the A/C going. Mary and Billie went inside the trailer to rest for a while. The event time was getting near. Mary and Billie had ridden in the grand entry and had paid their entry fees. Then it started to rain. Mary and Billie loaded their horses back in the trailer, still saddled, then went back in the sleeping area with Jim and Kattie.

"Well, what now?" asked Kattie.

"If it keeps raining, I'm not running," said Mary.

"Why?" asked Billie.

"Too dangerous," said Mary.

"For what, lightning?"

"No, for the horses on the wet ground. Are you willing to risk getting your horse hurt just for practice? I'm not," said Mary.

"She's right," said Jim. "But it's up to you, Billie."

"I want to run," said Billie.

"Okay," said Mary, "let's go get Toby ready. We need the wrap his ankles, front and back. You will have to start slowly coming into the first barrel, then speed up a little on the second, then open up on the third. Toby is going to want to run full out. You've got to hold him back."

Jim and Kattie sat back and listened as Mary instructed Billie. They couldn't believe this thirteen-year-old girl. "How does she know this, Kattie?" asked Jim.

"Okay," said Billie, "I will. Let's go." They unloaded Toby, and Mary got the wraps. She started wrapping his legs from his hooves to just below his knees.

Billie headed to the arena alley. Jim, Kattie, and Mary went to the stands. Luckily, the stands were covered in Cody.

"Okay, folks," said the announcer, "it's going to be sloppy, but here comes our barrel racers. Some have dropped out, but we have three ready to run. First up is a young lady from Nebraska, Ms. Hanna Smith." She came out of the alley full speed. She came to the first barrel, and her horse almost fell. They regained control as they turned the second barrel. She opened up, rounding the third, then headed home. "A 14.72," said the announcer, "with a close call on the first barrel. Next up is a young lady from here in Cody, a regular, Ms. Tammie Bright. Go, Tammie," said the announcer. She came out, turned the first barrel, then made the second barrel. She rounded the third too tight and knocked it over. "A 14.85," said the announcer, "plus 5 for a downed barrel. Okay, folks, we have a South Dakota cowgirl, Ms. Billie Hatcher."

Billie and Toby came in the arena at half speed. They made the first barrel, then picked up a little speed going to the second barrel. They cleared it as Billie opened Toby up. "Go, Billie!" yelled Mary as Billie rounded the third barrel. "Go, go, go!" said Mary.

"That's your winner, folks, a 14.56 in the mud," said the announcer. "Great job, Ms. Hatcher." The whole crowd all stood and cheered as Billie and Toby loped back in then out.

"Oh my god," said Jim as he hugged Mary and Kattie. "Let's go see her." They all headed to the trailer. Billie was there unwrapping Toby's legs. Billie stopped and ran to Mary. They hugged.

"You are the best," said Billie. "But if you knew how to do it and win, why did you not run?"

"I knew how to help you and Toby do it, not me and Bob. Bob is too strong in the turns and would have slid and fell, just like Hanna

Smith almost did. We will get you and Toby tomorrow night," said Mary. All four hugged.

Friday night, the sky was clear and the ground had dried out. There were ten entries. Billie was first, and Mary was sixth. Billie made her run with a time of 14.32. When it got to Mary's run, Billie was leading. Mary came out of the alley in a full run. Bob made the first barrel, then the second, rounded the third, and headed home. "A 14.00 flat," said the announcer, "for Ms. Plumber. It doesn't get much better than that, folks." After the night, the closest time to Billie's was a 14.56 by Hanna Smith.

Saturday morning, Hanna brought her horse to Mary and Billie's trailer. She knocked on the trailer door. Kattie opened the door. "Can I help you?"

"Yes, ma'am. My name is Hanna Smith."

"Nice to meet you. My name is Kattie Hatcher."

"I was told that you are a vet."

"Yes, I am," said Kattie.

"Well, my horse has hurt his leg somehow."

"Okay, let me look." Mary followed Kattie out of the trailer. The ankle on the left leg was swollen. Kattie felt the leg. "Easy, boy," said Kattie, "I know. Well, he has pulled a tendon. I'm afraid he is not going to run tonight."

Hanna was twenty-three and traveling alone. "What do I do?" asked Hanna.

"Let me put something on it to help the swelling and give him some antibiotics. It's going to take a while for it to heal, sweetie." The girl started crying. "Don't cry," said Kattie. "He'll be okay. It's just going to take a while." Mary was standing at the horse's head, rubbing his face.

Hanna said, "Rodeoing is all I have. I don't know what I'm going to do. I wait tables wherever I go to get by, but barrel racing is my life."

Mary spoke up, "Hi, Hanna. My name is Mary Plumber. I'll make you a deal."

"What kind of deal?" asked Hanna.

"I've got a four-year-old horse that I've been training for the barrel. If you will ride him this season so he can get some experience around crowds and other horses, I'll get your horse ready for next year."

"Okay, yes," said Hanna.

"When we leave tomorrow morning, you can follow us to our ranch in South Dakota with your horse. You can work with my horse for a few days, then take him on the road."

Hanna looked at Kattie. "Is that okay with you?"

"Horses are her business. I do cows," said Kattie.

"Great," said Hanna. "I'll be ready in the morning."

Saturday night, Mary and Bob ran a 14.10 and Billie and Toby ran a 14.20. Mary won two nights but had no score for the first night, so Billie was the event winner. She got a check and a buckle. The sisters were on their way to being ready for Cheyenne.

The next morning, Jim, Kattie, Billie, and Mary headed home with Hanna and her horse following behind them. As they drove along, Billie asked Mary, "Why are you going to let that girl ride your horse?"

"Well, I can't ride but one horse in competition, and he needs the experience. Besides, we cowgirls have got to stick together. Rodeo is all she has."

"I think it's a great idea," said Jim.

"Me too," said Kattie. "We should all help others if we can. By the way, your birthday is coming soon, Mary. What do you want?"

"I need a walker," said Mary, "so I can exercise more horses."

"One of those round things that you hook your horses to, and it walks them around and around?" asked Billie.

"Yup," said Mary, "that's what I want."

"Sounds good to me," said Jim.

"I'm a lucky mom," said Kattie. "Most moms haul their girls to dance lessons or cheer practice. Me, I just send mine to the barn." They laughed.

As they pulled up to the barn at Plumber's Gap, Kathy came out to meet them. "Well, how did you do?" she asked.

"Billie won the event," said Mary with a smile.

"Really?" said Kathy with shock in her voice.

"Yep."

"Who is that?" asked Kathy. Hanna pulled up beside them.

"Oh, that's Hanna. Her horse needs some help," said Mary. Mary went to the back of Hanna's trailer, opened the gate, and backed Hanna's horse out. She clipped a lead rope to his halter and led him into the barn, limping. She put him in a clean stall with hay and oats. Hanna followed her in. "Come meet your ride," said Mary. They walked to the next stall. "Here he is," said Mary. "I never gave him a name. He has one about a mile long on paper, but I never use those. I've just been calling him Blue Boy, because when I got him, he acted so sad and blue. But he is better now, aren't you, boy?"

"He is beautiful," said Hanna. He was a big bay-colored horse.

"In the morning, we will get you two started," said Mary.

Hanna said, "Can I ask you something?"

"Sure," said Mary.

"How old are you?"

"I'm fourteen," said Mary.

"Wow, so how do you know so much about horses?"

"I don't know," said Mary. "Our horse trainer and I have been working with the horses since I was about eight years old. I raised Bob, my horse, from a colt. He taught me most of it. We connected so deeply that he knows what I'm saying and I understand what he says. Horses don't talk with words, but they do talk with noises and movements. For some reason, I can understand them when they talk back."

"Well, I'll be going to town to find me some place to stay," said Hanna.

"You can stay here if you want," said Mary. "Just wait here." Mary walked to the tack room. "Kathy, is there any reason Hanna can't stay in the trailer at the mine this week?"

"No, not that I know of," said Kathy.

"Hanna," said Mary, "this is Kathy, our horse trainer. Kathy, this is Hanna."

"Nice to meet you," said Kathy.

"Unhook your trailer over there. Let me unload my horse, and I'll show you the trailer."

"Okay," said Hanna.

Mary unloaded Bob and put him in his stall and gave him some oats and hay. Mary walked to the house. "Mom, can Hanna stay in Troy and Kathy's old trailer this week?"

"That's fine," said Kattie, "but she needs to keep it clean just like it is now and buy her own food."

Mary went out to Hanna's truck. "Come on, and I'll show you the trailer." They got in Hanna's truck. They drove across the road to the trailer. Mary got out and unlocked the door. "Well, here it is."

Hanna walked inside. "This is nice," said Hanna.

"Mom said just make sure you keep it clean like it is."

"Oh, I will. Thank you so much." Mary told Hanna how to get to the nearest store, and Hanna took Mary back home.

The next morning, Mary was at the barn early taking care of the horses. She put Bob out in the lot to graze. She took Blue Boy out of his stall and put him in the round pen. Hanna came pulling up. "Morning," said Mary.

"Good morning," said Hanna.

"How was your night?" asked Mary.

"Great," said Hanna. "It has been so long since I've had a good bed to sleep in. After a long hot bath, it was wonderful."

"Well, if you want to get your saddle and tack, we will get started," said Mary. Hanna got her stuff and saddled Blue Boy up. "Just take him in the arena and ride him around for a little while. Let him get used to you." While Hanna was riding Blue Boy, Mary got out Hanna's horse and removed the raps on his ankle; some of the swellings had gone down. She put a heated paste on his ankle and then a new wrap. She then put him in the lot with Bob to graze. Hanna was getting a feel for Blue Boy turning and backing him up. Mary said, "Go ahead and lope him around the arena awhile." And Hanna did.

Mary went to the house; in a little bit, she came back. She told Hanna "Here" as she handed her a brown sack and a canteen.

"What's this?" asked Hanna.

"Lunch," said Mary. "You and Blue Boy ride down to the waterfall. There, you will see a trail leading down the valley. Follow it until you come to an opening stop by the creek. There's a big oak tree. Stop there and eat or nap, whatever you want to do. Let Blue Boy graze. I'll see you when you get back."

Billie was gone with Kattie to the clinic. She was going to be her helper today. She got to watch Kattie work on the animals and meet everybody there. Carol told Billie, "Don't let this get in your blood. You'll be cleaning up poop for the rest of your life." They laughed. A little girl and her mom brought in a kitten that was sick. Kattie told them that the kitten was dehydrated and needed an IV to get fluids in it and would need to stay a couple of days. The little girl cried. Billie hugged the little girl and said, "I'll personally take good care of your kitty." The little girl smiled as her mother led her out of the room. Kattie gave the kitten a mild sedative and started the IV. She handed her to Billie and told her to put her in a kennel and to check on her every hour.

Kathy showed up at the barn. "Where's your friend?" she asked.

"I sent her and Blue Boy out to bond," said Mary.

"So tell me how Billie beat you in Cody."

Mary laughed. "She's better than me, I guess," said Mary.

"Bull crap," said Kathy. "What happened?"

"Well, it was raining the first night, and I didn't think it was safe to run Bob. Billie wanted to run anyway, so I told her what to do, and she won. The next two nights, I won, but Billie got the overall win. It was bad wet the first night. That's how Hanna's horse got hurt. He slid and almost fell at the first barrel. She was pushing him too hard on wet ground."

"Are you and Billie practicing this afternoon?" asked Kathy.

"Yeah, Billie went with Mom to work today. When they get home, we will."

"Okay, I'll take the tractor and the drag and smooth out the arena," said Kathy.

Hanna and Blue Boy made it back in the middle of the afternoon. "Well, how was it?" asked Mary.

"Great," said Hanna. "Yawl have a beautiful place here, and Blue Boy is a sweetheart."

"Let's get him put up for a while," said Mary. "We're going to run this afternoon." They pulled his saddle off and brushed him down, then gave him oats and hay.

Troy's crew showed up at the barn with a load of hay. Mary told Ben which bay to stack it in. Kathy got the arena smooth, so Mary and Hanna went out and set up the barrels. Troy's younger hands were watching Hanna's every move. Ben said, "Yawl put your eyes back in your head and get that hay unloaded." Hanna knew they were watching and was putting on a show for them.

Kattie and Billie made it home around 6:00 p.m. Billie ran into the house to change clothes. Mary and Hanna got out Bob and Blue Boy and started saddling them. Billie came back out and got Toby ready. The hands finished with the hay and were leaving the barn. Kathy told Hanna with a laugh, "They are gone now. You can stop twitching your tail."

Hanna smiled. "Well, I had to make sure they noticed."

"Oh, they noticed everything about you," said Kathy.

The girls started riding around in the arena, warming up their horses. Hanna walked Blue Boy around the barrel pattern a couple of times. "Who goes first?" asked Hanna.

"I'll go first," said Billie as she headed down the alley.

Kathy lined up on the side with her stopwatch. "Anytime now," said Kathy.

Billie came running into the arena, turned the first barrel, then the second and the third. "Run, Billie, run!" yelled Mary.

"Not bad," said Kathy. "I got 15.45. Okay, your turn, Hanna."

Hanna eased down the alley, then came running back into the arena. Blue Boy made the first turn, then the next, then headed for the third barrel. He loped it and headed home.

"Wow, a 15.50. That's close, Billie," said Kathy.

Mary came running out of the alley wide open, turned the first, second, then third barrel.

"That's how it's done, girls, a 14.00 flat."

Mary said, "Okay, this time, I'm just going to watch yawl run. Maybe I'll see something."

Billie said, "Okay." She came running out of the alley, made the first turn, then the second.

Mary yelled, "Stop!"

Billie slowed down and walked her horse to Mary. "What is it?"

"Did you check his shoes before you got on him?"

"No," said Billie.

Mary picked up Toby's feet one at a time. "The shoe on the left rear is way loose."

"I'll go get Troy," said Kathy.

Mary told Hanna, "You go ahead and make your run." Hanna went down the alley, then came back out into the arena. She made the first turn, the second, and the third. Billie was timing Hanna.

"Good job, Hanna," said Billie. "A 15.36."

Troy and Kathy came back. Troy picked up the left leg, pulled the shoe off, filed and cleaned the hoof, then put the shoe back on. He checked the others and replaced a couple of nails.

"Okay, Billie, let's see if that helps." Billie came out of the alley, turned the first, then the second, and then the third.

"Way to go," said Kathy. "A 15.10, Billie, that's your best run ever."

"That's good, Hanna, for your first time on Blue Boy. Any one of these horses can run a 15.00 flat or better. Tomorrow I'll set up some pole for you, Hanna, and show you something."

"Okay," said Hanna.

"Let's put them up for tonight," said Mary.

Kathy asked Mary as Billie and Hanna rode off, "How did you know?"

"When Toby went into the left turn on the second barrel, I saw his leg muscle flinch, quiver, or whatever you call it. I saw it. Then when Billie was coming over to me, I heard the shoe clink."

"You are something else, Mary Plumber, really something."

The next day, Mary set up poles in the arena. She told Hanna, "Now this works for Billie and me, but I don't know yet if it will work for you. But it's worth a try. What I need you to do is help Blue Boy shift his weight. If you can do that, I believe he can put more into running and make better time."

"Okay," said Hanna.

"Let me show you on Bob first," said Mary. She walked Bob to the other end, then started at a slow lope, turning each pole. As Bob turned right, she leaned right, then as he straightened back up, she leaned left. When he turned left, she leaned left, then as he straightened back up, she leaned right.

Hanna said, "Okay, I see what you're doing." Hanna started running the poles in a slow lope like Mary did. When she got to the end, she stopped.

Mary said, "The faster the horse is going, the faster you move. It's all about helping the horse balance as he runs and turns at the same time. Just make about ten runs and concentrate on helping him turn. Feel his movements."

"Okay," said Hanna. Hanna made her runs, each time watching and feeling the way the horse moved and swayed around the poles.

"You feel it?" asked Mary.

"Yes, I do," said Hanna.

"You want to do the same thing on the barrels. Okay, let's unsaddle them and cool them off," said Mary. "We'll try it on the barrels this afternoon."

"Okay," said Hanna. Hanna helped Mary clean out the stalls and put down fresh chips. Then they went into the tack room and cleaned tacks and saddles.

That afternoon, Mary, Hanna, and Billie got ready to ride. This time, Mary went first. She ran into the arena, made the first turn and then the second, and flew around the third and headed home.

"Wow," said Kathy, "a 13.83. Way to go, Bob and Mary."

Then Hanna ran out of the alley. She made the first turn and the second barrel and then the third.

"Yes, yes," said Kathy, "a 14.18. Good job, Hanna. Now Billie's turn."

She came out and rounded the first, the second, and then the third barrel and then ran home.

"A 13.95. Way to go, Billie," said Kathy. "Yawl don't need me anymore with runs like that. Man, that's good."

Mary rode up to Hanna. "Did you feel it?"

"Yes, thank you so much. You are an amazing young girl," said Hanna.

"Well, I think you and Blue Boy will be okay now," said Mary.

"Yep," said Hanna. "There's an event in Billings, Montana, starting Thursday, and I need a check."

"Well, go get it," said Mary. "We will be in Cheyenne the week after next. Maybe we'll see you there."

"I hope so," said Hanna.

That night at supper, Kattie asked Mary, "Well, how is Hanna doing?"

"She's good," said Mary. "She will be leaving tomorrow, going to Billings, Montana, to an event."

"What about her horse?"

"Oh, his getting better. Still a little swelling, but no limp now."

"That's good," said Kattie.

"Yeah, Mary is letting her use her horse, and now she has taught her how to ride so she can beat us."

"She might beat you, but she's not going to beat me. I didn't teach her or you everything," she said with a laugh.

"So what do you think it's going to take to win in Cheyenne?"

"A 13.60 or 13.70," said Mary.

"Really?" said Jim.

"Yep. Billie ran a 13.95 today, and I ran a 13.83. We've got some work to do."

Rose spoke up, "How is your kitten, Billie?"

"She's good. That little girl's coming back to get her tomorrow. She'll be so happy."

"So how do you like working at the clinic?" asked Mary.

"It's great. I love all the different animals we see."

"Mom, will you talk to Troy about putting new shoes on Bob and Toby before we go to Cheyenne?" asked Mary.

"Sure," said Kattie. "Rose, are you going to Cheyenne with us?"

"I planned to. Somebody's got to keep the boy beat off these two cuties."

Mary said, "Yeah, right." Billie just smiled; she was at the age of thinking and talking about boys a little too much at sixteen years old. "Is Troy and Kathy coming?" asked Mary.

"I'm not sure," said Kattie. "You'll have to ask Kathy tomorrow."

"Okay, I will."

The next day, when Kathy got there, Mary asked her if they were going to Cheyenne.

"Do you want me to?"

"Yes," said Mary.

"Okay, then we're going."

Mary hugged her and said, "Thank you."

Cheyenne Frontier Days was a ten-day event. Kattie had already reserved a block of room months ago. Mary and Billie would be competing against Jane Harper, the six-time world champion of barrel racing.

"It's going to be fun," said Mary. "She may win it, but I'll be pushing her all the way. I'll be fine with being the fourteen-year-old girl who almost beat the world champion." They laughed. "But first, we must qualify to run. We better get to work."

"Okay," said Billie.

The next three days, Mary and Billie pushed their horses and themselves, but the best they could do was 13.72 for Mary and a 13.86 for Billie.

"Well, let's hope for the best. That's all we can do," said Billie.

"We will be in the top, I think."

Two days until time to go. They started to get all their tacks and saddles ready and loaded in the trailer. The next day, they loaded their horses and headed out on their five-hour trip to Cheyenne. Troy and Kathy followed behind them; they had left Tommie with Meemaw so they could have some time alone. They got there a day early and set up their trailer and a small round pen with a tarp over it for shade. Qualifying rounds were the next day. Once everything was set up, Kattie wanted to take everybody to town and show them the sights. She knew all the top spots to see and the best places to eat. After seeing the sights and eating, they went to the hotel and checked in. Troy and

Kathy volunteered to go back and stay in the trailer overnight and watch the horses. The next morning, Kattie, Jim, Billie, and Mary came to the trailer. Tryouts started at 12:00 p.m. Mary and Billie went to sign up.

Billie ran ninth, and Mary ran tenth. Jane Harper ran fourth. That was the only one they cared about, said Mary. They went back to get ready. Kattie, Jim, Troy, and Kathy headed to the stands to watch the tryouts. Billie and Mary rode to the arena, and they saw Hanna talking to Harper. They were laughing and talking like old friends. They eased up to Hanna.

"Hi, Mary," said Hanna. "Hi, Billie."

"Hi, Hanna," they said.

"Well, did you get your check?" asked Mary.

"I sure did," said Hanna. "Jane, this is Mary Plumber."

"Hi, Mary," said Jane.

"And this is her sister, Billie Hatcher."

"Hi, Billie."

"They are both very good," said Hanna. "But the little one is the one you better watch. She knows her stuff."

"When are you running, Hanna?" asked Mary.

"Eighteenth," said Hanna.

"Well, good luck," said Mary. "Hope you both do well."

"You too," said Jane.

When it was time for Jane to run, the best time so far was 15.52. Jane came out of the alley and made a perfect run; her time was 14.22.

"What?" said Billie.

"She's holding back," said Mary, "saving her horse."

"Are you sure?" asked Billie.

"I'm sure."

Billie got ready for her run. She had a perfect pattern, and her time was 13.80. "Wow," said some of the girls.

It was Mary's turn to run. She made her run, and her time was 14.00. "Well, we will see what happens," said Mary.

"Let's wait and see what the other times are," said Billie.

"Okay," said Mary.

Hanna's run was coming up. Nobody had been faster than 14.00, but Billie's. Hanna made her run, a 14.12.

"I can't believe this," said Billie. "Something's wrong."

The girls went back to the trailer. Kathy and Troy were there. Kathy said, "Yawl did good."

"Yeah, too good," said Billie. "Something's up."

Troy said, "You don't play your hand until you get your last card."

"What?" asked Billie.

"They are holding back," said Kathy, "waiting to see who stands out."

"Okay, well, we will find out in the morning who is running tomorrow night," said Mary.

The next morning, the judges had a list of the runners that night.

Thursday Night Barrel Racing

1. Billie Hatcher
2. Jane Harper
3. Mary Plumber
4. Cristy Jones
5. Carmon Houser
6. Hanna Smith
7. Rachel Adams
8. Jamie Spears
9. Bobbie Sims
10. Sara Taylor

For the two-night elimination, the two slowest combined times for Thursday and Friday nights would be eliminated. Only eight would run Saturday night, and the top six from Saturday night would move on to the finals, which would be held next Thursday, Friday, and Saturday nights.

"Well, Billie," said Mary, "looks like you get to set the pace for everybody else."

Hanna came by trailer to see Mary. "Are you ready for tonight?" asked Hanna.

"Sure," said Mary.

"What about you and Blue Boy?"

"Oh yeah, we're ready. We got second in Billings. Would have won it if Jane hadn't been there. She's tough to beat, but if anybody can beat her, you can," said Hanna.

"I'm going to try," said Mary.

"They are paying four places this year," said Hanna. "One of them is mine." She laughed.

"I hope so," said Mary. "If you win, Blue Boy will be worth a lot of money."

"Dang, I didn't think about that," said Hanna. "Don't sell my ride." She laughed as she rode off.

Mary went back inside the trailer. "Billie, let's talk about tonight," said Mary.

"Okay," said Billie.

"What do you think we should do?" asked Mary. "I think the top riders are going to be holding back to save their horses for the finals. We could do the same and try to stay about 15.00, or we can push it and make them do the same."

"Well, I'm first," said Billie, "Jane is second, and you're third. Why not let me push it this first run? If Jane holds back, then you hold back. If she goes all out, then you go all out," said Billie.

"Okay," said Mary, "you set the pace, and we will see what happens."

Billie and Mary mounted up and rode to the alley. They saw Jane and Hanna. "Good luck," said Mary.

"You too," said Jane.

Billie got ready.

"Ladies and gentlemen, your first barrel racer for tonight is Ms. Billie Hatcher. Come on, Billie, let's get this started."

Billie and Toby shot down the alley and flew by the timing light. They made the first barrel, then the second. As they headed for the third, the crowd had already stood up. They knew it was going to be good. Toby rounded the third barrel and headed home. As they crossed the light, the announcer said, "Oh my, what a way to start the night. A 13.80 run! Great job, Billie Hatcher. Well, that's a great run, but this next cowgirl is the six-time world champion and top-money winner of this sport, Ms. Jane Harper." Jane and her horse came flying out of the alley, hit the first turn and then the second, and rounded the third barrel. Again, the crowd stood up. The announcer said, "It's going to be close, folks. A 13.93 for Ms. Jane Harper. Two great runs back-to-back," said the announcer. "Okay, folks, we're just getting started. Next rider up is Ms. Mary Plumber."

Mary and Bob came out slinging dirt. Bob sat up and nailed the first turn. As they approached the second barrel, Mary felt Bob as he nailed the second barrel. As they ran for the third, Bob and Mary sat up and rounded the third like two dancers in perfect time with each other. "It's all you now, boy," said Mary. Bob kicked dirt ten feet high in the air as he flew by the clock.

"Just when I thought it couldn't get any better," said the announcer. "A 13.68, what a ride! Yawl got to let me catch my breath. Oh my, that's getting really close to the world record there, folks, real close."

Mary took Bob to the trailer. Billie and Toby were there. Mary got off and hugged Billie. "Way to go, sis," said Billie. "We got them scratching their heads now." They both laughed.

Kathy came running to the back. She hugged them both. "That was amazing," said Kathy. "You both beat the world champion. I'm so excited."

"That's just the first round," said Mary.

"Come on, let me help you take care of the horses so yawl can go watch the rest."

After taking care of the horses, Mary, Kathy, and Billie went to the stands. They went over to where Kattie, Jim, Troy, and Rose were sitting. They all hugged Mary and Billie. Jim gave them both a big kiss. "I'm so proud of you two." Mary sat down between Rose and Kattie.

"What now?" asked Rose.

Kattie turned and looked at Rose. "She has a plan. I know she does."

"Well," said Mary after taking a drink of water, "tomorrow night, we hold back and let Jane push her horse to win. We will still make the semifinals. Oh, here comes Hanna." Hanna and Blue Boy came out flying. They made the first and then the second. Mary stood and yelled "Go Blue Boy!" as they rounded the third barrel. "Go, go!" said Mary.

The announcer said, "A 14.00 flat, folks."

"Well, she's in fourth," said Mary. They stayed and watched the rest of the rodeo.

"The bareback horses are next," said Rose. "I like this event. This and bull riding."

"Okay, folks, in chute number 5, a cowboy from South Dakota, Mr. Paul Plumber."

Kattie said, "What? My god, that's my uncle's name."

The chute opened, and out came the cowboy and horse. The buzzer went off. They picked him up. "An 89.90 ride, folks," said the announcer.

"We got to find out who he is," said Kattie.

"Why?" asked Jim.

"Paul Plumber was my pop's brother's name who died years ago. That's whose gold I used to start my clinic. Oh my god.

"Calm down," said Jim. "We will find out. Come on, Troy, let's go meet this bronc rider."

"Okay," said Troy.

Troy and Jim headed down behind the chutes to find Paul Plumber. They stopped and asked one group if anybody knew where Paul Plumber was. "Who wants to know?" asked one of the guys.

Troy spoke up, "My name's Troy Petit."

"Oh yes, sir, Mr. Petit. He's right over there."

Jim looked at Troy. "Well, I rode broncs awhile," said Troy. They walked up to Paul.

"Paul Plumber?" asked Jim.

"Yeah, I'm Paul," said the young man as he turned around. "Oh, you're Troy Petit." He stuck out his hand.

"Nice to meet you," said Troy.

"What can I do for you?" asked Paul.

Jim said, "My wife is Kattie Plumber, now Hatcher. Well…"

"Yes, Mr. Hatcher?"

"And she heard the announcer call out your name and couldn't help but wonder. You see, Paul Plumber was her granduncle's name. Her dad was Tim Plumber."

"Oh, okay. Yeah, I don't know much about the history of that side of my family. My dad's name was John, after his grandpa Plumber, and he named me Paul, after his dad. That's really all I know. Is your wife Mary Plumber's mom?"

"Yes, and I'm her dad."

"That's great," said Paul. "She's famous around the circuit for her work with horses. They say she can talk to them. Well, that's what they say."

"I would love for you to meet my wife and Mary if you have time. How about lunch tomorrow? We can all meet in town," said Jim.

"Sure," said Paul, "that would be great."

"Thank you!"

Jim and Troy went back and reported to Kattie. She was so excited. Kattie told Mary how they were kin and the story of the Plumber bothers. She said, "They are the reason I built the ranch. My father entrusted me to do it."

"By the way, did yawl know Troy is a celebrity?" said Jim.

"No," said Kathy.

"Yeah. Troy said his name, and all the cowboys froze, and it was 'Yes, sir' and 'No, sir.'"

"Really?" said Kathy.

"Yep," said Jim.

"Well, I am not the only one," said Troy. "Mary is becoming quite well-known herself as the girl who talks to horses."

After the bull riding, they all went back to the trailer.

"I'll stay with the horse tonight," said Jim.

"Not without me, you won't," said Kattie. "Rose, you take Billie and Mary to the rooms."

"Okay," said Rose, "I will."

"Me and Troy will come back early in the morning so yawl can go rest," said Kathy.

As they all left, Kattie told Jim, "Take me into your trailer, cowboy. I'll be your buckle bunny." Jim laughed as he opened the door.

The next morning, Troy and Kathy showed up early. Kathy started tending the horses as Troy knocked on the trailer door.

"Okay," said Jim, "we're up."

"Almost," said Kattie.

"Oh, damn," said Jim, "we might be a few more minutes."

Troy and Kathy laughed.

Jim and Kattie finally opened the door. "Good morning," said Jim.

"Good morning," said Kathy.

"Yawl had fun last night?" asked Troy.

"Yes, Jim found himself a buckle bunny last night," said Kattie, smiling.

"What's a buckle bunny?" asked Kathy.

"I'll tell you tonight," said Troy.

"Well, Kattie and I are going to check on the girls. Yawl meet us at the restaurant for lunch," said Jim.

"Okay," said Troy.

"The restaurant is just across the road from the hotel we are staying in."

At noon, Jim, Mary, Billie, Rose, and Kattie walked over to the restaurant. Kattie had a table reserved. Troy and Kathy showed up as they were being seated, then Paul walked in.

"Hi, Paul, over here," said Troy.

In walked a tall light-brown-skinned young man who looked to be in his mid-twenties. "Everybody, this is Paul Plumber. Paul, this is everybody."

"Hi," said Paul.

Kattie stood up and walked over to him. "My name is Kattie Plumber Hatcher. My father was Tim Plumber. This is my daughter Mary Plumber, my daughter Billie Hatcher, and my daughter Rose. These are our good friends Kathy and Troy Petit. Let's have a seat."

Paul looked at Rose. She blushed but kept eye contact until he looked away. Mary saw it. She whispered to Rose, "He is kin."

"Not to me," said Rose, whispering back.

"So, Paul, who was your dad?"

"John Plumber Jr. My grandfather was Paul Plumber. My dad named me after him."

"Great," said Kattie, "so your grandfather and my grandfather were brothers. That makes us like second cousins, and you and Mary, third cousins."

"I guess so," said Paul as he looked back at Rose, who was still looking at him.

"So how long have you been rodeoing?" asked Troy.

"All my life," said Paul. "Well, since four or five years old." He looked at Rose again. "So Rose and I are third cousins," said Paul.

"No, not by blood. Rose is not my biological daughter, but she is mine just the same. She is a veterinarian."

"That's good," said Paul. Rose was wondering which part was good, the not being kin or the being a vet.

They finally ordered their food.

"I'm so glad we got to meet. My grandfather tried to find your father and his sister years ago."

"I'm glad we met," said Paul. "I've always wondered about the Plumber side of my family."

"So are you married, Paul?" asked Rose.

Paul hesitated as he chewed up his food. "No, ma'am. I just got me a piece of land off the reservation, hoping to build a house on it one day. With that and rodeoing, I don't have much free time for dating or anything."

Rose smiled. "I know how that is. I've been the same way." Paul smiled.

They all finished eating. Paul and Kattie exchanged phone numbers as they said their goodbyes. They all headed back to the arena to get ready for tonight's event.

Billie and Mary mounted up and headed to the alley. Mary told Billie, "Around 14.00, that's all you need."

"Okay," said Billie, "I'll try."

The announcer said, "Ladies and gentlemen, yawl ready for some more barrel racing tonight?" The crowd cheered. "Okay, get ready because here comes Billie Hatcher." Billie and Toby rounded the first barrel and then the second. Billie eased up a little as they came around the third barrel, then headed home. "A 13.99, folks," said the announcer. Jane headed to the alley as Billie came out.

Mary said, "Good job, Billie."

Jane made her run, pushing harder and harder. "A 13.65, folks, and great run."

Now it was Mary's turn. Mary and Bob came out fast, made the first two barrels, then coasted to the finish. "A 14.10," said the announcer.

Mary came out of the alley, smiling. She and Billie headed to the trailer. "That's all she got?" said Mary to Billie. "We got her now."

"Do you think we can beat that time?"

"No, but neither can she. She wasted her best run. Her horse can't do it again," said Mary. "That was all he had."

"I hope you're right," said Billie. They took care of their horses, then went to the stands and sat with the family.

Hanna was up next. She came out of the alley fast, made the first turn, then the second, and then the third. Mary stood up. "Bring him home!" yelled Mary.

"A 13.86. Great run."

Mary said, "Great run."

After the event was over, two riders were eliminated from the list.

Friday Night Total

1. Billie Hatcher   35.79
2. Jane Harper   35.58
3. Mary Plumber   35.78
4. Cristy Jones   37.56
5. Carmon Houser   36.80
6. Hanna Smith   35.86
7. Rachel Adams   36.10
8. Jamie Spears   37.43
9. Bobbie Sims   37.81
10. Sara Taylor   38.52

Sara Taylor and Bobbie Sims were eliminated after Friday night's event. The list showed the top eight. Two more would be eliminated Saturday night.

Saturday Night List

1. Jane Harper
2. Mary Plumber
3. Billie Hatcher
4. Cristy Jones
5. Carmon Houser
6. Hanna Smith
7. Rachel Adams
8. Jamie Spears

"Well, we are in the top four," said Mary to Billie.

"Yep, you were right. Now all we've got to do is get by tomorrow night."

"Rose, are you going to watch my new cousin ride tonight?" Mary asked with a laugh/

"Yes, I am. If he wins tonight, I'll go give him a big kiss."

"I dare you," said Billie.

"I double dare you," said Mary.

"Oh no," said Kattie, "Rose is acting like Kathy did when she met Troy for the first time."

"Yeah," said Kathy, "he is too old for you, Rose." They laughed.

"Nope," said Rose.

The announcer said, "Coming out of chute number 2, Paul Plumber."

Mary, Rose, and Billie yelled, "Go, Paul!"

The chute opened, and out came Paul. The buzzer sounded. Paul was picked up. He dusted off as the announcer said, "That's your leader, an 85.90. He's going to the semifinal, folks."

Mary said, "Go, Rose."

"Yeah, Rose, let's go," said Billie.

"He hasn't won yet."

"Oh no," said Mary, "he will be the winner of the past two nights."

Billie jumped up and grabbed Rose by the hand. "Come on, I'll go with you."

"No," said Rose.

Mary said, "Me too. Come on, Rosey." She grabbed the other hand.

"Kattie, help me," said Rose, "please."

"Yawl leave her alone," said Kattie.

About that time, Paul walked up and sat down by Rose. "Hi, Rose," said Paul. Rose's mouth opened, but no sound came out. "You want to go for a walk?" Rose nodded. Paul got up and took her hand and pulled her up. They walked up the stands. Mary and Billie giggled as they walked away.

After the rodeo, they went to the trailer. Rose was there. Rose said, "I'll stay with the horses tonight so yawl can all get some rest. No need to hurry back in the morning."

Kathy noticed that Rose's top two buttons were undone and her jeans were not zipped all the way up. "Okay, yawl, let's go before she changes her mind," said Kathy.

"Bye, Rose, see you tomorrow," said Mary. They loaded up and left Rose there.

Kathy told Troy, "I hope she has protection."

The next day was the semifinals and then a long break until next Thursday and the finals would start. Everybody showed back up around 10:00 a.m. the next morning. Kathy stopped and got Rose some breakfast. Rose was sitting outside when they got there.

"How was your night?" asked Kattie.

"It was fine," said Rose.

"Here," said Kathy, "I brought you some breakfast."

"Thank you," said Rose.

"You okay?" asked Kathy.

Rose smiled. "I'm good. Thank you."

"Okay then."

That afternoon, Billie and Mary got ready.

"What's the plan tonight?" asked Rose.

"Same as last night."

"Just try and stay in the competition," said Rose.

"We will." Mary and Billie mounted up and headed to the alley. "Okay, folks," said the announcer, "yawl ready for the semifinal event?" The crowd cheered. "Okay, folks, the six-time world champion, Ms. Harper." Jane and her horse came out hard; they made their run. The crowd cheered. "That, folks, was a 13.85. Great run. Next, get ready for Ms. Mary Plumber." Mary and Bob came out fast and stayed steady through the course. "A 14.25," said the announcer. "Okay, here comes Billie Hatcher." Billie and Toby came out fast, made the first two barrels, then headed for the third. They rounded the third and headed home. "Nice run," said the announcer. "A 13.95 for Ms. Hatcher."

Billie came out of the alley. Mary was waiting. "I hope this works," said Billie.

"It will," said Mary. "Did you hear her time?"

"Yes, a 13.85."

"Yeah, 0.20 seconds up. Let's go put up the horses and see how it comes out," said Mary.

They went up in the stands and sat with the others.

"Well, is your plan working?" asked Rose.

"I think so," said Mary. "We will see."

It was time for Hanna to run. She and Blue Boy came flying out of the alley. They made their run. "A 14.12," said the announcer.

"Well, she's third, and I'm fourth," said Mary.

After the event, two more were cut, Cristy Jones and Carmon Houser. The top six finalists were Jane Harper, Billie Hatcher, Hanna Smith, Mary Plumber, Rachel Adams, and Jamie Spears.

*****

"Out of chute number 7, your leader, Mr. Paul Plumber."

Paul came out riding hard, spurring every jump. The buzzer sounded. Paul missed the pickup man and hit the ground. Rose jumped up. Paul stood up, picked up his hat, and dusted it off. The crowd cheered. Rose sat back down holding her chest. Kathy looked at her and smiled. Rose smiled back.

The announcer said, "Still the leader, 87.40. Great ride."

In a few minutes, Paul walked up and sat down by Rose. "Hi, stranger," said Paul. Rose smiled and said hi. Paul took her hand and held it while they watched the other riders.

Mary came back from the restroom and sat down on the other side of Paul. "Good ride," said Mary.

"Thanks," said Paul. "What about you?"

"What?" asked Mary.

"Well, some say you're playing with Jane."

Mary just smiled. "I'm just a little kid. What do I know?" said Mary.

"Sure you are," said Paul. "What are you going to do now that the semifinals are over? Rest and lie around the pool? Watch the other events?"

"Mom, did you check on that stable for Bob and Toby?"

"Yes, they are full," said Kattie.

"I know a place," said Paul.

"Really?"

"Yes, not far from here. My horse is there."

"You have a horse?" asked Mary.

"Sure. I compete in roping and bulldogging, as well as bareback. But in this rodeo, the most money was in bareback or bulls."

"Do you ride a bull?" asked Rose.

"No, I tried it, but it's too hard on your body. I'll take you to my friend's stables after the rodeo."

"Thanks," said Mary.

When the rodeo was over, they all headed to the trailer. Billie and Mary loaded up their horses in the trailer. Jim and Troy took down the round pen and loaded it up. Paul pulled up in his truck with Rose by his side. "Yawl follow us," said Paul. They followed Paul.

About five miles out of town, he turned right onto an old gravel road. About a half mile down it, they came to an older house with a large barn and lots beside it. They pulled up to the barn. Paul got out and walked up to the house. A man came out to meet him. They shook hands, and the man went back inside. Paul walked over to Jim's. "Unload the horses. Let's put them up." Mary and Billie hopped out. "Just park your trailer over there by mine."

Jim looked and saw a two-horse trailer by the fence. "Okay," said Jim. Mary, Billie, and Kathy got the horses settled in.

"Just leave your feed and hay outside the stalls. No one will bother it," said Paul. "Tomorrow you can put them in that lot over there to graze awhile."

"Thank you," said Billie and Mary and gave Paul a hug.

"Let's go get some rest," said Kattie.

"What about Rose?" asked Mary.

"I'll bring her to the hotel after a while, if that's okay," Paul said, looking at Kattie.

Kattie walked over to Paul's truck. Rose got out and hugged Kattie. "Is this what you want, baby?"

"Yes, ma'am."

"Okay, then have fun. Love you."

"I love you too," said Rose.

Jim and Troy pulled out and headed to the hotel.

"Well, girls," said Kattie, "I'm very proud of you. We love you very much."

"We love you both too!"

The next morning at breakfast, Troy and Kathy said that they were going home for a few days to check on Tommie and the ranch. "We will be back next Thursday night for the start of the finals."

"Sounds good," said Kattie.

"You behave while I'm gone, Rose," said Kathy with a smile.

After breakfast, Jim, Kattie, Mary, and Billie rode out to where they put the horses. The place looked a lot bigger in the daylight, with nice rail fences and open lots with good grass. They pulled up to the barn. Mary and Billie jumped out and headed inside.

"Hey, Bob," said Mary, "how are you?" Bob nickered. "Okay, I'm going to let you out." She took a lead rope and clipped it to his halter. Billie did the same with Toby. They led them out to one of the big lots of grass and turned them loose. Bob found himself a spot and started rolling. He got up and went to eating grass.

The man came walking out of the house. "Hi, my name is Sam, Sam Pritchard."

"Nice to meet you," said Jim. "You have a nice place here."

"Yep, it's a lot of work, but it's a good place. My dad and I started this place ten years ago. Dad passed last year. We cater to the rodeo hands. He and I both used to rodeo some. I do some horse training, roping horses mostly. Paul said you folks are from South Dakota."

"Yes, sir," said Kattie. "We own Plumber's Gap there, and Jim has a breeding ranch in Montana."

"Plumber's Gap?" said the man. "Do you have Troy Petit working there?"

"Yes, sir. He runs the place," said Kattie.

"I know Troy. He's a good man," said Sam. "Tell them girls not to worry about coming back today. I'll put them horses up tonight for them. They can check on them in the morning."

"Thank you," said Kattie.

Mary and Billie spent the rest of the day in the pool or lying out by it. Rose was there until midafternoon, then she left with Paul. Kattie and Jim came out late afternoon and got in the pool. They all played in the pool for a while. Jim said, "Let's go dry off and change. I'm hungry." The girls got out and headed to their room.

Kattie looked at Jim. "Our girls are both growing up."

"Yep, and I don't like it," said Jim.

"Well, Dad, that's just part of it."

The next day, they went and checked on the horses, then went to the arena to watch some of the other events, like the chuck wagon races and such. It was like a big fair, a lot of people everywhere. They ran into Rose and Paul there walking along holding hands.

"Hi, Mary," said Paul. "How's the horses?"

"They're good. Thanks. We met Sam," said Mary. "He's nice."

"Yep, he's a good man. He will help you if he can."

"Rose, why are you holding his hand so tight? You afraid he might run off?" Paul laughed.

Rose smiled. "Yes, now that I've found him, I'm not letting him go."

"Come on, Mary," said Billie, "let's go see the bulls."

"The bull riders, you mean," said Mary as they headed to the pens.

That afternoon, they stayed around the pool again. They didn't see Rose much for a couple of days. She was off with Paul most of the time. Wednesday, Rose was there with Mary and Billie at the pool. Kattie came out and sat by Rose. "Hi, sweetie," said Kattie.

"Hi, Mom," said Rose.

Kattie put her arm around Rose. "Talk to me," said Kattie.

"I love him," said Rose.

"And?" said Kattie.

"I don't know," said Rose. "My head has been in the clouds for the last few days. This is not like me."

"Well, sweetie, your heart can make you do strange things," said Kattie. "Just look at me. All I ask is that you don't rush into anything. Just take your time. Have fun, but don't get swept away by it all."

Rose hugged Kattie and just held on to her. "I wish I was still fifteen," said Rose.

"Me too, sweetie," said Kattie.

The next morning, they went out to the stables to get the horses. Sam came out of the house. "I hear you girls are giving Jane a run for her money."

"We are trying," said Mary.

"Well, I think I might just come to watch that," said Sam.

Kattie paid Sam and shook his hand. "Thank you. I'm sure we will see you again," said Kattie.

"Anytime," said Sam. "Good luck, girls."

"Thank you," said Mary and Billie.

They made it back to the arena. Their spot was still open, so they backed in. They unloaded Bob and Toby, then helped Jim set up the round pen. Mary saddled up Bob, then climbed on.

"Where are you going?" asked Billie.

"I'm just going to ride around for a while. I need to go check on Blue Boy and then talk to Jane's horse." Mary rode off.

"Sometimes I think that girl is crazy," said Billie.

"Crazy like a fox," said Jim. "You listen to what she tells you. She's trying to help you."

"Oh, I do."

After about an hour, Mary came back to the trailer.

"Well, what did you find out?" asked Billie.

"Oh, Blue Boy's fine. Hanna's fine."

"What about Jane's horse?" asked Billie.

"He's okay for now. Jane has been working him every day," said Mary.

"Why?" asked Billie.

"First place is $10,000.00. She wants it bad."

"Holy crap," said Billie. "So what's the plan?"

"We run hard as fast as we can. Tonight, Jane is first, you're second, Hanna's third, and I'm fourth. No matter what Jane runs tonight, we run faster. After tonight, her horse won't be able to keep up with us. Now get ready," said Mary.

"What about Hanna?" asked Billie.

"We can't worry about her yet."

"Okay," said Billie.

The stands were full. The announcer welcomed the fans. He and the clown told some jokes; the clown had a dancing dog. Then the announcer said, "Okay, folks, let's see some barrel racing finals. We have six finalists. They will run three nights, and the best combined score will be the winner. The top four finalists will receive a check and a buckle for their efforts. Top prize is $10,000.00. So get ready, folks. We are about to see a race. First up, the six-time world champion, Ms. Jane Harper."

Jane came out of the alley fast, made the first turn and then the second, rounded the third, and headed home. The crowd cheered as she went back down the alley.

The announcer said, "A 13.72, folks. Great run. Next up is Ms. Billie Hatcher." Billie and Toby came out flying around the first two barrels, then the third. They opened up coming home. Toby was going so fast Billie couldn't get him to shut down until outside the back of the alley. The crowd knew her run was fast as they cheered. "A 13.63," said the announcer. "What a run. Folks, we got us a race here tonight. Next is Ms. Hanna Smith."

Mary told Billie, "Great job. We've got her now."

Hanna came out fast. She made her run. "A 13.78," said the announcer. "Another great run. These girls came to win tonight, folks. Next is Ms. Mary Plumber."

Mary and Bob came out at full speed. They rounded the first two barrels, and they rounded the third barrel. "Go, Bob, go," said Mary as they flew by the timing light.

"A 13.61, folks. Wow, what a run!" The crowd went wild. Mary and Billie were in the lead. The last two ran a 13.98 and a 14.03.

Mary and Billie had done what they needed to do. Troy, Kathy, and Tommie had just sat down before Billie's run. Billie and Mary brushed down their horses and put them in the round pen with hay, water, and oats. Then they headed to the stands. Kathy came running over to them. "You little shits, both of you." She hugged them. They went and sat with everybody else.

Kattie hugged them both with tears in her eyes. "I don't know how much more of this my heart can take," said Kattie.

"What now?" asked Rose.

"Now we win," said Mary.

Rose smiled. "I hope you are right."

The next night, Billie and Mary had their horses saddled and ready to go. They were both excited about getting this run behind them. They headed to the arena. Jane was there, ready to go also. The announcer started his intro as everybody got ready. The announcer called out Jane's name, and she took off down the alley. She made the first two barrels. As she rounded the third barrel, her horse slipped a little and bumped the barrel. It wobbled but stayed up. She ran through the timing light. "A 13.98," said the announcer. "Great run. Now Billie Hatcher."

Billie was smoking when she came out of the alley. Kathy and Kattie were standing and yelling at Billie. She made the first two barrels, then rounded the third. "Go, Billie, go!" Kathy yelled.

"A 13.60," said the announcer. "Great job, Billie Hatcher." Mary watched Hanna and the Adams girl talking before Hanna's run. "Next up, folks, Ms. Hanna Smith." Hanna came out fast, made her turns, and headed back. "A 13.80," said the announcer. "Another great run. Now our leader, Ms. Mary Plumber, folks. Give her a hand."

Mary and Bob came out hard. They flowed around the barrels like they were on rails, then headed home. "Go, Mary!" yelled Kathy.

"A 13.62, folks. Oh, these girls are on fire." The last two ran a 14.30 and a 14.05.

Jane now had a combined time of 29.70; Billie, 29.23; Hanna, 29.58; Mary, 29.23; and the other two were above 30. The announcer said, "Okay, folks, going into tomorrow night's final run, we have a tie for the lead, Mary Plumber at 29.23 and Billie Hatcher at 29.23. Give them a big hand."

Jim, Kattie, Rose, Troy, and Kathy couldn't believe it. "Oh my god," said Kattie, holding her chest and crying.

Mary and Billie took their horses to the trailer. They unsaddled them, brushed them down, took damp rags, and wiped them down to cool them off. "Great job, boys," said Mary as they wiped down the horses. "Yawl did so good." They put them in the round pen with extra hay and oats. "Yawl rest now," said Mary. "Just one more run."

They headed to the stands. The family was waiting. All along the way, fans were stopping them—the girls hugging them and the men shaking their hands. They felt like movie stars as they made their way to their seats. Kattie, Kathy, and Rose all circled them in a big group hug. When they let them out, Mary picked up Tommie. Troy hugged her and Billie. Jim grabbed them both with tears in his eyes. "I'm the luckiest man in the world right now," said Jim as tears rolled down his face.

"Aw, Dad," said Billie. "It's like you always say. You can do anything if you work hard enough at it."

"Well, you sure have, both of you." He hugged them again.

It was time for bronc riding. Rose was on the edge of her seat. All Paul must do to win the overall was make a qualifying ride tonight and tomorrow night. He would win $100,000.00 first place, enough to build his house. Paul was in chute number 3 tonight. He came out of the chute spurring. The buzzer sounded, and he scored an 84.50, a good ride. After the bronc riding, while they were getting the bulls ready, a horse came into the alley, making all kinds of noises, pushing and pawing at the gate.

The announcer said, "Somebody's got a loose horse here."

Mary looked up. "That's Bob," she said as she ran to the alley. Billie and Kathy were right behind her. She climbed over the rails and grabbed his halter. "Easy, boy," she said. "How did you get out?" She headed back to the trailer with him. He was throwing his head up and down, then when they get close, he pulls away. He runs to a spot in the gravel road and starts pawing the ground.

Troy and Jim caught up with them. "What is it?" asked Jim.

"He's trying to tell me something," said Mary.

Billie had gone to check on Toby. "He's gone!" yelled Billie.

"Oh no," said Kathy.

Jim and Troy got a light. They saw the fresh truck and trailer tire tracks in the road. Kattie went to call the police, then went to the announcer and told him what was going on.

The announcer said, "Okay, folks, we might have a horse thief. You better check your stock and make sure. We have one horse missing and another one loose." People started leaving the stands and going around back.

The sheriff got there. Mary had gotten Bob put back up; he was still upset. The sheriff took pictures and made a cast of the tire tracks, then started asking if anyone had seen a strange vehicle around. Then another man came up to one of the sheriff deputies to report his roping horse missing. They put out an alert to keep an eye out for a pickup and horse trail leaving the area.

Billie started to cry when she heard about the roping horse missing too. She knew then that Toby was gone. Paul and Rose showed up at the trailer. "What's going on?" They told them the story.

"That smells funny," said Paul. He went over to talk to Troy. Paul told Troy what he was thinking. "I'll go find out about the roping horse," said Paul.

In a little while, Paul came back. "Yep, it's what I thought."

"What?" asked Jim.

Paul said, "Jim, you and Troy come with me." They walked over to the trailer. A large group of people had gathered up around the area.

"Let's go inside where we can talk." They went in the trailer and closed the door.

"What's up?" asked Troy.

"Well, it turns out that the roping horse that's missing is in the lead in the roping event, and one of the leading barrel horses is missing and the other one loose," said Paul.

Troy spoke up, "They were taking out the competition."

"Exactly," said Paul.

"They tried to get Bob, Toby, and the other horse, but Bob got away," said Troy. "Then he came down the alley looking for Mary."

"Yep," said Paul.

"So we are looking for a calf roper and a barrel racing couple," said Jim.

"I think so," said Paul.

"Let's go tell the sheriff," said Troy.

They went and found the sheriff and told him their theory on what happened. "I think you're right," said the sheriff. "Let's talk to your girls." They headed back to the trailer with the sheriff. Mary and Billie were outside with Bob. Billie was still crying.

"Mary, Billie, the sheriff wants to talk to you."

"Okay," said Mary.

"Which of the other barrel racers do you think might want you two out of their way?"

"All of them," said Billie.

"Well," said Mary, "I don't think Hanna Smith would do anything like that or Jane Harper, but I don't really know the other two."

"Okay," said the sheriff, "if both you and Billie were taken out of the race, who would benefit?"

"The two girls on bottom. They are paying four places. With me and Billie gone, Jane and Hanna would move up, and they would get third and fourth."

"Do you know if either one has a boyfriend or husband who might be a roper?"

"Oh my god," said Billie, "it's Rachel Adams. Her Husband is Tony Adams. He is in third place in the calf roping."

"Good job, girls," said the sheriff. "Just keep it quiet. Don't say anything. We will be ready tomorrow night. They probably just took the horse somewhere to hide them until after tomorrow night. Then they plan to turn them loose so people will think they just got loose from the arena."

The sheriff left, and they were all standing around talking.

Kattie said, "Wait, roping horses…"

"What?" asked Jim.

"Sam said he trained roping horses mostly."

Paul spoke up, "You think Tony might have taken them out there? Well, there is one way to find out. Rose and I will go see."

"I'm coming too," said Troy.

"Okay, let's go."

They drove out to Sam's place. Sam came out in his underwear. "Damn, boys, it's 2:00 a.m. What's going on?"

"Did Tony Adams bring a couple of horses out here tonight?"

"Why hell, I don't know," said Sam. "I saw him and his wife come up about 10:00 p.m. Just figured they were bringing their horses back. Let's go see."

They walked into the barn, and they saw Toby in a stall by himself. Rose went over and opened the stall. He had a bad cut on his right shin that was bleeding. Paul told Sam, "I need to use your phone. Got to call the sheriff."

"Oh, hell, I guess I better go put on some clothes."

"Which one is the roping horse?" asked Troy.

"I don't know," said Rose. "But this horse ain't running no barrels anytime soon. Billie is going to be crushed. She is tied for first with Mary."

The sheriff got to Sam's place. Sam told him that Tony and his wife were keeping their horses there and that when they came up, he didn't come out. He just assumed they were bringing back their horses and that their two horses were still there now. The sheriff asked Sam if they could set up there and catch them when they came to get their horses. "Sure," said Sam. "Just don't shoot my house."

"I think we can catch them in the barn without any shooting," said the sheriff. "Yawl will have to leave these horses here until after we catch the Adams couple. Then yawl can have them back, hopefully, tomorrow morning."

Paul, Rose, and Troy headed back to the arena. The sheriff radioed ahead to one of his deputies to tell Kattie and Jim that the horse had been found. When Paul, Rose, and Troy got back, the spectators had cleared out. Rose told Billie and Mary about Toby's leg. Billie cried again. Mary asked Rose, "How bad is it?"

"Well, it's not going to cripple him, but he is limping on it when he walks. I'm sorry, Billie, but he doesn't need to run on it," said Rose. Mary took Billie inside the trailer, and they both crawled into one of the bunks.

The next day before noon, the sheriff came to the trailer. "We got them. They confessed. You can go get your horse. I've already told the roper. Sorry your horse got hurt in this."

"Thank you, Sheriff," said Jim. "We will be pressing charges." Jim was going to wake the girls.

Paul stopped him. "Just let me and Rose go get the horse so they can sleep. I can bring my horse back for Billie to use if she wants. He has never run the barrels, but he is fast."

"I don't know. Billie is pretty upset about it. She may not want to run."

"She hast to," said Kathy. "She is tied for first place in one of the biggest events in the country."

When Paul and Rose got back, Mary and Billie came out. They unloaded Toby and Paul's horse. Mary checked out Toby's leg. "Yep, it's deep. I don't think it got anything major. Put him in pain. I'll be back."

"Where are you going?"

"I've got to go talk to the judges."

"About what?" asked Billie.

"About you riding Bob tonight," said Mary as she ran to the arena.

"What is it?" asked Kathy.

"She wants me to ride Bob tonight," said Billie.

"That little shit! I knew she would come up with something," said Rose.

"She always does."

Rose started cleaning up the cut on Toby's leg while Mary was gone. After about forty-five minutes, Mary came walking back up. Rose, Kathy, Billie, and Kattie were all in pain with Toby; they were sewing the cut up on his leg.

"Well, what's the plan?" asked Rose.

"We are going to win this thing," said Mary.

"How?" asked Billie.

"We are both going to ride Bob."

"Oh, Mary," said Kathy, "that's a lot for one horse."

"Yep, but the judges moved Billie to first and then my ride until last so that Bob can get some rest in between."

"How did you talk them into that?"

"Well, we are tied. Her horse and my horse have the same combined time. There is no advantage."

"I think that will work," said Billie.

"How?" asked Kathy.

"When we practiced, Bob is always a little bit faster on his second run. I love you, Mary Plumber," said Billie as she hugged Mary. Mary and Billy got Bob ready. They put Billie's saddle on him first. Jim carried Mary's saddle to the alley. They headed to the arena. The announcer did his intro, then asked for the finalist to enter the arena. Mary got on Bob behind Billie as they rode in. The announcer said, "We have a few changes in this event. Last night was a sad night for our sport of rodeoing. We had some contestants who tried to increase their odds by stealing the top roping horse and the two top barrel horses. They have been caught, and the horses returned, but one of the barrel horses was injured, leaving one of the contestants without their ride. The judges were approached by Ms. Mary Plumber, who requested that she and her sister, Billie Hatcher, be allowed to ride the same horse in the finals. Because of the scores and the fact that Mary and Billie are tied for first place and that there will be no advantage for Billie to ride Mary's horse, the judges have agreed, if none of the other contestants disagree. As I call your name, reply with a yes for agree or a no for disagree. Harper."

"Yes."

"Smith."

Hanna was slow to respond, kicking the ground. Jane elbowed her. "Yes."

"Spears."

"Yes."

"Okay then, Ms. Billie Hatcher will ride first and Mary Plumber last. Take your places, ladies. Let's do some barrel racing." The crowd cheered.

Mary talked to Bob, "Okay, boy, we need your help. Toby is hurt. We need you to help us both to win, boy. Just do your best, buddy." Mary gave him a big kiss. "Okay, Billie," said Mary, "you set the pace."

Billie and Bob went flying down the alley. She felt Bob sat up for the turn. She got ready and followed his lead. They rounded the first barrel and then the second. As they headed into the third turn, she thought it was too fast, then she felt it as Bob rolled around the turn, then opened back up, throwing dirt behind them. They ran back through the alley and out the back. The crowd was cheering and yelling. She knew it must be good. "A 13.54," said the announcer. "Great ride, Billie. Okay, folks, her comes Ms. Jane Harper." She came out fast, made her run, and flew back through the light. "A 13.73," said the announcer. "Another good run. Now Ms. Hanna Smith." Hanna came out of the alley fast. Blue Boy nailed the first barrel and then the second barrel. She headed for the third. Blue Boy rolled around the third barrel, then headed home. "A 13.65. Great ride, Hanna. Now Ms. Spears." he came out hard and hit the first, then the second, then the third. She opened coming back. "A 13.87, whoa," said the announcer. "Now, folks, this little girl is riding the horse that got Billie in first. Her she comes, Ms. Mary Plumber."

Kattie stood up. "Go, baby, go!" she yelled as Mary turned the second barrel and headed for the third. They rolled around the third and headed back. Bob was lunging forward faster and faster.

"Ladies and gentlemen, your 1991 Cheyenne Frontier Days Barrel Racing Champion is Ms. Mary Plumber, by four hundredths of a second, a 13.50! Holy cow, what a ride! That's one for the record books, folks. Give her a big hand."

"A 13.50!" Kathy, Kattie, and Rose were jumping up and down.

"Oh my god," said Kattie.

As Mary came to Billie in the back, she picked her up, and she slid on behind Mary. Mary headed back into the arena. She and Billie made a victory lap, then headed out to the trailer. Billie was hugging Mary all the way back. "You're the best sister ever," said Billie.

"You're kind of special yourself," said Mary.

After the calf roping event, they had the barrel racing award ceremony while they got the broncs ready. "Okay, folks, your fist place winning gets this beautiful silver buckle and this giant check for $10,000.00, Ms. Mary Plumber. Second place gets this silver buckle and this giant check for $5,000.00, Ms. Billie Hatcher. Third place gets this silver buckle and a giant check for $4,000.00, Ms. Hanna Smith. And fourth place gets this silver buckle and a giant check for $3,000.00, Ms. Jane Harper. Give them a hand, folks. They rode their hearts out."

They stayed until the last bull ride. Jim was guarding the horses; he wasn't taking a chance with the first place and second place winners.

When the rodeo was over, Mary told Kathy, "I need your help."

"Okay," said Kathy. They headed out of the stands and around back. "Where are we going?" asked Kathy.

"To find Hanna and get my horse back." They walked to her truck and trailer; she was loading up Blue Boy. "Hanna!" yelled Mary in a tone Kathy had never heard before.

She turned and looked. "Hi, Mary," said Hanna. "Great job, girl."

Mary said, "I just wanted to let you know that your horse is ready to go now. You can come to get him next week."

"Great," said Hanna, "but I've got a rodeo next week. I was hoping to ride Blue Boy in it."

"No, I don't think so. I'm taking Blue Boy with me now. You come get your horse."

"But, Mary, you said I could ride him this season."

"Yep, and I thought we were friends."

"We are," said Hanna.

"I know that you were in on it."

"In on what?" asked Hanna.

"Stealing my horse."

"No," said Hanna.

"Yes, you were!" Mary yelled. "The Adams girl would have gotten third or fourth, but you would have gotten first." Mary was so mad she had her fist tight.

Hanna dropped her head. "I'm sorry, Mary, but I need the money. You and Billie don't."

Mary swung with all her might, hitting Hanna in the mouth, knocking her to the ground. "You take your check and come get your damn horse, and you better not ever come around me again." Mary walked over and opened the trailer gate, backed out Blue Boy, and led him away.

Kathy followed her; she had never seen little Mary so mad. Mary was six inches shorter and forty pounds lighter than Hanna, but in that moment, she was a giant.

"Some people you just can't help," said Mary, kicking the dirt as she walked off.

When they got to the trailer, Billie said, "Blue Boy, why do you have him?"

"I'm taking him home. Hanna is coming to get her horse next week."

"Do you think he is ready?" asked Rose.

"No!" said Mary. Kathy put her finger up to her lips.

They started packing up everything. Once everything was loaded, they headed home. Mary didn't say much on the way home. Billie was sleeping. Rose was with them on the other side of Billie.

"Well, what's your plan now?" asked Rose.

"Horse training," said Mary.

"Horse training?" asked Rose. "At fifteen years old?"

"Yep," said Mary.

"Do you think anybody will let you train their horse?"

"They should," said Mary.

"Why?" asked Rose.

"Because I trained the horses that won first, second, and third at Cheyenne this year."

Kattie busted out laughing. "She got you there, Rose. What are you going to do with Blue Boy now?"

"I don't know. Probably let Billie ride him until Toby heals. Maybe she can win a few more events on him this year. Then he will be worth more money next year."

"How much do you think he is worth now?" asked Rose.

"Well, I turned down fifty thousand tonight."

"What?" asked Jim.

"Really?" said Kattie.

"Yep. I was offered one hundred thousand for Bob."

"Holy shit," said Rose.

"I'm not ever selling Bob, but if somebody offers me one hundred thousand for Blue Boy. He's gone."

"I hope so," said Kattie. "That's a lot of money for a horse."

Chapter 6

More Horses

Mary Plumber, the horse trainer, had set her sights on building more stables there at Plumber's Gap to house other people's horses, along with another arena, lots, and pens. She wanted to put it closer to the highway. That way, they could keep their private barn, arena, and house secluded from the public as much as possible. Mary had agreed to put up all her winnings if her mother and dad match it. Of course, they agreed. They knew there was no holding her back once she set her mind to something. Billie, who was now seventeen, wanted to put her money down to buy a new car or truck; she couldn't decide.

Mary had her birthday and was now fifteen. Her mother got her the walker she wanted, but it hadn't been put up yet. Mary wanted to assemble it at the new horse stables when they were built. Mary asked Kathy to work with her at the new stables but was told quick by Kattie that Kathy's main job was taking care of the ranch stock but that she could help Mary in her spare time or in the summer months if she wanted too, though it would not become a requirement. Billie was going to Billings next week for a rodeo with Blue Boy; Mary was not going. She had too much to do before winter, she said. Jim was going to take Billie, plus Rose and Paul would be there. Paul was riding broncs there also; he needed another win to make the finals.

It was hay season on the ranch. Troy and his crew were work long days cutting, bailing, and putting up hay for the winter. Mary had asked Troy to fence in another 5-acre lot to grow hay for her new operation when he had time. "The ground must be cleared, fertilized, and planted before winter," said Troy. "It might take a while, but we will do our best."

Mary never did tell anyone else but Kathy about what Hanna Smith had pulled, but she hadn't forgotten. She liked Hanna and thought she was a friend, but greed and money took her over.

Although Hanna didn't help in the actual stealing of the horses, she planted the seed in the Adams's head and helped pick which horses to take. For that, Mary would never forgive her or trust her again.

The contractor had started clearing ground for the new stables. In the structure, there would be an office with a bathroom and shower, a wash stall for the horses, and another bathroom in the stall area. Then there would be a hay and feed storage area and tack room. Mary was excited to get started. Paul told her she should build some bucking chutes in the arena so cowboys could practice. She was not sure about that one yet, but she was thinking about it. She mainly wanted to work with people and horses that had issues together. There were a lot of horse trainers, but not many team trainers, which was what a horse and rider needed to be. Mary said, "You can take the best-trained horse in the world and put the best-trained rider on him, but if they don't connect, they are just a horse and a rider." *Team riding* was what she wanted to teach, and she thought she knew how. But she also wanted to help the problem horse with training issues too.

Billie and Jim made it home late Saturday night.

"So how did it go?" asked Kattie. Billie held up her buckle and check. Kattie hugged and kissed her. "I'm so happy for you. I'm sorry we couldn't go!"

"Where is Mary?" asked Billie.

"In her room, probably asleep," said Kattie. "She has been going from daylight to dark since you left."

"We saw where they had poured concrete in the front lot," said Billie.

"Yep, they are moving along fast," said Kattie. "They have a little girl pushing them. She has another crew coming next week to build the arena."

"Yep, she is hard to stop when she makes up her mind about something," said Billie.

"So, Billie, when are we going to pick out your car or truck?" asked Kattie.

"Monday, I guess. I think I'm going to get a truck. Dad and I have been talking about it."

"Good," said Kattie.

The next morning, Billie went to the barn to see Toby. His cut was almost healed, no more limping. Then she checked on Blue Boy. Mary came out of the tack room. "So I heard you beat them all," said Mary.

"Thanks to Blue Boy." said Billie. "I wish you were still racing. I miss you being there with me."

"I haven't quite," said Mary. "I'm just taking time off to get my stables built. I'll be ready next spring. I'll still train with you in the afternoons."

"I only need two more qualifying runs to make the finals," said Billie.

"Well, I'll make sure you're ready," said Mary. "And I'll go with you, but I'm not racing."

Billie hugged Mary. "Thank you, sis. I love you."

"Well, help me clean these stalls," said Mary.

"Oh, I just remembered Kattie needs me."

"Billie," said Mary.

"Just kidding," said Billie as she laughed. "Let's get to work."

The next day, Jim, Kattie, Billie, and Mary went to look at new trucks. Billie picked out one she liked. Jim wrote them a check. Billie and Mary loaded up in the new truck and headed back home the long way. Jim and Kattie went to eat out before going home. Kathy came to the ranch that night and told Mary about a big horse sale coming up next week. Mary told Kattie that she needed to go and see what they had. Jim said he would go and pull the trailer. Kathy and Troy wanted to go too, so they decided that the four of them would go. Rose was still seeing Paul on the weekends, except the ones when he had an event. Paul was working on his new house during the week, trying to get it built before winter. Mary's stables were going up fast; it wouldn't be long before they were ready. The arena was moving along. Also, the rails around the arena were up. Now they were working on three bucking chutes. She was also adding roping chutes. Kattie was a little worried about Mary being able to make enough money to keep it going once it opened.

Troy, Kathy, Jim, and Mary were on their way to the horse sale. Mary and Kathy walked through the back lots looking at the horses for sale; they were all packed in like sardines. They headed on in to wait for the sale to start. Jim and Troy had already gotten seats for them. The sale started. The first few horses were stock horses. Troy bought one for the ranch. Then they started running in some young green broke horse. That was what Mary was looking for. One was a two-year-old buckskin with good form. Mary bid three hundred. It went up to four-fifty. Mary went to five. "Sold," said the auctioneer.

A few more came through, then a nice three-year-old dun horse came out. "Four hundred," said Mary. The bids went up to six hundred. Mary bade up to six-fifty. "Sold," said the auctioneer.

Mary was excited. She had two young horses to train and sell. Then they started to run through some breed mares. One palomino mare heavy with a foal came through, bred to a palomino stud with a good bloodline. "Five hundred," said Mary, knowing it would take more, six, seven, eight all the way up to nine hundred. "One thousand," said Mary.

"Sold," said the auctioneer.

"One more," said Mary. After the mares, they ran through some stud horses. Mary just watched, then they brought in some paint horses. After about four or five came through, a four-year-old palomino and white pinto about thirteen hands high came through. "Six hundred," said Mary. Nobody else even bade.

"Sold," said the auctioneer.

"Well, let's pay for our houses," said Mary.

"What are you going to do with that pinto?" asked Kathy. Mary looked at her and smiled. "What?" asked Kathy. "Oh, you little shit, for Tommie?"

"Yep." Kathy hugged Mary.

They loaded up and headed home. Mary was happy. She got a couple of young horses to train and a foal on the way to raise like she did Bob, then the pinto she bought for Tommie. She would have to see what bad habits he had and get him trained. Kathy and Mary had decided not to tell Tommie until the pinto was ready for her to ride.

Billie, Jim, Kattie, and Mary were headed to Billie's next event in Colorado. She needed two more qualifying events to make the finals. They got there and set up. Mary helped Billie get ready, then went to the stands with Jim and Kattie. There were five riders who entered in the barrel racing, and one of them was Jane. Mary told Billie, "Don't even think about her. She is just another rider." Billie drew fifth. Jane drew second.

The first two riders were above 14.00. Jane made her run; her horse was faster than ever. "A 13.62," said the announcer. The next run was 13.90.

Billie came out on Blue Boy; they nailed the first two barrels. "Go, Billie, go!" yelled Mary. They rolled around the third barrel.

"A 13.60, folks. There's your leader." This was only a two-night event; the best of two nights would win.

Paul was set for the roping event coming up. The first roper was ready. He backed in the corner and nodded. The calf came out, and the horse fell in behind it. He threw his rope and caught the calf. A 7.80 run. Then Paul was up. He backed in the corner and nodded. The calf came out. His horse was on the calf. He threw his rope. The horse slid to a stop as Paul hit the ground, running to the calf. He tied up the calf's feet and threw up his hands. A 6.50 run. Two more ropers ran—one had a 7.50, and the other, a 6.90 run. Paul was in the lead. Paul also entered the bulldogging event. He missed steer, no score for the night. In the bronc riding event, he scored an 85.00, putting him in the lead for that event.

Jim, Kattie, Mary, Billie, Rose, and Paul all went out to eat after the rodeo. As they were eating, Paul asked Mary, "Well, didn't you add those bucking chutes like I suggested?"

"Yes, I did," said Mary.

"Good. I'll put out the word," said Paul.

Mary said, "I've got an idea for you, Paul."

"What's that?" asked Paul.

"Once you win the finals, why don't you buy some bucking stock? Then you can do some training at my arena for a small fee," said Mary.

"That might be something to think about," said Paul. "But I haven't won yet."

The next night, Billie was ready. Jane made her run, a 13.65. Billie came out fast, trying to beat Jane. She nailed the first barrel and then the second barrel, and she headed for the third. Blue Boy turned too tight and bumped the barrel, but it stayed up. They raced for the light.

"A 13.72. Boy, it's going to be close, folks. Billie Hatcher has 29.32, but Jane has 29.27, five hundredths of a second, folks. Let's see what the other two riders do."

"Jane wins, folks, by five hundredths of a second. Ms. Billie Hatcher gets second. Give them both a big hand."

Paul won second in the roping event and first in the bronc riding.

Billie told Mary, "I've got to find an edge over Jane. Our scores are too close every time."

"Well, next week, we will start working with Toby and see how he does. He had beaten her before," said Mary.

"That's right," said Billie. "He did. Good idea, Mary."

"You're welcome," said Mary.

The next day was Sunday. The Plumber and Hatcher family went to church to thank the Lord for all their gifts. After church, Billie and Mary went swimming and lay out by the pool. Jim was going to grill later. Kathy, Troy, and Tommie were coming out, and Rose invited Paul.

Mary's stables were ready; she had someone come out tomorrow to assemble the walker. The others should finish the arena next week. Mary was ready to start working with her new horses, especially the pinto she got for Tommie. Billie was going back to work at the clinic next week with Kattie and Rose. She would be a senior in high school this year and was thinking about going to veterinary school. One of Leann's sons just finished law school and was working with his aunt Sara in Deadwood.

Jim had the grill going. Kathy, Troy, and Tommie showed up. Tommie went straight to the pool with Billie and Mary. Troy went to help Jim at the grill and drank beer. Kathy was helping Kattie and Rose prep everything for the cookout.

Billie and Paul both had one more event before the finals. Paul had already qualified, but Billie needed one more place run. The event was in two weeks in Amarillo, Texas, a long trip from Lead, South Dakota. Billie knew that even if she won this event, the finals would just be for show. She had no chance for the world title. Jane already had it sewn up being the top-money winner. But now that she had her truck, she wanted a four-wheeler like Mary and Rose had.

That night at the cookout, plans were made for the rodeo in Texas. Jim would haul Paul's and Billie's horses in the new trailer. Paul and Rose would ride in his truck. Troy and Kathy were going to stay home and keep an eye on everything.

The next day, Mary got out Toby and saddled him up to see how he worked on his leg. Rose said, "It's completely healed now."

Mary started out slow, walking him around the arena. Then she went into a slow lope. "Good boy," said Mary. "You're doing good." She worked him for about an hour, then put him back up.

She got out the pinto and saddled him up. She put him in the round pen and worked him without a rider, then she put a fifty-pound sack of oats on his saddle and tied it down. She worked him some more; he never bobbled. Then she tried to spook him. Nothing bothered him; he stayed calm the whole time. She took the oats off and then the saddle. She brushed him down, talking to him the whole time. She picked up all his feet and cleaned them out; he never flinched. She walked around him, rubbing and touching him all over. Still nothing. "You're too good to be true," said Mary. "Why were you sold, buddy? Hey, that's a good name for you—Buddy. You and Tommie will be best buddies." She put him back up in the stall.

"Hi, Bob," she said as she opened his stall and brought him out. She hugged and kissed him. "Come on, let's go for a ride." She saddled him up and rode down to the new stables. The men were finishing up the dirt work in and around the arena; it all looked so good. She was about out of money now. She had a little left, but not much. She didn't want to ask her parents for more. "I know what to do, Bob," said Mary. "You and I are going to run in Amarillo."

That afternoon, Mary had the barrels set up and Toby and Bob saddled when Kathy got there. "What's up?" asked Kathy.

"Well, Billie and I are practicing this afternoon."

"Okay, why Bob?"

"Because I'm running too in Texas."

"You are?"

"Yes, I need some more money. I had enough to get everything built, but now I'm out," said Mary.

"You're not going to try to beat your sister, are you?"

"No, I'll let her win," said Mary with a laugh.

"You little shit," said Kathy.

"I put the pinto in the round pen. I want you to check him out."

"Okay, why?"

"Well, I worked him this morning, and I can't understand why anyone would sell him. He's perfect. I mean, just as a clam as he can be. I didn't ride him, but I worked him with a sack of feed. He is too good to be true. Go try him. You'll see."

"Okay," said Kathy, "I'll check him out."

Kathy went to the round pen and went inside. The horse walked right up to her. "Hey, boy," said Kathy as she reached out and rubbed his nose. "You are a sweetheart." Kathy picked up all his feet and rubbed him all over. She checked his teeth. She walked him around the pen with just her hand on his halter. "Good boy," said Kathy. She took the lead rope and led it over his neck and back; he never flinched. She clipped the lead rope to his halter and led him back into the barn.

Mary said, "Oh yeah, I named him Buddy."

"That's a good name," said Kathy. She tied him in the barn and went to the tack room. She came back with Tommie's saddle and bridle.

"What are you doing?" asked Mary.

"I'm going to fit this saddle and bridle to him, then you're going to ride him."

"Me?" asked Mary.

"Yes, you're the only one that can fit in Tommie's saddle." Kathy laughed. "I just want to see what he does when you mount up, not ride him."

"Okay," said Mary. "Tomorrow I'll put my saddle on him and ride him a little."

Once Kathy got everything adjusted, Mary put her foot in the stirrup and slowly swung over his back, her weight on his back. Her butt wouldn't go in the saddle. "Almost," said Kathy, laughing. Buddy never moved a muscle. Mary swung back off, then rubbed his face. Kathy said, "I don't understand either. Maybe we just got lucky."

"Maybe," said Mary. "I'll find out tomorrow."

Billie and Rose made it home. Billie went in the house to change. She came out to the barn. "Why is Bob saddled up?" asked Billie.

"Well, I thought we would repeat Cheyenne, except for this time, you get first and me second."

"Sounds good to me," said Billie. "Why did you change your mind?"

"I need some money," said Mary. "Okay then, sis, let's get ready. This will be the first time Toby ran scene he got hurt that night. Okay, Billie, you go first."

Kathy was set up with her stopwatch. Billie and Toby came out. Toby made the first barrel and then the second. He rounded the third. "Bring him home, Billie!" yelled Mary,

"A 14.00," said Kathy. "That's good."

Mary and Bob came out and hit the first, then the second, and then third. Billie yelled, "Go, Mary!"

"A 14.12. Not bad, girls. You run it again, Billie," said Kathy.

Billie came out fast—first barrel, second barrel, then the third.

"A 13.87," said Kathy. "Great job."

Mary came out hard and made the first, then the second, then the third.

"A 13.92. Another great run," said Kathy. "Okay, yawl cool them off."

Mary and Billie walked them around in the arena, with Billie talking to Toby. "What do you think, Mary?" asked Billie.

"I think you need to go for it this next run. Go all out."

Billie came back out faster than before. She nailed all the barrels and headed home.

"A 13.61. Wow, Billie, way to go," said Kathy.

Mary and Bob came out in sync with each other and floated around the barrel like one being connected.

"A 13.50. Damn," said Kathy, "that's six thousandths of a second off the world record, you little shit."

Mary said, "Now that we know that Toby is ready, the rest of the week, we can take it easy."

Mary and Billie walked them again to cool them.

"Good job, Mary," said Billie.

"Thank you," said Mary. "But don't worry. I'm not going to beat you in Texas, I promise."

"Oh, I don't care," said Billie. "I'm just glad you're racing with me."

Chapter 7

Amarillo by Nightfall

Four days before the event in Amarillo, as they were sitting down to eat supper, Mary announced that she was going to also run in Amarillo.

"Well, good," said Jim. "I know Billie's glad." Billie smiled and nodded.

"I thought you were done for the year," said Rose.

"I was, but I need some more money for my stables."

"I thought they were through with it."

"They are, but I need some operating money."

About that time, the phone rang. Kattie got up and answered it. Everybody heard her say, "Yes, she's her." Then she said, "Mary, phone."

Mary got up, and Kattie went back to the table. "Hi, this is Mary."

The lady on the other end said, "My name is Bobbie Spears, Jamie Spears's mother."

"Oh yes, ma'am," said Mary.

"I offered to buy a horse from you in Cheyenne. I think yawl call him Blue Boy."

"Yes, ma'am."

"Well, I still want him. I've been watching your sister on him, and I want to buy him for Jamie. Her horse has been injured. I'll give you $100,000.00 for him right now."

"Well, let me talk to my sister. Hold on." Mary laid down the phone. She walked over to the table. "Billie, are you sure Toby is going to be okay for you in Amarillo?"

"Yes, why?"

"Because I got a chance to sell Blue Boy."

"Aw," said Billie. "Okay, it's fine."

Mary went back to the phone. "Okay, I'll sell him," said Mary.

"Tomorrow?"

"Sure, I'll have him ready and all the papers. See you tomorrow." She hung up.

Everybody was sitting there looking at Mary.

"Well," said Rose, "how much?"

"Remember what I told you?" said Mary.

"No you didn't," said Rose.

"Yep," said Mary, "it's $100,000.00."

"Holy shit," said Rose.

"Well, you got money now," said Billie.

"Yep, but I'm still running in Amarillo though."

"Great," said Billie. "I need my sis with me."

"Oh," said Mary, "I've got to call Aunt Sara. I need a bill of sale written up."

"Come eat," said Kattie. "You can do that later."

That night in bed, Kattie told Jim, "I can't leave. Mary sold that horse for $100,000.00."

"I can," said Jim. "She is a very special girl. She's going to do just fine."

*****

"Amarillo, here we come," said Mary as they pulled out from Plumber's Gap.

"Yep, here come the Plumber's Gap girls," said Billie.

An hour later, they were both sound asleep as Jim drove down the road. They had to leave out about 4:00 a.m. to get there in time. Kattie was holding Jim's hand as they drove along. Jim was talking about the breeding ranch; he had four cross bull calves he was going to raise, then decided which bloodline to go with. It was a long process, but he hoped it would be worth it in the end. Jim still penned for his dad some and worked the roundups on some of the bigger spreads to help pay operating costs on the breeding ranch.

They got to Amarillo around 4:00 p.m. and got their spot set up. Billie and Mary went to pay their entry fees. They saw that Harper, Spears, and Smith had already signed up. This was a three-night event; they would have to come back later for tonight's draw. Paul and Rose were parked beside Jim. Paul had entered in three events—roping, bulldogging, and bareback. He was already qualified for the finals in bareback riding; he was just trying to make some extra money in the other events.

Mary and Billie went to make their draw. Jones and Houser had entered too, making seven riders. Smith got first; Houser, second; Jane, third; Spears, fourth; Hatcher, fifth; Jones, sixth; and Mary, last. They all went to get ready. Toby and Bob were already saddled and waiting. Kattie gave them both hugs and kisses and told them good luck. They mounted up, and Rose, Jim, and Kattie headed to the stands. Mary rode by Hanna Smith; she didn't bother to speak to her.

Hanna got ready. She ran down the alley, marking her first turn and then the second, and headed for the third. She started around the third and hit it, coming out on the other side, knocking it over. "A 14.85 plus 5 seconds," said the announcer.

"Well, she's out," said Mary.

"Next up, Ms. Carmon Houser." She came out fast, but her horse slowed down as they went around the first and second barrel. She headed for the third barrel, rounded it, and headed back. "A 14.95," said the announcer.

"Here she goes," said Billie. She turned the first barrel and then the second, and she headed for the third barrel, rounding it and heading home.

"A 13.87," said the announcer. "Great run. Next up is Ms. Jamie Spears on a new horse." Jamie and Blue Boy came out fast, turned the first two barrels, then raced to the third. They rounded it and headed home. "A 13.95. Another great run. Ms. Billie Hatcher back on her horse, Toby." Billie came out flying and made the first and second barrel without even slowing down. They headed for the third, then round the third and shot out the other side, flying home. The crowd was standing when the announcer said, "A 13.68, folks. What a run for Billie Hatcher. Ms. Cristy Jones is your next rider, folks." Cristy came out fast, made the first two barrels and then the third, and headed home. "A 14.25. Good run, Cristy," said the announcer. "Now, folks, your last racer is Ms. Mary Plumber."

Mary and Bob came out flying. They melted around the first two barrels, then raced for the third. They shot out from the third barrel. "Ease up, boy," said Mary, "ease up."

"A 13.82," said the announcer. "Great run, Mary. Okay, folks, your top four going into tomorrow night—Hatcher, Plumber, Harper, and Spears. Give them a hand."

Mary and Billie headed back to their trailer. They unsaddled and brushed their horses down. This time, they put the horses back in the trailer and put locks on the doors. They headed for the stands. They stopped along the way for burgers and Cokes.

"Great job, girls," said Jim and Kattie as they gave them a hug. Mary and Billie sat down to watch the roping. When the event was over, Paul was in second place for the night. He got third in the bull-dogging event. In the bareback riding, he scored an 82.00 and was in the lead.

After the bull riding, they all headed back to the trailer. Paul and Rose said they would stay in the trailer and watch the horses every night. Jim, Kattie, Billie, and Mary headed to their motel.

The next night, Smith ran a 14.36 for a total of 34.21, Houser ran a 14.65 for a total 29.60, Jane ran a 13.76 for a total 27.63, Spears ran a 13.78 for a total of 27.73, Billie ran a 13.70 for a total of 27.38, Jones ran a 14.22 for a total 28.47, and Mary Plumber ran a 13.69 for a total 27.50.

Paul dropped back to third in the roping but moved up to second in the bulldogging and still held the lead in the bareback riding.

The final night was here. They were paying four places; everybody wanted a piece of the pie. Hanna Smith started her run strong, then on the second barrel, she knocked it over. She finished her run in a slow lope and headed straight to her trailer. She knew she was done; she loaded up and pulled out. Houser came out fast, looking to make up some ground. She made the first, second, and third turn. "A clean run of 13.97, giving her 43.57." Jane was up next. She came out hard. She made the first barrel, and as she headed to the second barrel, she opened up, then raced to the third, rounded it, and headed home.

"A 13.62," said the announcer, "giving her 41.25. Here comes Ms. Spears." She came out rolling. Blue Boy was in true form. He nailed the first and second barrels, then headed for the third, rounded it, and flew home. "A 13.82. Great run," said the announcer. "Her total is 41.55. Your next racer is Ms. Billie Hatcher." She came out wide open. She was going for broke. She rounded the first two barrels and then the third and headed home like Toby was on fire. "A 13.60," said the announcer. "Her total is 40.98. Here comes Ms. Jones." She made her run. "A 14.00. Her total is 42.47. Your last rider, folks, the girl who talks to horses, Ms. Mary Plumber." They came out fast, and she and

Bob just coasted around all three barrels and then headed home. "A 13.65," said the announcer. "A total of 41.15. Your winner is Ms. Billie Hatcher at 40.98, second goes to Mary Plumber at 41.15, third goes to Ms. Jane Harper at 41.25, and fourth goes to Ms. Jamie Spears at 41.55. Give them all a hand, folks. They put on a show."

Paul got second overall in roping, he got third overall in bulldogging, and first in bareback. He was headed to the finals.

Billie qualified for the finals but said she wasn't going. "School is starting in two weeks," she said. "I've proven my point." Kattie asked what that was. "If I try hard enough, I can beat the best in the world."

Mary had a new sign ordered for the stables. It said:

Mary Plumber's Training Stables
Team Riding School
Plumber's Gap Ranch, Lead, South Dakota

Part 3

Chapter 1

Mary Plumber's Training Stables

Mary was glad to be back at home after Amarillo and glad that Billie was going to stop rodeoing for the year. Mary had the money she needed now to get started. She was setting up the stable office. Her aunt Sara had sent out one of her secretaries from the law office to help her get set up. Sara was handling all of Mary's legal requirements and writing her customer agreements. For now, Sara had agreed to send someone once a week to check the books and keep her up to date until things picked up and she could hire someone to keep the books. Mary found out there was a lot to operating a business of any kind. School would start back in next week, so she tried to do all she could now. Once school started, it would just be afternoons and weekends that she could work. Billie was going to work part-time after school at the clinic but would be off on weekends. She said she would help Mary on Saturdays.

Mary and Kathy had been working with the pinto and felt it was safe to give him to Tommie now. So this weekend, they were going to surprise her with him. Mary put the mare she bought out in the pasture until closer to time. The two young geldings she bought, she had been working in the round pen. She was hoping to make another Blue Boy out of one of them.

Mary told Rose to start pushing Billie to buy a four-wheeler so they could all ride this winter. Rose said she would. Kattie was spending more time at the clinic now since Billie was working there. Kattie told Mary to try to get her father more involved in the stables. He seemed to feel out of place at the ranch, and she wanted him to be happy there. Mary told her dad Friday night at supper that she needed his help with one of the young geldings. She wanted to train one for a barrel horse and the other for a cow pony, but she didn't know much about working cows. They were both broke to ride, just not trained for anything.

Jim said, "Sure, I'll help in the afternoons and on Saturdays."

Mary said "Thank you" and gave him a big hug. Kattie just smiled. "Oh, Mom, I might need to borrow a couple of calves to work with."

"Well, you make sure that they are heifers and not steers. I don't want you running the fat off my steers before I sell them."

The next morning, Jim came down to the stables. Mary was cleaning out stalls. "You ready to get started?" she asked.

"Sure," said Jim.

"Okay, I'll go get them. You go to the tack room and pick out a saddle," said Mary. She brought out the two horses.

"What do you want me to do?" asked Jim.

"Well, I thought if you would ride each one of them and work them a little to see if one has a natural knack for cows. I had Troy bring us two calves to play with. They are in the arena."

"Okay," said Jim. He looked the two horses over. "Let's try this dun first," he said. They put the saddle on him and adjusted the stirrups to fit Jim. Jim climbed on and headed to the arena. He rode the horse around the arena a few times, then cornered up the heifers. Each time they tried to get by, he would turn them back with the horse. The horse sat back on his hocks and rotated his front end from left to right. After a few minutes, Jim backed up, then took the horse to the middle of the arena. It took a few tries, but he got the horse to spin in place, then change directions. Mary was surprised at how fast the horse was picking it up. Jim stopped and walked the horse around the arena, then brought him out. "This one will be a cow horse," said Jim. "Let's see what the other one will do."

They took the saddle off the dun and put it on the bay. Jim climbed on. Mary brushed down the dun, then went to watch. Her dad was riding him around the arena. Then he cornered the calves again. They came right by him. The horse shied away from the calves. He set up again with the calves in the corner, but they came right back out. Jim took the horse to one end of the arena and ran him to the other end, then walked him around a couple of times. He brought him out of the arena. "There's your barrel horse," said Jim. "Maybe. He's sure not a cow pony."

It was close to lunch. They unsaddled the bay, and Mary brushed him down.

"Let's go eat a bite," said Jim. "We'll come back later."

"Okay," said Mary. They got in Jim's truck and drove to the house. They fixed some ham-and-cheese sandwiches and Coke to drink. Jim told Mary about the time he helped Kattie round up her cows at his place and how they sat under a big oak tree and ate a ham-and-cheese sandwich. "She was the prettiest thing I had ever seen," said Jim. "Still is." Mary smiled. "Okay," said Jim, "let's go back to work." They got back in the truck and headed back.

Mary put the bay in the round pen, and Jim saddled the dun back up. He took it back into the arena and started working the cows. Mary worked the bay in the round pen for about an hour, then put him on the walker. Jim was bringing out the dun. "I forgot about the walker," said Jim.

Mary took the dun, left him saddled, and put him on the walker. After a little while, Mary took the dun off the walker, unsaddled him, and brushed him down, then put him up. Then she went and got the bay, brushed him down, and put him up. She took out Buddy.

"What in the world are you doing with that?" asked Jim.

Mary laughed. She got Tommie's saddle out. "I got this horse for Tommie. She doesn't know it yet. Troy and Kathy are bringing her out here in a little while so I can give it to her."

"That's nice of you," said Jim. Mary saddled him up and got him ready for Tommie.

"Let's go in the office and cool off," said Mary.

"Sounds good," said Jim.

Mary opened the refrigerator and got two Cokes out. She handed one to her dad.

"Thank you," he said.

Troy, Kathy, and Tommie showed up. "Oh, this is nice," said Kathy as they came in the office. "I like this. You need to put up some pictures of horses and maybe your big checks."

"Hi, Tommie," said Mary. "What you are doing?"

"Nothing," said Tommie.

"Would you like to ride a horse?"

"Who, Molly?" asked Tommie.

"Let's go see," said Mary.

As they walked out into the alleyway, Tommie said, "A pony, Mama, a pony."

"Yep, it sure is," said Kathy.

Tommie walked over to Buddy. He dropped his head so she could rub his nose.

"His name is Buddy."

"Is he mine?" asked Tommie.

"Yes, if you'll be nice to him and help take care of him," said Mary.

"I will," said Tommie, "I promise, I will." She tried to climb up on him.

"Hold up. Let me help," said Kathy.

They set Tommie on Buddy, then led him to the round pen. Mary went inside with them. She walked buddy around, holding on to his halter.

"Let me do it," said Tommie.

"Okay, no running. Just walk him around," said Mary. Mary let go.

"Buddy, walk on now. Turn him. Okay, good. Now the other way," said Kathy.

"He is just my size," said Tommie, and she turned him again.

"Okay, now make him stop. Say whoa. That's it. Good job, baby girl."

"Look, Daddy," said Tommie, "I got my own horse."

"I see, baby. You be careful." She rode Buddy around and around for about forty-five minutes.

"Okay, let's brush him down and put him up." Mary led them back out an into the alley. She tied him up. "Okay, can you get off? Here, wait." Mary got a five-gallon bucket and turned it over and set it by Buddy. Tommie eased herself down until she touched the bucket.

"Good job," said Kathy.

They took off his saddle. Mary handed Tommie a brush. She had one also, and she showed Tommie how to brush the way the hair was lying, slow and soft. Jim was there watching the whole time. He had a tear in his eye. His baby girl was sure a great young woman.

Every afternoon, Jim came to the stables and worked with the dun horse. Kathy would bring Tommie after school and let her ride Buddy in one of the lots. One afternoon, Tommie was riding Buddy while Mary and Kathy were cleaning his stall. Mary was pushing a wheelbarrow out of the stables when she saw Tommie lying on the ground, flat on her back, with her arms laid out, not moving, with Buddy standing over her. Mary yelled "Kathy!" as she broke and ran to Tommie. She dropped to her knees, thinking the worst, as Kathy got there.

"What do yawl want?" asked Tommie as she sat up.

"Oh my god," said Kathy, "what are you doing?"

"I'm teaching Buddy how to lie down, Mama." Kathy and Mary both busted out laughing with tears in their eyes. Tommie led Buddy to the rail fence and climbed up the rails and onto his back.

After working with the dun for a week, Jim had Troy bring three more heifers to the stables. Jim worked the dun with five calves the next week. Mary had been working with the bay horse in the round pen. She was about ready to start working him on the barrels. Troy said he was going to start the fall roundup in three weeks. Jim asked if he could help him on the dun to give him some more experience. Troy said, "Sure, I'll be glad to have you along."

Kattie called the stables. Mary answered, "Mary Plumber's Stables."

"Mary, this is your mom. I need your help at the clinic. Get your dad to bring you. Hurry."

Jim and Mary jumped in the truck. When they got there, Kattie and Rose had a horse lying down in a trailer. "What's wrong?" asked Mary.

"We started to unload the horse, and she just lay down and just won't get up. All her vitals are fine. Rose said to call you."

"Okay, let me check her out," said Mary. She climbed into the trailer with the horse and started rubbing his face and talking to her. Mary turned and said, "Yawl go back inside and leave us alone for a while."

Jim said, "I'll stand by the building out of the way, but I'm not leaving you by yourself."

The others went back inside. Mary softly talked to the horse. "What wrong, girl?" asked Mary. "Oh, it's okay. They're not going to hurt you. I'm right here with you. See, it's okay." Mary lay down on the floor of the trailer with the horse and wrapped her arms around her neck. Jim was worried but stayed back. "You sweet thing," Mary was saying, "it's okay." Mary got up and walked around to the horse's head. "Come on, let's get this over with." She picked up the lead rope. The horse found her feet and stood up. "That's a good girl," said Mary as she rubbed the horse's face. "Come on, girl, let's go." Mary and the horse walked out of the trailer. Jim couldn't believe what he just saw. Mary led the horse to the clinic door and knocked. They opened the door, and she led her in. They pulled blood and did a pregnancy test. Then Mary led her back out and loaded her in the trailer, talking to the horse the whole time. She gave the horse a kiss and told her goodbye.

Rose came to Mary. "Thank you."

"You're welcome," said Mary.

"What was wrong with her?"

"She was just scared. She has never been here before."

Jim and Mary got back in the truck and headed home. Jim was still having trouble believing what he saw. Mary just kept doing amazing things with the horses time after time. No one could understand it, but it was real!

Chapter 2

The Roundup

Troy and his crew were getting ready to go at the bunkhouse. Jim came riding up on the dun.

"You ready?" asked Troy.

"Yep, let's go," said Jim.

They headed out to the falls. From there, they started up the old trail. Troy told Jim, "We're going to try and make it to the line camp tonight if we can."

*****

Mary set up the barrels in the arena and saddled up the bay horse. She started off just walking the barrel pattern repeatedly. Kathy came up with Tommie.

"Hey, Aunt Mary. Can I run the barrels with you?"

"You can walk the barrels with me," said Mary.

"Walk?" said Tommie.

"Yep, you must walk before you can run."

"Okay," said Tommie. Kathy helped her get Buddy saddled up, then helped her on.

"I've got to go to the barn and work," said Kathy. "Is she okay here?"

"Sure," said Mary. "I'll watch her."

Tommie came trotting into the arena. Mary said, "Okay, we are just going to walk the barrels a while. Later, I'll let you run them, okay?"

"Yep," said Tommie.

"Just follow me," said Mary as she started walking the bay around again.

After about six times around, Mary asked Tommie, "Do you think you remember how to go?"

"Yes," said Tommie.

"Okay, let's see you walk him by yourself," said Mary. Tommie took off walking Buddy around the barrels. When she made it back to Mary, Mary said, "Good job. Now this time, try trotting around them." Tommie took off again, this time trotting. "Good job," said Mary. "Okay, now make Buddy run around them. Tommie took off, and Buddy ran the barrels in a slow lope. "Great job," said Mary.

"I'm ready to rodeo now," said Tommie.

Mary laughed. "Not quite. You're only five."

"Well, when I'm six, I will be." Mary laughed again.

The sun was going down. "We better get them put up," said Mary.

"Okay," said Tommie.

*****

Meanwhile, Troy, Jim, and the crew had just made it to the line camp at the north end of the ranch. They started setting up camp for the night. Troy started a fire. Ben got out some beans and some ham steaks. Once the fire was ready, they put the beans on. After a while, they put on the ham. "Let's eat," said Ben. They all got a plate and started eating. Ben asked Troy, "How many you think we lost this year?"

"Hopefully, none," said Troy. "I don't want to have to send Jeff out looking for bears again." They all laughed.

"Bears?" asked Jim.

"Yep, we killed a big one last year." Then they told Jim the story.

Ben said, "I wish that bear would have gotten old Jeff there before he got that bull. I miss that bull." They all laughed again.

The next morning, they got ready. Troy told his men, "Okay, like last time, don't kill anything on federal land. You can shoot to scare it off, but don't shoot it. There is one hundred and fifty head in there. Let's go get them."

They all went through the gate to federal land and spread out. Troy and Jim headed to the meadow where they all drove them to.

There were about a hundred head already there. The men started slowly bringing them in—ten, fifteen, twenty, then five.

"Okay, that's all of them," said Troy. "Let's take them home."

They drove them through the trees to the gate. They put them in the catch pen for the night. They threw out feed then hay. Troy got the fire back going. They put the pot of beans back on the fire, and Ben pulled out some beef steaks.

*****

Mary finally had the bay running the right direction around the barrels. She was now working on speed. Tommie was outrunning her and the bay on Buddy, she thought.

Kathy was missing Mary at the barn. Mary was a lot of help there. Now Kathy was doing it all, except what she could get Pet to do. Good thing most of stock horses were gone on the roundup. Kathy came back down to the stables. "What are you going to do with that bull?" asked Kathy.

"Well, Mom told me to put him with some cows this winter since he's old enough to breed and to stop playing with him. I guess we can put him in one of the small winter lots for now. Troy can do what he wants with him."

"Sounds good to me," said Kathy.

The next morning, Troy, Jim, and the crew started pushing the cows down the valley. Jim took one of the men on one side, and Troy took one man with him on the other. Ben and Jeff kept the herd moving. A lot of cows came out on their own once they got started. Just before nightfall, they stopped and set up camp again.

"How is that horse doing?" Troy asked Jim.

"Good. He is coming along. By the time we get back, he should be ready to go."

"What is she going to do with the other one?" asked Troy.

"Make a barrel horse out of him, I think."

"That girl has a knack with horses," said Troy.

"Yep, it beats all I've ever seen," said Jim. "I didn't believe it, but she really can talk to horses. I've seen it firsthand."

"Yeah, Kathy is always telling stories about the thing she does with the horses."

*****

Mary got her first client. A lady and her daughter pulled up at the stables. Mary was in the arena working the bay horse on barrels. They came around and found her. Mary saw them and rode over to the rails. "Can I help you?" asked Mary.

"I hope so," said the woman. "My daughter wants to learn how to run the barrel. I bought her a high-dollar barrel horse, but they just don't seem to click together."

"Sure, I can help her with that," said Mary. "Bring the horse to me. I'll work with the horse during the week, then I'll work with both on Saturdays."

"How long will it take?" asked the lady.

"I can't tell you that. It depends on her and her horse."

"How much do you charge?" asked the lady.

"It's $40.00 per week boarding fee and $10.00 an hour for my time, about $150.00 a week."

"Okay, we will try it for a couple of weeks and see how it goes," said the lady. "We will bring the horse tomorrow afternoon."

"That's great," said Mary.

*****

The next morning, Troy, Jim, and the men started pushing the cows again. The herd was growing all the time. They were finding a few in the trees, but most of them were coming out on their own. They passed by the spot where they killed the bear last year. No sign of any. The older cows knew where they were headed and just eased along, eating as they walked.

The men heard a gunshot. Troy came out of the trees to Ben. "Not another bear, I hope," said Troy.

"Wasn't me," said Ben. "Sounded like it was on the side." He pointed the way where Jim was.

In a little bit, they saw Jim come out ahead of them. He had young deer on the back of his horse.

"Well, that's good," said Ben. "All we had left was beans for tonight."

"I'll go help him dress it," said Troy. "Yawl keep moving.

Jim and Troy pulled the deer up a tree and pulled its hide off, then dressed it out. They put the meat in cloth bags and tied it on the horses. They rode ahead to the next camp, stopped, and put the meat in the creek. Then they started a fire. The herd got to them just before nightfall. They set up camp for the last time. They would be home tomorrow. They grilled up deer meat to go with the beans. The men ate until they were stuffed.

*****

Mary told Kattie and Rose about her new client.

"That's great," said Kattie.

Billie said she would start helping Kathy at the barn after work. Once, Mary told them that Kathy needed some help.

Kattie asked, "Well, how is your dad doing?"

"Great," said Mary. "He took the new horse with him on the roundup. I just got to find another one for him to train. He is really good at it. I think he enjoys it."

"Rose told me that you could get that horse up the other day. I don't believe it," said Kattie. "How did you do it?"

"She was scared, Mom, like a human having a panic attack. Once I calmed her down and I convinced her it was okay, she got up."

"How did you know what was wrong, baby?"

"I can't explain it, Mom. I just knew."

About noon the next day, Kattie heard the cows bawling. She jumped up, grabbed the tea she had made and two glasses, and headed up to the catch pens. Jim and Troy came riding over as she pulled up. She poured them both a glass of tea and handed it to them. "Well, how did it go?"

"Good," said Troy. "No bears this year."

"Man, them cows are fat," said Kattie.

"Yep, they look good. We will get the steer separated so you can pick tomorrow."

"Sounds good," said Kattie.

Jim leaned down and gave Kattie a kiss. "I'll see you in little while," said Jim. "I'm going to help them pen these cows first."

"Okay, cowboy," said Kattie. Jim tipped his hat as he rode off.

Troy said, "Hey, you want some deer meat? Jim killed it."

"Sure, why not? It's better than bear meat," said Kattie.

After the penning, Jim brought the dun back to the stables. He unsaddled him and brushed him down. Mary came out of the office. "You can sell this one now," said Jim. "He's ready."

"Okay, good, I will," said Mary. "I've got another one coming, a stud horse."

"A stud horse?" said Jim. "You don't need to be fooling with no damn stud horse."

"I'm not buying him. He belongs to a client. He won't breed. They want me to see if I can help."

"Not no, but hell no," said Jim. "You're not even supposed to know about such things."

"Dad, I'm fifteen years old. Mom and I have had that talk. I thought you could work with him, Dad. He's a champion cutting horse if we can get him to breed one of our mares."

"Okay, fine, but you stay away from it. I'll handle him."

"Fine, I have a barrel horse and rider to help," said Mary.

"I already have a job, you know," said Jim.

"Yeah, I know. It's helping me."

Jim just shook his head. "I'm going to see your mother and tell on you, you little brat."

"Bye," said Mary with a laugh. "Tell her I said hi."

*****

Kattie picked out three steers for the orphanage, and Troy picked out two for the ranch. Two of his men loaded them up and took them to the meat-packing plant.

"How many?" asked Kattie.

"Eighty-seven steers, forty-two heifers, plus six at the stables," said Troy.

"Okay, sell the steers, and put the forty-two heifers in the lot with Mary's bull. We'll see what he can do," said Kattie.

"Yes, ma'am," said Troy as he rode off. Troy told Ben, "You heard the lady. I'll go call for the trucks."

Chapter 3

Winter

Billie bought herself a four-wheeler like Mary and Rose wanted. It hadn't snowed yet, but they had fun riding all over the ranch. As they rode along the creek near the falls one afternoon, Mary saw something in their tracks, something shiny. She stopped and got off her four-wheeler. She reached down and picked it up. Rose and Billie rode up.

"What is it?" asked Billie.

"It looks like a coin," said Mary, "a yellow coin." Billie and Rose got off too.

"Let me see," said Rose. "It is. It's a gold coin."

"Look, there's another one," said Billie as she picked it up. Rose picked up one too.

"Let's see if we can find more," said Mary. All three filled up their pockets with gold coins.

"Well, I think that's all of them," said Rose. "It's getting dark. We better go."

"Okay," said Mary.

They took their four-wheelers back home and put them up and went inside the house.

"Yawl are frozen," said Kattie. "Go stand by the fire and warm up."

They stood in front of the fireplace with their pockets bulging.

"What do yawl have in your pockets?" asked Jim.

"Oh yeah, look what we found." The girls started emptying their pockets onto the bar. Jim's jaw dropped.

Kattie said, "Oh my god, you found them."

"What?" asked Jim.

Kattie told them about the lost gold shipment that she and Troy found after the flood. Also, there were still over four hundred missing coins that they never found. The girls stacked them up and counted them. "Eighty-six," said Rose.

Kattie looked at the dates on some of them. "Okay, I need to call Sara." Kattie went to the phone. "Hey, sis, I need you to come out to the ranch. Okay, see you in a little while," said Kattie. She hung up the phone.

"Why do you need Sara?" asked Rose.

"Well, legally these coins belong to the P&P Gold Recovery Co."

"Who is that?" asked Mary.

"That's me, Aunt Sara, Kathy, and Troy. I need to see what we have to do to transfer ownership to each of you."

Sara knocked on the door. "Holy shit," said Sara when she saw the coins.

"Look what the girls found."

Sara picked some up and looked at the dates. "Okay, what do you want to do?" Sara asked Kattie.

"I want to give them to the girls. They found them."

"Okay, let's see," said Sara. "What about Troy and Kathy?"

"I'll talk to them," said Kattie.

"Okay, girls, divide them out, tweeny-eight each," said Sara. They did.

"That leaves two coins," said Mary.

Sara reached and picked them up. "These are legal fees. Yawl find some jars or something to put each stack in. Okay, I'm going to put your name on each jar." Mary handed hers to Sara. She wrote Mary on the lid. Rose slid hers to Sara. She wrote Rose on the lid. Billie handed hers to Sara. She wrote Billie on hers. "Okay, yawl each agree with the way the coins were divided?"

"Yes, ma'am."

"I'll draw up the transfer papers," said Sara. "You, Troy, Kathy, and I will have to sign them."

"Okay," said Kattie.

"Now I assume you want to put Mary's with her other coins?"

"Yes," said Kathy.

"What about Billie's?"

"I want to put hers up like Mary's, and she can get them at age twenty-one," said Kattie.

"Rose, since you're of age, you get to decide."

"How much are they worth?" asked Rose.

"Right now, from twenty-eight thousand to thirty thousand. If you hold on to them for ten years, they will double or triple that. That's what I would suggest," said Sara.

"Yes, ma'am, let's save them."

"Okay, they will be put in a safety deposit box in your name. You can get them whenever you want."

"Mary, yours and Billie's coins are under my care until you turn twenty-one, you understand?"

"Yes, ma'am."

"Oh, by the way, Mary, I had to take out some liability insurance on your stables in case someone or someone's horse gets hurt."

"Okay, thank you," said Mary. "That's good. I've got two new clients."

Sara hugged Kattie and headed for the door. "Bye, girls," she said as she walked out.

Jim said, "Well, yawl are some lucky little girls."

"We know," said Billie.

The snow finally came. The girls got so excited. Rose took off work at 3:30 p.m. so she and the girls could ride after school. They climbed on their four-wheelers, all bundled up with three layers of clothes, gloves, and hats. The snow had covered the ground and was still falling. Big beautiful flakes landed on their faces as they rode.

Jim was at the stables working with the stud horse in the round pen. Mary had had a shed built over it so it would be dry this winter. The stud horse was very antisocial to the point that he wanted to fight any horse he was near, even mares in heat. The owner was able to breed one mare through artificial insemination, but that cost a lot of money to do. So Jim was trying to work on the horse's attitude, but not having much luck.

Mary had one more session with the barrel racer and her horse this Saturday. They were now riding as a team and making runs in the low fourteens next season; they should do fine. Mary moved her pregnant mare back to the stables so she could watch her; she should foal in January. She was hoping Jim would have the stud horse ready by then. She was still working with the bay, trying to keep him in shape through the winter. Buddy had become a big pet. Mary let him run loose like a dog most of the time. He followed her around and tried to come in the office with her. He would nicker when someone came up, like a guard dog barking. Mary babied him and fed him treats when he minded her. Tommie cut ear holes in an old hat, and he only wore it for Tommie. If anyone else put it on him, he just shook it off. He would do anything for Tommie. Mary called them trouble and double trouble.

Thanksgiving would be next week. Kattie planned to have a big gathering of friends and family at the ranch. Jim had invited his mom and dad and his brothers and their family. Kattie had invited her sisters and theirs; Pete and Alice; Troy, Tommie, Kathy, and her mom; and Ben and his family. And Rose had invited Paul. Kattie, Alice, and Rose were cooking two big turkeys next week, along with all the other fixings. Jim and Troy were going to roast a pig on the pit. Kathy and her mom were making pies and cookies. They were shutting everything down from Thursday through Sunday.

Jim and Troy had made plans to go elk hunting at Jim's ranch in Montana the Monday and Tuesday before Thanksgiving. Jim really enjoyed spending time with Troy on the roundup. Mary had sold the dun horse Jim trained to one of Jim's brothers for $1,200.00 after Jim told him what a good horse he was. The bay horse's training was on hold for now. "It's just too cold," said Mary. Since there was no grass to eat, feeding and cleaning stalls were all she could handle right now anyway. Mary had started working with the stud horse some, not in the breeding department. She was trying to figure out why he was so mean around other horses. Alone, he was fine, easy to handle, but put another horse with him, he would go crazy. He was a beautiful horse, about seventeen hands, and would throw some pretty colts. Mary had been reading up on horse psychology but hadn't found anything yet that fit his behavior.

Thanksgiving came and went; so did Christmas and New Year's. It was not going to be long now before the snow started melting and the cows started dropping calves. Mary's mare that she bought had her foal last week, a beautiful little filly, a baby girl, said Tommie. The filly was a light brown now with four white stockings and a white diamond-shaped spot on her forehead. Tommie wanted to get in the stall with her so bad, but Mary said, "Not yet. Her mama might step on you or kick you." She probably wouldn't, but Mary wanted the mama and filly to have plenty of time to bond.

Tommie and Buddy played in the alley. Tommie was trying to get Buddy to fetch a ball. It was so funny to watch. Tommie would throw the ball, and Buddy would smell it and then walk away.

There was a steady drip of water from the roof's edge now as the snow and ice melted. It was getting a little warmer every day, but it was still too cold to not wear a jacket or coat. Rose had spent a lot of time out at Paul's place lately. Everybody felt like there might be a wedding soon. Billie was still working at the clinic after school and helping Kathy when she got home in the barn.

Mary got a call from a lady yesterday afternoon about a horse that wouldn't eat. Mary was thinking bad teeth. She and Jim were going out this afternoon after school to check on her.

Mary and Jim drove out to the lady's farm. The lady came out of the house, and she looked to be in her seventies. Mary introduced herself and Jim, her father. The lady's name was Margret. She said, "Let me show you the horse." They walked out to a small stall near the barn. She said, "The horses name is Nelly. She was my husband's horse. I don't know how old she is. My husband died three weeks ago. Even while he was sick, he still came out every day to feed and talk to Nelly. Since he died, she has not eaten a bite of food or hay. She'll drink water, but she just not eating."

Mary opened the gate and walked up to the horse. "Hey, girl," she said, "what's wrong?" Mary rubbed her face. She slowly opened her mouth, and Mary looked at her teeth. "Her teeth are not that bad," said Mary. "They need floating, but nothing that would keep her from eating. I would say she's around twelve to fifteen years old." Mary picked up some hay and offered it to her. No response. "Do you have a lead rope?" asked Mary. The lady walked over to the wall and got one off a nail on the wall. "I want to take her outside where there's more light." Mary clipped the lead rope on and walked her outside. She looked her over good. She picked up her feet and rubbed her underbelly. "Can I walk her down the road a bit?" asked Mary.

"Sure," said the lady.

Mary got the horse started down the road, then took the halter in her hand as they walked. "Tell me what's wrong, girl," Mary asked as they walked along. "I can't help if I don't know." The horse stopped. Mary wrapped her arms around the horse's neck, and the horse laid her head on Mary's shoulder. Mary started to cry. Big tears rolled out of both eyes. She just stood there holding on to the horse crying. The horse raised her head up. Mary stepped back. The horse had tear marks from her eyes to her nose. Mary wiped her own eyes, and they headed back down the road to the stall.

"Well, what do you think?" asked Margret.

"Did your husband wear a hat?" asked Mary.

"Yes, he did," said the lady.

"Can you get it for me?" asked Mary.

"Okay, I know right where it's at."

Mary led Nelly back inside the stall. The woman came out with the hat. Mary took it and put it up to the horse's nose. Then she rubbed it on the horse's face. "There, girl. He wouldn't want you to starve. You've got to eat, girl. You've got to stay strong. He took care of you because he loved you." The old woman had tears in her eyes. The horse reached into her trough and started eating. Mary stood talking to her as she ate. Jim was in awe.

As Mary and Jim left the barn, Margret came out behind them. "Hey, girl, I want you to do something for me.

"Yes, ma'am, what's that?"

"Well, I'm going to have a hard enough time taking care of myself. I want you to come back and get Nelly and take her to your place. She's yours now. You'll be doing me a favor," said Margret.

"Okay," said Mary, "I'll come get her next Saturday."

As Mary and Jim drove home, not a word was said. When they got back home and got out of the truck, Jim wrapped his arms around Mary and kissed her head.

Saturday, Jim and Mary went to get Nelly. They brought her back to the stables. Kattie came down to the stables. She looked Nelly over and then checked her teeth.

"I figured between twelve and fifteen," said Mary.

"More like eighteen to twenty," said Kattie. "So what are you going to do with this horse?" asked Kattie.

"Well, after I get her back on her feet and fattened back up and Troy get the mama cows and babies out to pasture, I think I'll saddle her up, lead Bob, and go out and find the mamas and babies and turn her loose. She can take Dawg's place looking after the calves all summer."

"That sounds like a good idea," said Kattie with a tear in her eyes. "I'd like to go with you if it's okay."

"Sure," said Mary. "It will be a few weeks."

Chapter 4

Out to Pasture

All the snow was gone. Green grass was growing high in the pastures. Troy and his crew were separating the cows, getting ready to put them back out to pasture. This year, they planned to put two hundred head on government land. They would put the mama cows and their babies in a field nearby until the calves were bigger and the rest in the north pastures. Troy's crew were coming out of the barn on their stock horses as Mary walked in. She needed another saddle from the main barn to take to the stables. As she walked in, one of the men was throwing his saddle on one of the horses, then he popped the horse's rump with his reins and told him to turn around. As he reached under the horse for the girth strap, the horse took a step. Mary could tell that the horse was scared; his flank muscles were flinching. The man popped the horse again as hard as he could and said, "Now stand still."

Mary couldn't stand it; she walked over and took the horse by the reins. She told the young man, "Don't hit this horse again."

He snatched the reins from her and said, "I'll do what I damn well please, little girl."

Mary pulled his saddle off onto the ground. As he turned to grab the saddle, she pulled his bridle off. Then she looked him in the eyes, fist clenched, and said, "Get your stuff and get out of my barn. You're not going to treat Plumber horses like that. You're fired."

The man laughed. "You can't fire me."

Troy had just walked in the barn to see what was going on. Troy said, "She just did. Now get your stuff and get off this ranch now." The man grabbed his saddle and bridle and headed out of the barn. Troy said, "Are you okay?"

"Yeah, just mad."

Troy laughed. "You were going to hit him, weren't you?"

"I was sure thinking about it," said Mary.

Troy and his men started moving the cows out to pasture. Mary got the saddle she wanted and headed down to the stables. The next day, Mary saddled up Nelly and the bay horse and put a lead rope on Bob. Kattie came down to the stables with canteens and sack lunches. Mary rode Nelly, and her mom rode the bay with Bob in tow. It took about an hour to get to the pasture where the mama cows and babies were. Then they had to find the cows. It was a 500-acre section. Just before noon, they found the herd. Mary unsaddled Nelly. Kattie told Nelly, "This is home for the summer. You look after them babies. You keep the wolves run off for me, okay?" Mary and Kattie both gave her a kiss, then turned her loose. Nelly walked out into the herd and started grazing. Mary saddled up Bob.

"Well, let's find a place to eat," said Kattie.

"Sounds good," said Mary. They went to the edge of the tree line and found a place to sit. They ate their sandwiches and watched the cows and Nelly graze.

Kattie asked Mary, "When you and your dad went to see Nelly because she wouldn't eat, what was wrong with her?"

"Well, I'll have to tell you the whole story. Nelly was the old man's horse. He died. His wife said that for years he and Nelly worked that farm. She pulled a plow and a wagon, pulled up stumps, and pulled hay equipment. She was a true farm horse that worked with him every day. She said that even after the old man got sick, he still got up every morning, walked through the snow, and took care of that horse. She said that he would sit and talk to Nelly while she ate her grain. When the old man died, the woman was so upset and busy with friends and family that she forgot about the horse. After three days, one of her sons was looking through the stall and saw Nelly. He gave her some hay and grain to eat. After two more days, everybody cleared out, except for the old lady. Her son told her not to forget to feed the horse and the milk cow in the barn. So she went out the next morning to check on them. The cow was fine, and she gave it more food. Nelly had not touched the feed or hay the boy had given her, but the woman gave her some more anyway. The next day, the food was still there. Every day the woman checked on her, but the food just sat there.

"A neighbor told her about me. She called and told me her horse wouldn't eat her feed. First thing I thought was bad teeth. When we got there, the first thing I did was check her teeth. They weren't that bad. Her ribs were showing, and her eyes were droopy. Her mouth was not sore. Her belly was not sore. She was just starving herself. I asked the lady to let me take her outside into the light, and I checked her feet. I then told the lady that I wanted to walk Nelly down the gravel road for a little way. She said okay. As we walked down the road, I kept asking Nelly to tell me what was wrong with her. Nelly just stopped in the road. I looked into her eyes. She made me so sad that I put my arms around her neck and hugged her. She laid her head on my shoulder. Mama, the horse cried. Big tears rolled down her face. I started crying too, then I realized she was mourning for the old man. Her only friend stopped coming out to feed her and talk to her every day. She didn't know why. If people knew what that horse and I talked about standing in that road, they would put me in the nuthouse.

"I took her back to the stall. I told her that the man took care of her for years because he loved her and that he wouldn't want her to starve. He would want her to be strong. He didn't leave her because he wanted to. He had no choice. She started eating again. The woman asked me to come back and get her, that she couldn't take of her.

"Mama, horses don't know about life and death. They just know when things change in their world. That's why I want to train horses and riders together as a team, *team riding*. If someone competes with a horse for, say, five years, they have that team bond, then all of a sudden, you buy that horse. You have a piece of paper that says you own that horse, but the horse is not yours until they get over losing their teammate and bond with you. Horses are born with a herd mentality. That can be them and other horses, them and cows, or them and people, but they must be part of a herd. A herd can be two or two hundred. Doesn't matter. Now that I've told you this, don't put me in the nuthouse," said Mary.

Kattie reached over and hugged her. "You are a very special young lady, Mary Plumber. You're not crazy."

"Well, I feel like it sometimes. There is still so much I don't understand."

"Well, let's go home, baby girl," said Kattie.

When they got back to the stables, Jim was there. "Well, how did it go?" asked Jim.

"Good," said Kattie. "It was a nice ride."

Mary said, "Dad, we need to find out the background on that stud horse. Something must have happened when he was young. We need to know what."

"Yeah, I think you're right. I've done all I know to do," said Jim.

The school year was almost over. Mary had decided not to rodeo this year. With the stables, it would just be too much. Once Billie found out Mary wasn't riding, she, too, said she wasn't riding. Billie wanted to work full-time with Kattie and Rose at the clinic. Mary and her dad, Jim, were enjoying working and spending time together every day. After years of not having him around, she didn't want to give that up for rodeoing or anything else.

Mary decided to try something. She put her mare on the walker and left the filly in the stall. She then put the stud horse on the opposite side of the walker and turned it on. The stud horse nickered and whinnied at the mare but could not get to her. Mary left them on the walker until he got quiet, then she put them up without feed. The next day, she put the stud on the walker with Bob. The same thing, he nickered and whinnied. Once he stopped, she put him up with just a little feed. The next day, she put the mare on the walker, then the stud and then Bob, with the stud in the middle. He really tried to show out, but all he could do was walk around and around. Once he settled down for a while, she put him up and fed him a little feed. The fourth day, she put the bay, Bob, and Molly on the walker with the stud. He only nickered once or twice, but Mary made him walk with the other horses anyway. When she put him up, she gave him a little more feed. The fifth day, she put him on the walker by himself. He kept looking around for the other horses. After about an hour, she put him up and left him in his stall and fed him his normal ration. She left him in for the weekend.

The next Monday, Mary put the stud back on the walker with the mare, Bob, and Molly. He nickered once when he first came out. The next day, when Jim got there, they saddled up Bob and the stud horse. They went into the arena, Bob in front and the stud horse following. They walked around the arena twice. Then Jim walked the stud up beside Bob. They walked around the arena, Jim and Mary rubbing legs. Then Jim moved to the front, and Bob followed. The next day, they did the same thing with Molly and the stud horse. No aggression at all. They put him in his stall and Molly in the stall beside him for the night.

The next day, Mary put Bob and the stud both in the round pen and worked them together. Jim ask Kattie to come check Mary's mare to see if she was in season. Kattie said yes. The next day, while Mary was in school, Jim got Troy to help him. They put the mare in the round pen and tied her. Jim led the stud horse in. The stud did what a stud was supposed to do. They put them both in the side grass lot together for the rest of the day. When Mary got home, Jim said, "You can call your client and tell him to come get his stud horse. Your mare is bred."

The man came to get his horse the next day. He asked, "Is he ready?"

Jim said, "Well, he has bred our mare yesterday. Mary said to tell you to keep him around other horse more."

"Okay," said the man. "Tell that girl to send me a bill. We will try him out."

*****

Rose and Paul had announced their engagement. They hadn't set the exact date yet, but it would be sometime after rodeo season. Paul wanted to try one more time at the bareback bronc riding championship. Last season, he got second. Paul wanted to raise horses on his place. He needed to win enough money to buy some brood mares and a stud horse. His land and house were paid for already, but he needed operating cash. Mary told Paul he could work for her parttime at the stables with roping horses. The stables had turned into a full-time job since school let out. Jim was spending more and more time there also.

The word had gotten out about Mary and her gift with horses, and business was booming. Jim told Mary that she needed to hire a stable hand to help with the stall cleaning and the feeding. Mary put ads in the local papers, but no response yet. She was hoping a young woman would respond. She hadn't had much luck dealing with cowboys in the past. But she didn't specify in her ads about male or female. Pete came to Mary and told her that he had a niece who lived in Rapid City with her parents because her husband ran off and left her with their young daughter. Pete said that she was a hard worker, and so was her ten-year-old daughter.

"I don't know," said Mary.

Pete said, "They can stay with us for now. You won't be sorry, I promise."

"Okay," said Mary. "Go get them. What's their names?"

"Selena is the mother's name. She is thirty years old. And Maria is her daughter's name. She is ten years old. I'll go get them in the morning," said Pete.

"Make sure she knows she'll be working for a fifteen-year-old shoveling horse crap," said Mary.

The next day, Pete came back with Selena and Maria. He brought them to the stables to meet Mary. Selena was a dark-skinned woman like Pete and Alice. The girl was lighter-skinned like Rose. Mary took Selena around the stables and showed her where everything was and explained to her what she needed her to do.

Selena told Mary her thanks and hugged her. She said, "My daughter loves horses. She will help."

"Okay," said Mary, "I'll see you in the morning bright and early." The next morning, Selena and Maria were at the stables early when Mary got there; they had already started to work. Mary jumped in to help. Maria worked right along beside them. Mary turned Buddy out to run loose. Maria couldn't take her eyes off Buddy. Buddy made his rounds aggravating the other horses, then came back to Mary. He knew Mary had treats in her pocket; she always did. Mary rubbed his nose, then gave him a treat. "Now go on, Buddy. We are working." Mary asked Maria if she had ever ridden a horse."

"No, ma'am," said Maria.

"If you're good to your mama, I'll teach you how, if it's okay with her."

Maria looked up at her mom. Selena just smiled and nodded.

Now that Mary had help, she could spend more time working with the horses. She had two barrel horses and a stock horse she was working with, plus exercising Bob and Molly. Jim was helping with the stock horse when he could, but just like before, Mary worked with the horse and then the horse and rider. The filly her mare had was growing fast. Now weaned from her mom, she needed to be worked with. It was a lot of hard work for a fifteen-year-old girl, but Mary loved every minute of it. Her biggest reward was when she could bring a horse and rider together as a team.

Chapter 5

A New Cowgirl

Jim had been separating his calves as they were weaned from their mothers. He now had twenty-five breeding-age heifers out of the big brown bull and twenty-five more yearlings. He was going to sell off all the older mama cows and just keep the young heifers and the bull. Next spring, he was going to breed the older ones to the bull, and their calves would be his new bloodline. He brought three steers from his ranch to Mary's stables to use for roping practice.

Kattie said it was time for a cookout. Everybody had been working hard and needed a break. What Kattie said would go most of the time. Jim, Troy, and Pete would oversee the grilling, and Kathy Kattie, and Alice would take care of the sides. Paul and Rose were bringing the drinks for the men and some of the ladies. Mary invited her new help Selena and her daughter to the cookout. Well, more like she told them to come. Mary dug through her old clothes and found a bathing suit that she wore when she was around Maria's age.

The men had the fire going. It took a lot of wood and beer to get a good bed of coals ready to cook on. The ladies were all in the house prepping everything for the meal. Mary, Tommie, Billie, and Maria were headed for the pool. Rose and Selena were out back talking about life and their childhood. Rose told Selena that this family was the kindest, caring group she would ever know. Jim told Troy about his new bloodline of cows that grew bigger and faster than any other breed. The steers grew from six to eight hundred pounds in just one year. Maria had never been in a real swimming pool before and was so happy. Mary and Billie treated her more like a little sister than just a worker's daughter. She didn't know how to feel; no one other than family had ever been so nice to her before. Tommie just hung on to Maria; she was closer to her age.

Kathy told the girls to get out of the pool and dry off as the food was almost ready. The girls got out and went inside the house and put on shorts and T-shirts. They went out back with everybody else. Troy said grace. The kids and women started filling their plates. After the women and kids were seated, the men filled their plates and sat with them. As they all ate, Billie and Rose talked about the clinic and Kathy, Mary, and Kattie talked about the stables. Everyone ate their fill. The girls went back to the pool to play more. This time, Rose and Kathy joined the girls in the pool. Kattie, Alice, and Selena sat and talked, while all the men stood around the fire and drank beer. It was a good day and a good night for friends and family.

Monday morning, Mary put a lead rope on Molly and led her over to Maria. She told her, "Today your job is to stay with Molly. She has been feeling lonely and needs company today. Don't leave her side. You can walk her, brush her, talk to her, whatever. Just don't get on her. At lunchtime, you eat with her. Can you do that?"

"Yes, ma'am," said Maria.

"Okay," said Mary, "I'll check on you two later."

All day long, Maria stayed with Molly. She led her all around the stables. Buddy followed them everywhere they went.

The next morning, Mary saddled up Molly and put her in the round pen. When Maria got there, Mary told her, "Come with me." Mary took Maria to the round pen. She told her, "Always get on a horse from his or her left side." She showed her how to put her foot in the stirrup and pull herself up. Mary adjusted the stirrups to fit Maria, then led her around the round pen. She explained to her how to make Molly turn and how to make her stop. Mary kept hold of the lead rope while Maria made Molly turn and then made her stop. Mary then made her get on and off Molly several times after making a round in the pen. Mary took off the lead rope and let Maria ride by herself around and around. Mary said, "That's enough for today. Let's put her up." Mary opened the gate and let Maria follow her on the horse to the alley. Maria got off Molly. Mary showed her how to loosen the girth and remove the saddle and then the bridle and where to put them. Then Mary had her brush Molly down and feed her oats and hay. Mary told Maria, "A cowgirl always takes care of her horse no matter what."

"Yes, ma'am," said Maria.

Mary then took out one of the other horses to work with while Maria helped her mom. Every day she did the same with Molly and Maria for a whole week.

The next Monday, Mary saddled up Bob and Molly. She had Maria mount up on Molly as she got on Bob. "Just follow me," said Mary as they headed down the valley to the falls. Mary knew Molly would follow Bob with no problem. Once they made it to the falls, they sat and listened for a while, then headed back.

When they made it back to the stables and got off, Maria said, "I'll take care of them." She took Bob's reins. Mary watched as Maria led the horses into the alley of the stables.

Selena walked up to Mary and gave her a hug, then said, "Thank you so very much."

Mary said, "Well, you better get ready. She's going to be a cowgirl. You may not thank me then."

"If she's happy, I'm happy," said Selena.

Maria watched as Mary ran the barrels on one of the horses; she was training. She had never seen anyone do this before. She had never been to a rodeo either. She was a city girl—or should I say, was a city girl—but now she lived on a ranch and was learning how to ride a horse. Paul and Rose were going to a rodeo this weekend in Billings; Paul was competing. Mary asked Jim if he would take her and Maria one night. Jim said, "Let me ask your mom. She may want to go also." Jim asked Kattie if she would go with them Saturday night, and she said she would. They got there just before the barrel racing started. Maria watched the girls ran the barrels and was amazed at how fast they went on those horses. Then she watched the calf roping and the steer wrestling, then the team roping. She never knew there were so many things you could do on a horse. Then there were the clowns and a dancing dog, the bronc riders, and the bull riders. She was in awe and in love all at the same time.

Monday, Mary let Maria saddle up Molly, and she saddled up Bob. She told Maria, "Come with me." They went into the arena. Mary told her, "Stay one barrel behind me." Mary started walking out the barrel pattern with Bob. Maria followed on Molly. Mary kept walking the pattern over and over as Maria followed on Molly. Then Mary said, "You and Molly stand over there, and I'll show you how it's done." Mary went back down the alley, then she turned and ran back into the arena. Bob sat up for the first turn and then the second as Mary shifted with him and then the third and headed home.

When she came back into the arena, Maria said, "That was fast, just like those girls at the rodeo. Can I try it?" asked Maria.

"Well, you need a different horse than old Molly there. She is too old for running barrels."

That night at supper, Mary was telling Billie and Rose about Maria wanting to run the barrels. Mary said, "I told her that Molly is too old, and I don't know if she could handle Bob."

"She can ride Toby," said Billie.

"Are you sure?" asked Mary.

"Sure. Somebody needs to ride him. He is getting too fat," said Billie.

"Okay, thank you," said Mary. "She will be tickled."

The next morning, Mary went to the main barn and got Toby and led him down to the stables. She told Maria, "Here's your barrel horse. Billie is loaning him to you for you to learn on. You take him and do just like you did with Molly. You spend all day with this horse. Tomorrow we will ride."

The next morning, Mary saddled up Toby for Maria and then saddled up Bob. They rode into the arena. Mary said, "Okay, just warm him up first." They rode around the arena at a half lope. Mary said, "Okay, go back down the alley and come out slow. Toby is going to want to run flat out. You will have to hold him back." Maria walked Toby down the alley, then he turned and ran out into the arena in a lope. Toby made the first barrel, then the second, and then the third. "Now let him go," said Mary. Toby flew back down to the alley. Mary said, "Okay, one more time. Faster." Maria came out again fast. She rounded the first barrel and then the second, with Toby getting faster and faster. They turned the third barrel, and then he opened up. "Great job," said Mary. "Now walk him around and cool him off."

The next morning, Mary set up the poles in the arena. She made Maria saddle up Toby by herself. When she finished, Mary was waiting in the arena. She rode in. "What's that?" asked Maria.

"Those are poles. It's called pole bending," Mary said. "Watch me." She and Bob zigzagged around the poles one direction and then came back the other. Mary rode up beside Maria. "Okay, as you ride through the poles like I did, feel the way Toby shifts his weight back and forth.

When he leans to the right and the left, you try to stay in time. If you lean too fast or too slow, you will throw him off time. You need to feel him adjusting just before he leans. When you feel that, you start leaning whatever direction he is going. Now try it, but this time, just sit in the middle and feel him shift under you."

Maria started slow, trying to feel Toby shift as he zigged and zagged between the poles. When Maria finished, Mary asked her, "Did you feel it?"

"I'm not sure," said Maria.

"Okay, do it again," said Mary. "You will know it when you feel it."

Maria and Toby started over. About midway, Maria felt it like a light coming on. When they finished, Maria said, "I felt it."

"Good," said Mary. "It works the same way in barrel racing. Run the poles a couple more times and try to get in time with Toby, then put him up."

The next day, Mary had Maria spend another day bonding with Toby. She had her ride him from the stables to the main barn and then back five times, each time changing her route. Then she kept him close to her the rest of the day. Mary gave Maria some treats to put in her pocket. "Here. As you go by the stalls, if the horse comes to the door, give them a treat. If they don't, just go on by. Watch Buddy. He will take you down for a treat. Next week, we will ride some more. You're doing good, Maria. Tell your mom I want to take you to town tomorrow. It's Saturday," said Mary.

"Okay," said Maria.

The next morning, Jim and Mary pulled up to Pete's trailer. Maria came running out and got in the truck. The three of them headed to town. They went to the clothing store. Mary told Maria, "You need some work clothes."

"But I don't have any money."

"Yes, you do. You've been working for me for a month with no pay. That will cover whatever you get today. Now come on." They picked out four pairs of jeans (plain Wranglers), four T-shirts, one nice Western shirt, and a cowgirl hat. Mary said, "Okay, now you need two pairs of boots, one for working in and one for dress. Oh, and socks." They picked out a plain brown pair of cowboy boots to work in and a pair of Tony Lama dress boots. Then they got her some socks and panties. Mary spent around $500.00 on her that day.

They went to the local café and ate lunch and then headed home. Maria was so proud of her new clothes and couldn't wait to show her mom. She hadn't had any new clothes in over a year. The sneakers she had been wearing had holes in them. When they got back to the trailer, Mary helped Maria get her stuff out of the truck. Maria took off into the house so excited.

The next Monday, Maria showed up in her new jeans, new T-shirt, and new work boots. Mary said, "Come here, Maria." She walked over to Mary, who was shoveling out a stall. Mary took a scoop of horse manure and threw it on Maria's new boots. "Now they are work boots," said Mary. "Go to work. This afternoon, we will ride."

"Okay," said Maria as she picked up a scooper and started working.

Selena came over to Mary as Maria was moving to another stall.

She gave Mary a hug. "Thank you," said Selena,

"Don't thank me. She earned those clothes," said Mary. "Like I told her, she worked for a month with no pay, just a few riding lessons. I can't pay her because she is too young, but I'll make sure she gets compensated for her efforts. As a matter of fact, I think it's time you and Maria had your own place. I'll see what I can do."

That night at supper, Mary told her mom that she thought Selena and Maria should have their own place. Kattie asked, "What are you thinking?"

"Well, I could put a trailer at the stables like Pete and Alice's."

"Yeah, or you could just let them live in the trailer at the mine," said Kattie.

"Could they?" asked Mary

"I don't see why not. It's just sitting there."

Mary hugged her mom and said, "Thank you!"

The next day, Mary told Selena that she wanted her and Maria to move into the trailer across the road. "It's already furnished and clean. The yard needs tending, but other than that, it's ready to live in. You can start moving after work. Pete will help you."

By the end of the week, Selena and Maria had the yard groomed and was all moved in. Selena asked Pete to take them to town Saturday to buy groceries and cleaning supplies. Selena also wanted some flowers to plant in the yard and a few pepper plants.

Billie had her eighteenth birthday last month. She didn't want a big event; just her, Mary, Kattie, and Jim went out to eat in Rapid City. Mary's sixteenth birthday was coming soon.

Chapter 6

Sweet Sixteen

Mary's sixteenth birthday would be in two weeks. She wanted to do like Billie and have a simple birthday.

"But it's your sweet sixteenth birthday," said Kattie. "It needs to be a special birthday."

"Oh, Mom," said Mary.

"But you only turn sixteen once," said Kattie.

"Okay, whatever you want. Just let me know what time and where to be. But I ain't wearing no silly dress or nothing like that," said Mary. "You can forget that." Kattie realized Mary sounded just like she did at that age.

That night, Kattie asked Jim, "What do you get a sixteen-year-old girl who has everything she wants?"

"I just don't know," said Jim. "Wait, I do know."

"What?" asked Kattie.

"Tickets to the world finals in Las Vegas," said Jim. "It's next month."

"That's a great idea," said Kattie. "She will love that."

"You know, Billie is going to want to go too," said Jim.

"Good," said Kattie. "We will all go. Paul and Rose are already going. Mary told me she didn't want a big event for her birthday. I told her the sixteenth birthday had to be a special day."

"Well, let's just get her a cake and then let her invite some people over to swim, and I'll grill hamburgers," said Jim.

Mary invited Billie, Rose, Troy, Kathy, Tommie, Maria, Alice, Pete, and Selena and, of course, Kattie and Jim. Mary told them all not to bring presents, except Kattie and Jim. They didn't tell Mary about Vegas; that was a surprise. Kattie made all the arrangements for the Vegas trip—airline tickets, hotel reservations, and rodeo tickets. She told Kathy and Troy so they could plan to look after things while they were gone. Pete and Alice could look after the house; Selena and Maria could look after the stables with Troy's help. The clinic could take care of itself, as it did most of the time. Kattie was excited since the girls were not doing rodeos this year. The family hadn't had any trips away from home.

Jim was helping Mary get through with her training before they leave next month, even though she didn't know it. The barrel horses were almost ready; the roping horse was coming along, but still not there. Jim asked Paul to bring his horse out next week so the horse could see what a roping horse should do. Jim got Troy and two of his hands to come help get the calves in and out of the chute.

Paul showed up, and he unloaded his horse and saddled him up. Paul rode into the arena. Jim was on the roping horse he was training. Jim told Paul, "You go first." Troy loaded a calf in the chute. Paul backed his horse up in the corner and nodded. The calf came out. Paul threw his rope around the steer's neck. His horse locked up, and Paul was on his way to the calf. The rope jerked the calf back, and Paul threw it to the ground and wrapped the piggin' string around its legs. Then he untied it and turned it loose.

"Great job," said Jim.

Paul herded the calf back to Troy. Troy opened the gate and let the calf in. "Your turn," said Paul as Jim backed his horse into the corner. Jim nodded. Troy opened the chute, and out came the calf. Jim threw his loop and caught the calf, but Jim had to stop the horse. The horse didn't do it on his own. Jim jumped off and ran for the calf. He threw it on the ground and tied its feet. Jim had to work extra hard because the horse didn't keep the rope tight.

"Okay, I see the problem," said Paul. "Let's try something. Let's both go at the same time. You rope the calf first, then I'll rope it. I'll get off and run down the rope. You stay on your horse, and after I throw the calf, you make your horse get the rope tight with mine. We are not worried about speed yet."

"Okay," said Jim, "let's try it."

Troy opened the chute. Jim came out first. He threw his loop and caught the calf. Paul came up beside him and threw his loop around the calf's neck as he slid off his horse. Paul's horse backed up until the rope was tight. Jim backed up his horse until his rope was tight. Paul wrapped the calf's legs, then untied them. They did the same thing three more times, then Jim tried it by himself. After Jim roped the calf, he slid off his horse and headed down the rope. The horse backed up to get the rope tight. "Okay," said Paul, "just do it about one hundred more times, and he should have it."

It was the day before Mary's birthday when Jim came to the stables from his ranch. He got off his truck with something under each arm. He yelled for Mary. He heard her say. "Around here." Jim walked around to the stalls.

"What have you got?" asked Mary as she walked up to him. "Oh, puppies! How sweet, Australian shepherd puppies."

"Yep," said Jim. "One is yours, and one is Billie's. Which one do you want?"

Mary looked at them both. "I'll take this one," said Mary. "She'll be our stable dog."

"Okay, I'll give the other one to Billie. She can keep it at the main barn."

"Thank you," said Mary as she gave him a hug. Mary yelled, "Maria, come here!" Maria came walking around the corner. Mary handed her the puppy. "Find a place to keep her here at the stable. Give her some water. I'll get her some food. It's your job to take care of her every day."

"Okay," said Maria.

The next morning was Saturday. Mary still went to the stables. Her party was going to be tonight. When she got to the stables, Maria was there putting out food and water for the puppy. "What are you doing today?" asked Mary.

"I thought I'd saddle up Toby and ride him some," said Maria.

"That's fine," said Mary. "I might ride with you later on Bob. I've got to work these barrel horses first," said Mary.

"Sure," said Maria. "Just let me know when you're ready." Maria got Toby out and saddled him up. She climbed on his back and headed out of the stables. Maria rode Toby up to the main barn and talked to Kathy a little while. Then she rode him back down to the stables. Mary had the barrels up in the arena. Maria went into the arena with Toby. Mary was in there with one of the barrel horses.

"Here," said Mary, "let me show you something."

"Okay," said Maria.

Mary showed her how to work the stopwatch. Maria moved over to the side where Mary told her to sit on Toby and timed her. Mary went down the alley, then came back running. As she passed Maria, she pushed the button. Mary made her run. When Mary came back by Maria, she pushed it again. "How fast?" asked Mary?

Maria said, "It's 14.30. Is that good?"

"For this horse, it is," said Mary. "Anything in the fourteens is a good run. Now give me the watch, and let's see what you can do."

"Okay," said Maria.

"Don't forget to lean with Toby. You've got to feel him sit up just before the turn."

"Yes, ma'am."

"I'm not a ma'am. I'm Mary."

"Okay. I'm sorry, Mary," said Maria. Maria headed down the alley, then turned and came out running on Toby. They headed for the first barrel. Toby sat up, and Maria felt it. They came out of the turn on the first barrel and headed to the second. She felt Toby sat up again. They popped out the turn on the second barrel. They headed for the third. Toby was wide open. Maria waited for it. She felt him sitting up for the big turn. They nailed it. Toby charged back home with Maria lying on the saddle horn.

"Yo-ho-ho!" said Mary. "Way to go, Maria. Great ride. That's the way you're supposed to ride. A 13.70, that's a money ride. I don't care where you are. Good job! Okay, let's get that other horse, and we will see what she will do. Here, take the watch."

Mary went and got the other horse. Maria set up where she was before. Mary came down the alley at a full run. When she passed Maria, she pushed the button. Mary made her run, and as she came back, Maria pushed the button again. Maria said, "A 14.10, Mary."

"That's good," said Mary. "These horses are ready to go home."

Mary and Maria rode out of the arena. Maria started brushing down the first horse. Mary unsaddled the second horse and brushed him down. They put them up and fed them. Mary reached over and hugged Maria. "Good job, cowgirl, good job." Mary got out Bob and saddled him up. She got on him, and Maria got back on Toby. They both headed out of the stables; they rode to Mary's house.

Mary stopped at her house and got off. "Here, hold Bob," she told Maria. "I'll be right back." Mary went in the house. In a little while, she came out with two sacks and two canteens. She put the sacks in her saddlebags and hung the canteens on her saddle horn. Mary climbed back on Bob. "Let's go," said Mary.

They rode on by the house to the falls and then down the creek. It was a beautiful day, not to hot, just right. They came to an opening there by the creek. Mary stopped Bob. "Okay, let's eat," said Mary. They both got off their horses. Mary got the canteens and sacks off Bob. "Just take the bridle off and hang it on the saddle horn," said Mary, "and turn him loose. He won't go far. We will let them eat too." The girls found a clean place to sit and started eating their sandwiches and chips.

"It's nice here," said Maria.

"I know," said Mary. "I love it back here. No noises other than nature sounds." She lay back on the ground. Then Maria lay back too. The clouds looked like big puffy pillows. Some shaped like animals, and some shaped like objects.

After a while, they got up and caught the horses. "Since we are back this far, let's go check on Nelly," said Mary. They rode to the gate of the mama cows' pasture. Mary opened it, and they both rode in.

"Where are they at?" asked Maria.

"We will have to find them," said Mary.

They rode off across the pasture, Mary calling for Nelly. After about thirty minutes of riding, they saw the herd and Nelly. Mary whistled, and Nelly looked and came running to her. Mary got off Bob and walked over and hugged Nelly's neck. "Hi, sweetheart," said Mary. "How are you?" Nelly was so fat. "Pasture life looks good on you, girl," said Mary. She and Nelly just stood there for a while as Mary rubbed her all over. "Well, see you later, girl. We've got to go," said Mary. Nelly turned and walked back to the herd as Mary got back on Bob.

The girls turned and headed back to the gate. Mary opened it again, and they rode out. Then they started back up the valley. As they rode along, Maria said, "That was a nice ride."

"Yep," said Mary.

They got back to the stables midafternoon. They unsaddled the horses and brushed them down. They put them up and fed them.

Maria said, "See you in a little while." And she started walking home.

Mary said, "Okay." She got on her four-wheeler and headed home.

Mary walked into the house. Sitting on the bar was a big cake with a horse on it and "Happy Sweet Sixteen, Mary." Mary took her finger and scooped up some of the icing around the bottom and stuck it in her mouth.

"Get away from that cake," said Kattie. Mary just smiled as she headed to her room.

Mary took a shower, then put on her bathing suit. She put on shorts and a T-shirt over it. Mary went back into the kitchen area. She picked up the phone and called the owners of the two barrel horses. She told them that their horses were ready to go and they could come get them.

Kathy and Tommie were the first to show up. Mary asked Tommie, "When are you going to come ride Buddy?"

"Well, I have to go to that dang kindergarten school every day. Mama won't come and get me so I can come with her."

"Kathy," said Mary, "you better stop being mean to this baby girl."

"I'll bring her Monday afternoon," said Kathy, "but you will have to watch her."

"That's fine," said Mary. "Oh, guess what, Tommie."

"What?" asked Tommie.

"I have a new puppy at the stables."

"Goody," said Tommie.

Jim and Troy showed up. They went out back and lit the grill. Pete and Alice came up as Kattie started getting the burgers ready to grill. Pete went out back with the men, and Alice started slicing tomatoes for the burgers. Billie had her own room now, like Rose. They both came out of their rooms. Selena and Maria showed up.

"Where's Paul?" asked Mary.

"He'll be here in a little while," said Rose. About that time, Paul knocked on the door. Rose walked over and let him in. She gave him a big kiss.

"Gross," said Mary. Paul headed out back too. Rose followed him.

Kattie had taken all the tickets and confirmations for their trip and put them in an envelope for Mary's birthday. Jim started throwing the burgers on the grill while he and the other men stood there talking. Rose came back in the house and reported that the burgers were on the grill. Kattie, Kathy, and Alice started taking all the condiments out back. Mary had said she wanted homemade ice cream for her birthday, so Troy had the mixer going.

Kattie opened the back door. "Okay, girls, come on, let's eat." Mary, Billie, Selena, Maria, and Tommie headed outside. They all started sitting down at the big table as Jim was taking up the burgers.

Once everything was on the table, Troy said the blessing and then said, "Let's eat."

The men sat back while the women and kids fixed their plates. Once they were finished, the men fixed their plates. After mostly everyone had finished eating, Kattie told Mary, "You said no presents. So this is for me, you, Billie, and your dad." Kattie handed Mary the envelope.

Mary slowly opened it and started pulling out the papers. She started reading them out loud. Mary said, "Vegas National Finals, yes!" She got up and hugged her mom and dad, then showed them to Billie. "We are going to Vegas, Billie."

Billie smiled. "Oh my god, this is great."

Tommie said, "Now can we go swimming?"

Mary, Billie, and Maria jumped up and said, "Let's go."

After a while, Rose and Selena joined the girls in the pool. They all swam until after dark, then got out for cake and ice cream. Everything was so good, and Mary enjoyed her birthday. She was so excited about the family trip.

Monday, the owners of the barrel horses came and picked up their horses. Mary got out the roping horse. Now that she knew about the trip, she was ready to get through with training for a little while. She took the horse into the arena. She roped one of the metal posts at the bucking chutes. She made the horse back up and tighten the rope. She then walked him to the post, rolled up her rope, and pulled it off the post. She loped him around the arena, then roped the post again, backing him up until the rope was tight. She repeated it about ten times. She unsaddled him and let him rest until Jim got there. Jim put his saddle on him. Troy came down to help with the calves. Jim worked the horse for about an hour. The horse was doing good backing up on his own.

"Well, what do you think?" asked Mary.

"I think after next week, he will be ready to go."

Mary and Jim worked with the horse the whole next week. By Friday, the horse was ready. He was in full auto mode—watching the calf and leaving the corner on his own, keeping the rope tight after the calf was caught. "Only one more thing to do," said Jim. "Go call the owner and see if he can come tomorrow. We will work with him and the horse awhile, then he can take him home."

The man came the next day Saturday. They both worked with him and the horse. Troy came and ran the chute and loaded the calves. After about five runs, Jim called. "Good, I think you're both ready," said Jim to the man. The man paid Mary and loaded up his horse.

"If you have any trouble, just let me know," said Mary. The man pulled out with his horse. Mary gave her dad a high five.

"What now?" asked Jim.

"Now we break a filly and get ready for Vegas."

Chapter 7

Viva Las Vegas

Kattie, Jim, Billie, and Mary walked into the plane to fly to Vegas and found their seats. Jim was the only one of them that had ever flown before. Kattie, Billie, and Mary were fine until the plane started moving, headed for the runway. They all tensed up a little, and when the plane started going down the runway with the engine revved up, they held their breath. Jim started laughing at the look on their faces. Kattie grabbed his leg. Billie and Mary were holding hands as the plane left the ground. "Oh, shit," said Kattie as Jim laughed harder. Once the plane leveled out, they took a breath and started calming down. Kattie hit Jim in the chest for laughing at them. "It's not funny," she said. "I thought I was going to have a heart attack, you ass."

The plane made it to Vegas and landed. They were so glad when it stopped moving. They made their way off the plane and into the terminal. They found their luggage and headed outside. Kattie paid for an airport shuttle to take them to their motel. She had reserved a suite with two bedrooms and four queen beds. The girls sat at the window of the main room and stared out. They were amazed at all the big buildings and all the people on the street. After Kattie got everything unpacked and put away, she said, "Let's go walk down the street and find a restaurant to eat at."

They took off out of the room. The girls liked the elevators, but not the plane. As they walked out of the hotel lobby on the sidewalks, they were in awe. As they walked down the sidewalk, wading through the sea of people, Kattie took the girls' hands. Jim said, "Here's a place. Let's eat here." He opened the door and let Kattie and the girls walk in first. "Table for four, please," said Jim as the receptionist walked up. She grabbed menus and led them to a table.

Jim pulled out Kattie's chair. The girls just sat down on their own and grabbed a menu. Everything was so nice.

Unbeknownst to them until they looked at the menu, this was an Italian restaurant. Mary said, "I can't pronounce these words, but it looks good in the picture."

Billie said, "Mary, look, spaghetti and meatballs."

"That's what I want," said Mary.

"Me too," said Billie, "with salad and bread."

"What about you, Kattie?" asked Jim.

"I think I'll get the shrimp alfredo with salad and bread."

"Okay," said Jim, "I'll get the lasagna with salad and bread."

After they were through eating, they went back out onto the sidewalk. "Come on," said Kattie as she grabbed Billie and Mary's hands. "Let's find our way back to the hotel." Jim followed them as they took off up the sidewalk. Once they made it to the hotel, they went into the lobby. Mary and Billie grabbed a handful of pamphlets of things to do there.

They all rested a little while, then it was time to head to the arena for the first night of the finals. Kattie called for a shuttle bus to come take them to the arena. The bus took them right up to the gate. As they got out, Kattie paid and then told him, "We will need you back when it's over."

"Yes, ma'am," said the driver. "I'll be right here when you come out."

Kattie showed their tickets. They gave each one of them wristbands to wear for the whole event. They went up into the stands; the arena had a roof over it. They found their seats; it was nice and cool inside the arena. The rodeo was about to start. The announcer had everyone stand up for a word of prayer. Then the grand entry started. Some of the riders were carrying American flags. As they circled the arena, they played the national anthem, then they stopped as everyone said the Pledge of Allegiance to the flag. Then they all rode out.

The announcer welcomed everyone to the National Finals Rodeo. The announcer said, "We have five finalists tonight in the barrel racing event. First up, Ms. Jane Harper, folks." Jane came out fast. She ran through her pattern. "A 14.00," said the announcer. "Next, Ms. Cristy Jones. Go, Cristy." She came out of the alley and made her run. "A 14.10, folks. Now Ms. Sara Taylor." Sara made her run. "A 14.15," said the announcer. "Next, Ms. Carmon Houser." She came out and landed the first two barrels, but she turned too close on the third and knocked it over. "A 14.45 plus 5.00," said the announcer. "Too bad. Okay, folks, last but not least, this little lady was the last to qualify, Ms. Jamie Spears. Folks, this little lady has had horse troubles for the last couple of years, but she has a good one now. Come on, Jamie, show them what you've got." Jamie came flying out of the alley. She made the first then the second barrel.

Mary stood up. "Go, Blue Boy, go!" yelled Mary as she turned the third.

Billie stood up. "Go, boy, go!" yelled Billie.

"A 13.80, folks. For Ms. Spears and her horse Blue Boy, give them a hand, folks. They are the leaders going into tomorrow night."

"Next, folks, we are moving to the south end of the arena for some calf roping. We also have five finalists for this event." Paul was one of the finalists in this event; he got a 6.85 for second place.

"Next, let's go back to the north end for some saddle bronc riding." After that, they went back to the other end for team roping, steer wrestling, and breakaway roping.

"Now, folks, if you will look at the chutes, we are about to see some bareback riding. Coming out of chute number 3 is the top-money winner this season. All he needs is to place in this event, and he will be your new world champion bareback rider. Okay, here he comes, Mr. Paul Plumber." The chute opened, and out jumped the horse. Paul spurred the horse as he jumped and bucked. The buzzer went off. The pickup men rode up beside him, and he crossed over. "Okay, folks," said the announcer, "this should be a good score. A 92.00 ride, folks."

After the event, the closest score was an 89.50. The clowns came out to get ready for the bull riding. While they were getting the bulls ready, the clowns were telling jokes and acting silly. They all watched the bull riding and then started trying to get out, along with thousands of other people. They finally made it out. Their bus was waiting. They jumped in and took off.

Mary said, "I think tomorrow night, we should leave as the bull riding starts."

"You might be right," said Jim. "It's crazy trying to get out of there."

Kattie said, "And your horse Blue Boy got the fastest time."

"He should have," said Billie. "Blue Boy is the third-fastest barrel horse I've ever seen."

"Who's the first and second?" asked Kattie.

"Bob and Toby," said Mary. "Maria got a 13.80 on Toby the other day, and she is a new rider."

They made it back to the hotel. The sidewalks were still full at eleven thirty at night.

The next morning, they all went downstairs to the hotel restaurant for breakfast. After breakfast, they went out sightseeing before the crowds came out.

By noon, they were back at the hotel and in their room. When it was time to head back to the arena, Kattie called for the shuttle bus again. That was what they called it, but really, it wasn't a bus, just a van with three rows of seats. The van took them to the front gate again. As they got out, the driver said, "I'll be here when it's over."

"Okay, thanks," said Kattie as they went through the gate and showed their armbands.

They made their way back to their seats. They were still dragging the arena. The stands were filling up fast. "I never knew there were this many people in the world," said Billie.

"Me neither," said Mary.

People were pouring in through the hole in the stand like ants coming out of a giant anthill. Things finally settled down, and the announcer welcomed everyone. They did the grand entry, the prayer, the national anthem, and the Pledge of Allegiance. "It's time for barrel racing, folks," said the announcer. "Ms. Jamie Spears is your first rider tonight. Come on, Jamie." She came out of the alley flying again. She made a clean run. "A 13.90," said the announcer. (Jane got a 13.98, Jones got a 14.00, Sara got a 14.03, and Carmon got a 14.12). "Ms. Jamie Spears is still your leader, folks," said the announcer.

They moved on to the calf roping event. Paul got second last night in this event. Paul was roping last tonight. When his turn came, the leading time was 6.80. Paul got 6.10, making him 12.95, good enough for first. After the team roping, steer wrestling, saddle bronc, and breakaway, they started the bareback bronc riding. Paul was in the lead but only needed to place to win the championship. Paul came out of chute number 5, spurring as the horse jumped. The buzzer went off. "Great ride," said the announcer. "Let's see what the score is. Okay, folks, a 95.00-point ride."

As they started getting ready for the bull riding, Kattie, Jim, Billie, and Mary got up and started heading out of the stands. When they got outside, the van was not there yet, then in a few minutes, they saw it coming. They climbed in, and the driver headed to the hotel. Once there, they got out and went inside. They went to their room. Kattie got on the phone and ordered pizza to be delivered to the room. The streets were just too crowded for them to go out.

The next night, the van came again to pick them up and take them to the arena. Once there, they went into the stands and took their seats. "Look, there's Jamie," said Billie. She and Mary went down to talk to her.

"Hi, Jamie," said Mary.

"Hi," said Jamie. "What are yawl doing here?"

"Just watching the show," said Billie. "You're doing great."

"Yes, but it's that horse Mary sold me. He is great."

"I knew he was a good one," said Mary.

"I haven't seen you two on the circuit this year," said Jamie.

"No," said Mary, "we've been too busy this year, and Billie is starting college next semester after she graduates next spring."

"That's great," said Jamie. "What about you, Mary?"

"I'm going to train great horses," said Mary.

"I bet you will," said Jamie. "Well, I got to go get ready."

Mary and Billie went back to their seats. They were playing the national anthem.

The announcer said, "Welcome, everybody. Yawl ready for the World Finals? Okay, let's get it started. The first rider tonight in fifth place is Ms. Carmon Houser. Give a hand, folks." Carmon made her run. "A 14.23," said the announcer. "Next up in fourth place, Ms. Sara Taylor." Sara made her run. "A 14.16," said the announcer. "Now in third place, Ms. Cristy Jones." She made her run. "A 14.03," said the announcer. "Okay, now in second place, Ms. Jane Harper." She made her run. "A 13.98," said the announcer. "Now in first place, Ms. Jamie Spears." Jamie and Blue Boy made their run. "A 13.78. And the winner of this event, Ms. Jamie Spears, on her new horse Blue Boy! Yawl give them a hand. Ladies and gentlemen, your 1993 World Barrel Racing Champion, Ms. Jane Harper."

"Well, that ain't no surprise," said Billie. "She does more rodeoing than anybody else."

Now it was time for calf roping. Paul had taken the lead for the event, but not the championship. Paul got a 5.90, sealing his win and getting him a check. After the other events, all that was left was the bareback and the bull riding events. Paul made his ride and scored an 86.50, making him not only the event winner but also the world champion bareback bronc rider. Paul now had the money he needed to start his horse ranch.

Mary was ready to get home; so was Billie. But they were not looking forward to getting back on that plane.

"Hey, Dad," said Mary. "Aren't you ready for a smaller truck?"

"I don't know. Maybe. Why?"

"Well, we can buy you a new one-half- or three-fourth-ton crew cab here and drive it home. I'll take the one-ton truck for the stables."

"Wait," said Kattie.

"Mom, do you really want to get back on that airplane?" Jim started laughing.

"No, not really," said Kattie, "but it's a long way by vehicle."

"Wait now," said Jim. "You mean you'd rather buy me a new truck than fly back home?"

"Yes!" said the girls in unison.

"Sounds good to me," said Jim. "Let's go find me a truck."

Kattie called the shuttle. The van met them out front of the hotel. "Where to?" asked the driver.

"To a car dealer or truck dealer."

"Okay," said the driver.

Jim and Kattie picked out the truck they liked, a three-fourth-ton crew cab with all the bells and whistles, automatic, A/C, FM/AM cassette player, and leather seats. Kattie wrote the dealer a check, and they headed back to the hotel.

The next morning, they loaded their luggage in the back of the truck and headed out. Kattie and the girls were so excited they would get to see sights they had never seen before. Mary told Kattie, "When we get home, find out how much Dad's truck is worth, and I'll write you a check. Sara says that the stables need to spend a little money before the end of the year anyway."

"What about that trailer you and Billie had to have?"

"We still need it. We might go back to rodeoing one day."

"Well, buy it from me."

"I'll have to think about that," said Mary.

"And I'll have to think about letting you use it next time you need it," said Kattie.

"Oh, okay," said Mary, "you win. I'll buy it too."

"Well, thank you," said Kattie.

"Thank yawl for my new truck. I love it. So fancy and clean," said Jim. "So what's your next project, Mary?"

"Well, I need to start breaking that filly," said Mary.

"Yep, that's going to be a nice horse one day."

"Oh, and I need to go get my driver's license next week," said Mary.

"Can you drive?" asked Billie.

"No, but Dad's going to teach me."

"I am," said Jim.

"Yep."

"Not in this truck," said Jim. "You need to learn to drive your one-ton."

"That's fine," said Mary. "Then I can drive you everywhere since you're getting so old now." Kattie and Billie laughed.

"Oh my lord," said Jim.

Well, they finally made it home. Everything was still standing. Troy came over as they were unloading. "Well, how did it go?" he asked Jim.

"Good," said Jim. "I got me a new truck out of the deal."

"How did you do that?"

Jim laughed. "The girls didn't like flying at all. Watching their faces as that plane took off, that was some funny shit. I laughed so hard it hurt."

"You hurt because Mom hit you," said Billie.

"So they bought me a truck to keep from flying back, but we had fun. Way too many people in one town for us though," said Jim.

"Yep, I went one time in my rodeo days. I didn't like it much either," said Troy. "Well, everything went good here. No problems. That woman Selena whom Mary hired is a go-getter. She and that girl got the stables spotless everywhere."

"Good," said Jim. "Mary will be happy about that. Oh, by the way, Mary needs somebody to teach her how to drive," Jim told Troy.

"Nope, not me," said Troy. "If she drives like she rides a horse wide open, I ain't riding with her."

Jim laughed. "Well, then this might be fun."

"It will be something. I don't know about fun," said Troy.

The next day, Mary started working with the filly in the round pen. She wore her down, then waited for the filly to come to her. The filly walked her way, but when Mary reached out to touch her, the filly turned back. So Mary ran her some more until she started licking her lips, then she let her stop and wait. The horse dropped her head and started walking to Mary as she stuck out her hand. The horse walked right up where Mary could touch her face. Mary rubbed her nose, then grabbed her halter. "Come on, little girl, that's enough for today." Mary put her up.

Chapter 8

The Colts

Jim came to the stables in the one-ton truck. "Come on, Mary, let's go riding."

"Okay, Dad," said Mary.

Jim got out and walked around to the passenger side and got back in. Mary got behind the steering wheel. Mary had driven a little, backing up a trailer and moving them out of the way, but never on the highway. "Okay," said Jim, "let's go to the falls.

"Sure," said Mary as she cranked the truck and backed out. She turned and headed down the driveway and drove past the house and down the wagon trail, as they called it. It was the truck trail now, but it did follow the same route as the old wagon trail. Once they got to the falls, Mary turned around and headed back, but then she drove right past the stables and out to the highway.

"Wait," said Jim. "What are you doing?"

"Going to get gas," said Mary.

"Oh, shit," said Jim as Mary took off down the highway.

"It's okay, Dad," said Mary as she laughed.

Mary drove the truck like she had been driving all her life. She pulled up to the pumps at a store in Lead, South Dakota. She got out and filled up the truck, both tanks. She walked into the store. Jim followed her into the store. Mary got herself a Coke and some peanuts; Jim got coffee. They walked to the counter. Mary said, "Just put it on Mama's account." And she signed the ticket.

As they got in the truck, Jim said, "Your mom's going to be mad."

"Why?" asked Mary. "You got a full tank of gas when you bought your truck. I just got mine." And she laughed. She cranked the truck up, and they headed back home.

The next week, Mary got here license, and she and her mom made their deal for the truck and trailer. Mary said, "I guess that covered the cost of Dad's truck." Kattie just smiled.

Mary was working with the filly everyday now. She had the filly where she came to her when she called her name. Mary let Tommie name the filly; she named her Diamond Girl. Jim came by the stables while Mary was working the filly. She was lying on the filly's back while walking her around in the round pen. Jim watched; he could see that Mary was talking to the filly but couldn't hear what she was saying. But he could tell the horse was listening to her. Jim walked up to the round pen.

"Hi, Dad," said Mary, "What you doing?"

"Just watching you," said Jim. "Why are you lying on her back like that?"

"Well, that's how I break a horse. By lying on them, I can feel it if they tense up and react before they jump or buck. It's also easier for me to get off and out of the way. I don't believe in letting a horse buck or jump with you on it. If she does, I'll run her in here until she doesn't want to anymore. Same results as bucking out one, just less chance of me or the horse getting hurt," said Mary.

"So what were you telling the filly as you lay on her back?" asked Jim.

Mary laughed. "I told her that if she throws me off, I will run her butt into the ground."

Mary worked her a little longer, then put her up and fed her. Mary worked with the filly every day for two weeks. She saddled her, put her foot in the stirrup, and lay across the saddle to get the filly used to her stepping up and putting weight on one side, never throwing her leg across the filly's back. The filly was still too young to ride. Mary was just getting her ready and making her easy to handle.

The next day, Mary saddled up Bob, then she saddled the filly and put a long lead rope on her. She led them out and climbed on Bob, holding the filly's lead rode. She wrapped the lead rope around her saddle horn and started walking Bob. At first, the filly pulled back and locked her legs; she didn't know about this other horse leading her. It was something new. Bob just dragged her along as she pulled back. Finally, she gave up and started walking as Mary headed to the falls. Occasionally, the filly would lock up, but Bob just pulled her along. By the time they got to the house, the filly had stopped fighting Bob and was following along behind him. Mary stopped at the house and tied Bob to the hitching post and tied the filly to the saddle horn. Mary got off and walked back to the filly. She rubbed her nose and talked to her. Mary then went inside. She got two apples and a canteen.

"Where are you headed?" asked Kattie.

"Down to the falls," said Mary, "with Bob and the filly."

"How is she doing?" asked Kattie.

"She's okay, a little hardheaded, but not as hardheaded as me," said Mary as she walked out.

Mary untied Bob and climbed on and started back out. The filly would still try to lock up and hold Bob every so often, but Bob just kept walking on. By the time they got to the falls, the filly's neck muscles were so sore from pulling that she wouldn't let the lead rope get tight at all. Once at the falls, Mary stopped and got off. She gave Bob an apple and then walked back to the filly. Mary took a big bite of the other apple, then held the piece in her palm and put it up to the filly's lips. The filly licked it, then took it from Mary's hand and chewed it up. Mary gave her another piece and gave Bob the rest, then climbed on Bob. They headed back to the stables. As they walked along, the filly kept slack in the lead rope. She never tried pulling back again.

Just before they got back to the house, Mary and Bob started trotting. The filly started trotting too. Then Bob went into a slow lope, and so did the filly. As they came back by the house loping, the filly was keeping slack in the rope and running. Kattie was watching through the window as they came by. The filly was now broken to lead by another horse.

They went to the stables. Mary unsaddled the filly and brushed her down. She then put some liniment on her neck and put her up. Mary then unsaddled Bob, brushed him down, and put him up. She gave him some treats. She went two stalls down and let Buddy out. She went inside the office and got a handful of horse treats. She came back out and gave them to Buddy one at a time. Maria came walking up and started rubbing on Buddy. Mary said, "Why don't you saddle up Buddy and go for a ride?"

"Sure," said Maria. She took Buddy by his halter and led him around to the alleyway.

The next day, Mary and Bob led the filly back down to the falls. The rope never got tight. She let the filly and Bob graze for a while as she lay in the grass and listened to the falls. Summer was about over; it was already getting cold at night. Time just seemed to go by so fast. Next year, at this time, Billie would be gone to college and Rose might be married. She would be all alone in the house with Kattie and Jim. Mary got up and called the horses. She climbed back on Bob, and they headed back to the stables.

Well, it was Monday again. Billie came home after work with Tommie. She let Tommie out at the stables. "I came to ride my horse," said Tommie.

"Well, it's about time," said Mary.

"Come help me saddle him," said Tommie.

"You go find Maria and get her to help you. Just ride him in the arena," said Mary.

"Okay," said Tommie. "You're not going to watch me ride?"

"Yes, I'll be out there in a few minutes. Just go get ready," said Mary. Mary went out just as Maria finished saddling Buddy. She led him into the arena as Tommie was jabbering. She helped Tommie get on the horse. Tommie rode him around the arena and then started running the barrels.

Jim came up. "What you doing?"

"Oh, just watching Tommie ride Buddy. What are you doing?" asked Mary.

"Well, I wanted to see if you had time to work a colt."

"Sure," said Mary. "Whose colt is it?"

"Aaron's, my ranch foreman. He bought this colt from a friend of his, a beautiful buckskin. He's is two years old, and he has been cut, but this horse is as dumb as a rock. Aaron has been trying to break him for two months now. He is broke to lead, and he can saddle him up, but if you go get on him, he goes nuts. He has broken two saddle trees by falling back on them. He'll rear up and just fall over backward. He asked me to talk to you a few weeks ago, but I was afraid this horse would hurt you, but after watching you with your filly, I see you know how to be safe."

"Okay," said Mary, "but it might take a while, and I'm not cheap."

"I know. I told him. But the horse is not worth anything the way he is now."

"Okay, bring him on."

The next day, Jim took Mary's truck and trailer to the Montana ranch with him. That afternoon, after Mary got out of school, he brought her the horse. "What's his name?" asked Mary.

"Bucket Head is what Aaron has been calling him," said Jim.

"That's not a name," said Mary. "He's a buckskin, so I'll name him Bucket."

"That's good," said Jim. "Aaron will like that, Bucket."

"All right, let's put him in a stall," said Mary.

After they put him up, Jim got in his truck and went home.

"Selena!" yelled Mary.

"Yes."

She walked up to the stall where Selena was at. "Don't get in the stall with this one until I figure him out," said Mary.

"Okay," said Selena.

"Where is Maria?" asked Mary.

"In the tack room."

"Okay, tell her to come. I'm taking you and her to town."

Mary got in the one-ton, turned it around, and backed it into its parking spot. Selena and Maria came out and helped her unhook the trailer. They all got in the truck. Mary headed out of the driveway.

"Are we going to Lead?" asked Maria.

"No, to Rapid City," said Mary.

"Why?" asked Selena.

"To get yawl and me some new winter clothes."

"Yeah," said Maria.

When they got to the clothing store, Mary bought the three of them new coats, coveralls, gloves, lined work boots, and insulated caps. Then she got the three of them some more jeans, flannel shirts, and long handle underwear. Mary paid for everything, and they loaded it in the truck.

On their way home, Selena told Mary, "Thank you so much."

"You're welcome," said Mary. "You wouldn't be getting much work done this winter if you're frozen."

The next afternoon after school, Mary started working with the new horse. She went in his stall with a pocket full of treats. She gave him a treat, then started brushing him and talking to him in a low, relaxed tone. She gave him another treat and picked up all four feet, then brushed him some more. Another treat and she brushed out his tail and mane, talking to him the whole time. She watched the horse's hind feet as she brushed and talked. Once he relaxed and took the weight off one hind foot, she knew she had him.

"Now, Bucket, tell me what's bothering you. You're such a pretty boy," said Mary as she gave him another treat. She brushed and talked to him for about an hour. She hugged his neck and kissed his face. Then she went out of the stall and latched it; he followed her to the gate and stuck his head out. "We will play some more tomorrow, Bucket," said Mary as she gave him the last treat.

The next afternoon, Mary put Bucket in the round pen and worked him for a while. Every time she let him stop, he would walk over to her and stand. She would rub him and talk to him; she gave him a treat, then ran him some more.

The next day, Mary put Bucket back in the round pen and worked him some more. She walked over to the side rails and let him stop. He turned and walked over to her. She rubbed his face and gave him a treat. Mary then climbed up on the round pen rails and eased onto his back and lay down with no saddle or anything. For a while, she just lay there still, talking to him and rubbing his sides. When she felt him relax one hind foot, she then slid off him slow and easy. She gave him another treat. "Good boy," she said, "good boy." Mary opened the gate and walked out as Bucket followed her to his stall. He walked in, and Mary closed and latched the gate behind him. He turned, and she gave him another treat.

The next day, she put him back in the round pen and worked him awhile. Again, she stood by the rails and let him stop. He walked over to her, and she gave him a treat. She climbed up the rails and eased onto his back and lay down. This time, it only took a few minutes, and the horse relaxed. Mary said, "Good boy." She then said, "Come on, boy." She gently popped his behind. Bucket started walking around the round pen. After a couple of rounds, Mary told him whoa, and he stopped. She slid off him easy and slow. Mary put him in the side lot to graze for the rest of the afternoon. Just before dark, she put him up in his stall and fed him. She told him, "Tomorrow we ride."

The next day was Saturday. Mary started early. Kathy was going to be there in case she needed help. She got Bucket out and saddled him up. She put him in the round pen and worked him for a while with his saddle on. Kathy showed up. "Well, how is he doing?"

"He's okay. He just needs training now," said Mary. "You ready to watch me?"

"Yep," said Kathy.

"Okay, here goes nothing." She put her foot in the stirrup, grabbed the saddle horn, and started easing up. Mary just had her toes in the stirrup and was ready to jump if she needed to. She eased up and put her full weight on the stirrup, saying, "Easy, boy, it's okay, easy." Then she swung her other leg over the saddle and sat. She put her other foot in the stirrup. Bucket just stood there. "Good boy," she said. No one else had ever sat on this horse. He knew nothing about raining or anything else. Mary just sat still until Bucket relaxed. "Now that wasn't so bad," said Mary. "Okay, Kathy, get that quirt and come inside."

Mary was rubbing his neck and talking. "See if you can get him to start walking around the pen."

Kathy walked up close to his behind. She laid the quirt on his rump and said, "Let's go, boy." Bucket started walking.

Mary said, "Okay, keep him going." After about three rounds to the left, Mary turned him. Kathy waved the quirt in front of him as he turned. Mary reined him. After one round to the right, Kathy turned him back to the left. Mary reined him again. Mary got him to loping. "Now," said Mary, and Kathy turned him. Mary reined him again. "Okay, stop him." Kathy stepped in front of him with her hands up as Mary pulled back on the reins. He stopped. "Good boy," said Mary as she rubbed his neck. "Okay, let me see if I can make him go."

Mary smacked her lips and said "Get up" and kicked him all at the same time. He started loping around the pen. Mary reined him back the other way, then made a lope around and turned him again. She stopped him, eased out of the saddle, and walked to his head. Bucket was breathing hard. She gave him a treat and rubbed his face. "Good boy," said Mary, then gave him another treat.

"That's pretty good," said Kathy.

"Yep," said Mary. "Monday, I'll put him in the arena and work him on some poles." Mary opened the gate and led him out into the alley and unsaddled him and brushed him down.

Kathy said, "Well, I'm going to go to the barn. I'll see you later."

"Okay," said Mary. "Thanks."

Mary got in her truck and drove to the house for lunch. Kattie said, "Hi, baby, what's up?"

"I'm hungry," said Mary.

"I've got leftover pork chops from last night."

"Yeah, that will be good," said Mary.

"So what's going on at the stables?"

"Not much," said Mary. "I've about done all I can do with my filly until she gets bigger. But Dad brought in a two-year-old gelding that belongs to Aaron. I've been working with him. I guess I'll have to buy me a couple more horses to work with. I made good money on the last two."

"Yes, you did. Here, baby," said Kattie as she set down Mary's plate.

"How is Dad?" asked Mary. "I don't see him much anymore."

"He is gone. Ever since we got him that truck, all he wants to do is drive somewhere." Mary laughed. "He plans to help Troy again this year on the roundup."

"That's good," said Mary. "When is it?"

"In three weeks, I think," said Kattie.

"Well, I need to go get Nelly just before the roundup and bring her home," said Mary.

"Have you seen her since we turned her out?" asked Kattie.

"Yes, she is as fat as she can be. Maria and I checked on her a few weeks ago." Mary finished eating.

"What are you going to do now?" asked Kattie.

"I think I'll go swimming. It might be my last chance before winter," said Mary.

"I think I'll go with you. That sounds good. And then I'll just lay out," said Kattie.

"Well, let's go."

When Billie got home, she came out to join Kattie and Mary. They swam and lay around the pool all afternoon.

Jim came home and walked out by the pool. "What's for supper?"

"Whatever you feel like cooking," said Kattie with a smile.

"Good, then we are going out to eat."

"Yeah," said the girls.

Monday afternoon, Mary had Maria saddle up Toby, and she saddled up Bucket. They walked them into the arena and closed the back gate. Maria got on Toby. Mary eased up on Bucket and swung over onto the saddle. Mary had the poles set up in the arena. "Okay, Maria, you and Toby go first. Not fast, just a short lope."

Maria started. She went zigzagging through the poles, then turned and came back.

"Now let's see if Bucket will do that." Mary got him started around the first pole. He turned opposite on the next. Bucket was trying to zig when he should zag, but they made it to the other end. Mary turned and started back. He did a little better coming back. "Okay, Maria, do it again." Maria started as Bucket and Mary watched her and Toby zig and zag through the poles, perfectly timing every turn. Then they turned and made their way back. Mary said, "See, Bucket, it's not that hard." Mary and Bucket started again. They wove through the poles. "That's it," said Mary. "Good boy." At the other end, they headed back, zigging and zagging. "Good boy," said Mary. She reached down and gave him a treat, then gave one to Maria to give to Toby. "Okay, Maria, run it." Maria took off running as she and Toby zigzagged through the course, then turned and came back. Mary lined up, and she and Bucket ran the course, not as fast as Toby but he ran. Mary said, "Okay, tomorrow we run barrels."

"Okay," said Maria.

They got off and led the horses to the alleyway. Both horses were soaking wet with sweat. They unsaddled them, then brushed them down and put them up.

The next afternoon, Mary took down the poles and put up the barrels. Mary took Bucket and walked him around the barrels. Then Mary had Maria run them at about half speed as she and Bucket watched. Then she walked the first two, then run him around the third barrel and run him back. Maria ran them again at half speed. Mary went back down the alley and ran Bucket out into the arena and around the first barrel, then the second, and then the third barrel and made him run full out coming home. "Good boy," said Mary as she gave him a treat.

"That was good," said Maria. "That was fast on the way back."

"Yes, he was," said Mary. "Okay, tomorrow we work cows."

"Cows?" asked Maria. "How do you do that?"

"You will learn how tomorrow," said Mary.

The next afternoon, Maria and Mary got both horses ready. Mary got Troy to put three calves in the arena. Mary and Maria rode into the arena. Mary said, "The idea is to get the calves in the corner and hold them there. They are going to try and get out by you. The trick is to keep them in the corner."

"Okay," said Maria. Mary and Maria got behind the calves and moved slow, pushing them into one corner. Once the calves realized that they were trapped, they turned and tried to run back out. Mary and Maria cut them off and pushed them back. "I see now," said Maria. Toby had worked cows before. Bucket was not sure what them critters were, but working with Toby, he saw what Mary was trying to do. Bucket started watching the calves as they tried to find a way out. One calf made a break for it. Bucket wheeled around and cut it off. Before long, all Mary had to do was just sit on him.

"Bucket is a natural cow horse," said Mary. "He has the instincts."

After about an hour, the horses were soaked with sweat and breathing hard. Mary and Maria stopped and let them cool off as they walked them around the arena. "Good job, Bucket," said Mary.

"You too, Toby, Maria said. "I liked that. Working cow is a lot of fun."

"It can be," said Mary, "but in a big herd, it gets intense sometimes, with cows bumping into you and your horse. There's a lot of noise too, but some horses just have it in their blood. I think Bucket is one of them. Toby started out as a cow horse, but Billie made a barrel horse out of him."

Mary continued, "Okay, let's try some roping and see how he does there." Mary got two ropes. She gave one to Maria. "Okay, find your loop, like this here. Slide it out to make the loop bigger. These are called breakaway ropes. You hook that small loop over your saddle horn, then when you rope the calf and it tightens the rope, that strip will break apart. Now let me try swinging this rope over Bucket's head. He may not like this." Mary took the tail end of the rope and run it between his ears. Bucket just shook his head and made it fall. Mary did it again. Bucket did the same. Mary then started swinging the tail of the rope round and round, making a swishing noise. Bucket took a step. "Easy, boy," said Mary as she kept swinging the rope.

After a few minutes, she stopped letting the rope hit his neck. Bucket flinched a little. "Okay, boy," said Mary, "let's try this." Mary hooked the tail of the rope to the saddle horn. She picked out a calf and started chasing it. The calf twisted and turned as it ran. Mary and Bucket stayed on it until Mary got her shot. She threw the rope, and the loop fell around the calf's neck. When the rope got tight, it broke loose. The loop got loose, and the calf ran out of it. Mary stopped, got off, and picked up her rope. As Mary rolled her rope back up. Maria picked her one out like Mary did. She threw her rope but missed. Mary and Bucket ran the calves back to the corner. Mary picked out another one. Bucket fell in behind it and stayed right on its tail. Mary dropped the loop over the calf's neck and pulled back hard on Bucket's bits. He slid to a stop, and the rope got tight and broke. "Good job, Bucket." Mary leaned down and gave him a treat.

Maria tried one more time. She picked one out. Toby got on its tail. She threw the rope. The rope fell over the calf's neck. Toby locked up and slid. The rope got tight and broke away.

"Good job, Maria. I'll make a cowgirl out of you yet." Maria smiled from ear to ear.

Jim came up and heard them talking. He walked around back to the arena. "What are you girls doing?"

"We are playing with calves," said Mary.

"Is that Aaron's horse?" asked Jim.

"Yep, this is him."

"You're kidding me," said Jim.

Mary told Maria, "Do it again." Maria picked out one and got on its tail. She threw her rope, and it fell over the calf's head around its neck. Toby locked up and slid. The rope got tight and broke away.

Jim said, "Good job, Maria."

Mary picked out one and put Bucket on its tail. Mary threw her loop around the calf's neck. Bucket locked up and slid. The rope broke away.

"I can't believe this," said Jim.

Mary said, "Watch this. Come on, Maria, let's pen them calves." Mary and Bucket started down one side and Maria and Toby down the other, slowly pushing the calves to the corner of the pen. As the calves got close to the corner, they tried to turn around. Maria and Toby turned one back on her side, then Mary and Bucket turned the other two. "Just hold them," said Mary to Maria. Each time the calves tried to come out, they turned them back. "Finally," Mary said. "Okay, let's put them in the pen." Mary and Maria pushed the calves right on in the pen, then Maria jumped off and closed the gate. Maria got back on Toby as she rode by Mary. They gave each other a high five.

Jim shook his head.

"Dad," said Mary, "open the gate to the alley, please." Mary got off and set the barrels, then got back on. "Maria, you go first." Maria went down the alley, then turned and came out flying. Toby sat up for the first barrel. Maria shifted her weight as they rounded the barrel and then the second. They flew to the third and nailed it, then headed back. "Way to go, Maria." As Maria came back out of the alley, Mary went down to it, then turned Bucket and headed back. They came out in a full run. Mary shifted as they popped out the other side and then the second barrel. They sped to the third. They zipped around the third barrel and flew back home.

"Oh my god," said Jim, "Aaron is going to flip out over this horse. That's amazing, simply amazing."

Mary said, "Well, I've got a couple more days of work with him. Tell Aaron to come get him next Saturday, or I'm going to keep him. He is a great horse, smart and fast."

"Aaron's not going to believe this."

"Tell him I need to work with him and Bucket for about two hours before he takes him, so come early." Mary and Maria walked their horses to cool them down. They unsaddled them and brushed them down.

Jim walked up to Mary in the alleyway. "I'm so proud of you," said Jim. "You took a useless horse and turned it around, and you took a little girl who had never been on a horse and made her a horse-riding fool." Mary gave Bucket a treat as she put him in his stall. Maria gave two to Toby and put him up. "What now?" asked Jim.

"We feed everything and then go home. Maria, don't forget to feed that puppy."

"I won't."

"I'll put up the tack," said Mary.

Jim was filled with pride. His little girl was a great young woman. She would never be a veterinarian or a lawyer, but she would be well-known for her abilities with horses.

Once everything was fed and watered, Mary told Maria her thanks and gave her a hug. "See you tomorrow."

Jim and Mary drove their trucks to the house. Mary went to her room to get a shower. Jim sat down at the bar. Kattie poured them both some coffee. Jim just sat there, not talking, just seeping his coffee. A small tear ran down his face. Kattie saw it. "What's wrong?" asked Kattie.

"Nothing," said Jim. "That's a happy tear. I am so lucky to have you and my girls, so lucky."

"Well, we are lucky to have you," said Kattie.

"Mary never stopped amazing me," said Jim.

"I guess she got that horse of Aaron's broke and trained," said Kattie.

"So much more," said Jim. "And she took a ten-year-old girl who had never been on a horse and made her… Oh, you would just have to see it."

Aaron came and got his horse.

Mary, Jim, and Troy were going to the sales tonight. Mary wanted to buy a couple of horses to train over the winter and sell next spring. She bought two young horses.

Troy said, "I'd buy all these horses if I could get you to train them for free."

"Well, that's not going to happen," said Mary. "Anyway, you're married to a horse trainer."

"No, I'm married to a horse exerciser and tender. You are the only true horse trainer I've ever met."

The roundup would be in a couple of weeks. Jim and Troy would be gone a few days. Tomorrow Mary was going to find Nelly and bring her home for the winter. She had two new horses to work with this winter and hoped to have them ready next spring. She planned to keep teaching Maria as much as she could over the winter. She seemed to have a real knack with the horses. Maybe one day she could be a barrel racer like Mary.

Chapter 9

Another Roundup

Well, it was roundup time. This year, Troy decided to take Pete along with the cook wagon so Pete could do the cooking for them to save some time. They were loading up the wagon with everything they could think of to take. Jim was so excited to go; he brought his horse from the Montana ranch to take with him. Like last year, they made it to the line cabin before nightfall. Tomorrow they would get the cows off the government land first, then start working their way back. The second night, Pete went on ahead to set up camp and start cooking. Once the herd made it to Pete, they stopped for the night. Pete had cooked a pot of beef stew and made biscuit.

Everybody gathered around the fire to eat. They went to picking at old Jeff about that bear again. Jeff said, "Yawl need a new story to tell. Yawl have worn that one out."

"I know a bear story," said Jim, "supposedly a true story. Now I wasn't there, and I only knew one of the men who was, and he told me this story."

"Let's hear it," said Ben.

"Now the guy who told me the story was named Mark. Now Mark had never been to Colorado, so when the opportunity came, he jumped at it. He had never been anywhere much outside of his home state of Louisiana. He loved to hunt and fish. He became well-known for his outdoor cooking skills. Although he worked in the oil field industry, on his time off, he was grilling and smoking meats or cooking a big pot of gumbo. Mark loved to cook for groups of people and hear them say that it's good.

"He said a local oil tool company was putting together a hunting trip to Colorado for some of their customers. Mark knew one of the men who worked for the company. His name was Bill. Bill was the one planning and organizing the trip and asked Mark if he would come along and be the camp cook. The company was going to fly in customers for a few days at a time and would pay for everything—hunting license, food, alcohol, and transportation. They would set up a large camp area with a cook's tent, a guide's tent, and a large tent for guests."

*****

Mark, Bill, and the eighteen-year-old son of one of the owners, Chase, loaded up all the equipment and supplies in two pickup trucks. One truck had a horse trailer behind it, with a horse and a mule inside. The other truck had a jeep behind it. They headed out going somewhere near Durango, Colorado, the morning of October 10, 1982. The estimated travel time was twenty-six hours driving straight through. Chase's father thought this trip would be a good chance for the boy to get some life experience and get him out from under his mom's coattail. To say he was a mama's boy would be an understatement.

They had to cross the Texas Panhandle, then turn up into Colorado. They traveled all day and all night and then got there around 2:00 p.m. the next day. They went to a campsite where Bill had camped before and started unloading the trucks. They managed to get one of the smaller tents up before dark to sleep in. The next day, they put up the other tents, installed the wood-burning heaters, and gathered firewood. Mark got the cook tent set up on the inside, with stove and supplies, a long table and chairs, and a sleeping cot in one corner.

The weather had been pretty, like clear fall days, but the morning of the fourth day, when they woke up, there was two feet of snow on everything. Their campsite was at 1,200 feet above sea level in the Rocky Mountain, miles from the nearest blacktop road. They soon learned that unlike in Louisiana, when it snows one day, then it's gone the next. In Colorado, when the snow comes, it stays all winter. The next day, the private plane flew into the Bay City Airport. Bill went to the airport to pick them up and bring them to the camp. They got to the camp just before dark. Mark had supper ready when they got there. After they ate, everyone got their cots ready and went to bed. Bill was taking them all on a hunt the next morning to an area he had already explored for elk sign. The next morning, Mark had breakfast ready when the men came in the cook tent, along with sandwiches for lunch that day. The men ate, and then they headed out with Bill on the hunt. That afternoon, they came back in around dark. Again, supper was ready, and they were ready to eat. None of the hunters had any luck that day. The next three days were the same. At the end of the week, Bill took those men back to the airport for their flight home. Bill dropped off three customers and picked up four more at the airport.

Bill and the new group of men made it to camp midafternoon. They unloaded their gear and set up targets and started checking their guns. This group were some serious hunters. There were two .300 Weatherbys and two 7mm rifles in their arsenal. They all worked for the same drilling company and worked together every day. One could tell they were a team. However, they did drink a lot. The next morning, they were up and ready to go while Mark was still cooking breakfast. They ate, then Bill and the four men headed out to hunt. By noon, Bill was back at camp on foot to get the horse and the mule. He told Mark that two of the guys had killed a couple of elks, and he was going back to pack them back to camp. Mark told Chase, "Well, we have meat coming. Looks like we will have elk tonight. Get us some scrub oak firewood and start a fire. We will need a good bed of coals to cook on tonight."

The men all made it back to camp just before dark. They started prepping the meat for storage. They gave Mark a big slab of elk meat to cut into steaks. Mark already had potatoes baking over the fire and a big pot of beans staying warm. Mark cut the meat up into about one-inch-thick steaks and rubbed them down. The men put up the rest of the meat in an ice chest. They packed them with snow. Everybody gathered around the fire as Mark threw the elk steaks on the fire. Each man had a plate ready to get their steak straight off the fire grate. As Mark put their steak on their plates, they got beans and a potato and started to eat. Everyone enjoyed the meal and thanked Mark for a great job.

Everyone was excited that two elk had been killed. Some people hunt for years before they get the chance to take an elk. The two men who killed the elks were very happy but now only had mule deer tags left. The problem now for Bill was that two of the hunters still wanted an elk and the other two now were after mule deer. The mule deer were normally at lower elevations than the elk and bear. Bill had showed Mark a spot back down the mountain where he had killed mule deer in the past. Bill asked Mark if he would take the two men down to that spot the next morning. Bill wanted to stay close to the other two hunters after elk, because once an elk is killed, you don't have long to get it out before a bear shows up. Bears are normally found in the same areas as the elk. The grizzly bear loves elk and moose meat. The mule deer are the prey of the wolves and mountain lions normally, although bears will eat mule deer, mostly brown bears, but grizzles like the bigger prey. Bears are never far away after an elk has been killed. It must be moved within a couple of hours. A grizzly bear can smell fresh blood for over three miles away.

The next morning, Mark took two men down the mountain to hunt, and Bill took the other two to hunt elk. They all came back to camp around dark. Mark got busy prepping for supper. Chase jumped in and helped. As the men sat around the fire, one of the men named Tim told the others that he heard what he thought was a bear grumbling around him today. He also saw some bear clawing signs on an aspen tree near him where he was hunting that day.

Bill said, "Well, you don't need to go back there tomorrow. If a bear got that close to you and wasn't afraid of your scent, that might be a problem. Most bears, like brown bears, will not get close to a man. If they smell him, they will go the other way. But grizzlies sometimes will, if you have entered their area or gotten too close to their young. Either way, it's not a good sign if a bear gets too close to a human."

The next morning, two men went back with Bill, and Mark took the other two back down the mountain. Bill took Tim to a new spot to hunt because of the bear, and Louis went back to where he was the day before. Dave and Carl were with Mark hunting mule deer. Around 9:00 a.m., Carl shot. Mark started his way. When Mark got to him, Carl was standing over a downed mule deer, smiling from ear to ear. "Well, look at you," said Mark, "an elk and a mule deer."

About 10:30 a.m., Tim shot. He was one of the hunters with Bill. Bill headed his way once he heard the shot. When he got to where he had left Tim, he couldn't find him. Bill called out for Tim. No answer. Bill called out again. He took off to get Louis to help him look for Tim. The rule was, if you get in trouble, to fire three times into the air. But no shots had been fired since the one shot Bill heard.

When he got to Louis, Bill said, "Come on, Tim is missing."

Louis jumped up. "What happened?" asked Louis.

"I don't know," said Bill. "I heard Tim shoot, but when I got there, he was gone."

"Okay, let's go," said Louis.

They went through the trees at almost a run back to where Tim was at. Bill and Louis searched the area, calling out Tim's name, but nothing. They found tracks in the snow and had started following them, but the snow was falling fast in big flakes, covering everything. They finally had to turn back before they lost their own track and could not find their way back. They headed back still calling for Tim.

Mark helped Carl get his mule deer loaded up in the back of the truck not knowing about Tim. Mark and Carl sat at the truck and waited for Dave to come out. The snow kept falling harder and harder. Mark was afraid that Dave might not be able to find his way out with all the snow. Mark told Carl, "I am going to get Dave. You stay here. If we get lost, I will fire three shots. You fire back so I can get my bearing."

"Okay," said Carl.

Mark headed out to get Dave. He met Dave about halfway. They turned and headed back to the truck. Carl had the truck running with the heater on. Mark and Dave got in the truck.

"Dang, it's cold out there," said Dave.

"Okay, let's go to camp," said Mark, "and get warmed up."

"Yep, I've got a deer to skin," said Carl.

Bill and Louis searched the area for any sign of Tim. All they found was Tim's bag by a tree. Louis said, "Bill, over here."

Bill went running. On the ground was blood, but they had no way of knowing if it was animal blood or human blood. Bill told Louis, "Let's go to camp and get the other men and the horse." They took off through the woods headed to camp.

When Mark and Carl and Dave got to camp, Bill and Louis were there. Bill was saddling the horse. Mark thought they had another elk to pack out. He walked over to Bill.

"Tim is missing," said Bill.

"What?" asked Mark.

"Grab flashlights and coats. We must go back and find him," said Bill.

Mark, Carl, and Dave took off to get light. Mark threw snacks in a bag, then grabbed a gallon jug of water. Mark asked Bill what happened.

"I don't really know," said Bill. "He shot, but we can't find him."

The men all went to where Tim had been seen last. They then paired up. They headed out to look for Tim with plans to meet back there in two hours. The snow had stopped for now, but all signs of any tracks were gone. It was getting darker and colder. At night at those elevations, the temperature could drop into the tens that time of year.

Bill and Louis found bear tracks in the snow, headed to the east, and they decided to follow them. They were hard to follow in the snow with the glare from the lights. Then they started seeing drops of blood between the tracks. "Oh no," said Bill.

"What?" asked Louis.

"That's not a good sign," said Bill. "That bear is bleeding. There is nothing more dangerous than an injured bear. God, I hope it is not a grizzly. Come on, let's head back to the meeting spot."

Carl and Dave, who had headed west, found nothing. The men headed back. Mark and Chase had already made it back. Once they all got back, they reported what they did not and did find. Bill and Louis told them about the injured bear sign they saw.

"Okay," said Bill, "let's head back to the camp and hope Tim made it back there. If not, we will make a new plan and let the rangers know that we have a man lost."

As the men headed back to camp thinking the worst, when they got close, they could tell that the campfire was burning bright. They took off running to the camp. It was Tim there at the fire.

"Bear," Tim said as they ran up. Tim was in a panic. He threw more wood on the fire.

"What happened?" asked Bill.

"Bear," said Tim, "big bear." He pointed to the woods.

"You are okay now," said Louis.

"No," said Tim, "bear here." He pointed to the woods again.

"Oh, damn," said Dave.

"The bear is here. He is telling us the bear is here now," said Bill. "It followed him back here."

Mark said, "I will get coffee going. Carl, hold a light while I get some coffee." Carl shone a light so Mark could grab the coffee from inside the cook tent.

Louis got Tim to sit down by the fire. Bill grabbed some wood and started three more smaller fires about ten feet away from the big fire. Bill said, "Everybody stay between the fires. Nobody goes out without someone with a gun guarding them. Nobody!"

*****

"That should be enough tonight. It's a long story," said Jim.

"When did that fellow tell this story?" asked Ben.

"In 1985," said Jim. "I was young. He was hauling cattle then and brought a load to my dad. He had come through Colorado. I told him I always wanted to go hunting in the Rockies. That's when he told me the story. He said he would never go back in those mountains again. I'll tell yawl some more tomorrow night." They all went to bed with bellies full, thinking about bears.

The next morning, Pete had coffee going and bacon frying.

"Yawl get up," said Troy. "Let's eat and get moving." The men ate, then saddled their horses and headed out. Troy and Jim stayed to help Pete get the wagon loaded up. Then they headed out to catch the crew, with Pete following with the wagon. About midday, Pete caught up with the herd. Each man came by the wagon, and Pete handed them a sandwich to eat on the way. Pete then went on by them and the cows to the next camp spot. Just before dark, the herd made it to camp. Pete had supper cooked and coffee. The men took care of their horses, then sat around the fire to eat.

"Tell us some more of that story," said Jeff.

"Let him eat first," said Troy.

Jim finished his meal, then poured himself a cup of coffee and sat back down. He took a sip of coffee. "Okay, where was I at?"

"They were at the fire," said Clark.

*****

They heard the bear growling out in the trees. They could hear it scratching a tree. Bill took his rifle and shot in the treetops in the direction of the noise, but the bear just moved to another spot. Bill did it again, but the bear just moved again. Tim had calmed down after drinking some coffee and warming up. Tim said the bear started circling him while he was hunting. "It was like it was stalking me. It kept getting closer and closer."

"What kind of bear?" asked Bill.

"A grizzly, I think. All I know is, it is huge. When it got close, like thirty feet away, it turned and looked straight at me and pawed the ground like a bull. I raised up my gun, put my crosshair in the middle of its chest, and shot. It let out a loud groan, then turned and run off. I was so scared I jumped up and started running. I ran for like fifteen minutes before I realized I didn't know which way I was going. I stopped, and once I got my heart to slow down, I got out my compass and figured out which way to go. I walked forever until I came out on the road leading here. I knew where I was and started up the road. Just before I got here, I heard the bear out in the tree beside me. I started running. I got here and started throwing wood on the fire. It started circling me again, just growling. It stopped when yawl came up for just a minute. What are we going to do? It is after me. It wants to kill me."

"Calm down," said Bill. "We are not going to let it get you. We just have to make it until daylight, then we will kill it. Mark, you and Dave take the first watch so maybe some of us can get some sleep. Louis and Carl will relieve you two in three hours. Chase and I will take the last watch. I'm sure Tim is not going to sleep, but he can lie down and rest. Everybody just keep the fires going. There are blankets in the cook tent. One man with a light, one man with a gun, and third man to carry the blankets. Come on, let's go." They got the bedding and brought it out by the fire.

Mark and Dave stood watch with lights and their guns. The bear kept slowly circling and growling the whole time. Mark told Dave, "Looks like the dang thing would just lie down and die." Then they heard crashing and tearing sounds coming from the guest tent.

"It's in the tent," said Dave. They both turned and started shooting at the movement of the tent. They heard a loud moan and then a growl as the bear came out of the tent and headed straight for them.

Out of bullets, Mark grabbed a burning limb from the fire and hit the bear across the face, turning it around. The bear headed back into the trees. Everyone was awake now. Mark and Dave reloaded their guns.

Bill said, "We've got to get some help." The bear was growing louder now than before.

Louis said, "Let me take Tim down the mountain in the jeep and find a phone to call the rangers."

"That's a good idea," said Carl. "Maybe the bear will leave us alone if Tim is gone."

"Okay," said Bill.

"Hell, let's all leave," said Louis. "We've got the trucks too."

"I don't know," said Mark. "A grizzly bear can run thirty miles an hour. We can't go that fast on that road, especially at night."

"He's right," said Bill. "Here's what we will do. Dave, you drive one of the trucks. Let Carl get in the back with his rifle. Louis, you drive the jeep with Tim in it. Mark, you drive the other truck with Chase in the cab. I'll ride in the back with my rifle. We'll put the jeep in the middle and get the hell out of here as fast as we can."

"Let's go," said Louis. All the men took off running to the vehicles. They all jumped in, cranked up, and headed out. They pulled out of camp and started down the rocky road.

Not far out of camp, Carl started beating on the cab of the truck. "What?" asked Dave.

"The bear, it's running along beside us."

"What?" asked Dave.

"Speed up," said Carl.

About that time, the bear turned and ran straight into the side of the jeep like a rhino and flipped it over and off the road.

"Holy shit," said Mark as Bill shot at the bear. Then Dave stopped, and Carl shot.

Tim and Louis were thrown from the jeep. Louis was bleeding from his head, and Tim was knocked out, still on the ground. Dave backed up to the jeep.

"Oh, damn," said Carl as the bear hit the driver's side door at a full run, caving the door in and throwing Carl out of the back of the truck. Dave crawled out the truck on the passenger side.

Bill yelled, "Everybody get in this truck! Hurry!" Everybody ran to the other truck. Bill yelled, "Go, Mark, go!"

"Wait, where is Tim?" asked Louis.

"Damn," said Bill. "Get him. Hurry."

Louis and Dave ran over to get Tim.

"Where is he?" asked Dave.

"He was right here," said Louis.

"Shit," said Dave. They took off back to the truck.

"The bear got him," said Louis. "He's gone."

"Damn," said Bill. "Mark, get us back to camp."

The men ganged up at the fire. Mark started first aid on Louis's head.

"What now?" asked Carl.

"We've got to get Tim back," said Bill.

"He's dead," said Dave.

"I don't think so," said Bill. "Bears will take their prey to a safe spot and hide them."

"What do we do? How are we going to get him back?" asked Carl.

"At daylight, we'll go back to the other vehicles. We'll get out there and start tracking that bear. Louis and Chase will take the truck into town for help and bring back the rangers."

At first light, the men loaded up in the truck and headed back down the road. When they got to the jeep and the other truck, all but Louis and Chase got out.

"Hurry," said Bill to Louis.

The four men started searching the area. Bill said, "Over here." The other men ran over. "Look," said Bill, "you could see where something had been dragged across the snow."

They started following the trail deeper into the trees. They were seeing blood all the way, but it was droplets, not smeared, like if it was coming from Tim as he was dragged. They knew the bear had been shot at least twice, but they didn't know where. They kept following the trail, with Carl in the back watching behind them. About a hundred yards in the trees, Carl heard something. "Hey, guys," said Carl. "There is something back here."

Everybody stopped and pointed their guns. "What is it?" asked Dave.

"I don't know, but it's following us."

"It's that damn bear," said Bill. "It is hunting us now!"

"What do we do now?" asked Dave.

"We keep looking for Tim and keep watching our backs. Tim could have been hidden anywhere, in a brush pile or anywhere," said Bill.

"We need to kill that damn bear," Mark told them, "before it kills us."

"What are you thinking?" asked Bill.

"Give me some more ammo, and I'll go after the bear. It can't hunt you if it is hunting me. I'll lead it off in another direction," said Mark.

"That's crazy," said Carl.

"No, that's the only way you're going to find Tim." Mark got some more ammo and headed back the way they came. About thirty yards away, he could hear the bear growling. He eased up as close as he could to the bear downwind. He could see the bear. It was bleeding from its left shoulder, and blood was dripping from its head. Mark was trying to get a clear shot at the bear, but he turned, and all Mark could see was his behind. The bear started moving in the direction of Bill and the other men. Mark got up and walked upwind of the bear. He found a spot and waited for the bear to come. Mark could hear the bear coming. He got set, the bear came over a ridge, and Mark put the crosshair right between the bear's eyes and squeezed the trigger. The shot rang out, and the bear fell in its tracks.

"Yes," said Mark. Mark eased over to the bear, poked it with his gun barrel, and the bear didn't move. Mark headed back to Bill and the other men to see if they had found Tim yet.

Louis and Chase made it to the rangers' station and reported the bear. They told them about Tim and the bear and what had happened. The rangers started rounding up men, horses, and dogs. Once they got their team together, Louis and Chase led the rangers back to the jeep.

Mark was trying to find the drag trail that Bill, Carl, and Dave were on, but he wasn't sure which direction. He had made so many turns. Finally, Mark found the trail. He followed the trail until he got close.

Bill yelled, "Mark, over here!"

Mark got to them, and they had found Tim. He had been mauled, and it looked like he had a broken leg and a broken arm. They were dragging Tim out of a brush pile. He was awake, but not talking. Once they got him out and gave him some water, they all picked him up, one on each side and one holding his head, and they started carrying him out.

The rangers had found the same trail and was working their way down it.

"Hey, over here!" said Bill as the rangers got to them. They got everybody back to the road. They flipped the jeep back over. Bill and Mark told the rangers the whole story about the bear. The rangers loaded up Tim and Louis and took them down to the road to meet the ambulance. The rangers called for two wreckers to get the truck and jeep.

One of the rangers told Mark that they needed him to take them to the dead bear. "Okay," said Mark, "I'll try." Mark and two of the rangers headed back down the trail. Mark found his tracks in the snow where he turned off the trail. They were following them until they found where Mark had sat waiting for the bear. They followed his trail to where the bear was lying, but no bear, just the impression of the bear and some blood.

"Oh, hell," said one of the rangers, "we have got to get out of here now."

They turned and headed back as fast as they could. When they got back to the road, the other rangers asked, "Did yawl find it?"

"No, get everybody in a vehicle, and let's go. We can't stay here. We need more help."

The ranger got on the radio and called in. He said, "Stop the wreckers. We've got to barricade this road. We need to get all the other hunters out of this area. We have an injured grizzly bear on the loose."

The ranger got Bill, Mark, Chase, Dave, and Carl off the mountain. They put them all in a motel in Bay City. Louis was already there. Tim was still in the hospital.

Later, after cleaning up and getting some sleep, Mark went to Bill's room. "Man, I don't know how this is possible," said Mark.

"I don't know either," said Bill.

"How can a bear be shot three times, once in the chest and twice in the head, and still be alive?"

Bill asked, "Was your gun zeroed in at one hundred yards?"

"Yes," said Mark.

"And how far was the bear from you?"

"About thirty yards," said Mark.

"You missed it," said Bill. "At thirty yards, you were shooting two and a half to three inches high."

"Damn," said Mark. "I didn't think about that. I should have aimed at the tip of its nose. I must have grazed its head because it dropped in its tracks and didn't move."

*****

"Okay, that's a good stopping point," said Jim. "I'll finish it tomorrow night. Everybody needs some sleep." They all curled up and went to sleep.

The next morning, they ate and headed out. Again, Troy and Tim helped Pete. The men pushed the cattle through the valley. More and more were joining them as they moved along. Again, Pete came through around midday and passed out sandwiches, then headed on to the next camp spot. When the herd got there, Pete had a big pot of chili cooked. The nights were getting colder already. The men took care of their horses and then filled a bowl and sat at the fire and ate.

"How many head do you think, Troy?" asked Jim.

"Over five hundred," said Troy. "Kattie may have to sell off some older cows. We can't let the herd get too big."

"You're right," said Jim. "I'll talk to her about it." Jim finished his bowl, then got some coffee and sat back down. "Okay, let me finish this story."

*****

Bill called the main office. "They are sending the plane for Chase, Carl, Dave, Louis, and you to take you home."

"I'm not leaving," said Mark, "not until they kill that bear and Tim gets out of the hospital."

"Okay," said Bill, "I've called and rented a car for them. I need you to go with me to get it and bring it here for them to drive to the airport."

"Okay," said Mark.

Bill and Mark went to the hospital in Durango to check on Tim. He was awake and sitting up. His leg was in a cast, lying in a sling; his arm was in a cast also.

"Hey, Tim," said Bill.

Mark walked over and took Tim's good hand. "How you feeling?" asked Mark.

"Well, the pain meds are working so far. Did you get that bear?" asked Tim.

"No," said Mark. "The rangers are out looking for it now. I shot that bear at about thirty yards. I had my crosshairs between its eyes. As soon I pulled the trigger, it dropped in its tracks. An hour later, it was gone. I must have grazed that damn bear."

Tim said, "I know. I shot it in the chest, and it just ran off growling."

"That bear is not normal," said Bill. "The last I heard, the rangers had a helicopter with a sniper in it trying to track the bear down and kill it."

"That bear is smart," said Tim. "I moved two hundred yards from where I was hunting, and that damn thing came and found me. It was stalking me. It wanted to kill me. Me and Louis came up here three years ago with another group. We had no problem with bears. Hell, our guide kill one, an old sow bear."

"You came here before?" asked Bill.

"Yes, Louis and I."

"And you hunted the same area?"

"Well, not the same exact area. About two miles west of where we are this year."

"Holy shit," said Bill. "Did that sow bear have cubs?"

"No, well, I mean, when we went to help the guide get the bear, there were a couple of young bears hanging out in the area, maybe two years old. They would stand up on their hind legs and look at us over the brush. The sow wasn't suckling or anything like that. These cubs were half grown. That's why he shot the sow. He had been watching the two smaller bears for two days. The big bear came out. She was huge, like a big boar bear."

"Oh, shit," said Bill and Mark at the same time.

"What?" asked Tim.

"Okay, now tell us," said Bill, "so you and Louis went with this guy to get the bear he shot?"

"Yes!"

"And you helped dress her?"

"Yes! We all three crawled around on the ground skinning her, then cut her up and packed her out, along with her hide, a huge hide. It probably weighed a hundred pounds or more with the head."

"Was there snow on the ground?"

"No, not yet. We left the next morning, which was the last day of our hunt."

"Okay," said Bill, "what was the guide's name?"

"Ahh, Tom… Tom… Tom Paterson. That's it, Tom Paterson," said Tim.

"Do you know how to contact him?" asked Bill.

"Well, I did, but he's dead now. He was mauled and killed by a grizzly bear up here last season," said Tim.

"Oh, shit, said Mark, "shit, shit, shit, you have got be kidding me."

Bill just shook his head.

"What?" asked Tim.

"Don't you see? The bear is one of the cubs. He knows your scent, yours and Louis's scent."

"Damn."

"He killed the guy who shot his mother last season, and now you two show up back in his area. That's his dream come true. I've got to call the rangers." Bill picked up the room phone and dialed the number to the rangers' office. He told the ranger chief the whole story about the guide and Tim and Louis.

The ranger said, "We will get Louis out of the motel and to a safe place. You keep Tim there. I'll send a backup to guard the hospital."

"Do you think that's necessary?" asked Bill.

"Hell yes," said the ranger. "Not only do we have an injured bear but we also have one that wants revenge. That's why we can't find the bear. He is hunting those men in town now."

"Oh, shit," said Bill.

"Exactly," said the ranger.

When one of the rangers got to the motel, unbeknownst to him, the bear was already there hiding outside, behind Louis's room, in some tall grass. There was a window above the A/C unit on the back side of the room. The ranger knocked on the room door. Dave, who was sharing the room with Louis, opened the door. The ranger told Louis, "I need you to come with me."

"Okay, what for?"

"We have reason to think the bear is looking for you here in town."

"What?"

"Yes, please come with me."

"Okay," said Louis, "let me grab my bag." Louis walked to the back of the room near the window and reached down for his bag. The men heard glass breaking as the bear came through the window and grabbed Louis by the neck. The ranger pulled his sidearm and shot at the bear three times. The bear dropped Louis and jumped back out the window and hit the tall grass, leaving a blood trail.

Dave ran over to Louis. "Louis!" he shouted, but Louis was dead. The bear had gotten his jugular and ripped it open; he died in seconds. "Oh, shit," said Dave.

The other men, Chase and Carl, came running over. "What happened?" they asked.

"The bear got Louis," said Dave.

The ranger had gone to his truck to call in. The rangers' station called Tim's room. Bill answered the phone. The ranger told him that Louis was dead and that they were sure the bear was headed their way. "Damn," said Bill as he hung up the phone. He told Mark, "I need you in the hall."

Mark got up, and they went outside the room. "What?" asked Mark.

"Louis is dead," said Bill. "The bear got him at the motel."

"Shit, are you serious?" asked Mark.

"Yes," said Bill. "The rangers think the bear is headed this way."

"How...how can a bear do this?"

As they stood in the hall, two rangers walked up. "Where's Tim?" they asked.

"In this room," said Bill. The men started in the room.

"What are you doing?" asked Mark.

"We've got to move him to the basement," said one of the rangers.

A nurse was making Tim's equipment mobile. They rolled Tim out into the hall and down to the elevator. They took him down into the basement to a room that had no windows.

"What are you going to do?" asked Bill.

"We have four sharpshooters on the roof of this three-story building and six more officers on the ground. The local police are blocking all the roads and helping evacuate this hospital. The ones who can't leave are being moved down here, and ICU has two guards in there. We are going to kill this damn bear, hopefully before he gets in the building. Yawl just sit tight. I'll let you know what's going on."

Two hours went by. No word. Another hour went by, then they heard three pops, like fireworks. The door opened, and a ranger stepped in. "We got him."

"All right," said Tim,

"Great," said Mark.

"Thank God!" said Bill.

In a couple of hours, they moved Tim back to his room. Everything had calmed down. The rangers had loaded up the bear to be hauled off. The police officers opened the streets back up. The ranger chief came by Tim's room to personally check on him and to assure him that now he was safe and he could rest easy tonight. Tim, Mark, and Bill all shook the ranger's hand and thanked him for everything. As the ranger headed out of the room, he turned and looked at Bill. "You boys don't forget to go back up and clean up that campsite before you go home."

"Oh yes, sir," said Bill. "We will." The ranger left.

It was almost dark. Bill told Mark, "Let's get the others and go out to eat. I'm starving. I haven't eaten in three days."

"Okay," said Mark, "let's go. You want us to bring you anything back, Tim?"

"No, I'm good. I'm going to sleep now and sleep for a week."

Bill and Mark left and headed out of the building.

Tim was almost asleep when he heard glass breaking. The bear came through the window, grabbed Tim, and dragged him out of the bed, then bit his neck, breaking it. The bear then climbed back out of the window and ran off.

Bill and Mark heard the hospital alarms going off. They turned and ran back in. The nurses were standing in the doorway of Tim's room. Bill squeezed by them. A doctor was standing over Tim. "He's dead, guys. He's dead."

Bill and Mark walked out. Bill called the rangers. "Yawl killed the wrong bear," said Bill. "Tim is dead."

"What?" said the ranger. "We're on our way."

The ranger got there, and they checked the room with the local police. The ranger said, "It was a bear, all right. We are not going after him at night. We found a blood trail leading into the trees. I'll leave some men here overnight. We will start tracking him down at first light."

The next morning, the ranger started their search. Within an hour, they found the bear dead about two hundred yards away from the hospital. The bear had finally bled to death from all the gunshot wounds.

Chase, Carl, and Dave got on a plane for home that morning. Bill and Mark went back to camp to load everything up. On the way, they stopped and got the other truck that had a new door and the jeep that was repaired. It took them two days to get everything broke down and loaded up. They hooked up the horse trailer, then loaded the mule and horse, and then headed down the mountain.

Bill and Mark went by the rangers' station on their way out to let them know that they were gone. The chief called them into his office. "Have a seat," he said. "I want to show you something."

"Okay," said Bill.

The chief slid two photos across his desk. "Have a look at them." The men looked them over.

"Okay," said Bill.

"You see anything different between those two pictures?"

"No," said Mark.

"I do," said Bill.

The chief smiled. "What do you see?"

"These are two different bears," said Bill.

"Give that man a gold star. Yes, what else?"

"Well, one of them has a graze mark across the top of its head and a shoulder wound and has been gut shot. The other one has a wound in its chest and has also been gut shot."

"Yes, two bears. This one was killed first outside the hospital. He had a chest wound, a gut shot, and had been shot by the ranger's pistol three times in the chest area in the motel room while killing Louis. The other bear with the head wound and shoulder wound and gut shot was found dead the next morning after killing Tim in the hospital. One mama with two cubs! Revenge is a powerful thing," said the ranger.

Then Mark said, "Before you mistreat someone's mother, the first thing you need to know is how many sons she might have and how long they will carry a grudge!"

*****

"Holy shit," said Jeff, "I know I won't sleep tonight." Everybody just laughed.

The next day, they made it back home with the herd. Kattie could hear the cows and went to the catch pens with tea and glasses. Jim rode over when she pulled up. She poured him a glass of tea. "Hey, baby," said Kattie. Jim leaned down and gave her a kiss. Then Troy rode up. She poured him a glass of tea. "Well, how did it go?" asked Kattie.

"Good," said Troy, "really good. There's a lot of beef up there. I'll give you a count tomorrow."

"Okay," said Kattie. "Have fun." She got back in her truck.

The next day, Kattie went back to the pens. "How many?" she asked Troy.

"Five hundred and forty," said Troy. "Eighty-six steers."

Kattie went over to the steer pen and picked three to send to the orphanage. "Three this year," said Kattie. "And keep three for the ranch. Sell the rest."

"Okay," said Troy. "What about the herd?"

"I don't know yet," said Kattie. "Jim and I will talk about that some more."

"Yes, ma'am," said Troy.

The next day, Kattie came out to the pens and found Troy. "Well, I've made up my mind. Well, Mary made up my mind for me. She said the best thing would be to pregnancy test all the cows we weren't sure about, and if they are not pregnant, sell them. That way, you won't be feeding them through the winter for nothing."

"That's not a bad idea," said Troy. "That way, we can cut down the herd size and cull out the nonproducers. Let's check the young heifers first. If they didn't get bred, we will cut them out. If we have older cows not bred, let's check the records and see if there is a pattern."

"Okay," said Kattie, "I'll set up to get some help from the clinic out here. Maybe next week. The ones we feel for sure are bred, let's go ahead and separate them."

"Okay," said Troy, "Tell Mary that she had a good idea for once." Troy laughed.

Chapter 10

Snow, Snow, and More Snow

Mary bought two horses at the sale. One of them was for Maria, but she hadn't told her. She was not sure yet which one she wanted her to have. Mary was going to work with them awhile before she decided. Maria had become Mary's sidekick; she followed her wherever she went, soaking up everything Mary said and did. Maria's birthday would be in two months, on December 5. She would be twelve years old. Mary planned to give her one of the horses for her birthday. Mary was so proud and happy with Maria; she worked harder than anyone else on the place, except Mary.

It was the first of October, and it was already cold. They were predicting snow any day now. From all reports, this winter was going to be a rough one. Mary had a contractor at the stables installing heaters in the alleyway and some of the stalls. They were also wrapping heavier insulation on the water lines in the barn to keep them from freezing. Troy had the tractor ready with the snow blade on it so they could keep the driveway clear, from the blacktop to the stables, house, and barn. It was like everyone was rushing to get ready for a major snowstorm.

Maria was doing her daily chores with her helpers Buddy and the blue heeler puppy. They were following her around to each stall. Buddy was trying to get into her pocket because he knew she had treats. The puppy liked the horse treats too. Maria told them, "If yawl don't stop, you're not going to get any treats." The puppy sat down and looked up at her. Buddy put his head on her shoulder. "Fine, here," said Maria as she gave Buddy and the puppy a treat. "Now go on, you silly kids. I've got work to do."

Mary was working with one of the new horses, Dusty, a beautiful buckskin gelding. He seemed to be very smart. He was green broke when she bought him and had trust issues. She had been working on that. She hoped he would turn out to be the one for Maria, but she was still undecided. Mary was having a new saddle made for Maria, with matching breast collar and bridle. They were putting her name, Maria, on the back ridge of the seat.

On October 27, the snow started to fall and didn't stop until November 3. The whole ranch was white. Troy cleared the driveway. The state was clearing the roads, and school was shut down until next Monday. Billie, Rose, Mary, and Maria were riding in the snow every day. Maria was riding behind Mary. It was so cold, but they loved it. They had built snowmen all over the place—one in front of the house, one at the barn, and two at the stables.

Monday, Rose went back to work, and the girls went back to school. Mary was still working with the buckskin in the afternoons. She had him calmed down. She had rubbed on and touched every inch of his body over and over. She had him broke to lead and had been lying on him bareback. He was ready for the saddle. Mary had Troy scoop all the snow out of the arena, but the ground was still too wet. She was afraid they might fall if she worked him in there. The alley was one hundred feet long and thirty feet wide, so she was going to work with him in there.

Mary saddled up the buckskin and rode him around in the alley, working on his stopping and turning. Dusty was a natural spinner. Mary would make him spin to the right and then to the left. He was good at it. He could also slide. She would run him from one end to the other and break him. He would drop his hips and slide. By the end of the week, she could run him down the alley and then say whoa, and he would lock up and slide. Mary was happy with how he was doing but wanted to work cows and run the barrels with him. But it was just too wet, and she didn't want to take that chance. Dusty was a four-year-old and was smart. Mary decided to let Maria start working with him some, hoping they would make a bond. If they did, then Dusty would be Maria's horse.

The next week, Mary told Maria, "I want you to start feeding Dusty. Every other day, I want you to take him out and ride him here in the alley. That way, I can start working on one of the other horses."

"Okay," said Maria.

The next horse she wanted to work was a solid black filly, no color anywhere, just jet-black. She was a three-year-old and, like Dusty, was only green broke. Mary was going to call her Midnight. She had good shape and form, long legs, and black eyes. She was not that easy to handle, so Mary was not sure about her yet.

Maria started working with Dusty, brushing and talking to him like she had watched Mary do a hundred times. She would lie on his back in the stall and rub his neck and sides. She would give him treats. Within a week, Dusty would follow Maria wherever she went with no rope. She would saddle him and ride him in the alleyway, giving him voice commands each time she had him turn or stop. She started eating lunch with him, Buddy, and the puppy every day. Dusty loved peanut butter sandwiches. Maria started working with him on lying down in the stall, then she would lie on top of him, talking and rubbing him the whole time. Dusty was falling in love with this little girl, and she with him. Maria would ride him, spin him, and break him under the alleyway.

Then came more snow. It snowed for two weeks, higher and heavier than before. All the roads closed; as did the school. Kattie shut down the clinic except for emergencies. It was like the whole world just stopped outside of Plumber's Gap. Mary and Kathy's jobs didn't get to stop. The livestock still must be cared for no matter what. Mary loaned Selena to Kathy for a while. She and Maria were taking care of the stables. Troy was making some of the hands help with the stock horses at the barn.

Maria's birthday was finally here. The weather was cold, but there had been no more snow for a couple of weeks. Mary and Selena decided to have Maria's party at the stables. Just cake and ice cream for a small group. Selena invited her uncle Pete and aunt Alice. Mary invited Troy, Kathy, Tommie, and Billie and also her mom and dad. They all met up at the stables midafternoon in the alleyway. Once everyone finished their cake and ice cream, Mary told Maria, "I have a surprise for you." Mary went around the corner and led Dusty with a brand-new saddle and bridle. She held out the reins and said, "Here, he belongs to you now."

Maria started crying with her hands over her mouth. She said, "Really, he's mine?"

"Yes, ma'am, he is yours. Happy birthday."

Maria ran over and hugged Mary, then hugged the horse. She then started looking at the saddle. "Oh, how beautiful," said Maria. "And my name is on it. Thank you, thank you." She gave Mary another hug.

"I think she likes it," said Kattie.

"Oh yes, ma'am," said Maria. "I love it."

Spring finally came. The snow and ice were melting slowly. Most of the roads were clear and open. Mary said, "Come on, Maria, let's go to town. I haven't had a hamburger and fries in months."

Maria said, "And a milkshake."

They jumped in Mary's truck and headed to town. They went to the store in Lead and ordered two large cheeseburgers, two fries, and two chocolate shakes. When they brought their food out, Mary ordered another large cheeseburger, fries, and strawberry shake to take to her mom. They finished eating. Mary paid and grabbed the to-go order, and they headed back home. Mary drove to the house and told Maria, "Take this to Mom."

"Okay," said Maria. Maria came back out. "Your mom said thank you, thank you!"

Mary turned and drove back to the stables. She was now working with the black horse all the time. Midnight was doing great, but she still could not get in the arena with her. The water was dripping off the roof, and the grass was peeking through in places. Maria was still working with Dusty in the alley when Mary was not in there. The cows were starting to calve. It would not be long until it was time to worm, vaccinate, and tag the calves, then they would start moving the cows back out to pasture.

Finally, all signs of the snow and ice were gone. The arena had dried out, and Troy had tilled it up and spread it out for Mary. Mary had Troy go ahead and put new shoes on Dusty and shoe Midnight for the first time. Today after school, Mary and Maria were going to ride them in the arena. Mary set up the poles. Maria wanted to use one of the old saddles and save her new one, but Mary said, "No, you need to get it broke in."

"Okay," said Maria.

Mary had Maria run the poles on Dusty, something new for him. She walked through them the first time. Then she loped him through the course, zigzagging around the poles. Then Mary walked Midnight through them. She was not sure about those things at all, but Mary made her lope through them the second time. Then Maria did it again, this time faster. Dusty was picking it up fast. On the way back, he was zigzagging on his own. Mary made Midnight run again, making her zigzag through the course faster and faster. She didn't pick it up as fast as Dusty, but she was better each time.

Mary said, "Okay, let's move the poles and set up the barrels."

"Okay," said Maria.

Once they had the barrels set up, Mary walked Midnight through the barrel pattern, and Maria followed on Dusty, doing the same. After about three times, Mary said, "Okay, let's run 'em. I'll go first." She rode down the alley, then turned and came back fast. Midnight hit the first barrel, but it didn't fall. They made it around the second barrel and then the third barrel. Mary opened her up coming back.

Maria went down the alley, then came back out on Dusty wide open. She turned the first barrel, then the second, and the third and then flew back home. Mary got ready for another run on Midnight.

Before they started, Mary talked to her. She told her, "Don't be afraid, girl. Just do what's natural to you. You run the course. I'll just ride." They went down the alley. They came back out. This time, the horse was not waiting for Mary to guide her around the barrel. Mary felt her sat up, and she got ready. They popped out of the other side of the barrel. Mary said, "That's it, girl. You run 'em." They made the second turn. "Now go," said Mary. Again, Mary felt the horse sat up, and she got ready. They nailed it. "Go, baby, go," said Mary as they flew back home. "Good girl," said Mary as she rubbed her neck and gave her a treat.

"Wow," said Maria, "that was good."

"Yep, now you do it."

Maria went down the alley, then turned and came back. Dusty was lunging ahead as he reached out with his front legs and pulled himself and Maria across the ground. They nailed the first barrel, then the second, and then the third. "Go, boy, go," said Maria

"I think we got a couple of barrel horses here," said Mary.

"Yep, me too," said Maria. "Dusty is fast in those turns."

Mary said, "Yes, it's his short legs. He's built just like Bob and can hold those turns."

"Well, I'm happy," said Maria.

"Are you?" she asked Maria.

"Yes, I'm happy," said Maria.

"Let's cool them off, then put them up. Tomorrow we will play with calves."

"Oh, good," said Maria. "I like that."

The next day, Troy brought five calves to the stable and put them in the arena for Mary. After school, Mary and Maria saddled up and got ready. They rode into the arena. Mary and Maria eased the calves back into the corner. Mary held them as the calves made a break for it. The girls turned them back. One got by. Mary said, "Let it go. Hold the rest." Midnight, who had long legs, was having trouble turning fast enough to stop the calves, but Dusty was right on time wheeling back and forth as the calves tried to get by. Mary had to keep Midnight pointed toward the calves, but Dusty never took his eyes off them. They worked them for about twenty minutes, then Mary said, "Let them go."

They didn't know it, but Troy and Jim were watching them work the calves.

Mary got her rope off her horn and made a loop. Mary told Maria, "That one." She pointed. Maria eased into the group, then ran it out. Mary fell in behind it and threw her rope, catching it around the neck. When the rope got tight, it broke away.

Then Maria said, "That big one there." She pointed. Mary eased her horse into the group and pushed it out. As it came by, Maria fell in behind it. She threw her rope and dropped it over the calf's neck. When it got tight, it broke away. Maria spun Dusty a couple of times in celebration, then they got their ropes and did it again.

"Okay," said Mary, "let's each pick one and separate it from the group and hold it as long as we can."

"Okay," said Maria. Mary let Maria get hers out. She then cut hers out. Maria and Dusty stayed right on top of the calf, moving every time the calf moved. Mary was keeping hers away from the group, but she was having a harder time.

Finally, Mary yelled, "Let them go!" And they stopped as the calves ran by and joined the others. "Okay, let's cool them off," said Mary as they rode them around the arena.

Troy and Jim walked up to the rails. Midnight, the black horse that Mary bought, was lean and a little poor-looking when she bought her. Now she was filled out and muscled up, and she had shed her winter coat. Her coat was a shiny black. "Is that the same horse you brought for $500.00?"

"Yep, you told me I was crazy."

"Man, that's a pretty horse," said Troy.

"She is for sale," said Mary.

"What about the buckskin?" said Jim, picking.

"No!" said Maria.

"What do you want for her?" asked Troy.

"Who's buying, you or Plumber's Gap?"

"Me," said Troy. "I'm going to take her home with me."

"For you, $850.00."

"Sold," said Troy.

"Okay, she is yours." Mary looked at Maria and said, "Let's put them up."

The next day, Mary started working another horse she bought locally, a little strawberry roan horse that was only two and a half years old and not broke at all other than halter broke. She was sweet-natured but knew nothing yet. Mary saddled up Bob, and Maria saddled up Dusty. Mary put a lead rope on the roan horse and wrapped it around her saddle horn. They took off down the valley, by the house, and headed to the falls. The roan pulled back a little but figured out soon she was a losing battle. Once they made it to the falls, they stopped for just a minute, then headed back to the stables. Mary put the young horse in the round pen and worked her for about an hour, then put her on the walker.

Maria got out Mary's filly, saddled her up, and put her on the walker with the roan. Paul and Rose came to the stables. Paul asked Mary if she had time to work with some more horses.

"Sure," said Mary. "What you got?"

"Well, I bought a couple of brood mares that have been bred but now are hard to manage. I want to get them gentled down before they have their colts."

"Sure, we can do that."

Paul said, "Okay, I've got them in the trailer." Paul backed his trailer up to the alleyway. He opened the trailer and took the first one out. She jerked and pulled as Paul tried to lead her.

Mary said, "Hold up." She walked up to the horse, rubbed her noise, and looked straight into her eyes. Then Mary said something to the horse. Mary took the lead rope from Paul and led the mare into a stall and gave her a treat. Paul just stood there in awe. "Okay, get the other one," said Mary.

Paul got out the other horse. She tried to spin and kick Paul.

"Whoa," said Mary as she walked up to the horse and rubbed her nose. The horse tried to turn to kick Mary. "Watch out," said Paul.

Bob was still saddled. Mary got on Bob and looped the lead rope around her horn and dragged the mare out to the round pen and then inside. "I'll start with this one," said Mary.

Paul asked Mary, "Whose roan is that?"

"She's mine," said Mary.

"What are you going to do with her?"

"I'm going to break and sell her," said Mary.

"Call me when she is ready. I may be interested in her."

"Okay, said Mary.

Paul and Rose left. Mary went out to the round pen. She went inside the pen and started running the mare around and around. Mary ran her until she started licking her lips. Mary let her stop. The horse just stood there. Mary walked toward the horse. The horse turned her butt in Mary's direction. Mary popped her on the butt and ran her some more. After about thirty minutes, she let the horse stop. The horse was exhausted. Mary waited, but the horse just stood there. Mary walked up to her. The horse was breathing hard. Mary reached out her hand and rubbed her nose. Then she gave her a treat. She stood there rubbing the horse and talking to her. Mary turned and walked to the gate, but the horse just stood there. Mary smacked her lips and said, "Come on." But the horse didn't move. Mary opened the gate and walked on out, leaving the horse in the round pen.

Mary went and took the filly and the roan off the walker and put them up.

"What now?" asked Maria about the mare.

"Well, she is hardheaded," said Mary. "We will let her stew for a couple of hours. If she doesn't do better next time, she can spend the night in there."

After about two hours, Mary went back into the round pen and stood on one side across from the horse. The horse just stood there like a kid, mad from being punished. Mary walked over and popped her butt with the quirt. The mare started running again. Mary turned her and made her run the other way for a while. Then she stopped her. Mary stood in the middle of the pen. Mary took out a treat and held it in the palm of her hand. The horse took two steps and stopped. Mary didn't move. The horse took two more steps. Mary still didn't move. Then the horse walked up and took the treat. Mary rubbed her nose and face, talking to her. She gave her another treat, then clipped the lead rope to her halter. Mary led her around the pen a couple of times, then took her out the gate. She led her to an empty stall and put her inside. Mary gave her some oats and hay for the night.

Mary had been working with Maria and Dusty on the barrels some. She told Maria that when they could run consistently in the fourteens, she would take them to a rodeo and let her run. They had been running in the mid fourteens and low fifteens for a while now.

Mary had Paul's two mares ready to go; they were both changed horses, nothing like they were when they got here. Mary had the roan horse broke and gentle, but she hadn't trained it for anything yet. Paul came to get his brood mares. Mary walked to the gate of the one that always tried to kick. The mare walked up to her. Mary snapped on the lead rope and handed it to Paul. Paul walked her to the trailer. The horse loaded up on her own. Then Mary brought out the other one with no lead rope, just her halter, and said, "Load up." And she did.

Paul said, "Rose told me you could work wonders with horses, but that is unreal. What about the roan?"

"She's $1,000.00," said Mary.

"Okay," said Paul, "bring her on."

"Maria," said Mary, "bring the roan."

Maria opened her gate and said, "Come on, girl." The horse followed her to the trailer. Maria said, "Load up." The horse stepped up into the trailer.

Paul paid Mary and told her, "Thank you. I'll be spreading the word."

*****

Mary told Maria, "Let's get you ready for a rodeo. There is one next month in Billings, Montana." Mary worked with Maria and Dusty. Maria could ride, and Dusty could run, but they were still not connecting with each other. Mary said, "We are going back to the beginning. Starting Monday, every afternoon, when you get here, you stay with that horse until you leave. Brush him, ride him, lead him around, whatever, but don't leave his side."

"Okay," said Maria.

The next week, Mary worked with her filly while Maria worked with Dusty. At the end of the week, Mary told Maria, "Okay, tomorrow is Saturday. We are going to run barrels."

The next morning, Mary set up the barrels. Maria saddled up Dusty and rode into the arena. Mary sat up on the side with her stopwatch. Maria and Dusty went down the alley, turned, and came back fast to the first barrel, then the second, then the third and home.

"A 14.80," said Mary. "Okay, yawl both come here. Dusty, you have got to let Maria know when you're going to turn. Maria, you've got to feel him shift and then help him get out of the hole if you're ever going to win anything." Mary walked up to Dusty. She pulled his head down and whispered in his ear. "Okay, do it again," said Mary, "but this time, do it slow. Feel the shifts, then react."

Maria and Dusty went to the edge of the alley, then headed to the first barrel. This time, Maria felt it when he sat up. She never had that problem with Toby; she always felt it, but Dusty's reaction was so smooth that they were hard to feel. Then they turned the second barrel. She felt it again. Then the third. "I felt it that time," said Maria. "He is just so smooth it's hard to feel."

"Okay, just concentrate on Dusty. Don't worry about the barrels. Dusty knows how to run the barrels. I want you to try this. When you come to the barrel, close your eyes and feel each barrel. Close your eyes. Trust Dusty. Trust that he can make the run without you. Be one with your horse."

"Okay, I'll try," said Maria. They rode down the alley, turned, and came back. When they got to the first barrel, Maria closed her eyes. She felt Dusty sat up for the turn. She was ready. They headed to the second barrel. Again, she closed her eyes. Dusty arched his back a little just before the turn. She felt it again. They headed for the third barrel. This time, she felt it with her eyes open. They headed home.

"A 14.65," said Mary. "That's better. Okay, run it one more time. This time, just concentrate. You both have a job—his is to run and yours is to ride. Don't just sit there. Stand up in those stirrups, lean over, and ride."

"Okay," said Maria.

They rode down the alley, turned, and came back flying. They hit the first turn. "Perfect," said Mary. Then the second. "That's it!" yelled Mary. Then the third. "Yes!" said Mary. "Now run, Dusty, run." Dusty slid to a stop at the end of the alley. They came walking back out into the arena. Mary had her head down looking at the watch.

"Well, what?"

"A 13.90," said Mary. "Great run, you two. That's what it takes."

Maria smiled from ear to ear with a tear in her eyes. She jumped off and hugged Dusty and gave him a treat. They worked on barrels every afternoon until it was time to head to the rodeo event in Billings.

Mary got Jim to drive the truck and trailer and haul the horses. Mary was taking Bob so she could ride with Maria in the grand entry and be there with her in the alley. Kattie and Selena were also going. It was a three-day event, and first place would get $5,000.00 and a buckle. They left out early Thursday morning. Mary had her mom make reservations. It was like old times when Mary and Billie were riding.

As they got there, Jim found a place to park the trailer. They set up the round pen and unhooked the trailer. Mary and Maria put their horses in the round pen and gave them some hay. Mary said, "Come on, Maria, let's get you signed up." They walked to the arena and found the sign-up table.

"Well, hi, Mary," said the promoter of the event. "It's good to see you."

Mary said, "I want to sign up my friend here, Maria."

"You're not riding?" asked the man.

"No, I'm just here to help her. This is her first real event," said Mary.

"Well, I figured surely you would compete since you're one of our sponsors."

"Here, young lady, fill this out," said the woman at the table as she handed a clipboard to Maria.

The promoter pulled Mary to the side. "I really need you to ride."

"Why?" asked Mary.

"Because we only have two other riders."

"Who?" asked Mary.

"Jane Harper and Jamie Spears. I guess your girl will be guaranteed third place no matter what."

Mary laughed. "We didn't come for third place, Tom. Okay, I'll ride, but we won't be third," said Mary.

"Well, all right then," said Tom.

Mary and Maria went back to the trailer to get ready.

"Well, did you get her signed up?" asked Kattie.

"Yes, we're all set," said Mary, then mounted up and headed to the alley.

"Are you running too?" asked Maria.

"Yeah, there are only two other girls who entered, but they are the top two in this sport right now. But you and I are going to show them something."

As they rode up to the other girls, Mary said, "Hi, Jamie."

Jane turned and said, "Shit, what are you doing here?"

"Oh, I'm just here helping a friend. This is her first real event."

"Oh, that's good," said Jane.

The grand entry started. Maria stuck close to Mary the whole way. Then they had the prayer and Pledge of Allegiance and the national anthem, and they all rode out. Kattie, Jim, and Selena were in the stands; they didn't know Mary was competing too.

"Ladies and gentlemen, are yawl ready for some barrel racing?" asked the announcer. The crowd yelled. "Okay, let's get started. First up from New Mexico, Ms. Jane Harper. Jane is ranked number 1 again this year. Let's go, Jane." Jane came out of the alley fast, rounded the first barrel and then the second, and headed for the third. As she came back by the timer, the announcer said, "A 14.35, folks. Okay, next up from Wyoming, Ms. Jamie Spears." Jamie came out hard on Blue Boy. She made her rounds and ran back by the timer. The announcer said, "A 14.40, folks."

Mary started laughing. "What is it?" asked Maria.

"They're just give this thang to us. They didn't think you were a threat. Now go get 'em."

"Next up, a new cowgirl representing one of our sponsors from South Dakota, folks, Ms. Maria Sanchez." Maria and Dusty came out fast. They nailed the first barrel and then the second. Dusty flew to the third barrel, and they headed back home. The crowd stood up as she passed the timer. The announcer said, "A 13.98, folks."

Mary was watching Jane's and Jamie's faces when the announcer called Maria's time and busted out laughing.

"Okay, folks, we have one more ride for this event. She sponsored this event, so first, let's thank her for that. From South Dakota and Mary Plumber's Stables, welcome, Ms. Mary Plumber." The crowd cheered. Mary and Bob came out with Bob slinging dirt. They nailed the first and second barrels and headed to the third, rounded the third, and headed home. Kattie and Jim were yelling for her. The announcer said, "Folks, a 13.65 run for Ms. Mary Plumber and her horse Bob."

Mary came back out of the arena. Jane and Jamie were gone. Maria was waiting. "Great run," said Maria.

Mary laughed. "I want you to learn from that," said Mary. "Don't ever underestimate your competition. Let's go put these boys up." They unsaddled and brushed their horses down and gave them some hay and oats and fresh water.

Mary and Maria went to the stands to join the others. They stopped and got hamburgers, chips, and Cokes. Selena gave Maria a big hug, and Mary hugged her mom and dad.

"I didn't think you were running," said Jim.

"Well, when Tom told me that Jane and Jamie were the only entries, I couldn't help it. It's not every day you get to show up a world champion." Jim just laughed.

After the rodeo was over, Mary went and found Tom, the promoter. She asked him if he had anybody she could hire to watch her horses overnight.

"Sure," said Tom. "I'll get you somebody."

Mary handed him a key to the trailer. "Thanks," said Mary as she walked to her trailer.

"Okay, let's go," said Mary. "Tom is going to get someone to watch the horses."

"Great," said Kattie.

The next day, they came back to the trailer. They took care of the horses. Mary told Maria, "The other girls will be riding hard tonight trying catch up. You need to run a 13.60 or 13.70 to lock it up. I'm going to run around 14.00. The plan is for you to get first and me to get second. But if you don't have a good run, then I've got to go faster to keep them out of first."

That night, Jane came hard; she ran a 13.90. Jamie ran a 14.10, Maria ran a 13.69, and Mary ran a 13.98. Mary and Maria were still holding the lead. Mary got somebody to watch the horses that night, plus all day the next until they got back so she and Maria could swim and lie around the pool the next day.

That night going into the final event, Jane had 28.25, Jamie had 28.50, Maria had 27.67, and Mary had 27.63 with the lead. The girls lay out by the pool until noon. They all went to eat, then headed back to the arena. They took care of their horses. Mary was coaching Maria the whole time, telling her, "You need to be 13.70 to win." They got their horse ready and headed to the arena. Jane and Jamie wouldn't even speak to them.

The announcer said, "Okay, folks, it's time for the final events. Give a big hand for Ms. Jane Harper. Jane came out smoking. She made the first two barrels and then the third and headed home. The announcer said, "A 13.73, folks, giving her a 41.98. Next up, Ms. Spears." Jamie came out. She made the first two barrels and then the third and headed home. The announcer said, "A 13.85, folks, giving her a 42.35. Now the new young cowgirl, Ms. Maria Sanchez." Maria and Dusty came out, burning up the dirt. They nailed the first two barrels and then the third and flew back home and through the alley. The announcer said, "A 13.72, folks, giving her a 41.39. Now for the last runner of the event, give a hand for Ms. Mary Plumber." Mary and Bob came out fast. They make the first two barrels, then as they rounded the third and final barrel, Mary pulled back on Bob and walked the rest of the way, waving her hat. The announcer, the judges, and all the fans stood up and cheered as she walked out of the arena. "What a classy move," said the announcer. "Ms. Mary Plumber, folks, give her a hand. She sponsored this event."

"Maria Sanchez, folks, gets a check for $5,000.00 and a silver buckle. Ms. Harper gets second place and $3,000.00. And Ms. Spears gets third and $1,500.00."

Mary and Maria took their horses to the trailer. They unsaddled them, then brushed and fed them. They then went to the stands. Kattie hugged Mary, Selena hugged Maria, and then Mary hugged Jim. He had a tear in his eyes. Everybody sitting around them stood back up and clapped for Mary.

As they sat down, Maria told Mary, "You could have won."

Mary hugged her. "It wasn't about winning for me. I just wanted to show them that I could. You're the new cowgirl in this family!"

Part 4

Chapter 1

Maid of Honor

Well, Billie would now be going to college in Cheyenne, Wyoming. She would be studying to be a veterinarian, like Kattie and Rose. Jim was sad to see her go, but happy she was following her dream. For now, he still had Mary and enjoyed working with her at the stables. They had a lot of fun together. Mary loved bossing him around, although most of the time, she was just joking. Mary was now seventeen years old and a senior in high school. Maria was now thirteen, a teenager. She was still working with Dusty on the barrels. She had asked Mary to rodeo with her this next season. Mary hadn't made up her mind yet; there was a lot going on at Plumber's Gap.

Troy was talking about retiring and getting a few cows of his own. He and Jim had been talking about Jim's new bloodline of cows. Jim hoped he would build a herd of them. Kattie and Jim had been talking about who was going to run the ranch if Troy did retire. Ben was as good as gold and a great cowhand, but he was not that much younger than Troy. Also, they felt that if Troy retired, Kathy would want to spend more time at home with Troy and Tommie. They would then need someone to work the barn and care for the stock horses. But for now, the big event was Rose and Paul's wedding. In just three weeks, Rose and Paul were getting married. Rose had asked Mary to be her maid of honor. They were planning a small wedding at Mary's stables; they want to get married on horseback in the arena.

Billie had taken a week off from school and came home to help with the wedding. She was also a bridesmaid, along with Selena and Maria. Tommie would be the ring bearer, and Paul had asked a rodeo friend of his to be the best man. All the participants of the wedding would be on horseback, including the preacher. Mary had Selena and Maria cleaning and washing down everything. They were getting down all the dust and spiderwebs, then Mary had someone coming to spray the whole thing with insect and fly spray. The reception would be at the house. Troy and Pete were going to roast a pig out back. The wedding would be at three o'clock that afternoon and the reception directly after. Kattie was so happy for Rose but felt bad that her girls were leaving her, all but Mary. Mary said, "I ain't never leaving Plumber's Gap, not for more than a few days anyway."

The day had come. Mary and Maria had all the horses saddled and ready. Now they could go get dressed for the wedding. The girls were all wearing the old-timey white lace bloomers under their dresses because of being on horseback. Not only for padding but to also keep some things hidden from view. Kattie had the wedding march recorded and ready to play. First, the preacher came out of the alley into the arena. All the guests were sitting in white chairs. He rode to the end of the arena in front of a beautiful arbor decorated with white roses. He turned the horse and faced the alleyway. Then Paul and his best man in black tux came out into the arena. They turned their horses and stood on the preacher's left side, facing the middle.

Kattie started playing the march. In came Tommie on Buddy. Buddy was draped with a blanket made of white roses with Tommie wearing a white gown with a train that touched Buddy's back. Tommie and Buddy stopped, facing the preacher, then came the maids—Mary and Billie side by side in front, then Selena and Maria side by side behind. They circled and stopped on the right-hand side, facing the middle. Then came Rose and Pete. Rose was on Molly, and Pete was on a stock horse. Both horses were draped with rose blankets, like Buddy's. Rose was dragging her train across the sand in the arena, and her veil was held by a ring of white roses on her head. Such and beautiful sight with her light-brown skin.

The preacher started the service. Kattie and Alice were both already crying. Then the preacher said to Paul, "You may kiss your bride." They leaned over to each other and kissed. The maids circled and headed out, with Tommie following. Then Pete and the best man circled and headed out, and then Paul and Rose left side by side holding hands, with the preacher following.

Mary, Maria, Kathy, and Billie gathered all the horses and started putting them up as everyone else headed to the house to change clothes for the reception. Once all the tacks were put up and the horses were put away, they headed to the house also.

The reception was great. Everyone had a good time. Paul and Rose danced. The best man kept flirting with Billie, and he did get her to dance once, but that was it. Mary danced with Jim and Troy, and Billie danced with Jim, and Troy danced with Tommie. Paul and Rose left for parts unknown; they never would say where.

The next day, Selena and Maria got busy loading up the rented chairs and arbor in Mary's trailer so she could take it back. Jim and Pete cleaned up out back, and Kattie, Mary, and Alice got the house back in order.

"Dang," said Mary, "weddings are a lot of work."

"Yes, they are," said Kattie, "but Rose will remember hers for the rest of her life."

"Okay, well, I've got to go take those chairs back to town. I'll see you later." She kissed her mom.

That night at supper, Mary asked, "Well, what are we going to do about Troy and Kathy?"

"Well, your father and I have been talking. If Troy is going to leave, we need to be ready, so we are thinking about building a barn and bunkhouse across the road on that 40 acres. Your dad can move his operation there and shut down the Montana ranch for now. He can bring his crew here and manage both with Ben's and Aaron's help. What do you think, Mary? asked Kattie.

Jim said, "I'll still be around to help you some. I won't need to drive to Montana every day."

"Sounds good to me," said Mary. "What about the stock horses?"

"We will have to hire somebody," said Jim.

"We need another couple. Pete and Alice are getting old. They won't be able to work many more years. They are family," said Kattie. "We are not going to run them off, but they need help now."

"Okay," said Mary, "why don't I put a new trailer there at the stables for Selena and Maria? It will be a tax break for the stables, then Dad can let Aaron and his help stay in the trailer there. You won't need to build a bunkhouse right now, just a barn. If we find a couple for the stock barn, we can put another trailer there or build something."

Kattie looked at Jim. "Okay by me," said Jim.

"Me too," said Kattie.

"Okay, I'll order a trailer tomorrow," said Mary. "I'll just have figure out where to put it."

"I can help you with that," said Jim.

"Good. Tomorrow then," said Mary.

Mary got a new three-bedroom double-wide trailer for Selena and Maria. Then they would set it up on the north side of the stables close to the highway and far enough away from the stables to cut down on the smell and the noises. That was Jim's idea. Selena and Maria had made a nice home out of the old trailer across the road, but this one would be even nicer, said Selena. Jim had hired a contractor to start construction on the new barn across the road. Troy said he would stay on Plumber's Gap until after the roundup this fall. That would give Jim time to get his operation moved. Kathy said she would stay until school was out next spring. She wanted to make sure someone was ready to take over the care of her horses.

Mary was in her office when the phone rang. She picked it up. "Plumber's Stables, Mary speaking."

She heard, "Hey, sweetie."

"Well, hi there, Tom, what's up?"

"I just wanted to check in on you. I haven't heard from you since you showed them girls in Billings last year." Tom was a rodeo promoter and stock contractor out of Oklahoma. He put on rodeos all over the Northwestern United States and some as far down as Texas. Troy knew him from his rodeo days and introduced them to each other about three years ago. They hit it off from the start. He got her to sponsor some barrel racing events last year.

"You looking for sponsors?" asked Mary.

"Always," said Tom. "But that's not why I called. I've got a horse I want to send you."

"Oh, okay," said Mary. "What's wrong with him?"

"That's what I want you to figure out. He has been one of my top bucking horses for the last three years. Now it's like he has lost his fight and just half bucks. Nothing like he used to be."

"Okay, send him on. I'll see if I can find out."

"You riding this year?" asked Tom.

"Well, don't know yet. I'd like too. Maria wants too."

"That little girl who won in Billings?" asked Tom.

"Yep," said Mary.

"I tell you what, if you and that girl will run the barrels in my events this season, I'll add $500.00 to each pot."

"Okay," said Mary. "If you do, I'll sponsor the breakaway events."

"Deal," said Tom. "I'll send you that horse in a couple of days."

"I'll be looking for him," said Mary.

Mary went out to the arena where Maria was and said, "Get Dusty ready. We are running in at least eight events this season. I need your mom to sign a release form. I'll get mine to sign one for me."

"Yeehaw!" said Maria as she spun Dusty around and around in a circle.

That afternoon, Mary gave Selena a blank consent to sign for Maria, and Mary took one home for Kattie to sign that night.

"I guess you and Maria are barrel racing this season," said Kattie.

"Well, Tom said he would add five hundred to each pot at his events," said Mary. "He is putting on eight rodeos this season. I'll pay all the travel expenses. You and Dad can just enjoy getting away."

Kattie looked at Jim. He just smiled. She turned back to Mary. "Okay, give me the form."

"Oh, by the way, Dad, Tom's sending one of his bucking horses in a couple of days for us to work with," said Mary.

"Do what?" asked Jim.

"It will be okay, Dad. It's just a horse." Mary laughed as she walked away. Jim shook his head, and Kattie started laughing.

Two days later, a truck and trailer showed up with the horse Tom sent for Mary to work with. He was a big tricolored horse, about sixteen hands, with huge muscled legs and thighs. His shoulders and neck were also huge. But he was as gentle as a lamb to handle and right away loved Mary's treats. Mary rubbed him all over his face and told him, "We are going to be great friends. We will spend a lot of time together." Mary put him up in one of the empty stalls for the night.

The next afternoon, Mary put him in the round pen so she could watch him move around. She first let him walk around each direction, then trotted him a little both ways. She tied him to the rail, then rubbed him all over, except for his privates, filling for knots or growths under the skid. Tom said that his vet had drawn blood from him for testing but found nothing wrong. Mary turned him back loose and tried to run him. A slow lope was all he would do and only for a few feet. Mary tied him again. She looked at all four feet; they were clean, no cut or bruised frogs, and shoes looked fine. "What's wrong with you, boy?" asked Mary. She put him back in the stall.

She went into her office and called Tom. He answered, "What's up, sweetie?"

"Well, I've been looking at your horse," said Mary. "Did you change his diet over the winter or add anything?"

"No, don't think so," said Tom. "We started our spring training workouts on our horses just like always, but he just wasn't the same."

"Okay," said Mary, "just checking. He seems fit, but something's wrong. I'll figure it out." "I hope so," said Tom.

The next afternoon, Mary put him in the side lot and let him graze. She sat nearby him on the ground and just watched him. As he grazed along and stepped and turned, she watched his movement. Nothing. He looked perfect.

The next afternoon, Mary got the paint horse out again. She led him around with her as she cleaned out stalls. She noticed occasionally he would reach his head back under his belly. Once, he even took his hind foot and pawed at his belly, like a dog after a flea or something. Mary reached under and felt in the area she thought he was trying to reach. Nothing. As she was moving her hand around. She bumped a knot by his private parts, and he let out a quill and sidestepped away from her. "Easy, boy, I'm sorry," said Mary as she stood up and rubbed his face. "You got something going on down there, don't you?"

Rodeo contractors use mares or cut their male horses and make geldings out of them. But this boy had got problems around his male part. Mary put him back in his stall and fed him. That night, Mary told her mom about it. Kattie told her she would come to the stables in the morning to look at him.

The next morning, Kattie came to the stables. Mary got the paint out of his stall and put him in the alley. Kattie took a flashlight and looked where Mary said the knot was. "Yep," said Kattie, "he's got something going on there. We will have to tranquilize him and lay him on his back. Let's take him to the clinic, where it's more sterile and has better lighting."

"Okay," said Mary, "I'll hook up the trailer and load him up."

Mary and Kattie got in the truck and headed to the clinic in Deadwood. On the way, Kattie asked Mary, "What are your plans after graduation next week? I know you're rodeoing this fall, but what about next year? Have you thought about college?"

"I know you want me to go," said Mary, "but somebody's got to keep you and Dad in line." She laughed. "I may change my mind later, but for now, I want to keep doing what I'm doing," said Mary.

They pulled up to the clinic. Mary parked to one side of the drive. She went to the back to unload the horse, while Kattie went inside to get things ready. Kattie opened the side door, and Mary led the horse in. They ran a wide sling under his belly and hooked it to an overhead hoist. They raised it up close to his belly, then Kattie gave him the shot. In about five minutes, he was having trouble standing. They raised the hoist up to catch his weight. One lady had his head over her shoulder holding it up. After he was out, they eased him down onto a padded frame. One lady still had his head, and two others were pulling his legs out to one side. Once he was lying on his side on the pads, they unhooked the strap from the hoist. Kattie stepped on a foot pedal mounted to the floor, and the frame started lifting the horse up. Once the horse was at the height Kattie wanted, she stopped. They then put small padded slings around his ankles and hooked them to the hoist and rolled him onto his back. They unhooked the sling on one hind leg and folded it out so the belly would be exposed, then tied it off.

Mary watched in awe as her mother and the assistants worked around the horse. Kattie touched the area in question and felt the knot. She circled the area with a white marker. One of the others rolled a portable x-ray machine in and set it up. Everyone had stepped behind a protective curtain. Then they all came back to the table. There were wires and tubes hooked to the horse as they watched a screen. Kattie went to look at the x-ray. She came back. "Okay," she said, "he has a cyst up inside his remaining sac flap that's inflamed. Let's get it out." Kattie took a scaffold and started to cut the flap back. As Kattie was working, she was talking to her staff. "That's why we don't leave much sac flap when we cut a horse. This horse was probably thrown on the ground when he was a yearling, cut with a pocketknife, and turned loose. There, I got it. Clean this out really good," said Kattie. "I'll send this to be tested. I don't think it's anything, but we'll see."

They eased the horse back on his side, then let the table down. They hooked the big strap back to the hoist and picked him up and moved him away from the table. Then they started waking him back up. In a few minutes, fifteen to twenty, he started trying to find his feet. The floor was covered with a thick rubber pad. They started easing off on the hoist to let him stand but kept him lifted some so he wouldn't fall. Once he got his control back, they let off the rest of the way with the hoist.

Mary was standing at his head, talking to him. "Hey, boy, you're okay." He tried to turn his head. "Just look at me, boy. You're good," said Mary. She clipped the lead rope back on him, and they removed the sling.

"Take him out back in the lot and let him drink some water. "Don't let him lie down."

After about an hour, Kattie told Mary, "You can load him back up now, and we will take him back to the stables." Mary led him to the trailer and loaded him up and tied him short to keep him from trying to lie down on the way back.

Once they made it back to the stables, Mary unloaded him and put him in his stall. "What now?" asked Mary.

"Well," said Kattie, "we watch the area and keep it clean. Tomorrow you can work him in the round pen to keep that area loosened up and work the soreness out. I should get the tests back in a couple of days on the cyst."

"Do you think that's why he wouldn't buck?" asked Mary.

"Sure, it is. Where it was located, it wouldn't have bothered him much just walking around. But running and bucking, that cyst was attached to his belly liner. When he moved, bucking or running, each time the belly skin moved and shifted, it pulled on that cyst until it got inflamed around it. There was no infection in the area. It was just an aggravation of the tissue around the area, like a rock in your boot rubbing your foot each time you step until you get it out. Once you do, it's still sore for a while, but it will go away. He'll be fine now once it heals back up."

For the next week, Mary worked the paint horse every day in the round pen. He would now run and turn and twist with no problem. Mary called Paul.

"Hi, Mary," said Paul.

"I need your help," said Mary.

"Okay, what do you need?"

"Well, you know those bucking chutes you had me build?"

"Yes, I remember."

"Well, I need you to use one of them. I have the horse. I just need you to ride him," said Mary.

"Okay, when?" asked Paul.

"Tomorrow," said Mary. "It's Saturday."

"Okay, how about 4:00 p.m.?" said Paul.

"Okay, bring your gear with you," said Mary.

"Okay, see you tomorrow," said Paul.

The next afternoon, Mary had Troy and Jim recruited to be the pickup men for this one-horse rodeo. When Paul got there, they were already waiting. Mary had the paint horse in the alley. Paul and Rose came into the alleyway. "Holy shit," said Paul. He walked up to the horse and rubbed his face. "Hey, Moon Beam."

"Moon Bean?" said Mary.

"Yep, that's his name. What are you doing with him?" asked Paul.

"Tom brought him to me. He wouldn't buck anymore, but I think we got him fixed."

"Really?" said Paul. "This horse here is a bucking fool. I've made a lot of money with this horse. Well, let's get set up."

Mary took Moon Beam and loaded him in the chute. Kattie, Billie, Kathy, Maria, and Tommie were all there to watch the show. Ben and Carl were there to help with the chute and to help Paul rig up. Paul had everything ready; he started easing down onto Moon Beam's back. He tucked his chin and nodded. The gate swung open, and out came Moon Beam and Paul. Moon Beam jumped into the air and kicked his hips up. As his hide hooves hit the ground, he reared and jumped again as Paul spurred Moon Beam's shoulders. Each time Moon Beam jumped, he kicked higher and harder than before. Jim was watching the time. After eight seconds, Jim and Troy moved in to pick Paul up. He slid on behind Jim as Troy rode in and pulled the girth off Moon Beam. Moon Bean made a lope around the arena, then stopped and walked over to the chute.

Paul told Mary, "I don't know what you did, but there is nothing wrong with that horse. If anything, he bucks harder than before."

"Good," said Mary. "Thank you so much. That's what I needed to hear."

Troy told Paul, "That was one hell of a ride."

"Yes, it was," said Paul. "That's a good horse."

Jim said, "Let's go drink a beer and cook something."

"Sounds good to me," said Paul.

Mary went into her office and called Tom. "Hey, sweetie," said Tom, "what's up?"

"Well, you can come get your horse. He is ready to go."

"Are you sure?" asked Tom.

"Yep," said Mary. "Paul Plumber just rode him. He said he bucked harder than ever."

"What was wrong with him?" asked Tom.

"He had a cyst on his privates. I'll send you the vet report."

"Well, good job, girl. I'll send after him Monday. Thanks for your help."

"Anytime," said Mary. She went back out to the arena and got Moon Beam and put him in his stall. She brushed him down and gave him some food. Then she went to the house, where everyone else had gone.

Graduation ceremony for Mary's school was Monday night. She would be graduating high school. Even though she never really liked school, she did very good. She had been a straight A student since the first grade. Mary never had any problems at school; she didn't bother anybody, and nobody bothered her. But Mary was always the one who hung out with the lonely girls, the ones whom no one sat with or the ones others picked on. Once Mary took them under her wing, everybody left them alone. The teachers called them Mary's lambs. If any of them had grade or behavior problems, the teachers told Mary, and she fixed it. They didn't know how and didn't ask. Mary not only had a knack for understanding horses, she was good with other girls. Mary graduated valedictorian of her class. All her lambs graduated as National Honor Society members.

Chapter 2

Rodeoing

Now that Mary was out of school, she was concentrating on barrel racing again. She and Maria were practicing every day. They had their first rodeo in two weeks in Oklahoma. Billie was home from college for the summer. Mary asked her to compete with them this season, but Billie wanted to work at the clinic this summer. She said she didn't have time for rodeoing anymore. Maria was getting better and better every day, and so was her horse Dusty. They were finally working as a team. Mary thought they were both ready and hoped they could put a good show on for Tom.

Wednesday morning, they loaded up everything but the horses and got ready for Oklahoma. It would be a long trip. They would leave out late this afternoon and drive straight through and get there sometime in the morning. Kattie and Jim would swap out driving. Once they got there and set up, they would go to the motel and rest. Tom would have somebody watch their horses; that was part of his and Mary's deal.

They got to the arena about midmorning, unloaded the round pen, and set it up, then unload Dusty and Bob. They unhooked the trailer and headed to the motel to get some rest. Around 4:00 p.m., they headed back to the arena to get the horses ready for tonight. Mary and Maria went to the sign-up table, paid their entry fees, and signed up. Tom said, "Well, you did make it. How was your trip?"

"Long," said Mary. "How's your horse?"

"His great," said Tom. "You will get to see him tonight. Are you entering the breakaway event?"

"Hadn't plan to. Remember, I'm the sponsor."

"Well, what about that girl?" asked Tom.

"Her name is Maria," said Mary. "And that's up to her."

Maria said, "Sure, I'm not scared."

"Well, then sign her up," said Tom. "I only have two entered. She will make three."

Mary and Maria went back to the trailer to get Dusty and Bob.

"What do I do in the breakaway?" asked Maria.

"Just like we do at home. The only thing is, they have a rope up that your horse runs through. You can't break the rope before the calves clears the chute. That's the only difference. Just rope the calves as fast as you can and break Dusty. The rope does the rest."

Mary and Maria rode to the alleyway. There were four other girls who entered in the event. Mary didn't know any of them. She spoke to them all and told them good luck. One of the girls was in her late twenties, and Mary could tell she thought she was better than the rest of them. Just the kind of girl Mary liked to compete against. Mary smiled at Maria. Mary had drawn third, and Maria fifth, both good spots. They started the grand entry. Mary and Maria both carried a flag. They circled the arena in opposite directions as they played, and a girl sang the national anthem. Then they stopped in the middle, one facing one way and one facing the other, as everybody said the Pledge of Allegiance, then the prayer for all the animals and the participants in the rodeo. Everybody made a lope and headed out of the arena. The announcer came on to pump up the crowd.

A girl named Jill had the first run and was ready in the alleyway. The older girl was second; her name was Pam. The announcer called for Jill, and she took off into the area and around the first barrel, then the second, and the third. She came running home. The announcer said, "A 14.80 to start things off, folks." The announcer called for Pam. She took off down the alley. She had a good-looking horse. She came out into the arena, cleared all the barrels, then headed home. "A 14.35," said the announcer. "Good run." Pam just smiled when she came back by Mary. That was probably not the smartest thing to do. They called Mary. She and Bob flew down the alley, Bob slinging dirt behind him. They nailed the first barrel and then the second. Once they rounded the third, Bob lunged back to the alley. "A 13.98," said the announcer. After Mary got Bob shut down, she walked him past that Pam girl, but this time, she didn't smile, and neither did Mary. The fourth girl made her run and scored a 14.50; her name was Clare. Now it was Maria's turn. They called her name, and she and Dusty bust out of the alley flying around the barrels, then back home. "A 13.75," said the announcer. "Great run." The sixth and last girl's name was Page. She came out fast, but she and her horse were fighting each other at the barrels. "A 15.40," said the announcer. "Okay, folks, we will see how they do tomorrow night."

Next, they had the calf roping, then the bulldogging, and then team roping. It was now time for the breakaway roping. Mary went with Maria for support. The announcer said, "Folks, I want to introduce you to the sponsor of this event. There on the big palomino, Ms. Mary Plumber from South Dakota. She has a stable there in Lead, and she works with problem horses. If your horse has a problem and is still breathing, she can probably fix it. Okay, folks, let's see some girls breakaway roping."

Page, one of the girls who ran barrels, was first. They released the calves, and she came out and missed her calves. The next girl was out of Texas and looked like a boy. They released her calves, and she came out and let the calves get ahead of her. She threw and caught the calves. "A 10.50," said the announcer. Maria was up next.

Jim nudged Kattie and said, "Watch this."

They released her calves. Maria came out right on the calf's tail and dropped her loop over its head. Dusty locked up and slid his hind end, and the rope popped. "A 6.80-second run, folks. There's your leader going into tomorrow night. She also turned the fastest time on the barrel racing tonight. Give her a hand, folks."

Jim said, "I told you."

"Where did she learn that?" asked Kattie.

"That's what she and Mary do for fun. That and pinning calves," said Jim.

"You're kidding," said Kattie.

"Nope, and they are both good at it too, really good."

"Well, we shouldn't be surprised. Our girl is special," said Kattie. "Yes, she is," said Jim.

The next night, Maria ran a 13.95, Mary ran a 13.68, and Pam ran a 14.08. The others were in the high 14s and low 15s. Mary was now in the lead with 27.66; Maria, second with 27.70; and Pam, third with 28.43. Maria scored a 6.50 in the breakaway roping. No one else was even close.

Saturday night, the crowd was even bigger. Some of them had heard about the girls from South Dakota running the barrels in the 13s. Clare ran first. She made her run, a 14.80. Then Page ran a 14.87. Then Jill ran a 14.45. Pam went for broke and ran a 14.28. Maria was next.

Mary told her, "You set the pace. We have them beat if we run around 14.00 or lower. Don't take a chance on knocking over a barrel. Be smart. Make a clean run, and you will win."

"Okay," said Maria, "I will."

The announcer called for Maria. Sher and Dusty came out strong, then made first barrel, the second, and then the third. They crossed the light. "A 13.80," said the announcer. "Now, folks, here comes Ms. Mary Plumber." Mary and Bob came out hard. They made the first two barrels, then the third. They headed home. "A 13.96," said the announcer. "Maria is the winner, folks. Mary gets second, and Pam gets third."

Later, Maria scored a 7.20 in the breakaway roping and took first place in it too. Maria took home two buckles and two checks and was a very happy little girl.

As they headed back to South Dakota, Jim told Maria, "Well, you are the big winner in this trip."

Mary said, "I'm very proud of you, Maria."

Rose and Paul came to the ranch with an announcement. Rose was expecting a baby. Kattie was so excited for a baby. Alice and Pete were also so happy for her. What wonderful news. Mary was happy for Rose and Paul but would be happier if it was a new colt that she could play with. She knew nothing about a baby. Mary gave Rose a big hug and told her congratulations, then headed to the stables. Billie was holding Rose's hand and smiling from ear to ear. She and Rose had become very close after working together at the clinic. Everybody hugged Paul. Jim and Pete shook his hand. They told him, "Your life is about to change forever." Then they laughed. Maria was in the huddle of girls. She was so happy for her. As did Selena, Rose's cousin.

The next rodeo would be in Nebraska, not as far away as Oklahoma but still a good way off. Mary and Maria were ready for it. Maria got two checks of over $6,000.00 from the last rodeo. She gave them to her mom. She hoped to win some more in Nebraska. Mary told her, "If you make good, clean runs, you will win. As far as the breakaway event, you will be hard to beat. You're that good."

Mary got second place and a check for $2,000.00, barely enough to pay for the trip. But for her, it was not about the money or the fame; she was proving a point: a good horse and a good rider working together can and will beat a great horse and a great rider not working together every time. Maria and Dusty were living proof of that. Not a great horse or a great rider but a team that could be unbeatable.

Mary and Maria proved it again in Nebraska. Mary took first in the barrel racing; Maria took second. Maria took first in the breakaway roping. Again, she would be hard for anyone to beat. One of the girls competing in the breakaway wanted Mary to train her and her horse at her stables. Two of the barrel racers wanted her to work with them also. Mary was setting up a weeklong team riding school. She was going to charge $1,200.00 for the week for each person. She would board the horses at the stables, but the girl would have to get their on-motel rooms.

The two barrel racers came in on Sunday afternoon and brought their horses to the stables. They were rooming together in Deadwood. The other girl was coming first thing in the morning. Mary was going to let her work with Maria on breakaway roping. Mary would work with the two barrel racers. But first, they would all work with Mary on the fundamentals of team riding.

Monday at 8:00 a.m., Mary and all the girls were there and ready to get started. Mary set up the poles in the arena, then had each girl run the poles. After they each had their turn, Mary got the girls altogether. "Now you're all probably wondering, *Why does she have us running poles?* I'll tell you. I want you to learn to move with your horses as they work no matter what the event. In rodeo, each event is a team sport. Bull riding is scored half for the rider and half for the bull. Same with bronc riding, and bareback riding. In the other events, it's man and horse working against the clock as a team. I want you each to run the poles at half speed and feel your horse move under you. Feel them shift their weight on each turn."

They all took their turn, each girl running in a slow lope, trying to feel their way around the poles. Mary asked each one if they felt it. They all said yes, but she wasn't sure. She asked them to do it again, this time to shift their weight with their horse. She watched them as they ran the poles. Once they finished, she had them put their horses up.

Once they were done, Mary told them she had asked Salena to fix them lunch at her trailer. Mexican food. Selena was great at cooking authentic Mexican food, which Mary loved. They all walked down to Selena's house, along with Maria. Selena had everything ready—chips and salsa, fajitas, refried beans, and guacamole. Them little skinny girls ate and ate and ate until they were ready to pop. They each hugged Selena and told their thanks. Mary told the girls all that she knew. They were too full to ride. She said, "Just go to your rooms and rest and come back tomorrow morning."

The next morning, Mary took them all on a ride through the valley, even Maria. When they got back to the stables, she had them unsaddle their horses and led them into the arena. Mary told them to slowly rub their horses all over with their bare hands and talk to them softly. She told them to talk to their horses like they would talk to a good friend. The girls started laughing. Mary asked, "Do you want to win or just compete?" They stopped laughing. "Look, I know it sounds strange. Most of you have been told since you were little to show your horse who's boss. They know who the boss is. They know who feeds them, who takes care of them, and in return, they let you ride them. They want to be your friend, your equal, your partner. You don't believe me, do you? I'll show you." She motioned at Maria.

She brought over three folding chairs and put them facing each other. Mary said, "Okay, rub your horse's nose and give it a kiss." They did, then Maria led all three horses to the end of the arena. Mary told the three girls to sit down in one of the chairs, and they did. Then Maria removed the lead ropes and let the horses go. As the girls sat in the chairs, Mary said, "Don't say anything. Just ignore them." The horses wondered around the arena, then slowly started walking one by one to the girls. Each horse walked up behind their owner and stood there. "Now when your horse touches you or nickers, turn around and rub their nose," said Mary. "Talk to them and look them in the eyes."

One horse put his nose over its owner's head and nibbled her hair. Another horse nickered and pawed the ground, and the third laid his head on his owner's shoulder. They all turned in response to their horses, rubbed them, and talked to them. Mary said, "You see, they are not just stupid animals." One of the girls started crying; she could see the care in her horse's eye. "A dog may be man's best friend, but a horse is a girl's best friend. All day long, your horse will run until he or she falls dead from exhaustion if you ask them to. They depend on you to take care of them, and in return, they will work themselves to death for you. But you have to do your part. You have to lighten their load when you can. Now let me and Maria show you how this will help you and your horse. Maria is the smallest, so we will use her as the rider."

Mary said, "One at a time, I want yawl to let Maria ride piggyback." The girls started laughing. The first girl got Maria on her back. "Okay," said Mary, "walk in a circle to the left." As the girl turned left, Maria leaned to the right. The girl tried hard to turn. "Now," said Mary, "make a circle to the right." As she did, Maria slightly leaned right with her. "Now which was easier?"

"The right," said the girl, "when she leaned with me. I see what you're talking about."

"Now the rest of you, do it so you will understand. There are little things you can do as a rider to lighten your horse's load and make him or her faster." They all let Maria ride on their backs. "Now let me explain another trick. When your horse goes into a hard turn, like with going around a barrel, if you concentrate, you can feel the horse getting ready for the turn. Going in, you lean with him, but coming out, you lean the opposite way to help him get back up right. Now put your horse up and feed them. Tomorrow we see if you can use what I've shown you."

The next morning, Mary, Ben, and one of the ranch hands were there to help Maria and the breakaway roper Jane work on her roping. Mary took the other two girls up to the barn so they could run barrels in that arena. Mary said, "Okay, I want yawl to walk the barrels first and feel your horse's movements under you."

Kara, one of the girls, went first, then Amy, the other girl, went second, then Mary followed on Bob. Mary went to the right side of the arena near the alleyway and set up to time them. Meanwhile, Maria and Jane were setting up to start roping. Mary said, "Okay, Kara, you're up first." Kara walked her horse down the alley, then turned and came back running. She rounded the first barrel kind of sloppy, then recovered and did better on the second. "Feel your horse!" yelled Mary as Kara made the third turn and headed back. "A 15.80," said Mary. "Okay, Amy, let's go." Amy came flying out of the alley, nailed the first turn, then the second. She looked good heading for the third barrel but hit it and knocked it over. "A 15.10," said Mary. "You had a good run going until you hit that barrel."

Amy said, "My horse hit the barrel."

"No," said Mary, "yawl hit the barrel. Do you want me to tell you why?"

"Why?" asked Amy in a mad tone.

"Because when yawl was coming out of the turn, you didn't lean away from the barrel to help him back up. Now, Kara, what happened to you on your first barrel?" asked Mary.

"I forgot to lean," said Kara.

"Yep, but then you did good on the second and third," said Mary. "It's all about working with your horse and helping them. Kara, run it again. This time, relax and feel the turns." Kara came out faster. She turned the first barrel. Mary yelled, "Good job!" She turned the second. Mary yelled, "Yes!" Then she nailed the third. Mary yelled, "Push him! Yes. A 14.60. Great run, Kara. Now Amy's turn. I know you can do it."

Amy came out. She nailed the first barrel, then the second. She pushed her horse to the third barrel. The horse turned the barrel, and on the back side, Amy threw her weight away from the barrel. Her horse stood up and flew back home. "A 14.50. Great job, Amy. That's in the money, girls."

Mary got Kara to time her. Mary went down the alley, then she and Bob came flying back down. They nailed the first and the second barrels. Bob picked up speed going to the third, then nailed it and lunged home, throwing dirt. "A 13.80," said Kara. "Oh my god, Mary." They all came to a huddle in the middle of the arena.

Mary said, "Look, I don't want to discourage anyone, but if you and your horse can't run in the mid fourteens to the high thirteens, you are wasting your time and money."

Maria and Jane had made four runs, each in the single digits. Mary left Kara and Amy perfecting their runs while she rode down the stables to check on Maria and Jane. Mary rode up to the rails outside the arena. Jane was setting up to make another run. Jane nodded, and they released the calf from the chute. Jane's horse broke the rope and zeroed in on the calf. Jane threw her rope and looped the calf's head. Her horse stopped, and the rope broke away. "Good job," said Mary. "That was a 6-second run."

Maria set up and nodded. They released the calf. Maria threw her rope by the time she got to the end of the chute. Her rope dropped over the calf's head. She set the loop, and Dusty sat down. "Wow," said Mary, "great job, 4.80 seconds. Jane, you're not going to beat that. Yawl pack it up for today. I'm taking everyone out tonight, yeah." Mary rode back up to the barn to get the other two girls. They took their horses back to the stables and put them up and feed them. Mary said, "I'll pick yawl up at the motel around 6:30 p.m. Mary put up Bob and fed him, then went to the house to get ready.

"Hi, Mom," said Mary as she walked in the house. "Have you heard from Billie?"

"No, not this week. Why?"

"I just wondered," said Mary. "I miss her a little bit."

"Rose and Billie had gone to a veterinarian convention in Las Vegas. How are the girls doing?" asked Kattie.

"Good," said Mary. "Tomorrow is the last day, then they will be leaving the next morning. I'm taking them out to eat tonight. You and Dad want to go?"

"No, us old folks will just stay around here. What are you going to do after they leave?" asked Kattie.

"Wild horses," said Mary.

"Wild horses? What wild horses?"

"I'll tell you later. I've got to get a shower."

Kattie thought to herself, *What in the world is that girl getting into now?*

Mary came back through the house. "I'll see yawl after a while," she said as she went out the door. Mary went and picked up Maria, and they headed to Deadwood. They stopped by the motel and picked up the three girls. They went to the steak house there in town. Mary knew the waitress.

"What can I get yawl to drink?" asked the girl.

Jane, the oldest at twenty-two years old, said, "Five beers." She handed the waitress her ID.

"Okay, I'll be right back." The waitress came back and set all five of the beers in front of Jane. "I can't serve them to the other girls, but she can do what she wants with them." They all took one, even Maria, and turned them up. "What can I get yawl to eat?"

"Steak," said everybody.

"And five more beers."

Mary said, "Me and her"—pointing at Maria—"want Coke with our food."

"Me too," said the other two younger girls, then they drank the first beers down.

By the time the waitress brought the next round to the table, Maria was slurring her words and giggling. "She's drunk," said Jane. "No more for her." They all laughed. They brought out some rolls.

Mary said, "Here, Maria, eat this roll. It will soak up some of that beer. Well, did yawl learn anything this week?"

"Yep," said the girls, "a lot."

"Good," said Mary.

The waitress brought their steaks, and they all dug in. They ate like they had been fasting for a week. The food helped Maria sober up. By the time she was finished eating, she was fine. They sat there and talked for a while about cowboys and rodeos, then Mary paid for their meals, and they left the restaurant. Mary dropped the girls off at their motel, and she and Maria headed home.

The next day, the girls spent all day riding and practicing there runs over and over. At the end of the day, Mary told them all they did great and to spread the word. The two girls who were traveling together decided to go ahead and leave out. They only lived about three hours away. Jane, the roper, put her horse up for the night and said, "I'm going to party tonight. I'll see yawl tomorrow sometime." They all gave Mary and Maria a hug and left.

Mary said, "Come on, Maria, let's go swimming."

They got in Mary's truck and headed to the house to go swimming. Kattie came out and asked Mary about the wild horses she said something about. Mary said, "Wyoming is rounding up wild horses. They are asking horse trainers from all over to volunteer their services to train some of them to sell so they can raise money to feed the other horses in the wild horse reserve. Once the horses are sold, the state will give use a receipt showing it as a donation to the wild reserve for a tax break."

"Wow," said Kattie. "So how many are you getting?"

"Six," said Mary. "They want to try and get fifty to sell for at least one thousand each. Each trainer gets to keep one of the six."

"When?" asked Kattie.

"I go next week and pick out my six, then they will deliver them to the stables. Will you go with me, Mom?" asked Mary.

"Sure," said Kattie.

"Great," said Mary.

*****

Mary and Kattie pulled up to the roundup location in Wyoming. The ten trainers would all be given six number tags with the same number on them. Ten numbers were put in a hat, and each trainer reached in and picked their number. Mary pulled out number 3. The trainer with number 1 picked first, and their picks were tagged by the roundup crew. When Mary's turn came, she told Kattie to pick three, then she would pick three. Kattie picked three nice-looking horses, one paint and two duns. Mary picked an Appaloosa, a red roan, and a gray.

Kattie took Mary out to eat lunch before they headed back home.

Jim had his breeding operation all set up now at Plumber's Gap; he had Arron running things there. Ben was handling things and in charge of the cattle ranch now. Rose and Billie made it back from Vegas. They had a good time but were glad to be back at the clinic. Rose was showing more and more. In her last doctor's visit, she found out she was having a boy.

Maria and Mary started setting up the cow pens to put the mustangs in when they got there. The horses arrived that afternoon, and they unloaded them in the catch pen. They had already put out hay, grain, and water. Once the truck left, Mary told Maria that they get to keep one horse out of the six and for her to pick it. Maria watched the horses move around the pen. Finally, she said, "The Appaloosa."

"Good choice," said Mary. "Tomorrow we get him out so he can be cut."

"Are you sure you want to cut him?" asked Maria. "He is beautiful."

"Yes," said Mary, "he will still be beautiful."

The next day, Mary and Maria coached the Appaloosa into the chute so Kattie could do the honors. Once the Appaloosa was tranquilized, vaccinated, and dewormed, they turned him out into a separate lot. Once he lay down, Kattie went to work on him. While he was out, Mary put a halter and a short rope on him. "Okay, Maria, now he needs a name. Not Spot," said Mary with a laugh.

"Okay," said Maria, "we will call him Dakota."

Mary looked at her mom. Kattie said, "Sounds good to me."

"Okay then," said Mary, "Dakota it is. Now let's get out of here before he gets up. He's not going to be happy. Now let's get the red roan in the chute so we can give her the shots, then we will get the rest one at a time."

"Okay," said Maria.

By the end of the day, they had them done. Tomorrow they could start working with one of them. Mary told Ben that she needed a couple of his hands to help them with the horse for a few days. Mary tried to get Paul to help, but he was busy with his own horses.

The next morning, Carl and a new hand, Tray, came to the stables to help Mary. Carl told Mary, "This is Tray. He is new, but he knows horses. Tray, this is Mary Plumber, and that's Maria. They train horses and do some rodeoing."

Mary told Carl, "I need to rope that roan and get her down so I can put a halter on her."

Carl and Tray got ropes and went into the lot. Carl threw his rope but missed. Tray threw his and caught her, then Carl threw again and caught her. They let her fight the ropes for a while to wear her down. She finally fell. The guys ran over and got on her to keep her down. Mary and Maria ran out and put the halter on the roan, then Carl and Tray turned her loose in the lot with Dakota. Since these horses had never been touched by human hands before and not halter broke, this was the only way. Next, they got the gray horse and did the same. Tomorrow they would get the other three.

The new hand, Tray, kept smiling at Mary. She asked Maria, "What is he looking at?"

Maria laughed. "He is looking at you. He likes you."

"No, he doesn't," said Mary.

"Yes, he does," said Maria.

"Well…well, he needs to stop. It makes me uncomfortable. Maria just laughed again.

The next day, they caught the other three horses and put halter on them. Mary tied short ropes to the halters just long enough to reach the ground so they would step on them. This would make their neck muscles sore and make it easier to halter break them. These horses had a long way to go yet before they could be handled.

Jim came by to see the new horses Mary got; he was impressed as to Mary and Kattie's picks. "Those are good-looking horses," Jim said. "Let me know when they are ready to ride, and I'll help you."

"Thanks, Dad," said Mary. "I will. It might be a while. They are pretty rank right now."

"You will tame them down, I'm sure," said Jim.

"Maria and I have one more rodeo to compete in, and then we are through for the season," said Mary.

Together the girls had earned over $100,000.00 rodeoing. Mary had earned over $40,000.00, and Maria had earned over $60,000.00. Maria competed in two events, barrels and breakaway. Neither girl finished less than second at any competition. They could both easily compete more and go to the world finals and probably win first and second. One day Maria might do just that, but for Mary, it was all about her stables and horse training.

Mary would turn twenty next month, and Maria would be sixteen in October. Mary started paying Maria her salary last spring. Maria had put back all her earning from the stables and the rodeos. She hoped to save enough for college by the time she graduated high school. Mary and Maria went to the rodeoing in Billings, Montana, the last one of the year for them. Mary took first in the barrels, and Maria took second, but Maria took first in breakaway roping.

Now with rodeoing behind them, they could concentrate on breaking horses. Mary called Kathy to see if she wanted to help. Kathy said, "Sure. I'll come get one of them." Kathy showed up. Mary had Carl and Tray there to help load.

"Which one do you want?" asked Mary.

Kathy looked them over. "I'll take the paint horse," said Kathy.

"Okay," said Mary. Carl and Tray ran her into the loading chute for Mary. They forced her into the trailer. "Keep me posted," said Mary to Kathy.

"I will. I'll have Tommie riding her in a couple of days," said Kathy with a laugh.

"Yeah right," said Mary.

Carl and Tray helped the girls get the Appaloosa into the round pen, then they put the roan in the arena. Maria started working the Appaloosa in the round pen, while Mary went into the arena with the roan. Mary ran the roan around and around the arena until she saw her licking her lips. Mary told her whoa. Mary slowly walked up to the horse with her hand out. Just before Mary got to her, she took off. Mary ran her around the arena three more times. "Woah!" she yelled. The horse stopped. She was sweating and breathing hard. Again, Mary walked to her. She reached out and touched her nose. The horse pulled her head back. Mary got a treat from her pocket and reached out again. The horse smelled Mary's hand, then Mary opened it. The horse took the treat. Mary got another treat out, then took a step back and held her hand out. The horse took a half step forward, then stretched out her neck, smelling the treat. Mary stood there until she stepped closer, then gave her the treat. The horse started to relax some and swished her tail. Mary reached in her pocket and got another treat. This time, she held out both hands. As the horse reached for the treat, Mary reached for the short hanging rope. Once the horse realized Mary had the rope, she pulled back. "Whoa," said Mary. "You're okay." Mary stepped up and gave her the treat, then rubbed the horse's nose. "See, that's not so bad," said Mary. "Easy, girl." She gave her another treat. Mary turned and pulled on the rope. The horse pulled back, but her neck was so sore she gave way. Mary slowly took step after step until the horse was following her with the rope loose. Mary stopped and let go of the rope. As Mary walked to the side gate of the arena, the horse followed. Mary opened the gate and stepped out, closing it behind her.

Mary went to the round pen to check on Maria and Dakota. Maria took ahold of Dakota's rope, but every time she pulled on it, he pulled back hard. Mary went to the tack room and came back with a lunge line. "Here, said Mary, "put this on him." Maria eased over to the rails and took the rope. She put it on her shoulder, then eased back over to Dakota. She gave him a treat and got the short rope again, then slowly snapped the lunge line to his halter, then let go of the short rope. She gave him slack, then popped his hip with the quirt and made him run some more while she held the rope. After a couple of rounds, she jerked the rope and said whoa, then the horse stopped and turned toward Maria. She slowly walked to the horse, taking up slack. She rubbed his nose and gave him a treat. Again, she tried to lead him, but he pulled back. Mary said, "Just hold the rope tight on his neck. He will give up." Maria pulled hard on the rope like playing tug-of-war. Finally, the horse stepped toward her. "You got him now," said Mary. "Just keep it up."

Mary went back to the arena. She stepped into the arena and whistled. The horse turned and looked at her. Mary said, "Come here, girl." The horse just looked at her but didn't move. Mary reached into her pocket and pulled out a treat. The horse just watched her. Mary said, "Okay." Mary turned her back to the horse and leaned on the rails. The horse nickered. Mary said, "No, you come and get it. I'm not walking over there." The horse nickered again. "No," said Mary, "you've got to earn it." Slowly the horse stepped toward Mary, then stopped. Mary just stood with her back to the horse. Mary said, "I'm not afraid of you. Why are you afraid of me? Come over here."

After about ten minutes, the horse slowly walked up to Mary's back and nudged her with her nose. Mary slowly turned around and held out her hand. "Are you going to be a good girl now?" She rubbed her nose. Mary took the short rope and led her around the arena, then stopped and rubbed her neck and shoulder. Talking low and slow, Mary told the horse what she was going to do before she did it. The horse stood there as Mary rubbed her back and her hips, all the way to her tail, then worked her way back to her head and gave her another treat. Mary started down the other side and worked her way to her tail again. "Good girl," said Mary. Mary led her over to the rails and clipped a lead rope onto her halter. Mary took the short rope off. Mary led her out of the arena and over to a stall. "Here's your new home for a while." She gave her some oats.

Mary went back to check on Maria. She had Dakota leading around the round pen. He was still a little spooky, but getting better. Mary stepped into the round pen and walked to Maria. "Here, let me see him for a minute." Maria handed Mary the rope. Mary walked with him, talking low and slow. Maria couldn't hear what Mary was saying, but she could tell the horse was listening to her. His walk became relaxed, and his tail swished as he walked. Mary told Maria to open the gate. Mary led Dakota out of the round pen and into a stall. "Get him some oats," said Mary. "He has earned them."

Maria saw that the roan was already in a stall. "How did she do?" asked Maria.

"About like him. But I don't want to push them too hard yet. They know what's coming. We will get the other two out tomorrow and see how they do. I think they are going to be easier. They seem pretty calm."

The next day, they got the two duns, one in the round pen and one in the arena. Maria got into the round pen and worked the horse a little while, then stopped her. Maria walked over to the horse. She never moved; she let Maria grab the short rope and rub her nose. Maria pulled on the rope, and the mare started walking with her. They made a couple of rounds, then Maria removed the short rope and clipped on a lead rope. Maria tied her to the rails and went to the tack room and came back with a saddle blanket. Maria came back and eased up to the horse. She rubbed her nose then down her neck. She eased the blanket onto the horse's back. The horse never moved. Maria thought, *I don't believe this.* She moved the blanket around on her back. Maria thought, *Let me try something else.* She leaned down and grabbed the horse's left front leg at the hock. The horse picked up her leg. Maria said, "Oh my god, this horse was a tamed horse at one time." She made her way around the horse, picking up her feet.

Mary was in the arena with the other dun horse. She had gotten the horse to let her rub on her some, but she was still spooky. Mary move around her, talking and touching her.

Back in the round pen, Maria decided to see just how tamed this horse was. She went back to the tack room and came back with a saddle and bridle. She eased the saddle onto the horse's back. She didn't move. Maria tried the bridle, and the horse took the bits with no problem. Maria cinched up the saddle, untied the lead rope, and slowly climbed onto the saddle. The horse just stood there as calm as she could be. Maria eased her heels into the horse's ribs and smacked her lips. The horse started walking. Maria walked her around the pen, then urged her into a lope, then pulled back on the reins, and she stopped. Maria thought to herself, *This horse ran off and joined the herd, or someone turned her loose.* Maria got off and opened the gate. She led the horse out of the round pen. They walk over to the arena gate.

As Maria and the horse stood there, Mary looked up. Maria said, "Well, I'm through with mine. How about you?"

Mary came walking over to the gate. "No way," said Mary.

Maria laughed. "Yes way." She walked beside the horse and climbed on. Mary came out of the gate and started rubbing the horse's nose. Maria said, "This horse was tamed at one time. I don't know how she got with the mustangs, but I picked up all her feet. She took the bits with no trouble."

"Holy cow," said Mary. "Well, that's good. We just need to fatten her up and build up her muscles. Go ahead and put her on the walker. Leave the saddle and bridle on her. Good job, Maria. This one I got is not easy at all. She is scared to death. I'm just trying to calm her down."

The next day, Maria got out Dakota and tied him in the arena. Mary got out the gray horse and put her in the round pen. Maria went back and got the tamed dun and put her back on the walker for a while. Maria went by the tack room and got a saddle, blanket, and bridle and took them into the arena. Maria started working Dakota in the arena, running him around one direction, then the other. Once he was tired and licking his lips, she stopped him. She clipped the lead rope back on him, then tied him to the rail. She got the bridle, and after four attempts, she got him to take the bits. Then she took the blanket and rubbed him with it, then slowly put it on his back. She went back and got the saddle. Dakota didn't like the looks of that thing at all. He wouldn't let Maria get close to him with that monster. Maria left him tied to the rail and went to see Mary. She was working with the gray horse. Maria told Mary about the trouble she was having with Dakota.

Mary said, "Run him some more. I'll come help in a few minutes."

Maria went back to the round pen with Dakota. She unclipped the reins from the bridle and then unclipped the lead rope. She started running Dakota again until he was breathing hard and licking his lips.

Mary came around to the round pen. Mary told Maria to stop him. Mary walked up to him and clipped on the lead rope. Mary hugged Dakota's neck, then whispered in his ear, and then kissed his nose. Mary told Maria to bring the saddle and blanket. Mary took the blanket and put it up to Dakota's nose, then eased it on his back. She then took the saddle from Maria and gave her the lead rope. Dakota pulled away when he saw the saddle. "Woah," said Mary, putting her arm around his neck. Mary put the saddle under his nose, saying, "Whoa. Now easy, boy." Dakota sniffed the saddle, then calmed down some. Mary let go, then moved to his side and eased the saddle onto his back. Mary just let it sit there until she walked around him, rubbing him and talking to him.

Finally, she reached under and got the girth and cinched it up. She clipped the reins back on and put them over his neck. Mary took the lead rope from Maria, then said, "You're up." Maria moved to his side and put a foot in the stirrup. Slowly she pulled up and stood in the stirrup, then slowly swung her leg over and sat in the saddle. Mary was talking to Dakota and rubbing his nose. Mary started leading him around with Maria on his back. Until he relaxed and started swishing his tail, Mary stopped and handed Maria the lead rope. "Just walk him," said Mary. Maria nudged him in the ribs, and Dakota started walking. After a few rounds, Maria turned him with one rein while holding the other against his neck. Over and over she worked him on turning and stopping. Mary said, "Now stop him, get off, then get back on. I'm going back to the gray horse. Just keep working with Dakota." Mary had the gray leading well, and she seemed very smart.

For the next six weeks, Mary and Maria worked with the mustangs. They had them all riding. Maria was working with the roan horse on breakaway roping and with the tamed dun on cow pinning. They were both coming along well. Mary was working the gray horse on the barrels and the other dun on cow cutting and pinning. The gray was running in the low fifteens but doing well. The dun was a natural cutting horse; she seemed to have a keen knack for outthinking the cows and anticipating their next move. Mary said she could be the best cow horse she had ever worked with.

Mary had Jim come down to the stables to ride the horses one last time. Kathy brought back the paint horse. She was so beautiful. "Here, Jim, try this one," said Kathy.

Jim said, "Okay, what can she do?"

"Anything you want her to," said Kathy.

Jim climbed on and made a couple of lopes, then put her into a spin, and then changed directions. "Great job," said Jim. "Yawl really did good. Those are some fine horses."

The day of the auction was tomorrow, so Mary, Maria, Kattie, and Kathy were going to deliver the horses back to Wyoming. The next morning, they were loading up the five horses at the stables when Kathy called. She told Mary that she was sorry, but Tommie was sick, and she couldn't go. Somebody else would have to show the paint. Jim was there helping them load up. He spoke up and said, "I'll go."

"What?" asked Mary.

"I'll go with yawl to Wyoming."

"Great," said Mary. "Let's go. Everybody load up."

Once there, they unloaded the horses and penned them so the bidders could come around and look at all the horses before the sale.

As the sale started, each trainer showed the five horses they trained as the auctioneer called for bids. Most trainers came out and walked around the arena and turned the horses, ran them a little, then backed them up. Most sold from $800.00 to $1,200.00 each.

When it came Plumber's Gap's turn, Maria came out on the dun. She cut one cow out of a group of eight, held it in place, then penned it. The dun sold for $3,000.00. Jim came out on the paint horse. He ran her to the end of the arena and slid her, then came back to the middle and put her in a spin. The paint sold for $4,800.00. Maria and Jim set up barrels. Mary came out on the gray horse. She nailed the barrels at a 14.48 time. She sold for $5,000.00. Next, Maria set up on the roan for breakaway roping. The calf came out, and Maria threw her rope—a 6.60. She sold for $3,600.00. They turned the cow's loose again. Mary came out on the other dun horse. Mary pointed her at one of the cows. They cut it out of the herd. Mary and the dun held it, then pushed it to the other end of the arena and held it again, and then pushed it back to the other end and penned it. She sold for $8,000.00, top money of the sale. Mary not only trained good horses, she helped raise money for a very good cause.

As they made their way back home, Mary was proud that she was able to help save more wild horses by taming a few.

Chapter 3

Mary's Roundup

Well, summer was about over. Maria had started back to school. Mary had her days alone again. Mary liked this time of the year. Things slow down, and days were shorter. She looked forward to the holidays and spending more time with her family.

The roundup would start soon. Mary was going to help this year. The last time she went, she was only five years old and had to ride with her mom. The herd was a lot smaller then, and it only took one overnight stay to get them back from the pasture where they kept the mama cows now. But now with more cows, it took all the Plumber's Gap's land and some government land to feed them through the summer months. Jim thought it was time Mary learned the trail and how they round up the cows and bring them home to the winter lots. One day she might have to lead the roundup for herself with the ranch hands. Mary was excited about it. She thought it would be fun camping at night and riding all day. She had been working cows with the Appaloosa. She wanted to take him on the roundup.

Rose had her baby boy, six pounds, eight ounces. Paul was ecstatic, a proud daddy, if there ever was one. They named the baby John Paul Plumber Jr. Rose said they would call him Junior. Although Rose was not Kattie's real daughter, Kattie claimed Junior to be her first grandson. Pete and Alice were now great-grandparents and were very excited also. The baby had dark black hair and light-brown skin and his mother's eyes. Mary thought he was the sweetest thing she had ever seen and wanted to hold him all the time. Billie felt the same way and called herself Aunt Billie. She and Mary fought over whose turn it was to hold him. Jim told them that they were going to wear the skin off that baby, wagging him around. Paul couldn't stop kissing Rose and thanking her for their beautiful boy.

The next day, Kattie sat on her porch wrapped up in a blanket and seeping on coffee. She looked out over the field at the waterfall, thinking about how everyday things kept changing. She felt so blessed by God for all the things she had and for her family and friends. She had fulfilled her father's family dreams of the ranch that they always wanted—Plumber's Gap.

Mary and Dakota were ready to go. Her saddlebags were packed and tied, along with her rainsuit. She met Jim, Ben, and the ranch hands at the bunkhouse, where they finished loading the wagon with supplies. Tray, the new ranch hand, could only smile when he found out Mary was going on the roundup. Mary saw him watching her and smiled back at him.

"Let's go," said Jim.

They headed off down the trail by the house and past the falls to the gate going into the main pasture. They kept following the main trail along the creek to the back end of the of the Plumber's Gap land. It was almost dark when they got to the back gate and the line camp. They set up camp and built a fire to cook on. Ben put on a pot of beans and a pot of coffee. Carl and Tray unloaded the rope to put up a picket line for the horses overnight. Jim and Mary set up their tent. They would be staying together on this trip.

The next morning, they all crossed over to the government land. Ben and his crew hit the woods, while Jim and Mary went to the meadow. Jim and Mary started counting the cows that were already there in the meadow, ready to go home. There were 130 cows in the meadow out of the 200 they put on the government land. Slowly more cows entered the meadow, three and four at a time, until there was over 150 cows grazing in the meadow. Midafternoon, the hands started coming in with groups of 10 or more until they had all 200 together. After a short break, they started moving them to the back to the gate and the lots at the line camp.

Ben stoked up the fire so he could cook supper. Ben put the beans and coffee back on the fire. Jim got out some beef steaks. He threw them on the hot grate. They could hear the meat sizzle as it landed, and the smell filled the air. They all sat around the fire talking about the day they had and all the things they saw. Carl said he saw a big elk on the north ridge. Ben asked Jeff if he saw any bears out there with a laugh.

Jim said, "Meat's ready. Yawl come get it."

Mary noticed how Jim seemed to be in his elements out there. He was the prime example of a true cowboy—slim, tall, and rugged-looking, with a soft voice. She thought to herself, *That's my dad.* Mary saw Tray looking at her as they ate, but she didn't let on that she noticed.

After they ate, Ben asked Jim if he had any stories to tell this year, like the bear story he told last year. Jim said, "Well, I can't top that one, but my grandfather told me one about a Lakota Indian boy years ago."

"Let's hear it," said Ben.

*****

Back in the early 1800s, when the Indians still owned this land, not only in South Dakota but also in North Dakota, Wyoming, and

Montana, there was a tribe of Lakota Indians who lived near here. There were thousands of buffalo roaming these lands. For a young teenage Indian boy to become a man and be allowed to have his own teepee, he must prove he's ready to support himself and help support his tribe. He must kill many elk and deer, then bring them back to his tribe, or he could kill one buffalo by himself and bring back the tongue as proof. The women of the tribe would then go out and process the meat and hide, then bring it all back to their camp. Wild buffalo were very hard to kill in those days. All the Indians had bows and arrows and spears to hunt with. It would take many arrows and spears to bring down one of these huge beasts. Normally, it would take a hunting party of eight to ten braves to bring down a buffalo. Like any other wild animal, a wounded buffalo was very dangerous and could be deadly by hooking or stomping the braves.

A young Indian boy, sixteen years old, wanted to prove his manhood to the chief. He had killed many deer and small animals. The boy's name was Gray Owl, and he was in love with the chief's daughter, Willow Leave. The boy had captured and broken eight horses to give to the chief for Willow's hand, but each time he tried, the chief said, "You're not ready yet." So Gray Owl told the chief he would go out and bring back the tongue of a buffalo to prove his manhood. The chief nodded his approval. Gray Owl gathered some skins to sleep on and some food and water. He tied it on his back and jumped on his horse. The buffalo were many miles away this time of year and always moving to find more grass. Gray Owl knew the trip would be hard, but he never knew just how hard it would turn out to be. He rode across the open planes for miles and miles, only seeing prairie dogs and rabbits along the way. At night, he would sharpen his arrowheads and spears, hoping the next day would be the one. As he lay there under the stars trying to sleep, he thought of Willow and how much he cared for her. Gray Owl had three spears and ten arrows in his arsenal, plus his skinning knife. More than enough to kill anything, he thought.

Next morning, just over the rise, he saw the herd. He could not believe his eyes. Thousands of buffalo covered the land as far as he could see, like ants moving in all directions. He eased back below the rise to make a plan of attack and build his courage up; the sight was overwhelming, to say the least. He decided he would hold the spears in one hand and have his bow over his shoulder and try to ease as close as he could, lying on his horse's back, then make his move. Gray Owl slowly moved in on the buffalo. His heart was pounding so hard and loud he thought it might scare the buffalo away. As he got within about one hundred yards of the herd, one bull buffalo spotted him. He and his horse stopped. The buffalo pawed the ground, then went back to grazing. Gray Owl slowly moved in some more, keeping his eyes on the herd. When he got within about fifty yards of the herd, he let out a yell and charged the herd. The buffalo broke into a stampede as he rode up beside the large bull that stopped him. He stabbed it with one of the spears. The buffalo turned into the herd and disappeared. He picked out another large bull and speared it. This time, the buffalo turned away from the herd, and the race was on. It was all he and his horse could do to keep up with the bull as it ran. Finally, he got up beside the buffalo and sank the last spear. The buffalo turned and headed back to the herd. Gray Owl grabbed his bow and put two arrows in the buffalo's shoulder. The buffalo started slowing down as Gray Owl followed along with the bull, hoping it would fall. Out of nowhere, the first buffalo hit Gray Owl's horse in the side and hooked its belly and flipped Gray Owl and his horse over. Gray Owl scrambled to his feet. His horse was down. The buffalo stood over him with the spear still in its shoulder. Gray Owl shot three arrows into the buffalo's ribs. The bull turned and started walking off. Up ahead, he could see the other buffalo on the ground. Gray Owl checked his horse; the horse had a punctured wound in its belly. The main herd of buffalo had cleared out. The plains were empty other than Gray

Owl, his horse, and the two buffalo—one down but still alive and one still up and a threat but badly wounded.

Gray Owl took grass, dirt, and water and made a paste to fill up the hole in his horse. Pulling and coaxing, Gray Owl got his horse back on its feet and gave it some water. This had been a long fight. It was midday. Gray Owl and his horse were exhausted, but he had done what he came for with one buffalo down and bleeding out. Nothing to do now but wait. Gray Owl sat in the shadow of his horse, trying to cool off. He had traveled for two days to find the herd. Now he must send a message to his tribe. He got up and gathered up dry limbs and grass and started a fire. He then gathered green grass and brush to make smoke. With a blanket, he sent plumes of smoke into the blue sky repeatedly.

Back at his camp, his father was worried about his son and was hoping he was okay. Then one of the women said "Look" as she pointed to the sky. "It's Gray Owl," his father said as he ran to the chief's teepee. The chief came out and looked up, then told the women to gather their things. He sent a small group of braves along with them for protection and to help haul back the meat.

Gray Owl walked over to the downed buffalo. It was barely alive. Gray Owl jumped on its back, reached down, and cut its throat. The other buffalo had dropped down to its front knees. Gray Owl eased up close and put two more arrows in it.

Night came. Gray Owl sat by the fire under the stars and ate dried fish he had brought with him. He had given his horse the last of the water. He lay back and closed his eyes, thinking his fight was over. About midnight, he was awakened by horse nickering, whinnying, and the sound of growling. He jumped up and grabbed his bow and a burning stick from the fire. Wolves had found his buffalo. He ran after them, shooting one with his bow and chasing the others with the burning stick. One of the wolves circled around him and leaped on his back, knocking him down. The other wolves piled on him, biting, clawing, and dragging him. Gray Owl finally got to his knife and started stabbing at the wolves. They started limping off one by one until the last one collapsed on top of him. Gray Owl pushed the wolf off and slowly got to his feet. He made it back to the fire. He was bleeding from his head, face, arms, chest, and legs. He put more wood on the fire, lay down, then passed out.

The next morning, Gray Owl woke, his horse standing over him. He was in so much pain he didn't know what hurt the most. After three tries, he made it to his feet. The second buffalo was now dead. Gray Owl took his horse and a rope and rolled each buffalo over so he could remove the guts and entrails. Then he split the sides of the mouths and removed their tongues. He left the heart and livers inside the carcass. He cut a hole in each tongue and ran a string through them. He hung them over his horse's neck. He pulled his horse up close to one of the buffalo, then stood on it to help him get on his horse. He pointed his horse back the way they came. As he passed over the rise, he could see in the distance his people coming for the buffalo. As he got closer to them, he put the string with the tongues on it around his neck and sat up straight as he and his horse walked by them. He was covered in blood from head to toe. His horse was the only way they could tell who he was. They yelped as he rode by, wearing not one but two buffalo tongues around his neck.

When his tribe got to the buffalo, they found two large bull buffalo and six dead wolves on the ground. Gray Owl made it to the river, where he stopped and let his horse drink and graze while he sat in the cold water and washed off the blood. He and his horse spent the night there.

The next morning, they headed home. Just after dark, he rode up into camp and stopped in front of the chief's teepee with the two tongues hanging around his neck. The chief came out, and Gray Owl handed him the buffalo tongues. The chief held them up and said, "You're ready now."

Gray Owl's father helped him down from his horse and carried him into their teepee. He was so proud. His mother went to work cleaning and tending his wounds. Gray Owl slept for two days. He was awakened by the sound of yelps and people talking. He got up and walked outside. There by the teepee flap were two huge buffalo hides and six wolf pelts.

Over the next two weeks, Gray Owl's mother and some of the other women worked on the hides while he and his father cut poles for his new teepee. Once the teepee was finished, Gray Owl gathered his eight horse, one buffalo skin, and two wolf pelts and went to the chief's teepee. The chief and his daughter came out of their teepee. Gray Owl handed the chief the ropes holding the horses. Everyone gathered around as the chief looked the horses over, then looked at the skins. His daughter, Willow, smiled as the chief put her hand in Gray Owl's hand and then nodded his approval.

*****

Jim stretched his arms over his head and said, "So, Tray, if you keep looking at my daughter that way, it might cost you eight horses and your hide." Mary and Tray blushed, and everybody else laughed. Mary and Tray had never talked much, but it was obvious that there was an attraction between them. "Let's get some sleep," said Jim. "We got a long day ahead tomorrow."

"The next morning, Jim and Mary took the right side of the ridge up in the tree line, and Carl and Tray took the left side, while Ben and the others pushed the main herd down the valley. As they moved along, the herd kept growing as cow after cow joined the herd. Just before dark, Ben stopped the herd and ganged them up for the night. The men set up camp and started a fire. Jim and Mary came into camp. Mary tended their horses. Carl and Tray came in right at dark. Ben had coffee and beans going on the fire. Jim threw some elk meat on the grate from his and Troy's hunt last year in Montana. Everybody gathered around the fire. It was cooling off fast. They all started eating.

Ben said, "Well, Jim, you got another story?"

"No, I'm about storied out. "What about you?" said Jim. "Tell us about Jeff and his bear."

"Oh, that's not much of a story, but three years back, it was Troy, Carl, Jeff, me, and three other hands who are gone now. We were not far from here. Back then, we just had one man on each side working the trees. The bear is the reason we have two on each side now. I was pushing the herd with Troy and the others. Carl was working the left side, and Jeff was on the right. All of a sudden, Jeff came running out of the trees yelling something, which we found out later was bear. He crossed the creek and headed out across the valley. Following him was a huge grizzly bear."

"Yeah," said Jeff, "and the bear was gaining on me." Everybody laughed.

Ben said, "So I pulled my rifle out and shot the bear, but it didn't slow him down. If anything, he got faster. I cocked another shell in and was going to shot again, and Troy fired his rifle. The bear folded up and slid about ten yards. I rode down to the bear and shot him in the head. If Troy hadn't stopped that bear, I think he would have caught Jeff's horse. It was close, bad close."

"Yeah," said Jeff, "I thought I was a goner for sure. I never knew a bear could run so fast."

"But it ended well. We ate bear meat the rest of the trip and ground up the rest for chili meat."

The next morning, they pushed on, Jim and Mary back on the right side. Dakota was doing great. He had turned out to be a good cow pony. He was sure-footed on the rocks as they rode the ridge. As they pushed the cows out of the trees, Mary just held on as Dakota did all the work. After the first morning riding the ridge, he had figured out what the job was and how to do it.

Jim told Mary, "That horse don't even need you."

"Nope," said Mary, "I'm just along for the ride." Jim laughed.

That late afternoon, Mary noticed Jim's horse favoring his right hide foot. "Hold up, Dad," said Mary. Jim stopped. Mary got off her horse.

"What is it?" asked Jim.

"Your horse," said Mary. Mary picked up the foot and cleaned it out. "Well, he's done," said Mary.

"What's wrong?" asked Jim.

"His frog is cut. Must have been one of these rocks. Let's take him out to the grass." Mary got back on Dakota, and they headed out of the trees. Ben had already stopped the herd. They rode on up to the camp. Mary picked up the foot again and showed Jim the cut.

"No more rocks for him," said Jim.

Mary pulled the saddle off and took Jim's horse to the creek. She led him out into the cold water and told him, "Just stand here for a while, boy." She took off his bridle and turned him loose. The horse just stood there as she walked off.

"What now?" said Jim.

"Just wait," said Mary as she got on Dakota. "I'll be back," said Mary as she rode off into the herd of cow. Midway, she saw Nelly in a group of yearlings. She whistled. Nelly threw up her head and looked at Mary. Nelly started making her way to Mary. "Hey, girl," said Mary as she put a rope around her neck. "I need your help, girl. Come on with me." Mary led her out of the herd and up to the camp.

"Is that the horse that old woman gave you?" asked Jim.

"Yup, that's Nelly."

"Man, she's fat and pretty."

"You can ride Dakota tomorrow. I'll ride her. Just let your horse walk with the cows."

"Where is my horse?" asked Jim.

"Standing in the creek, soaking his foot," said Mary. "Here." She handed Jim a lead rope. "Go get him out. Jim took the rope and went after his horse.

The next morning, Jim put his saddle on Dakota, and Mary saddled up Nelly. Everybody spread out and started moving the cows down the valley. Jim had tied his horse to the wagon so he could walk in the grass as it moved along. Old Nelly wasn't very fast, but she walked steady as they moved along the ridge. Most of the cows had figured out by now that it was time to go home and were coming out on their own. This would be the last full day on the trail. They hoped to be back at the ranch by noon tomorrow.

As Jim and Mary were moving along the ridge, Jim whistled at Mary. Mary eased up to him. He had pulled his gun out. "What is it, Dad?" asked Mary.

He pointed up ahead. "There was a dead yearling on the ground almost covered up with grass and dirt. Big cat," said Jim as he was looking around. They eased up closer to the carcass. Jim got off Dakota and went after the ear tag, holding his reins. The mountain lion came running out of the brush and jumped at Jim. Jim jumped sideways away from the cat. Nelly reared as the cat came by her and Mary. The cat spun around to come back, but before it could, Dakota was stomping it into the rocks with his hooves. The cat had no chance to recover from the mustang's attack. With a flurry of final strikes to the head, the cat lay lifeless on the ground.

Jim was in awe of what had just happened. The horse stood over the cat, watching for any movement. Mary eased up and took Dakota's reins. "Wow, boy," said Mary as she pulled him away from the cat. Jim cut the ear tag and put it in his shirt pocket. He took his rope and put it around the cat's head. Jim climbed back on Dakota and started dragging the cat out of the trees into the valley. He removed the rope, and they went back in the tree to look for more cows. Jim told Mary, "This is one hell of a horse."

Mary just smiled and said, "I know, and no, you can't have him." She laughed.

At the end of the day, when they got to camp, Jim got Tray and the wagon and went back to get the cat. They loaded the ninety-plus-pound cat in the wagon and headed back.

"I have got a story to tell tonight," said Jim. The crew walked up to the wagon.

"Oh my god," said Ben, "that's a big cat."

"I'll tell yawl the story after we eat, but a mountain lion is no match for a mustang."

Ben had the fire going and coffee on. "We are out of beans," said Ben.

"Good," said Carl. "I can't take much more of Tray's gas." Tray blushed.

"I've got more elk meat," said Jim, "or do yawl want to eat that cat?"

"That's a no," said Carl, "on the cat meat." They all laughed. They sat around the fire and ate as Jim told them about the cat attack and how the mustang ran in and killed that cat.

The next morning, the last leg home. Just before they made it to the ranch, a light snow started to fall. Jim stopped at the house. Mary took Nelly, Dakota, and Jim's horse to the stables, brushed them down, put them in stalls, and fed them. Mary went to the house, stripped off her clothes, and crawled in a hot tub of water and fell asleep. She was exhausted from trip. Suppertime, Kattie went to get her and found her sleeping in the tub. She helped her out and dried her off and helped her into bed.

The next day, Kattie went and picked out the steers for the orphanage. It always made her feel good to help them.

Tray caught Jim at the catch pens and asked if he could talk to him a minute.

"Sure," said Jim. "What is it?"

"Well, sir, I want to ask for your permission to ask Mary out on a date."

Jim laughed. "Well, I don't know that it would matter to Mary what I said, but I don't have a problem with it. Just remember, Mary has never been on a date, and if she agrees, it will be on her terms. She is the most independent girl I've ever known, next to her mother."

The next day, Tray went down to the stables to talk to Mary. "Hi, Mary," said Tray.

"Hey," said Mary.

Tray said, "I was talking to your dad yesterday, and I asked him if it would be okay to…aw…well, if he cared if I asked you out. He said it would be up to you."

"He's got that right," said Mary under her breath. "Out where?" asked Mary.

"Well, I mean on a date."

"I know what you mean," said Mary. "Where?"

"Oh, well, we could go out to eat in Deadwood."

Mary was silent. Finally, Mary asked, "When?"

"Tomorrow night," said Tray.

Mary looked him dead in the eyes. "Okay, but you try anything, I'll break your nose."

"Yes, ma'am," said Tray.

"And don't call me ma'am," said Mary. Tray turned and walked away, smiling from ear to ear.

The next night, Mary wore jeans and a nice Western shirt with polished boots. Tray came to the door wearing the same. Mary made him come in and wait with her mom and dad while she pretended to be getting ready. Mary came out, and Tray smiled. A small tear formed in Kattie's eye. Her baby was going on her first date. She was beginning to think it would never happen. Mary had never shown interest or talked about a boy until Tray came along. They said their goodbyes and walked out the door. Kattie hugged Jim. "It will be okay," said Jim. "Mary can take care of herself."

Chapter 4

The Kiss

The following Monday, Maria and Selena asked Mary about her date Saturday night. Mary just smiled and said, "It was okay."

Tray would make it a point to come by the stables every day to fix something—a gate hinge, a hayrack, or a loose stall panel—anything to see Mary. They would laugh and talk some as he worked and she cleaned stalls. After three or four weeks, they went out again, this time to where a band was playing, and they danced repeatedly. The first real snow came, and Mary went by the bunkhouse and picked up Tray on her four-wheeler. They road all over the ranch—Mary driving, of course—through the snow and across the creek. Tray became the hand who volunteered for anything Jim wanted done around the ranch. Jim told him one day, "Tray, I'm not the one you have to impress." He laughed. Tray smiled but kept doing it anyway. Mary liked the thought of having someone thinking about her all the time but was still unsure.

Kattie told Jim one night, "That boy's got it bad."

"Yep," said Jim. "He acts just like I did about you."

Kattie smiled. Well, I think it's time we invited him to Sunday dinner. I'll tell Mary to invite him," said Kattie.

"Okay," said Jim, "whatever you think."

Winter came in with a roar. Snow covered everything; icicles hung from every roof. In the afternoons, after his ranch work, Tray still came to the stables to see Mary and help her if she needed anything. One afternoon, while working in one of the stalls, Mary was leaning over Tray, watching him work on a gate. As he finished and started to stand up, Mary put her arms around his neck and gave him a kiss. They both just stood there looking at each other. It was their first kiss, for both of them. Mary started to break away, but Tray pulled her back and kissed her back. Mary turned and said, "I've got to go." She headed up the hill through the snow to her house. Tray picked up his tools and headed back to the bunkhouse, smiling.

That night, Mary lay in bed thinking about what had happened. She couldn't believe she did that. She thought of how it felt when Tray pulled her close and kissed her back. Her mind was telling her to break free, but her heart and body was telling her to stay in his arms. In the end, her mind won over her body. She knew she wasn't ready yet for what she didn't know.

The next morning, after her dad left for the bunkhouse, Mary told her mom about the kiss. She asked her for advice about the feelings she had. Kattie said, "Mary, we have had this talk."

"No, Mom, not that. How do I know? Why did I kiss him like that? I don't understand," said Mary as she started to cry.

"Oh, baby," said Kattie, "don't cry. You're okay. There is nothing wrong with you, honey. It's normal to be confused at first. These are all new feelings for you, sweetheart. The only advice I can give you is, don't make the mistakes that your dad and I made. Leave nothing unsaid and no question unanswered. If there is something about him you want to know, you ask him. If he asks something about yourself, tell him. Don't sugarcoat anything. If you can't be open and honest with each other about everything, he is not the one. Like you did yesterday, always let your mind control your heart. If you love him, over time you will know. If you don't, just let him go." Mary gave her mother a hug and walked out going to the stables.

That afternoon, when Tray came to the stables, Mary took him into the office and said, "We need to talk." Mary looked at Tray and asked him. "Do you like me?"

"Yes," said Tray, "very much."

"Do you like kissing me?"

"Yes," said Tray.

"Why?" asked Mary.

"Because I think you're beautiful, and I really like being around you, and I respect how hard you work," said Tray.

"Do you want to ask me something?" said Mary.

"Well, do you like me?" asked Tray.

"Yes," said Mary.

"Why did you kiss me?" asked Tray.

"Well, honestly, I don't know. I mean, I like you, and I think you're good-looking and all, but that wasn't like me. I've never kissed a boy before or wanted to," said Mary.

Tray said, "It was my first kiss too."

"Okay," said Mary, "we can kiss, but nothing else. No touching, no feeling, no nothing."

"Okay," said Tray, "I promise." Tray leaned in and gave her a kiss. She kissed him back. "I'll wait for you as long as it takes," said Tray.

"Now let's get to work," said Mary. "By the way, I like chocolates and flowers." She walked out the door.

The winter was long and cold, but before it was over, Mary was looking forward to Tray's afternoon visits. As spring came, so did the thaw. There was a constitute drip from the roof edges. The days were getting longer again, and the grass was peeking through the snow.

Mary started exercising her horses again and putting them on the walker. Maria was going to graduate from high school this spring. Mary knew she had plans for college and was looking for more help at the stables. Pete and Alice planned to retire this summer, and Selena was going to take Alice's place at the house. So until Mary could get more help, she was not starting any new projects this spring. Mary worked the stables in the morning and rode her horses in the afternoon. Sometimes Tray rode with her. They had become very close and spent all their free time together.

One afternoon, on one of their rides, they stopped to rest the horses and let them graze on grass. As they sat on a big rock nearby, Tray told Mary he had a question. "Okay," said Mary, "what?"

"Well, I know we have only known each other for a few months, but I know I love you, Mary." Mary blushed. "I know I want to spend the rest of my life with you," said Tray. Tray got up and then got down on one knee. He reached into his pocket and pulled out a box.

Mary asked, "What are you doing?"

Tray said, "Mary, please, will you marry me? Be my wife, Mary. I promise I'll be good to you." He opened the box; there was a beautiful ring inside.

Mary was stunned. She looked at the ring, then looked at Tray. Mary started to cry. So many things ran through her mind. Finally, she said, "Yes, yes, I'll marry you."

Kattie cried when Mary showed her the ring. Kattie asked, "Mary, are you sure?"

"Yes, Mama. I love him. I wasn't sure for a while, but now I know, and I know he loves me."

"I'm so happy for you, baby, but I've got to say this. Sometimes when a young girl has sex for the first time, she thinks—"

"Mom, Mom, we haven't done anything," said Mary. "We have only kissed. We have both agreed that we will wait until we are married. It will be the first time for both of us, and we want it to be special."

Kattie smiled. "Well, baby, you have always known what you want. I love you, and I will support you in anything you do."

"I know, Mom. I love you too."

"Have you told your father yet?"

"No not yet. I thought I would tell him tonight at supper. I told Tray not to say anything until I have told you both," said Mary.

"Why don't you invite Tray to supper? Yawl can tell him together."

"Okay," said Mary, "I will."

That night after supper, Mary said, "Dad, Tray and I have some news." Jim looked up. "We are engaged."

Jim smiled and said, "Well, that's no big surprise. I've been watching you two for months now." Jim got up and gave Mary a hug and a kiss, then shook Tray's hand.

"So when?" asked Kattie.

"Next year," said Mary. "We're not in any hurry, and I want a June wedding."

"That's great," said Kattie. "That will give me time to get ready."

"Nothing fancy, Mom. Just a simple country wedding."

"Tray, do you have any request about the wedding?" asked Kattie.

"No, just as long as Mary is there."

"Aw." Mary kissed Tray. "I'll be there," said Mary as she walked away. Then she said with a laugh, "Maybe."

Winter came then went, and another roundup was made. Mary encouraged Maria to go to college and study accounting so she could come back to the stables and manage them for her. Mary and Tray would be getting married soon. Kattie and her sisters had made all the arrangements. Alice and Pete moved out of the trailer at the barn when they retired last year, and Selena moved into it to be closer to the house. Mary and Tray would live in the double-wide Mary put by the stables for Selena and Maria for a while. Maria came home last Christmas with a boy she met in school. She stayed two days then left. No one had heard from her since. Mary got to see Maria for about thirty minutes in those two days. When Mary found out she had already left without saying goodbye, she was hurt. Mary swore she would never help anybody again who were not family. Billie spent all her time with Rose at the clinic now and had also met someone in Deadwood she was dating. Seemed like Tray came along at just the right time for Mary.

Mary Plumber and Tray Scott were married at her mother's house. Just family was invited, except for Kathy, Troy, and Tommie. Tray's mother and father were there. Tray and Mary Scott spent a week in Yellowstone for their honeymoon. Kattie was glad to see them come back home. She couldn't wait to help Mary set up the double-wide. Mary helped with roundup again this year, but this time, she and Tray shared a tent. Jim and Kattie decided to sell off Kattie's herd. Cattle prices were higher than they had ever been before. Kattie and Jim were getting older, and Ben wanted to retire soon, plus Aaron was getting older too. So they sold all of Kattie's herd and would move Jim's special herd to the ranch next spring. Mary gave Maria's horse Dusty to Tray to use on the ranch. Maria never came back to the ranch. Selena got word that she had dropped out of school and moved to Denver, Colorado, with her boyfriend. Mary was still looking for help at the stables but was being very selective. Her trust level was very low.

Summer came, and Ben retired. Jim made Carl foreman over the hands, including Tray. Mary asked Jim why he didn't make Tray foreman. Jim said, "He's not ready yet. His time will come. I figure he will take my place one day as manager." They moved Jim's cattle across the road to Plumber's Gap Ranch and turned them loose.

Mary found out in September of this year that she was going to have a child. Tray was excited, and Kattie and Jim were happy as well. But it didn't slow her down any. She still worked every day at the stables and riding her horses. At six months, Kattie begged her to stop and let them put one of the ranch hands at the stables. Mary said no. At eight months, Mary changed her mind and let Kattie and Jim put a ranch hand at the stables. On May 2, Mary gave birth to a healthy seven-pound baby boy.

They named him Timothy Wayne Scott. Kattie was so proud of her new grandson. He had Jim's eyes and nose, and she didn't want to put him down. Tray kept saying, "It's my turn now. It's my turn Maw-Maw."

Kattie looked at him. "I'm not Maw-Maw. I'm Mama Kat. Here," she said as she handed the baby over to Tray.

The next few weeks, Kattie never left Mary's side. She made them stay with her and Jim so she could help with the baby. Kattie sat holding the baby in her arms, remembering how she used to hold Mary the same way. Kattie thought of how life was a great big circle. Mothers have daughters and daughters have sons and sons have daughters, and the world keeps turning over and over. A new generation begins as the old one fades away. God's plan works.

Mary asked her mom, "What am I going to do with a little boy? I know nothing about boys."

Kattie hugged Mary and pulled her close with a smile. She said, "Baby boys are easy. Little girls like you and I were are hard. He will love you more than anyone else ever could. A mother and son's bond is unbreakable."

Mary told her mom that she would be going back to the stables next week. She felt like she had been lazy long enough. Kattie said, "Mary, I built this big house because my grandfather wanted a house big enough for the whole family to live in. Please, won't you, Tray, and the baby move in with me and your dad? Billie is still here. I wish Rose was. There is more than enough room here. I'll watch the baby while you're at the stables working, please."

Mary said, "Okay, let me tell Tray, but I don't want you to spend all your time with the baby. Once I come home in the afternoon, you're off-baby duty until the next morning."

"Okay, I promise," said Kattie. "Thank you! We will get you a new bed for your room."

"No, Mother, I will get Tray and I a new bedroom suite for our room. Timothy can have my old bed one day when he is older. Now I can hire somebody to work the stables with me, and they can stay in the trailer," said Mary.

Mary put signs out all over town. An elderly couple responded to her signs. They had three grown kids who had married and moved off. The couple were in their late fifties. They had both been raised on a farm and knew animals and hard work. Mary told them to let her get the rest of her stuff out this week, and they could move in this weekend. The man was Greg, and his wife was Gale. They looked like they need a job as bad as Mary needed help. Mary told herself that she would not get attached as she had done in the past.

Tray was not real sure about living with Jim and Kattie, but he really didn't have a vote. Leann, Kattie's sister, had sold the store a few years back and was helping raise her grandchildren. Her oldest son was a lawyer and worked with Sara, Kattie's oldest sister. Sara never married. No one knew why. She had always had men friends. Sara, now ready to retire with no children, was selling the law firm to Leann's son. Sara had sold off most of her father's properties in town and split the money with her sisters.

Mary still worked with problem horses and riders at the stables. She still sponsored rodeo events for Tom. Mary Plumber was still considered to be one of the best horse trainers who ever lived. Nelly died last winter. They buried her beside Dawg on the hill. Bob was too old to run barrels anymore, but Mary was not ready to put him out to pasture yet. There had never been a horse and rider with a stronger bond than theirs; they truly loved each other. Mary still rode Bob to the falls and let him graze while she lay in the grass. Mary told Bob, "One day when he is older, we will bring Timothy with us." Fourteen months after having Timothy, Mary was with child again. This time, she wanted a little Kattie.

The End

www.ingramcontent.com/pod-product-compliance
Lightning Source LLC
LaVergne TN
LVHW091617070526
838199LV00044B/828